THIEF OF ALWAYS

"Nature's fury has nothing on the fire of desire and passion that burns in Kim Baldwin's *Force of Nature*! Filled with passion, plenty of laughs, and 'yeah, I know how that feels…' moments, *Force of Nature* is a book you simply can't put down. All we have to say is, where's the sequel?!" — Outlookpress.com

"'A riveting novel of suspense' seems to be a very overworked phrase. However, it is extremely apt when discussing… *Hunter's Pursuit*. Look for this excellent novel." — *Mega-Scene Magazine*

"A…fierce first novel, an action-packed thriller pitting deadly professional killers against each other. Baldwin's fast-paced plot comes…leavened, as every intelligent adventure novel's excesses ought to be, with some lovin'." — Richard Labonte, Book Marks, *Q Syndicate*

"In a change of pace from her previous novels of suspense, Kim Baldwin has given her fans an intelligent romance, filled with delightful peeks at the lives of the rich and famous… the reader journeys into some of the hot dance clubs in Paris and Rome, and gets a front row seat to some very powerful sex scenes. Baldwin definitely proves that lust has gotten a bad rap. *Focus of Desire* is a great read, with humor, strong dialogue and heat." — *Just About Write*

Visit us at www.boldstrokesbooks.com

THIEF OF ALWAYS

by

Kim Baldwin
and Xenia Alexiou

2009

THIEF OF ALWAYS

ISBN 10: 1-60282-049-X
ISBN 13: 978-1-60282-049-4

This Trade Paperback Original Is Published By
Bold Strokes Books, Inc.
P.O. Box 249
Valley Falls, NY 12185

First Edition: February 2009

Credits
Editors: Jennifer Knight and Stacia Seaman
Production Design: Stacia Seaman
Cover Design By Sheri (graphicartist2020@hotmail.com)

Acknowledgments

The authors wish to thank all the talented women at Bold Strokes Books for making this book possible. Radclyffe, for her vision, faith in us, and example. Senior Consulting Editor Jennifer Knight, we are happy to have found the treasure that is your talent. Your personal attention this to book, and the Elite Operatives series, is deeply appreciated. Editor Stacia Seaman, for making every word the best it can be. Graphic artist Sheri, for another amazing cover. Connie Ward, huggable BSB publicist and first-reader extraordinaire, and all of the other support staff who work behind the scenes to make each BSB book an exceptional read.

We'd also like to thank our dear friend and first-reader Jenny Harmon, for your invaluable feedback and insights, and BSB author JLee Meyer, for teaching us how to read. And finally, to the readers who encourage us by buying our books, showing up for personal appearances, and for taking the time to e-mail us. Thank you so much.

❖

My cherished friend Xenia, I'll never be able to thank you enough for entrusting me with the joyous task of co-authoring your stories. I'm honored and deeply touched by your faith in me, and hold you close to my heart.

For Marty, for everything. Forty years of friendship and so much more. Your encouragement started me on this path, and I'm forever grateful.

For my father, your love knows no bounds. And my brother Tom, for always saying yes when I need a ride to the airport.

I also have to thank a wonderful bunch of friends who provide unwavering support for all my endeavors. Linda and Vicki, Kat and Ed, Felicity, Marsha and Ellen, and Claudia and Esther. You are family, and near or far, I hold you always close to my heart.

Kim Baldwin, February 2009

As always, a very big thank you to my wonderfully supportive family and friends.

Dennis, I sincerely don't know what I'd do without your constant encouragement and eternal optimism. Esther, Nicki, Steven, Mirjam, Zus and the Amsterdamse Posse, Georgia, Elia, Giorgo, Vaso, Dimitri and Vasiliki. I am forever grateful for your support and enthusiasm. I couldn't ask for better friends.

Mom, Dad, and Sis. I don't know what I'd do without you. You are my biggest reward and comfort. Thank you for everything.

In a category of your own, Kim, you are a precious friend. Your patience, trust, and belief in me have given me wings.

And last but not least, a big bow of appreciation to all the readers out there who make writing one of the most rewarding things I've ever done. YOU ALL ROCK.

Xenia Alexiou, February 2009

Dedication

This book is dedicated to Claudia.
You are my reason, my always, my shadow, my "without a doubt."
Είσαι η ψυχή μου.

Ξenia

If you are going to lie, lie for a friend.
If you are going to steal, steal a heart.
If you are going to cheat, cheat death.

—Anonymous

CHAPTER ONE

Basel, Switzerland
Friday night, February 8

"You never said," Allegro whispered in her earpiece.

"Never said what?" Nighthawk replied. His voice was tight from the strain of his exertions.

"If you scored the other night." Allegro descended, dangling by a thin cable attached to the lightweight harness around her legs, waist, and shoulders. She wore tight black pants and a black turtleneck, not thick enough to ward off the chill of Switzerland in February, but necessary for the task. And good motivation to hurry, because she despised the cold.

The darkened bedroom beneath her, seen through her infrared specs, was the best access point of the house because it had the least security, alarmed beams but no cameras. Above her, on the flat roof, Nighthawk braced his feet against the frame of the skylight as he slowly lowered her into place. They had been monitoring the home—two stories of ultra-modern glass and whitewashed brick—for the past week. Fortunately the place was surrounded by tall conifers for privacy and was far enough from neighbors that their twilight break-in would not be seen.

The homeowner, a diplomat, had just departed for Prague. An earlier call to his office had confirmed he was to be there through the weekend. There was plenty of time to locate and steal their target, a dossier containing the names of a Serb death squad involved in an infamous genocide case against the Bosnians.

"Yeah, I scored."

"Liar." Allegro couldn't suppress a chuckle. "She was way out of your league."

"Watch it, hot shot. I have you hanging by a string."

Thin red rays of light surrounded her. "Is this guy paranoid or what? The place is swamped with beams."

"Money'll do that to ya."

"So will guilt." Allegro landed softly on thick carpeting and came face-to-face with herself in the mirror of the dresser. She studied her reflection as she unclipped from the wire. "I look so threatening in a ski mask."

"Is that how you get the ladies in the sack? By putting the fear in them?"

She glanced up. Nighthawk grinned down at her from the skylight. He was an op who could blend in well in any environment. Average height and weight, dark hair, and no distinguishing features to remember, except for the gold tooth that showed itself only when he smiled.

"Did you just add jealousy to your list of shortcomings?" she teased.

He shook his head. "You know, someday…"

"I'd love to sit and chat about your sex life, or lack of it," Allegro said, "but I've got work to do."

Her agility and infrared glasses enabled her to avoid the beams with relative ease. She crouched under some and jumped over others until she reached the door to the hallway. Once there, she opened the small pouch attached to her chest, retrieved a mini periscope, and slipped half of it under the door.

The revolving camera on the opposite wall was pointing in her direction. She waited for it to complete its cycle and counted. When it was once again aimed at the bedroom door, she withdrew the periscope and counted down until she could safely open the door. As the camera was moving past, she belly-crawled across the hardwood floor, out the door, and down the hall as fast as she could, snaking in and out of the vertical beams and carefully avoiding the horizontal ones mere inches above her head.

The stale stink of cigar smoke greeted her as she reached the den.

She slipped inside and scanned the room with her penlight until she spotted what she was looking for, a reproduction of Corneille's *Femme Verte VII*. Negotiating the beams, she made her way to the painting and gingerly took it down, placing it at her feet against the wall.

"Bingo." She took off the glasses and pushed up her ski mask.

"You found it?" Nighthawk asked.

"Yup."

"*And?*"

"Well, I don't see the attraction," she replied. "Why paint her green?"

"Funny. Real funny."

"Oh, yeah, the vault's here, too." She trained her light on the small steel door she'd uncovered. The hiding place was so predictable. This was not a job she would long remember. The missions that lingered in her memory were those where the target had a little imagination and she had to be on top of her game. Cracking a safe was only interesting when the EOO couldn't tell her the exact location and it wasn't in the first places anyone would look, behind a painting or beneath the floor of a bedroom closet. She didn't get much satisfaction from doing jobs a second-rate burglar could pull off.

"Get busy, slick," Nighthawk said. "I'm freezing up here."

"I'll be out in ten." Allegro fit the stethoscope in her left ear and twisted the combination dial, listening for the telltale clicks that would help her discover the contact points.

"You're that good, huh?"

"No, just that horny. I have a date and I want to be on time." There was pathetically little challenge to the task. She quickly cracked five of the six digits. "Almost there."

"What the hell? Damn." Nighthawk's jovial tone was gone. "Change of plan. He's coming back. You have five minutes to get out of there. Otherwise, abort."

"Are you sure it's him?"

"I have him in my sights."

Allegro carefully spun the dial in the opposite direction, listening intently.

"Four minutes, thirty-six seconds," Nighthawk said.

"I can tell time. Now be quiet so I can hear what I'm doing."

She smiled as the final wheel clicked into place. The dossier was nestled beneath a jewelry box, along with a handful of other documents. She photographed what she needed with a small digital camera, returned the folder as she'd found it, and pulled the ski mask down. "Okay, I'm moving out."

"Not the way you came. Initial location is too exposed to pull you back up through the skylight."

"I'm waiting for an alternative."

"I thought you were the all-knowing guru," Nighthawk said. "I'm working on it. Sit tight."

Allegro could hear the faint click of his handheld navigator as he searched the layout of the house, seeking an alternative escape route. "I'm getting bored."

"Shit." His tone rose slightly. "We don't have a choice. I'm going to have to cut the power line."

"You don't have time for that, and there's probably backup power as well. Go back to the van and guide me from there."

"How you going to get out of there, Houdini? The place is surrounded with cameras."

"Leave that up to me. Now go."

"One minute, twenty-eight seconds until he enters," Nighthawk said.

"Stop already with the human clock routine." Allegro slipped the infrared glasses back on. The alarm beams reappeared, the nearest one a few feet behind her. "You're making my brain bleed."

Car tires crunched on the gravel in the front of the house. In a crouch, she hustled under the first few beams, then climbed onto the diplomat's desk. Like a predatory animal interrupted during its feast, she froze, muscles tightening, her senses hyperalert. The slightest sounds were amplified as she braced for a calculated leap. Her precision jump over the next pair of beams brought her to the doorway. The rush of adrenaline was intoxicating. Her heart hammered and her clothing clung damply to her skin. Using her periscope, she checked the camera in the hallway and waited for the right moment. She would have only ten seconds to negotiate her way past several more beams to the end of the hall and around the corner.

"He's parking in the garage and entering the house through the kitchen, as usual," Nighthawk reported. "You have less than a minute to get out."

In eight seconds, she reached the end of the hall and turned the corner, where she paused, hidden from the cameras. To her immediate left a staircase led to the ground floor, the obvious choice, but the steps were riddled with thin beams of red. It would take too long to escape through them. On either side, waist-high railings enabled her to surveil the ground floor. She leaned over and, in a quick, assessing glance, took in the position of the cameras below and the crisscross pattern of infrared beams.

Calculating the drop and the timing, she took a deep breath, grabbed hold of the railing, and pushed herself over, hanging there briefly before dropping to the left of one of the beams. Ignoring the brief flash of pain in her shins and ankles, she ducked quickly back into a crouch and moved through the living room and dining room toward the kitchen. Her time was about to run out. There was one cam in the kitchen, mounted above the doorway. As she stood beneath the device, counting, she heard the motorized hum of the garage door. He was coming.

When the camera swiveled away, she shot across the room. "I'm in the kitchen," she relayed to Nighthawk in a whisper.

"Are you crazy? I told you he was coming in through there."

"Relax. I know what I'm doing."

"You're not to hurt him. I repeat, you are *not* to hurt him."

"We sat at the same briefing. I got the message the first time." The sweat on her forehead left a damp circle on the ski mask.

The camera began its slow pivot in her direction. Five seconds until it reached her. Allegro heard his key in the lock on *four*. He entered the kitchen and fumbled for the light switch on *two*, and she slipped silently between his back and the door, catching a whiff of his musky cologne.

The garage was dark, but moonlight spilled through the narrowing space beneath the automatic door as it descended. She had only seconds before her escape route closed. She bolted across the concrete floor and dove for the gap, sliding through without an inch to spare.

"You got some balls, lady," Nighthawk said once they were safely ensconced in the van. "Balls, and a whole lot of luck."

"Luck's got nothing to do with it. We've been watching this house for a week. So when you said he was coming in through the kitchen, I knew I was golden."

He looked at her, one eyebrow raised. "Are you going to tell me you timed the garage door?"

"Are you going to tell me you're surprised?" she asked cockily.

He snorted. "Freak."

"Amateur."

Her voice betrayed her heady relief. Although she'd had no choice in the life she was leading, she often wondered what she would have chosen under different circumstances. Would she have wanted an ordinary life, even if it were a possibility? The answer was always the same. No. She wasn't cut out for a dull existence, working nine to five, going home to watch TV or look after a family. If she'd been able to make the choices most people made, she would still have ended up doing something similar to what she did now.

Allegro stared out the van window as they left Basel behind and entered the long stretch of dark highway that wove southeast through pastureland and thick forests. An occasional farmhouse or distant village provided the only lights. She recognized that the Organization had formed much of who and how she was, but she also knew she needed the challenge. She craved the excitement and intensity of her work. Moments like the one in the diplomat's kitchen made her feel alive.

❖

An hour later, Nighthawk parked the van in front of the entrance to the Marzili, a vast green space in the city center of Berne that featured swimming pools, a tree-shaded park, and an old-fashioned funicular. Jammed on weekends when the weather was nice, the park was nearly deserted on this cold winter evening. Allegro entered alone, strolling at a casual pace until she came to the lit fountain as instructed. The middle-aged man standing there wore only one glove. He held the other in his hand.

She approached from behind. "*Il fait très froid ce soir. N'est-ce pas?*" It's very cold tonight, don't you think?

The man turned to face her. "*Trop froid pour un gant,*" he replied. Too cold for only one glove.

Allegro retrieved the memory card she'd taken from her camera, slipped it into an envelope, and left it on the edge of the fountain. Without another word, she headed back to the van. After changing their clothing and ditching the vehicle, she and Nighthawk returned by tram to their hotel in Berne's medieval old town, where they'd been playing cozy couple for the past week. They were now typical Americans on vacation, dressed in sneakers, jeans, and sweatshirts, happily returning from drinks somewhere and, from all appearances, planning more intimate fun in their shared room.

The three-and-a-half-star tourist hotel was comfortable but not posh. Its eighteenth-century exterior blended in well with its surroundings, the façade the same arcaded sandstone as nearly all the buildings on the quiet, cobbled street. Recent renovations had thoroughly updated the interior. Their room was spacious and bright, the furniture was modern, and they had a view of the Aare River.

They'd barely closed the door when Allegro's cell phone rang. She checked the caller ID, although she knew who it was. It was twenty-thirty—eight thirty p.m.—and Montgomery Pierce, Chief Administrator of the Elite Operatives Organization, was always prompt. She flipped the phone open, greeted him with, "Mission completed," and listened to a few instructions before closing the cell and stripping off her clothes. She was naked by the time she reached the threshold to the bathroom.

Before she could make it inside, Nighthawk turned from where he'd been staring out the window and queried, "Are you going to share further orders or make me guess? Can we head back?"

Allegro pivoted to face him, enjoying the blush that spread rapidly over his cheeks. "Well, let's see, I have about ten hours to get showered, dressed, and laid. So, yeah, we have to head back. We've been booked on an oh-seven-hundred flight tomorrow and Monty wants us in his office by twenty-two-hundred sharp for a debriefing." She snapped her fingers as if a sudden realization had hit her. "Hey, what do you know? Someone finally wants to de-*brief* you, pal. Goes to show you, there's always hope."

After a quick shower, she pondered what to wear for her date. Her options were limited, considering she'd packed only the bare essentials for the job, and besides, whatever she chose would be irrelevant. Her clothes would be on the floor ten minutes after her arrival at the woman's house. She threw on her last pair of clean jeans and a short-sleeved black turtleneck. No need to bundle up since the car would be warm in no time and she would soon be in her date's bed, or on the couch, floor, counter, or whatever. She checked herself in the mirror one last time and grabbed her brown leather jacket and the keys to the rental Camaro.

She made the necessary cell phone call as she took the stairs down to the street. "Hey, beautiful. It's Mishael."

"*Bon soir.* You're not going to cancel, are you?" The female voice on the other end was heavily accented. "I have been looking forward to getting you naked since I laid my eyes on you two days ago."

Allegro smiled as she propped the cell phone between her shoulder and ear and unlocked the car. "How could I possibly cancel on such a beautiful woman? I'm calling because I'm running late."

"Just for that, I'm going to expect you to make tonight worth my wait."

"I think I can manage that...and more." She left the garage and guided the Camaro toward the highway.

"Do you really think you can make it up to me, Mishael?"

"As a matter of fact, I know I can make it up to you," Allegro promised before disconnecting. She turned the music up full blast and pressed harder on the accelerator. This was what she loved the most—speed, loud music, and more speed, until the world made sense. The music was so loud she didn't hear her cell phone, but she felt the vibration on her lap and checked the caller ID. "Perfect," she muttered as she flipped open the phone. It wasn't like she had anything better to do tonight. "Allegro 020508."

The instructions were brief, the change of plan nothing unusual. She and Nighthawk were expected in Venice ASAP and would receive further instructions upon arrival. That should have been the end of it, but Allegro was never one to adhere strictly to protocol.

As she turned the car around, she replied, "Sure, no problem. I mean, who doesn't want to turn down a sex-filled evening with a beautiful woman?"

CHAPTER TWO

Amsterdam
One Week Earlier

A small gold plaque engraved HANS HOFMAN, ADVOCATE was the only indication of commerce within the seventeenth-century brick mansion on the prestigious Prinsengracht, at Amsterdam's city center. Icy rain and high winds had driven most people from their bicycles, so the trams were packed, but Hans Hofman had no transportation concerns. The law office was one floor below his spacious apartment.

His appointment this morning was with Countess Kristine Marie-Louise van der Jagt, and for the occasion he'd taken exceptional care in his appearance. Not to impress her, for he knew Kris did not expect anyone to make a fuss over her title. It meant little to her, being hereditary not earned. She had no desire to exploit a noble rank bestowed upon an ancestor in appreciation of his wealth. Hans had selected his best navy suit and favorite tie solely because of his fondness and respect for the young woman, whom he considered his niece.

Having arrived early for their meeting, he sat at his desk to wait for her, absently caressing a brown, leather-bound diary as he stared down at the diamond beside it. He hadn't remembered the gem was so large, and such a brilliant blue. But then he'd seen it only once, very briefly, more than sixty years earlier when he was just a youth of twenty-one, working as an aide for Kris's father, Jan van der Jagt. When they'd last spoken of the diamond, Jan had lied to him, claiming the stone had been broken up and sold decades ago. Hans wondered why he'd kept it hidden away all these years, since he seemed so desperate for money.

The brown leather diary might provide an answer, but so far, Hans could not bring himself to read it. He'd been more than Jan's wartime aide and, later, his attorney. They'd been the closest of friends for most of their lives, and he wasn't anxious to learn new unpleasantries about the man. The one guilty secret he'd kept since the war years haunted him enough.

Kris was due any moment, so Hans rose from his chair and locked the diary in his filing cabinet with the rest of the family's records. Though he was well aware that father and daughter had not been close, he suspected Kris might be curious about the journal if she learned of its existence. Jan had left instructions that she was not to see it.

Settling his friend's estate was proving to be anything but routine. Hans had known of Jan's safe deposit box, of course. That was fairly standard. Many of his clients gave him authority to access their bank vaults in the event of their deaths. But he'd expected to find nothing more than the usual will and papers, along with perhaps some family heirlooms or jewelry. Instead, he'd found Jan's instructions and details of a hidden safe at Jan's estate in Haarlem. The blue diamond and the diary were there. It seemed Kris knew nothing about the gem or the vault.

When he heard a car pull up outside, he peered out the window. Kris was getting out of a taxi, so he hurried to the door to admit her. After the prerequisite pleasantries, he handed her the diamond and briefed her on what he'd learned of its possible significance.

Kris held the stone up to the light, awed by its size and brilliance. A dark, steely blue of exquisite clarity, the gem was Mazarin cut and weighed in at 15.8 carats. "So we know it's of high quality, very old, and possibly a match for one of the rarest, most famous diamonds in the world?"

"Apparently so," Hans confirmed. Their exchange in Dutch was familiar, without the formality of language reserved for mere acquaintances.

"So many questions," she mused aloud. "Jesus, it has to be worth a fortune. How did my father come to have it?"

"Your father is the only one who might have told you that, I'm afraid."

Kris's otherwise ordinary if privileged existence had been

shattered by a whirlwind month of changes. Her father's unexpected death from a heart attack had left her feeling disoriented. Although they were never close, he was a constant in her life. And when she returned to the Netherlands for the funeral, she was shocked to learn that he'd left an estate millions of euros in debt, with her as executrix to deal with it. Not only must she find a way to pay the massive stack of bills, she also had to come up with the funds to pay for her mother to remain in a private psychiatric institution.

Hans Hofman had advised the immediate sale of the two family residences, the estate in Haarlem where she'd grown up and the villa in Venice that had been her home since she'd turned eighteen. She loved living there and hated the idea of leaving. Selling it would not be difficult; homes in Venice's San Marco neighborhood were highly sought after and she'd kept the place in good condition. But she'd received yet another shock with her first look at the Haarlem mansion. She hadn't visited in more than three years, and to save money her father had let the staff go and refused even routine repairs and maintenance. The place suffered badly from neglect and would need a lot of work before it could be put on the market.

None of these problems came close to surprising her the way the diamond did. The gem seemed the obvious solution to her monetary problems. She was astonished that her father hadn't sold it so he could live more comfortably, and that he'd kept its existence from his family. Placing the diamond back on its velvet cloth on the attorney's desk, she said, "So this was in a vault my father never mentioned and you are quite convinced it's this Blue Star. How can we verify that?"

"I took the gem to a friend of mine to have it privately appraised," Hans said. "He worked for one of the big diamond concerns here until he retired. It's such a unique piece that he recognized the similarity to the Blue Star quickly, but of course that didn't make sense, so he consulted an expert in Arabic antiquities, Professor Bayat at the Allard Pierson Archeological Museum of the University of Amsterdam. Bayat is checking into it and will get back to us as soon as he learns anything. This may take some time."

"But how is it possible that there are two of them?"

"It's not," Hans replied. "If this is the real Blue Star, then the centerpiece of the Persian crown in Kabul must be a replica. A fake."

"That's unbelievable. It's been on public display for decades. Seen by thousands of people. How can the Afghans not know theirs is a fake?"

"That's a very good question." Hans smoothed his tie. "I hoped you might be able to sell it discreetly, or have it recut and sold as smaller pieces. But my friend refused to consider that because of its possible significance. Any reputable cutter will likely say the same. Perhaps that's why your father hung on to it."

"How in the world did Father come to have it?" she asked again. "I can't believe he never told you." Hans had served with her father in a Dutch squadron of the British Royal Air Force and the two men had remained close friends. She doubted they had many secrets from each other, especially one as significant as this.

"He didn't tell you, either, it seems," Hans remarked.

"Strange, considering he never missed an opportunity to flaunt his achievements," Kris murmured.

That he hadn't shared this with her directly was no surprise, since he rarely communicated with her at all. As a child, she'd tried to get him to spend time with her, but her attempts inevitably ended the same way. Her mother would try to convince him to do just that, and they would argue until Wilhelmina van der Jagt fled to her room in tears, leaving Kris's father, alone and drunk, in his study. The few times they'd spent together as a family were either in Haarlem during the holidays, surrounded by relatives and pretentious friends, or in Venice, throwing parties to impress associates and locals. Although the geographic location and guests varied, the topic of conversation was consistent: her father's wartime heroics. The fact that he'd never bragged about the diamond when he had an audience was out of character, as he was never shy about showing off.

"I don't think he wanted anyone to know how he obtained it," Hans said.

Kris was too intent on the stone to respond to his carefully worded evasion. "Well, we can't do anything with it until this professor decides whether it's the real thing. And if it is?"

"Provenance is the issue. As far as I know, there are no papers or bill of sale to indicate your father had clear title to the diamond."

"So, if it's the genuine Blue Star, the Afghans will want it returned?"

Hans nodded. "Its history as a Persian relic dates back hundreds of years and the crown would be much less viable as a tourist attraction if everyone knew the center stone was a fake."

"So if we have the real thing, it won't yield a cent for the estate. Wonderful." Kris glanced at her watch. "I should probably head to the airport soon. My return flight to Venice leaves in a couple of hours. Do you have those papers you wanted me to sign?"

"Yes, right here." Hans set a folder of legal documents before her, and she quickly dispensed with the business that had necessitated this brief visit to her home country.

"I'm going ahead with the Carnival party on Friday." She got her coat and readied to leave. "The invitations had already gone out and it was too late to cancel. I just hope everyone is out of the villa by the next morning, because the movers are set to arrive at ten. Once they've finished I'll head back to Haarlem the same day. Could you see that there is Internet service at the house? I'm in the middle of a couple of jobs."

"I don't think it's been disconnected since your father's death, but I'll make sure. What do you wish me to do with the diamond?" Hans asked.

"Well, I don't have the time to arrange a safe deposit box before I leave and since I'll be returning directly to Haarlem, it would be more convenient to have it there in case the professor needs to see it again."

"The vault is certainly well hidden," Hans assured her. "The diamond's been safe there all these years."

"For now, it will do. Could I prevail upon you to put it back there while I'm in Venice?"

"Certainly, I'll drive up tonight. Here's the combination." He wrote some figures down and handed these to her along with another sheet of paper, explaining, "A list of the repairs needed at the estate."

Kris scanned the document. "This is worse than I expected." The appraiser had outlined a litany of renovations necessary, including a new roof, electrical and plumbing work, flooring, exterior and interior painting, and landscaping. "I have some savings, but not enough for such extensive work. And even if the Venice property sells quickly, it will take some time to close and get the funds from it."

"Let me see about hiring someone for you," Hans offered. "I know a handyman who does this kind of thing for cash. That could save you on taxes. He works for a plumber friend of mine."

Kris kissed him good-bye in the Dutch way, three times, left cheek, right, then left again. "Bless you, Uncle. That would be a big help. I'll see you when I get back."

CHAPTER THREE

Kabul, Afghanistan

Like most traditional Afghan men, Culture Minister Qadir had eschewed the recent—and in his view, obscene—habit of some to adopt a surname, either for dealing with the West or for easier recognition. He had no need of either. He was a devout Muslim. He loathed the democracies that sought influence in his part of the world and did everything in his considerable power to support the Holy War aimed at bringing down the infidels. Qadir wore the traditional turban and chapan, a loose robe embroidered with colorful silk thread. As he stroked his long, graying beard, he considered the gift Allah had presented to him.

"You are correct, Professor Bayat," he informed the man speaking to him from Amsterdam. "This is a matter of extreme delicacy and utmost importance. You are quite sure?"

"Yes, the jeweler who contacted me to authenticate the gem recognized it, and after examining it myself, I believe it to be genuine. Of course I have not confirmed that since it still needs to be officially authenticated by our government."

"The *Setarehe Abi Rang*," Qadir said softly. A lengthy silence followed. Neither man attempted the extended pleasantries normally expected of associates who hadn't spoken in months. "And how was this matter left?"

"The diamond belongs to a Dutch countess. I expressed my doubts about its authenticity and provenance and told the jeweler I would investigate and get back to him."

"You have acted wisely by calling me," Qadir said. "The severity of this matter, I am sure, has not escaped you. There cannot be two *Setarehe Abi Rangs*, and since we have the real one here in our country this other stone must be a copy made from a genuine diamond. The discovery could cast doubt and cause great turmoil."

"Yes, indeed," Professor Bayat said with dismay. "What is your advice, Minister?"

"Do you know how this woman acquired the diamond and who else's hands it may have passed through?"

"No. I have not talked to the family in person."

"Very well. When you do, you must urge her to keep this very quiet until we have decided how to deal with the situation. Now, I need the name of this countess."

As he took down the information, he wiped a mist of perspiration from his brow. The *Setarehe Abi Rang* had surfaced at last. And a loyal patriot had paved the way for its swift return. It was his duty to seize the chance to eliminate the only threat to his government's long deception. But Qadir couldn't do this alone. He sent for two men he trusted implicitly: Yusuf, Deputy Minister of Arts, and Azizi, a loyal soldier in the Afghan National Army who had proven his discretion and versatility on a number of prior occasions.

Yusuf was one of the few who knew that the centerpiece of the Persian crown was only a replica, since his duties included overseeing the exhibition of the Afghan national jewels. He would find out if any inquiries had been made in Kabul about the authenticity of the gem on display. Meanwhile, Azizi would be dispatched to recover the real diamond from Countess Kristine Marie-Louise van der Jagt. The woman, of course, would have to vanish, also.

❖

Allard Pierson Archeological Museum,
University of Amsterdam

Professor Rafi Bayat stared down at a picture of the Persian crown and its renowned centerpiece, still incredulous. The cut, the color, the dimensions. He'd been certain the gem he'd just seen here in Amsterdam was the real *Setarehe Abi Rang*, or Blue Star, but Qadir had assured him that the legendary diamond was still in the crown. Could there possibly be two stones exactly alike? Rafi glanced around his cluttered office as he grabbed his coat. He'd only been in Amsterdam for two years, but the items he'd accumulated suggested a lengthy entrenchment in the Dutch capital. His bookcases overflowed with reference material, archeological tools, and small mementos of the digs he'd joined, most of them in the Middle East. He'd worked hard to gain credibility and respect in his field, but had never expected to be at the center of a find that could attract worldwide attention. Unwanted attention. For he understood the implications of the discovery of this look-alike diamond and the possible repercussions for his homeland, and first and foremost, he was true to his heritage.

As he headed out for his appointment with the countess's attorney, Rafi considered carefully the best approach to take with Hans Hofman. It was rush hour in the city, and the bike lanes were crowded with commuters on this sunny morning, so he stuck out his hand to signal his turn to the line of bicycles behind him as he turned onto the Prinsengracht. His primary task for this meeting was to ensure that the countess kept quiet about her diamond's uncanny resemblance to the Blue Star. But although he knew the Afghan authorities were now conducting their own investigation into the matter, he was unable to stop thinking about how he could help. If he could clear up the mystery concerning the striking similarity between the two gems and quickly discredit the newly discovered diamond, he would be doing an invaluable service for his country. No one was in a better position to do so. He had the expertise needed, and the van der Jagt family seemed cooperative. He hoped the countess's attorney would give him a place to start.

Rafi locked his bicycle to a rack beside the canal and smoothed his short black hair with his hand before mounting the steps to Hans Hofman's office. The man who greeted him was much older than he'd envisioned. Hofman was in his eighties, certainly past the age that most men retired from the legal profession. But despite his outward appearance, the attorney had the vigor and agility of a much younger man, and showed no sign of diminished mental acuity.

"Thank you for coming," he said as he led Rafi down a hallway and through an outer reception area into a well-appointed office. "I hope you have news for us?"

"No verification yet." Rafi settled into a leather chair opposite the man's desk. "It doesn't appear your stone can be the Blue Star, but it will take some time to investigate this mystery. In the interim, we must be discreet. I'm sure you would not wish to create a political problem between our countries."

"I understand," Hofman said, affirming Rafi's expectations. The Dutch could be counted upon to respect the cultural sensitivities of others. This made them easy to deal with, and exploit, if necessary.

"Now, it will help me a great deal if you can tell me what you know about how the countess acquired this gem?"

Hofman swiveled his office chair and gazed out the window overlooking the canal, his face in profile. "She inherited it from her father, upon his recent death. Count Jan van der Jagt was a colonel in the air force during World War Two." He paused for a long while, seemingly pre-occupied with his thoughts. "He acquired it in 1946 from a Nazi lieutenant he turned in to authorities."

"Do you know name of this lieutenant?" Rafi asked.

"Why is this important?"

"Because I am personally going to try to track the origins of this stone. If we are to prove conclusively that the real stone is in the possession of the Afghan people we will need to authenticate the rival stone's history."

"I see." Hofman faced him with a tired expression. "At this point there is nothing I can do to stop you from proceeding?"

"But why would you want to?" Rafi reasoned. "I would think that it will help both of us to get to the bottom of this. Do you not wish to be free to sell the diamond?"

"The countess needs the money, this is true. But we don't know if she will have any claim to this treasure, you see. And I stand to expose her father…my friend."

"I am afraid I don't understand."

"Count van der Jagt did what was necessary to survive that dreadful period," Hofman said. "In times of war we do things we may later regret."

Rafi gave the attorney a look of compassion. "Ah. I promise to be very discreet with my inquiries."

"Thank you. Would you do me the kindness of passing on any information or questions concerning…the German directly to me?"

Hofman gestured dismissively with his hand. "I do not want Ms. van der Jagt involved."

"Of course. I will respect your wishes."

"The Nazi's name was Geert Wolff," Hofman supplied. "He was with the Gestapo and was tried at Nuremberg. To the best of my knowledge, he took the diamond from a wealthy Jew who was sent to Auschwitz. Wolff was executed, and one must assume the man he stole the diamond from is no longer alive, God rest him."

"A most horrific period for so many." Rafi got to his feet and extended his hand. "I appreciate your candor, Mr. Hofman. I will be in touch."

CHAPTER FOUR

Venice, Italy
Friday, February 8

The private plane the EOO had arranged flew Allegro and Nighthawk from Berne to Venice in eighty minutes. They met their contact in a dark, quiet street away from the city center. Carnival was in full swing, and they could hear the distant shouts and laughter of the revelers who filled the streets and canals. Although they were in an area where they could meet with relatively little fear of being seen or overheard, they still remained on the move, walking as they talked. Nighthawk strolled at Allegro's right, and the contact was on her left. He reminded her of Dilbert, all glasses and cartoon-geeky. She remained silent for the most part during the briefing, carefully listening.

"Here's the file that was recently put together on the van der Jagt family." The contact handed her a thin folder. "It's a fairly brief account but will have to do for now. The countess's code name is Rocky and this is Operation Vanish."

Allegro slowed her steps as she opened the dossier to the first page. The usual mundane specifics were there, but thankfully the report was not as elaborate as some, so she was able to scan it quickly. Kristine Marie-Louise van der Jagt. Age: 38. Height: 5'8". Blond hair, blue eyes. Occupation: Web designer. Her education and employment stats followed, along with information on her parents.

"What if the stone's not here in Venice?" Allegro glanced over at the contact. "As far as I can see there's no..." She trailed off and stopped dead as she flipped to the next page.

"There's no what?" Nighthawk asked, and when she continued to stare at the page in her hands, he jabbed her lightly on the shoulder. "Hello? Anybody home?"

"Proof, there's no proof," she said in irritation. "Is this really her?"

Nighthawk leaned in and studied the countess's picture. The four-by-six color photo might have been an advertisement for a modeling agency or cosmetics firm. Kristine van der Jagt was smiling an enigmatic smile. Her fair skin was flawless, her shoulder-length wheat blond hair shimmered in the sun. She was breathtaking.

"She sure is hot. Can I keep the picture when we're done?" Nighthawk tried to grab the folder, but Allegro slapped him on the hand.

"Down, Fido. This isn't one of your porn centerfolds. Besides, if anyone gets to keep this picture, it's me."

The contact cleared his throat. "Can we get back to the subject?"

Allegro tore her attention away from the photo with great reluctance. "So…" she summarized as they resumed walking, "I have to get into this woman's villa, pass unnoticed through all the guests, search for a possible safe in a cellar with limited access, and hope that there's a diamond worth millions in there. Then extract it. And nothing in this little plan screams 'dodgy'?"

Ignoring her sarcasm, the Dilbert look-alike replied blandly, "We don't have the luxury of a long planning period. Even though there's probably only a remote chance the diamond is here, the residence must be searched. The movers and estate agents will be all over the place tomorrow morning. Tonight is a sort of farewell to daddy's mansion and money, which means that whatever is worth anything to the van der Jagts will be leaving with Rocky tomorrow."

"Why can't I wait until the guests leave and she's gone to bed?" Allegro asked.

"It's Carnival. Who's going to be sleeping tonight?"

"My kinda party."

"Think you can manage without getting sidetracked?" Nighthawk teased.

She winked at him before returning her attention to their contact. "How soon do you want me in there?"

"We have to move fast." He handed Nighthawk a navigator memory card. "The layout for the house. You'll be able to move most freely around the interior if you pass as one of the masqueraded guests."

Allegro grinned. "Can I go as a cat burglar?"

"No," both men replied.

❖

Southwestern Colorado

Montgomery Pierce stared out his window at the blizzard raging beyond his office, obscuring his splendid view of the Rocky Mountains and the immense Weminuche Wilderness Area. The snow covering the remote, wooded landscape was thigh deep, perfect for winter survival training but a pain in the ass for everything else. Still, he had no doubt the esteemed visitor due any minute would somehow make it through to the Elite Operatives Organization campus. If the deputy director of the Military Intelligence Service was trying to get to them for an assignment in this weather, it meant he was acting under orders from brass at the Pentagon. In anticipation, Monty had invited the two other members of the EOO's Governing Trio to sit in on the briefing. It took a vote of any two of them to dispatch a member of their Elite Tactical Force on a dangerous mission and he'd already obtained their approval for the Venice operation, based on nothing but a phone call from Norton, who was waiting out a blizzard at the time. They needed more information before Monty was willing to commit resources on the broader operation Norton had alluded to.

"If Norton himself is coming in all this mess, this must be pretty big," said a voice from behind him.

Joanne Grant, Director of Academics, was good at reading Monty's mind. They'd grown up together at the Academy, had been ETFs in the same graduating class, and he'd been in love with her for nearly four decades. Since emotional attachments of any kind were discouraged in their line of work, he'd never once acted on those feelings, but he noticed every little detail about her.

She placed a cup of coffee on the small oval conference table and sat down. Today her white hair was styled a little differently than usual, swept away from her face. It made her neck appear longer, and accentuated her high cheekbones and vivid green eyes. Monty sucked in his stomach, as he did whenever she was around. He also made sure those damn bifocals he'd come to depend on were nowhere in sight. There was little he could do about his thinning blond hair and pale skin, a by-product of his Scandinavian heritage. He hoped his look was mature and distinguished, not middle-aged and well past his prime.

"I don't know much more, just that this is a high-priority, time-sensitive European operation. The usual."

David Arthur, Director of Training, joined them, brushing snow from his winter white camo fatigues. When he took off his white skullcap, his copper-colored crew cut stood out in stark contrast. "Sorry. Got held up in explosives class. Anything from Venice yet?"

Monty checked the time. His intercom buzzed twice, confirming that the guard at the front gate had just admitted Major Cliff Norton. He drew the blinds, a habit whenever anything of importance was being discussed.

As soon as he'd joined them at the conference table, the major, a balding career soldier with a dour expression, flipped open his briefcase and got right to the point. "This is it." He withdrew a photograph and tossed it toward Monty. Grant and Arthur leaned closer to study it. "The Blue Star Diamond," Norton continued. "This rock is supposed to be in the Persian crown, on exhibit in Kabul. But a source in the Afghan government claims the diamond in the crown is a fake and the gem in the possession of the Dutch woman is the real thing."

"My operatives are presently attempting to steal not just any diamond, but one that will create political heat with Muslims?" Monty concluded, wondering what the tradeoff was. "Why is the U.S. getting involved in this?"

"We have intelligence that the diamond is about to be stolen by another party and sold to finance al-Qaeda," Norton replied. "Our informant is in a position to return the stone to the crown, where it belongs."

"Making the Afghans happy," Grant noted.

"Yes, and in exchange we'll get information about an imminent terrorist threat to be launched from Afghanistan against Western targets."

"How reliable is your source?" Monty asked.

"He's always delivered, so far. But this time there's no money changing hands. He says it's his duty."

"Did you try offering more cash for information on the threat?"

"We've exhausted that option," Norton said. "Look, we don't give a damn about the rock, and whether or not it returns to the goddamn crown, but this a code-red situation. Our assets in Afghanistan are on standby and we can move in as soon as you do your part."

Monty picked up the photo and brought it closer to his face. "If they come up empty in Venice, what are we looking at? A vault in the ABN AMRO?"

The major withdrew a dossier from his briefcase, opened it to the relevant page, and set it beside a print of the photo he'd e-mailed five hours earlier, when the orders were given for Operation Vanish. "Kristine Marie-Louise van der Jagt. Her late father had a safe deposit box in Amsterdam but it's been emptied, and she doesn't have one of her own that we can find. So we think the gem is likely to be in a mansion in the Netherlands if it's not at the Venice location. Bottom line is, we have to get it ASAP. We're not the only ones after it."

"Understood," Monty said.

Norton pointed to another address in the file. "That's her lawyer's office in Amsterdam. He's settling the estate and is close to the family, so that might be the best place to start if the stone isn't in Venice."

Monty nodded. "I'll get someone on it."

Once the major had departed, David Arthur asked, "Do we keep Allegro on this? We could assign Domino to the Netherlands end, since this is time critical."

"I don't want to send in a second-tier crew and possibly clue in our competition," Monty responded. "Allegro's our best in breaking, entering, and retrieving. She has that instinct." He didn't have to explain what he meant. They were all well familiar with the ETF's profile and accomplishments. She had an uncanny ability to figure out where people hid things, to locate what others could not. "Hell, I think she could find Bin Laden if we asked her to."

"Let's just hope she doesn't leave a trail of destruction behind." Arthur glanced down at Allegro's file. "She's great at what she does, even irreplaceable, but she's so damn fearless and cocky about her abilities, she overestimates herself. One of these days, she'll overreach and we'll be cleaning up after her. Trying to break that one was one of the most challenging things I've had to do."

"All that and you didn't succeed," Grant joked. "But her heart's in the right place, and she's very dedicated to us."

"She wasn't and still isn't easy, that's for sure," Monty agreed. He'd just received a new pile of her speeding tickets, proving the point. "But she's always delivered, no matter the circumstances. Nighthawk is with her. He won't let her mess up."

Arthur chuckled. "Poor bastard."

The comment elicited one of Monty's rare smiles. He reached for his cell phone. "She's high maintenance but she'll deliver."

"That's what I'm afraid of." Grant's expression turned glum. "Her inexorability will someday be the end of her."

❖

The dimly lit streets around the Piazza San Marco were crowded with revelers, many in exquisitely ornate leather or papier-mâché masks and the traditionally opulent and colorful period costumes that celebrated the rich history of Venice or Commedia dell'Arte characters. There were also ample partygoers in more modern dress, masquerading as animals and clowns or barely disguised beneath whimsically decadent garb. Many were headed to private parties, staged events, and balls. The rest were content to join the tourists mingling among the street performers, an abundance of musicians and jugglers, acrobats and fire-eaters, and small theatrical troupes.

From the balcony of her second-floor bedroom, Kristine van der Jagt observed the merriment along the pedestrian walk in front of the villa and in the canal, which was crowded with boats. The din from the celebrations was deafening. It was nearly eleven p.m. and her first guests would arrive any moment, but already she was bored senseless. The annual Carnival affair had never really held much appeal for her, yet she kept up the family tradition, and now she wondered why. For her mother, it had been an escape from her loneliness; for her father, an opportunity to boast and impress. But Kris had long ago ceased to derive any real pleasure from such hedonistic pursuits, and tonight, especially, she was in no mood to entertain. It was likely her last night in the villa and she couldn't bear the thought of leaving. The charming fifteenth-century home was more than her residence. It was a refuge, a stark contrast to the cold and lonely mansion in Haarlem where she'd grown up. Venice was warm and colorful, a city in love with life. Romance hung in the air, and though she'd not found it here herself, as she'd once hoped, the atmosphere was full of promise and she'd never stopped believing something magical was possible.

There was no more beautiful view in the world than the one from her balcony. Every morning, she had her coffee here, usually in time to catch the sunrise. If the weather was good, she settled into a lounge chair with her laptop, pausing often to admire the way the sunlight made diamonds on the canal or to listen to the gondolas passing by, their drivers serenading the tourists or regaling them with the rich history of the ancient city.

The recent upheaval in her life, with the death of her father, the hopelessness of her mother's mental health, and her critical financial situation, had left her feeling even more alone than ever. And now she was about to lose the only thing in her life that kept her sane. She vowed to mingle with her guests only as much as required tonight, escaping when she could to enjoy, in solitude, the final hours in her precious villa.

The dress she wore gave no hint of her disinterest in the coming gala. She'd always lived according to form, and it was expected that a hostess at Carnival be the center of attention, with the most splendid and eye-catching costume of all. So she'd chosen a magnificent gown of deep purple velvet, with a high slit up the side to show off her legs and a bustier of gold lace that displayed her high, round breasts to perfection. Her blond hair was pulled up in a French braid and adorned with purple feathers in the same hue as her dress. Because she found the full-face masks so typical of Carnival too warm and confining, she'd chosen a half-mask of gold, decorated with more purple feathers and fine bead pearls.

At the sound of her name being called, she looked down at the crowd below. Several guests, unrecognizable in their masks and elaborate period costumes, waved up at her as they approached the front door to the villa. She sighed as she waved back perfunctorily, grateful that the half-mask and the shadows on the balcony hid her true feelings. If only for the moment, no one who saw her could distinguish heartache from happiness.

❖

Allegro emerged from the costume store and stepped down into the boat their contact had supplied. Nighthawk stood waiting for her. "Not a word out of you," she warned when his stare turned into a broad smile.

She'd chosen the traditional eighth-century attire of the *bauta maschile*. Over a white lace shirt and black-and-white filigreed knickers, she wore a black velvet cloak. A matching tricorner hat, white leggings, black buckle shoes, white gloves, and a white half-mask completed the ensemble. Traditionally worn by a man, the costume would allow her to move quickly, and on her five-foot-eight frame, with her small hips and slim build, it concealed her identity well. Her dark brown hair, which normally hung to her collarbones, had been tucked beneath the hat. Unless someone paid attention to the details—the long eyelashes beneath the mask, the feminine curve of her lush lips, the rise of breasts beneath the shirt—she would pass for a male.

"I was only going to say you look…dapper." Nighthawk was barely able to contain his laughter. He looked every bit the typical American tourist, with his Boston Celtics jacket and a camera around his neck. "Are you picking me up?" he asked, testing the earpiece as he paddled ineffectually toward the van der Jagt villa.

"Loud and clear." Allegro gazed up at the fifteenth-century villa, an impressive showpiece even in a city abundant with splendid, historic buildings. Each architectural detail had been lovingly maintained or restored: the marble balcony with its Byzantine wrought-iron accents, the Gothic arches above the quatrefoil windows and heavy wood door, the delicate traceries etched into the stone of the façade.

Leaving Nighthawk stationed in the canal, she cruised into the mansion with a half-dozen other costumed guests, through the grand foyer, with its ornate crystal chandelier and wide marble staircase, and into the salon decorated with Oriental carpets and heavy Italian furniture dating from the late nineteenth century. She received no second glances. The olive skin and caramel eyes of her Persian heritage helped her blend with the preponderance of Italians present. Mingling discreetly, she scanned the crowd for the lady of the house, engaging no one but noticing everything.

When a booming male voice behind her proclaimed, "*Buena sera, Kris,*" she turned and saw a woman dressed in purple, with her fair hair done up in a braided crown on her head. The coloring and height matched their description of van der Jagt.

"I've spotted Rocky," she informed Nighthawk, moving away before she could be noticed. Now that she knew where the countess was, and that she was engaged with her guests, it was time to get down to business.

"I've got you," Nighthawk relayed, tracking her on the navigator.

She let him guide her down a hall and through a small sitting room to the courtyard, where a handful of hearty guests braved the chill, sipping wine and preening for each other in their elaborate costumes. The courtyard was a private green space shared by the van der Jagt villa and three neighboring homes. It was inaccessible from the outside. Allegro frowned as she glanced about. According to the layout their contact had provided, she should be at the entrance to the cellar.

"Don't see the way in," she said in a low voice. "I'm here, but the entrance has been sealed. It's all brick, and fairly new."

"Damn. Well, he did say these blueprints were thirty years old. There has to be another way down."

"I'll find it." Allegro backtracked, cautiously opening the doors in the hallway, always conscious of the occasional guest who happened by. A bathroom. A closet. A small guest bedroom. She ducked inside a den. The room was dark, but she could make out a desk, bookshelves, a stocked bar, and two doors. One led to another bathroom, the second to a narrow staircase leading down. "We're in," she reported, closing the door behind her and clicking her penlight on.

The cellar she entered bespoke the age of the villa more than any other place in the house. The walls were ancient brick and the wooden beams above her, obviously hand hewn, were dark and cracked from centuries of moisture and expansion. Allegro inhaled a damp, earthy smell reminiscent of a cave. Built into one side of the long, narrow space were several six-foot-high wooden racks for bottles of wine and spirits. Half were filled. Numerous wood crates were stacked opposite, some with bottles nestling in packing material.

She was pleased to discover that, though the blueprint was outdated, at least the information about the vault was accurate. The bill of sale, dated 1996, confirmed that the van der Jagts had invested in a freestanding Phoenix safe, a combination dial model, and that's precisely what stood against the far wall. A newer safe would've required more tools than she could comfortably have sneaked in under her cloak. This one needed only her penlight, stethoscope, a pair of latex gloves, and ten undisturbed minutes.

She worked quickly. The diamond wasn't there, only a few pieces of jewelry, nothing too valuable, and a thin sheaf of documents. She relayed the bad news to Nighthawk, adding, "I'm exiting now."

She put her hat and mask back on and selected a bottle of wine from the rack to explain her presence should someone happen to catch her coming back up the stairs. When she entered the den, she immediately picked up a scent. Lavender. The room was so dark she didn't see her at first, standing near the window some twenty feet away. It wasn't until the woman moved that Allegro picked up her location. Eyes adjusting, she made out the profile with the help of the light coming from the window. It was Kristine van der Jagt. The countess had removed her mask.

"*Buena sera,* Kris," Allegro said, deliberately lowering her voice a notch.

"Kris as in Kristine? Shit. She's there?" Nighthawk's voice sounded scratchy.

Van der Jagt tilted her head, studying her wayward guest, obviously trying to figure out who, beneath the mask, had just addressed her like an old friend. She responded in Italian, hers not quite as perfect as Allegro's, asking what she was doing in the cellar.

Allegro raised the bottle and explained, in perfect Italian, "Looking for more wine."

"Who are you?"

"Let's see you wing this one, slick," Nighthawk said in her ear.

Allegro made a show of studying her costume, then smiled her most charming smile. "Who do I look like?"

Kris laughed and commanded, "Take off your mask. I want to see you."

When she didn't immediately comply, the countess reached for a nearby lamp. But as soon as her intent became clear, Allegro quickly closed the distance between them and wrapped her hand over Kris's just as she reached the pull chain. "No."

This close, she could make out van der Jagt's delicate features in the moonlight streaming in through the window. And more, the cleavage formed by the bustier in the dress, the round swell of breasts, the smooth skin of her shoulders and chest. Her perfume, a mix of lavender and something Allegro couldn't identify, was intoxicating. It was risky to prolong the conversation any further or reveal any more of what she sounded and looked like, but she needed to distract the woman.

She skimmed her fingertips up Kris's arm to her bare shoulder, then slowly, provocatively, down her chest to the valley of cleavage. She smiled at the sudden intake of breath she felt and heard. Next, she traced a path across the top of one breast, over to the other, then up to the warm, soft flesh of Kris's neck. When Kris leaned her head back and closed her eyes, relaxing into the caress, Allegro kissed her at the hollow of her throat.

"Sei così bella," she whispered, between kisses. You are so beautiful.

❖

When Kris opened her eyes, the woman was gone. Something about her—oh yes, she was dressed as a man, but Kris had sensed instantly that the figure was female—something about her had intrigued her at once. The hint of humor and charm in their brief exchange, the woman's apparent resolve to keep her identity secret, and most of all, her bold yet teasing caresses. It was not her habit to succumb to a stranger, but Kris had melted into the light touch and sweet kisses as though she'd been starving for them. She'd almost folded against the stranger's velvet cloak when those soft lips pressed delicately against her neck. She could still hear that husky voice repeating, *"Sei così bella,"* first against her throat, and then on another sensitive spot, beneath her ear. Another kiss had followed, a tongue dancing lightly above the hollow of her breasts. When the lips withdrew, Kris had moaned at the loss and waited, breathless, for more. She must have stood there alone, composing herself, for several minutes before returning to her party.

She spent the rest of the evening searching rooms and approaching guests with similar costumes, even long after she realized her efforts were futile. Part of her refused to believe that the stranger who had invited her to forget her sorrows, and who'd made her heart pound with the lightest kiss, had left without a trace.

CHAPTER FIVE

Berlin, Germany
Saturday, February 9

Manfred Wolff had a face like a bulldog and a body to match, his arms and legs disproportionately small in relation to his ample girth. When he sank into his leather chair by the fireplace, he filled it completely and his feet didn't quite touch the floor. He shared his spacious three-bedroom apartment in the city center with his mother, who was sitting opposite in her wheelchair. She had long ago lost her mind to dementia, and her only pastime these days was either staring out the window on the sunny warm days or at the fireplace during the cold German winters. Manfred was happy that the tedious routine of his profession allowed him to concentrate his attention elsewhere, especially now that he needed to take care of her.

More than ever, his mind was not on balancing someone's books today. His meeting with the foreign professor who had telephoned was imminent, and he sat in anticipation, staring at the fire, tapping his fingers on the carved wooden armrest. When his mother coughed, he glanced sideways to see if she needed something. She raised her hand as if to say that she was all right. Even in her eighties, frail and emaciated, she was still a strong authoritative figure, the only parent he had ever known. But as strong and determined as she might have been, he never stopped missing the presence of a father.

As had become his habit in the past year, he studied her features as if to imprint them in his memory. He knew it wouldn't be long now before she was gone. Once again, he was lost in the family resemblance. Their bodies couldn't be more different, but anyone could see they were mother and son. Every facial feature, from the dark blue eyes to the round scoop of jaw and upturned nose, was the same. Even the dark brown hair had aged the same way, to a mixture of salt and pepper. The only thing he'd inherited from his father was his stubby height and penchant for obesity. His mother, in her prime, had been tall and svelte.

Her deterioration saddened him. He knew how much she hated being dependent upon him. She was a survivor, someone to look up to, and he'd spent his life making sure she could view him with the same respect. The chime of the doorbell ended his reverie and he pushed his bulk from the chair to answer it.

Their visitor was dark haired and dark skinned, in his forties, and dressed in a navy suit, though of inferior material and badly in need of pressing. He seemed tentative and nervous, though he tried to mask it with a professional tone. "Thank you for seeing me on such short notice, sir."

"I could hardly refuse, Professor Bayat." Manfred led the man to the living room and introduced him to his mother, then gestured toward the couch. "Quite a tantalizing bait," he remarked as they took their seats at opposite ends. "A valuable diamond that once belonged to my father."

"I know this may be a delicate matter, Mister Wolff," the professor began. "My understanding is that your father acquired the gem during the war from a Jew who was sent to Auschwitz."

Manfred tried not to bristle. He was all too aware of how Nazi officers were perceived after the war, and he viewed such carefully worded references as subtle condemnations. "Who has it now?"

"A woman who inherited it."

"Van der Jagt. Yes?" His mother had remembered the name, from the trial, but they'd never known whether the Dutch colonel had a family. Manfred had been certain the man must have sold the diamond long ago, and that it was gone forever.

"I'm afraid I'm not at liberty to disclose who I am representing, Mr. Wolff," the professor said. "I'm not here to judge your father's actions, merely to seek the history of the diamond."

Manfred bit back an angry response. "Van der Jagt took everything my father had," he said calmly. "Then turned him over to be tried and executed. My mother, pregnant with me, was thrust into poverty. And you expect me to help you?"

Professor Bayat looked down at his feet. "Many horrific things happen during war, sir," he said in a quiet voice. "I do not wish to offend you, or your family. Or stir up unpleasant memories. I am merely an academic seeking to trace the historic significance of this stone."

Which might make it more valuable in the end, Manfred concluded, and perhaps that was reason enough to help. His mind worked quickly as he weighed the possibilities opening before him. Like this professor, he needed to know more. If he had to provide some information in exchange, he was willing. His father had told his mother the name of the Jew who'd owned the diamond. Like van der Jagt, the name was forever burned into Manfred's brain. "The diamond came from a man named Moszek Levin. He was a watchmaker in Prague."

"Thank you for your time, Mister Wolff." The professor got to his feet. "I'll not bother you further."

After he'd shown the visitor out of the apartment, Manfred paced the living room in agitation for a few minutes, then took a folder from the bottom drawer of his work desk. From this he extracted the yellowed sketches his father had done of the wartime treasures he'd confiscated. The diamond had been detailed with exquisite care.

All his life, Manfred had dreamed of vengeance and now, finally, his opportunity was at hand. His only regret was that his mother was too far gone to fully appreciate their opportunity for justice. Her bitterness over the Dutch colonel's betrayal and what it had done to their family had eaten away at her like a cancer, just as his father's beliefs had found natural root in Manfred. Instead of reading him fairy tales, his mother had tucked him into bed every night with her account of the treachery that had kept him from knowing his father.

During the days of the Nuremberg trials, when Nazi officers were being hunted down en masse and imprisoned or executed, Manfred's father had done what he could to avoid detection, letting his beard grow and dressing beneath his status. Geert Wolff had made plans to escape the country on a ship bound for America, and on that fateful day in 1946, to anyone who saw him, he was just another impoverished German citizen, heading home with meager groceries. But he had the misfortune to run into the Dutch colonel on the street. He'd known at once, from the look in the colonel's eyes, that he'd been recognized. He couldn't remember where they'd first met, or how, but their wartime encounter had been enough that the RAF officer knew him immediately. Two policemen were standing not ten meters from them, and Geert knew the officer was going to call out to them. All was lost. In desperation, he grabbed at the colonel's arm and hustled him around the corner.

"Keep silent," he urged as the colonel's aide looked on without a word. "I'll make you a rich man."

The Dutch officer shook him off at first. But Manfred's father had begged. *Begged.* "Please. My wife is pregnant with our first child. Come with me, my home is not far. Let me show you."

It took some convincing, but the colonel accompanied Geert back to the apartment, and in the end, he'd accepted the paintings and other treasures that had once belonged to rich Jews who had tried to bribe their way to safety. The Dutchman took everything, so much bounty that he and his aide had to bring their car to transport it all away. With the wartime plunder went Geert's most treasured prize, the diamond that was supposed to buy the Wolffs a new life.

The very next day, as they were packing to flee, the colonel returned with the police. It was that image Manfred's mother had burned into his brain. The colonel, at the door, pointing. The words, "That's him."

Less than two months later, Geert Wolff was convicted and put to death. Manfred's mother had done her best to provide for him, but he'd suffered a wretched childhood. Raised in poverty, and ostracized by neighbors and schoolmates who wanted to distance themselves from their own Nazi pasts, he'd grown into a man obsessed with righting a horrible wrong. And though it'd taken more than six decades, perhaps there was a reason. For he now had the power and money to rectify this injustice, and the right kind of friends to call upon.

He picked up the phone and dialed the leader of *Arische Bruderschaft*, the Aryan Brotherhood, Berlin's most powerful underground neo-Nazi group.

❖

Amsterdam

"I'm freezing my ass off," Nighthawk complained. He was waiting outside in the dark blue Volkswagen Passat they'd rented at Schiphol Airport.

"This shouldn't take long. All the files are very organized," Allegro said. She'd succeeded in getting into Hans Hofman's office with little effort.

Nighthawk yawned loudly in her ear. "Jesus, this has been a hell of a long night. I'd like to get some sleep eventually."

"Eventually being the key word." She skimmed through the attorney's files. "I'm hoping we get lucky later."

"I'd say you got your share of luck last night."

"I'll admit, that one is hot."

The memory of that soft neck against her lips made it difficult for Allegro to concentrate. In those brief moments, so close to Kris van der Jagt, she'd almost forgotten herself and she still wasn't sure why. Something in the countess's eyes had lingered with her, a sadness that piqued her interest. She'd found herself wondering why, on such a festive occasion, Kris seemed so uninterested in her own party. Her father's death, obviously. But then why not cancel? Why surround herself with people so absorbed in their own lives they didn't care enough about their hostess to wonder why she'd slipped away to be alone?

Kris van der Jagt had the loneliest eyes Allegro had ever seen.

"Got anything?" Nighthawk prompted and she forced herself back to the business at hand.

"Blueprints to the house in Haarlem." She took out her small digital camera. "According to this, it dates back to the sixteen hundreds. The place is huge. We'd better get going if we want to search the place before she arrives from Italy."

She returned the file to its folder in the lawyer's cabinet and extracted a leather-bound journal. Untidy handwriting covered the first page. *Amsterdam 12 April, 1939. Ik vrees dat ik morgen weg moet. De Duitsers komen eraan...* Allegro continued to leaf through, reading lines here and there. *Berljn 16 December, 1946. Hij wist dat ik hem had herkend...toen ik de diamant zag...*

"It's her father's war diary, and there's mention of the diamond in here," she relayed, photographing each page. Pressed for time, she only snapped the first pages that referred to the diamond. Much of the early part of the journal dealt with Jan van der Jagt going off to war. In later pages the gem was mentioned over and over. The references made no sense to her when skimmed out of context. Someone had been recognized, Jan had seen the diamond, and later he referenced that it was in his possession. There was no hint about what he'd done with the gem.

"If tonight doesn't pan out, I'm going to have to come back here and photograph the rest of this," she said, packing up.

"Let's hope we just find the stone. I hate reruns."

❖

During their half-hour drive to the van der Jagt estate outside Haarlem, Allegro studied the blueprints she'd photographed. "These are dated 1975. That's when they did some renovations to the tower."

"Tower?" Nighthawk stole a quick look at her. "What is this place, a castle or something?"

"Twenty-three rooms, your rectangular square two-story, with a cellar. The tower is a four-story square, added later to the front corner of the house."

"Is there a safe?"

"Maybe. According to this, it's in the cellar. Built in. Pretty traditional with these old homes."

The estate was in the countryside, out of sight of the nearest neighbor but close to the road. They parked the car a short distance away behind some brush and approached on foot. The house was whitewashed brick with light gray brick accents around the rectangular windows, and a charcoal slate roof. The tower had a dome top the same color, with a tall wind vane in the shape of a V, currently pointed east. Low hedges along the front had been planted in an elaborate pattern of rectangles, but their once-perfect symmetry had suffered from long neglect, as had other topiary around the place. There were no vehicles parked outside.

Adjacent to the house and tower was a long, narrow building of dark brown brick. It was clear from the wide, arched wooden doors spaced along one side that the structure was designed to house livestock, probably horses. There were no signs of current occupants. Several motion detection lights were positioned at the front of the house and a security camera was aimed at the front door. A glance over the six-foot wooden fence around the back confirmed a similar setup at the rear of the house.

"That looks like the best access point, if we don't want to have to cut power." Allegro pointed to a second-floor window of the tower, reachable from the roof of the barn. With daybreak fast approaching, they didn't want to alert the countess or any staff that someone had broken in, just in case they needed to return.

With a boost from Nighthawk, Allegro climbed up and peered through the window to see if there were any cameras. When she found nothing, she studied the glass and frame with her penlight. It didn't seem to be wired, and to her relief no alarms sounded when she jimmied it open. The window gave her access to what appeared to be a small sewing room, furnished with an older machine, dressmaker forms, baskets of yarn, and other relevant sundries. The place had a musty smell, as though it hadn't been used in some time. She proceeded through the room with caution, careful to surveil for security devices. She spotted a camera at the end of the hall she then entered, but it wasn't turning, nor was the light on alert.

"I can see cameras and sensors, but they've been deactivated," she told Nighthawk.

"Sun's coming up soon," he reminded her unnecessarily.

"Yeah, yeah. I hear you."

"Where are you now?"

"In the kitchen." She saw another camera, also not working. "This doesn't make sense. Why would they disable the security if they had something this valuable in here? Either because the diamond's *not* here, or…" She paused to consider. "Well, the family's up to its eyeballs in debt. Maybe they eliminated their security monitoring to cut down on expenses."

Allegro used the blueprint to make her way to the front of the house, where the door to the cellar was located. Every room she passed was accounted for on the schematic. She stayed close to the walls, ticking off the doorways against the picture on the back of the camera, until all of a sudden it didn't make sense.

"This is strange. I'm supposed to be standing in front of a room that's not here."

"It's an old map and a four-hundred-year-old house. How accurate can it be?"

"Yeah. You could be right." Continuing to the end of another hallway, she found the door to what the blueprint indicated was the cellar. It was locked. Once again, she took out her pick and opened it with little effort. "I'm about to enter the cellar."

The underground level was very dark, so she turned on a small headlamp. The cellar was huge, extending under most of the many rooms above. But despite the room's immense square footage, the family had managed to jam it full of a variety of treasures and trash. There were old paintings and hunting decoys, broken pieces of furniture, bicycles and Lord knew what else in endless boxes and barrels. Allegro glanced into the nearest container. It was filled with tubes of acrylics, spray cans of paint, and well-used camel hair brushes. One of the van der Jagts was obviously an amateur artist. She wondered if it was Kris.

"Whole lot of junk down here. Don't these people ever throw anything away?" She studied the camera blueprint again and turned toward the wall behind her. "Okay, good news is, I found it." The built-in metal vault was not just old, but ancient, with a locking mechanism she'd never come across before, though she'd seen something similar in a book during her EOO training. The safe was covered in cobwebs and its door was ajar. "Bad news is, it's bare."

"Someone beat us to it?"

"No, it's not even locked. From the looks of it, it hasn't been used in years."

"Then you'd better start with the rest of the house," Nighthawk said. "Dawn is an hour away."

"You know, you have to quit with the human sundial thing. I'm capable of telling time." Allegro made her way back to the first floor, pausing to examine the wall she'd passed on her way to the cellar. She knocked experimentally. The dull thud of her fist sounded like concrete. She continued to knock along the wall until she came to a spot that sounded hollow. From the small pack she was carrying, she withdrew a portable radar scope. About the size of a telephone handset, it could see through twelve inches of concrete. When she held it in front of the wall, solid objects showed up as green shapes against the black screen. She could clearly make out a small room not much bigger than a walk-in closet, maybe six by four feet. Inside was a rectangular object about the size of a safe. "Son of a bitch. I knew it."

"What do you have?"

"I've found the safe, but I can't get to it."

"She'll be here soon."

"Keep your shorts on."

When she'd eliminated the three interior adjacent walls as possible access points, she made her way back to the cellar. Negotiating her way through the junk to a point directly beneath the walled-in room, she directed her headlight up to study the ceiling. It was low enough to reach by standing on a chair. The concrete above her was new and in stark contrast to the surrounding ancient brickwork. This had obviously once been the way to get in and out of the hidden room, but the entry had been sealed up in recent years, just like the one in Venice. There had to be an alternative entrance. But where?

"Check something for me," she told Nighthawk. "Go to the southwest corner of the house and make sure there's no possible hidden entry there from the outside."

"Roger that."

While he searched, she headed to the den and skimmed through the documents in the desk, looking for any reference to the diamond or the safe.

"Nada," Nighthawk reported back. "And the clock is ticking."

"I'm gonna punch *your* clock if you don't keep quiet and let me work." She picked up a handwritten note on the lawyer's letterhead, about repairs to the mansion. Reading it, she began to formulate an idea. "Coming out," she informed Nighthawk.

As she headed back toward the tower, she glanced at her watch. It was seven thirty a.m. in Amsterdam. Eleven thirty p.m. in Colorado. She grinned. With luck, Monty Pierce might already be asleep.

She got him on the phone as soon as they were back in the car and safely away from the estate. "I've located the safe, Monty, I just need to find a way to get to it."

"I'm sure that won't be a problem for you, of all people," the EOO Chief replied. His voice was groggy. "Good work. You can tell Nighthawk I want him here in forty-eight hours. I need to him to get ready for another job. I'm sure you can handle this alone."

"In other words, I'm to remain here solo, without eyes and ears on the outside. An open target of sorts."

"I'm sure you'll manage."

"I don't have a choice."

❖

Hans Hofman wanted to arrive at the van der Jagt estate before the handyman he'd hired, so he could get a good look around the place and prioritize what needed to be done. As he approached the gravel drive he was surprised to see a woman walking alone in the same direction. American, he guessed from her faded jeans, hooded sweatshirt, and baseball cap. As he drove past, he glanced at her face. She was older than the typical vacationing student seen on the streets of Amsterdam. Probably in her early thirties. He parked in front of the house and got out, but remained where he was, staring at what was once a grand example of seventeenth-century Dutch architecture, now a worn and faded vestige of its former self. He couldn't believe that Jan had let it come to this. There were no other cars, so Kris had evidently not yet arrived from Venice.

The woman from the road stopped in front of him and offered a cheerful greeting. "They told me in town that I could rent a horse out here, real cheap," she said after he'd mumbled a hello. "Is this the place?"

"The family used to own horses, but they were never for rent." Hans was pleased his assessment had been correct. Her accent was distinctly American.

"So this is not your house?"

"No. It belongs to a dear friend."

"Maybe I should ask him."

Allegro took a couple of steps toward the house. She knew the elderly man had to be Hans Hofman. In the note left inside the mansion, he'd indicated that he'd be by the estate today, and his appearance confirmed everything she knew of him. He'd served in World War II, which would put him in his eighties, and he wore the type of conservative business suit common to those in the legal profession. His large nose and lack of any discernable jawline evidenced his Dutch heritage.

"That won't be possible. My friend passed away a month ago." Hofman's attention was back on the house. "The house now belongs to his daughter. She's due to arrive today."

Allegro stood beside him and they both stared up at the house. It was obvious he'd once been very close to the owner. Pain and sadness were evident in his expression and slumped shoulders. "I'm sorry for your loss," she said. "It's a beautiful house."

"It used to be. It's falling apart now. She simply can't afford it, but so much needs to be done before she can sell it." He said the last more to himself than to her.

"It's on the market?"

"More or less, but she can barely manage to pay for the repairs to get a decent price on it."

"You know, in the States you can have cheap handymen come in and do wonders. Maybe she could try that," Allegro suggested.

"It's not as simple in the Netherlands. Officially, hiring someone who isn't licensed is not legal."

"Unofficially?"

Hofman smiled at her eager tone. "If I didn't know better, I'd say you were looking for work, young lady."

"The wisdom of your years would make that assessment correct." Allegro produced her most charming smile. "I came here a month ago. Started out in Amsterdam and thought I'd spread out, know what I mean? Anyway, I want to stay here for at least another month and I'd rather spend my cash on something more interesting than hotels."

"I see."

"So…I figure if you need help and I can provide that help…well, in my book that's serendipity." She stuck out her hand. "The name's Angelica Whitman. Call me Angie."

"Hans Hofman. Well, Angie, you look strong and healthy enough. Are you handy?"

"Carpentry, painting, plumbing, roofing, some landscaping, and electrical work. You name it, I can do it."

His smile got broader. "You don't say."

"I don't even require much in the way of payment. I'm good with a room and a meal now and then. So, do we have a deal?" she pressed eagerly. "I mean, you can cut me loose if it doesn't work out."

"I think we have a deal. And if you need transportation, you're welcome to use Jan's bicycle. It's in the barn." Hofman reached into his pocket for a set of keys. "Why don't we have a look inside? You can tell me what you think."

Before they could move, a van with a logo painted on the side pulled up and parked next to them. The driver, a blond, sturdily built man in his thirties, got out and greeted the lawyer.

"Angie, this is Jeroen," Hofman said, shaking the man's hand. "You'll be working with him."

CHAPTER SIX

Kris was absolutely and thoroughly exhausted to the bone, physically and mentally. Glancing in the rearview mirror, she could see that she looked it as well, with dark circles under her puffy eyes. She'd had to shoo the last Carnival guests away so the movers could get started, and the cleanup from the festivities had taken all the energy she could muster.

Returning to the Haarlem estate was not something she was looking forward to. Memories of the last time she was there, after her father's funeral, were still too fresh and she dreaded the idea of all that had to be done to fix up her childhood home before it could be sold. But her current fatigue exceeded her misgivings. All she could think about was how wonderful it was going to feel to finally lie down and sleep.

She was driving her father's Renault Clio, a far cry from the luxury cars he'd favored in more prosperous times. Her mind flashed to the many times she'd ridden this stretch of highway in the backseat of his Jaguar, her eyes stinging from the smoke of his cigar. Almost unconsciously, she cracked the window. There was never any conversation during their outings as a family. Her father brooked no distractions when he was enjoying himself behind the wheel of one of his sports cars. But although he was able to tell by the slightest noise if anything was amiss mechanically, he never had an ear for anything she or her mother had to say.

Kris pulled into the drive and parked. As soon as she did, her body, as if awaiting its first opportunity to really relax, went leaden. She had two large suitcases with her; the rest of her things were being shipped from Venice. Gathering the last ounce of her strength, she hauled the bags through the front door and across the foyer toward the salon. The bedrooms required climbing stairs. The salon had a nice, inviting couch. When she turned the corner into the front room, however, she was so tired it took her a few seconds to realize the furniture had been moved to one side. The floor was covered with white dust and chunks of some kind of material. She was still trying to figure out what the debris was when she was blindly tackled from the side and sent flying. Her bags left her hands and she crashed against the wood plank flooring so hard it knocked the wind out of her and sent a flash of pain shooting up her elbow to her shoulder.

"What in God's name?" she sputtered once she could regain her breath.

She gazed up into a pair of caramel-colored eyes. A woman was lying on top of her. An attractive woman, she had time to register. With dark brown hair, olive skin, even features, and a very mischievous smile.

"Hi, there," the woman said in English. She was American, from her accent. She cocked her head to scrutinize Kris as openly as Kris was studying her. "I'm Angie."

"Would you kindly remove your hand from my breast and get off me?"

"Oops. My bad." The stranger chuckled as she stood and brushed herself off. "By the way, I saved your life. In my country that's a good thing." She extended a hand to help Kris up.

Ignoring the offer, Kris got to her feet without assistance. "What exactly are you doing in my country, and in my house for that matter?" The woman was covered in the white dust. Looking down at her own clothes, Kris noted that she was, as well.

"I'm fixing your ceiling, at the moment, so it doesn't rain on your pretty little head. I take it you're the lady of the house?"

"Not by choice," Kris said, more to herself than the stranger, as she took in the mess at her feet. There was now a very large chunk of plaster where she'd been standing only seconds ago. This Angie woman apparently had indeed just saved her from serious injury…or worse. Kris's irritation faded a little. Rubbing her shoulder, she said, "I thought Hans had hired a man."

"He did," a male voice interjected from above. She glanced up and for the first time noticed the handyman, who was perched atop a ladder near the high ceiling. "Hoi, Kris. I'm Jeroen. Sorry, we didn't expect you to be here." He twisted his head to address the American. "Great reflexes, Angie."

"Yeah, lucky for me, Jeroen, or we'd both be out of a job," the American replied cheekily. "So, lady of the house, how about some dinner to show your gratitude?"

"What are you saying?" Kris asked.

"Room and board, that was the agreement." Angie picked up a small crowbar to resume what she'd been working on. "And I don't know about you," she said, looking up at Jeroen, "but I'm famished."

They both smiled at Kris expectantly.

Room and board? Could this nightmare get any worse? "I don't remember agreeing to anything of the kind," she told her savior. "And you look healthy enough to fix your own meal."

"Fine." The woman headed to the ladder. "We'll get our own dinner."

Kris retrieved her purse from where it had landed when she'd been tackled. "American!" she called out. The woman paused halfway up the ladder. "Here. Catch." She tossed her car keys. "Take my car to get to town. You can pick up something there." She crossed to the doorway of the salon, where she stopped to retrieve her wallet. "And here's your dinner money," she said sarcastically as she threw forty euros on the floor. She was two steps into the salon when she heard the American call after her.

"Angie. The name's Angie."

She never turned nor replied, but smiled broadly at the irritation she'd provoked in the woman's tone. It felt good to knock that smugness out of her voice. *Pretty little head? Get me some lunch?* She wondered who this arrogant American was, and why Hans had hired her. Kris dropped onto the couch. Her exhaustion was getting worse by the second. She searched in her coat pocket for her cell phone and dialed Hans Hofman.

He picked up right away, and she launched into him in Dutch. "Where did you find her and why am I buying her dinner?"

"Angie?" he replied brightly. "Charming, isn't she?"

"Charming?" she snapped. "Try arrogant and smug. I think she expected me to bow to the greatness that is her."

Hans laughed. "Yup. Sounds like her. Give her a chance, Kris. I think you'll like her. She really *is* charming, you know."

Kris was unmoved. "Where did you find her?"

He explained the chance meeting and the agreements made about payment for the job.

"So I have to take her in, feed her, and be at her beck and call?" Kris let her tone convey her unhappiness with the arrangement, but her uncle continued as though he hadn't noticed.

"You could also give her a hand with the repairs," he suggested. "The job will go much quicker with everyone working."

Kris went quiet, lost in thought. She stared at the grandfather clock across the room, listening to the seconds tick away.

"Are you still there?" Hans asked finally.

"I used to have a life, you know. How could Father have screwed it all up like this? How did I end up in this situation?"

"Serendipity," he said. "That's what Angie called it."

❖

The guest room Kris had chosen for her was on the second floor at the end of the hall, as far away from Kris's bedroom as possible. It was comfortably furnished and had a view overlooking the side of the estate, but it hadn't been cleaned in months. Dust covered every surface and a dank odor pervaded the space. Allegro opened the windows before settling on the bed to pore over the diary pages she'd photographed.

The contents of the journal provided insights into the complicated man who was Kris's father and detailed how he'd acquired the diamond one December day in 1946. According to the diary, Jan van der Jagt had recognized German Lieutenant Geert Wolff when they'd encountered each other on the street. He'd just been staring at the man's face on a flyer during a briefing. Wolff was one of a number of Gestapo officers still at large and believed to be living in Berlin. Van der Jagt was anxious for his share of the glory afforded those who tracked down Nazi war criminals and brought them to justice. His diary chronicled his inner turmoil over the bribe the German offered him to keep silent. He'd been a loyal Allied officer, Jan claimed, unwavering in his duty until that day. But the war was over and the conflict had devastated his homeland, stripping him of his wealth and most of the family estates.

His once-prestigious noble title was meaningless and he had a wife to consider.

Allegro read each page slowly, mentally translating the Dutch text.

> *I didn't trust Wolff. I thought he was speaking out of desperation in order to get me somewhere alone where he could kill me. But Hans was with me, and so I went to the Nazi's apartment. Hans stood guard outside, ready to call the police if I didn't reappear.*
>
> *But Wolff wasn't lying. He had a cellar full of treasures, and he offered me all of it—paintings, sculptures, silver, jewelry. And a diamond, more glorious than I had ever seen. I knew where he'd gotten it, and how. But what was I to do? The RAF paid nothing, my wife was living in a drafty basement apartment, and I was scrambling to keep food on the table. And here he was, offering a way to lift us from that wretched, meager existence and regain all we had lost. Were we not victims of war as well, and entitled to some compensation?*

Jan had struggled all night with his decision, he claimed. His betrayal of his country and sworn duty ate at his conscience. And although he knew Hans would keep silent about the matter, the bribe might come to light in some other way, and he might be brought to trial himself. Most of all, he worried that, if he let Wolff escape, the German might resurface to reclaim the looted possessions and perhaps retaliate against his family.

> *I knew if I turned him in, it would be his word against mine so I returned to his apartment the next day with the police. Not for the glory. I did it to protect my family. Everything was for them.*

Allegro frowned. The pages she'd copied provided no help in finding the vault. She'd have to return to the lawyer's office to photograph the rest. She closed the windows, settled beneath the plush comforter, and was quickly asleep.

When her alarm clock went off three hours later, she lay in bed staring at the ceiling, wondering why they could spend money sealing up entrances and hiding vaults, but not invest in a heating system sufficient for a house this big. Having to get up at one a.m. in order to search the drafty old mansion was bad enough. Worse was that she'd been in the middle of a wonderful dream when the shrill warning went off—she was in England, testing out a brand-new Ferrari on the track at Silverstone.

She forced herself out of her warm, cozy nest and hurriedly donned sweats. Her back ached from the ceiling renovations. The sooner this assignment was over, the faster she could return to her much more satisfying civilian job as a Formula One race-car mechanic.

The house was quiet except for the occasional creak of the ancient wood flooring beneath her feet, and the overly loud ticking of the grandfather clock in the salon. She returned to the walls surrounding the hidden room and checked each again thoroughly. Although he was back home in the States, she could hear Nighthawk saying, *This is ridiculous. What do you think you're going to find? A revolving wall?* The truth was, she didn't have a clue what she was hoping to come across. Maybe all entrances had been sealed simply because the safe was empty, and hadn't been used for centuries. Even if there was a way into the sealed chamber, she had no proof that anything would be in there. Too many ifs and maybes, but she couldn't take the risk of not finding out.

She decided to go back to the cellar and have a better look. Halfway down the hall, she heard the floor creak. She froze and immediately turned off her small penlight. Coming straight at her in the dark was Kris. There was no point in turning away or trying to hide. She couldn't do so undetected. A better approach was to confront her, before Kris saw her and thought she was sneaking around.

"Couldn't sleep either?"

Her only answer was a shriek and something that came flying her way.

"Kris, relax, it's me," she said as she ducked. But Kris had started to run in the opposite direction as if she hadn't heard, still screaming. Allegro ran after her but slipped on something on the floor. Skidding wildly forward, she groped for a doorknob and managed to break her fall. Within seconds, she was running after Kris again, and when she caught up she grabbed her by the arm from behind. "Damn it, stop screaming. You're going to wake the dead. It's only me."

Kris jerked around. "What in the hell are you doing creeping around in the dark?"

"I was in the kitchen looking for something to eat. I didn't want to wake you up so I didn't turn on the lights. Besides, what were you doing in the dark?"

"I had just finished making myself a sandwich and was taking it back to my room." Kris stepped to the wall switch and turned on the lights in the hall.

It was then Allegro got her first good look at the woman she'd terrified. Kris was wearing black silk pajamas with a matching robe. With her long, blond hair tousled from sleep, she looked entirely too kissable. Allegro noted her empty hands and glanced past her down the hall. The sandwich contents were strewn in a trail behind them. Bread... cheese...salami...and the mayonnaise she'd apparently slipped on.

"When they say mayonnaise isn't good for you, they're not kidding. I almost broke my leg." Allegro rubbed her knee.

"Fortunately, you survived."

"Do I detect regret in your tone?"

"Turn on the lights from now on," Kris said. "Next time I might hurt you."

"Why don't you like me?" Allegro asked. "I'm only here to help, you know."

"I don't dislike you. Actually you leave me indifferent, Ms....er... Now, if you don't mind, I'm going to clean up this mess and get some sleep."

"The name's Angie," Allegro called after her. How hard could it be to remember that? If she could get used to it, why couldn't Kris?

CHAPTER SEVEN

Sunday, February 10

When dawn broke, Allegro rolled away from the light streaming in through the window and buried herself farther in the blankets, steadfastly refusing to rouse. There was still ample time to get her morning jog in before Jeroen arrived to resume work. Her stomach growled. Then her nose caught a whiff of... *Aww. She's up making breakfast for me. How sweet. Maybe it's a peace offering.* That thought, however, was immediately followed by the realization that the kitchen was too far away for her to be smelling bacon. She sniffed the air again. No, she swore she could smell...

She opened her eyes and found the source on her pillow. What she was smelling was the salami that must have been plastered to her hair all night. Kris had certainly gotten a good look at her when she'd turned on the light, but she hadn't said a word or cracked a smile. Had the woman no sense of humor at all? Allegro frowned. She needed Kris to open up to her, because she would know where the diamond was. Humor and charm weren't working, so perhaps it was time to try a different tack.

The city of Haarlem was just two miles from the estate, so it took Allegro only a half hour to jog the distance. The day was cool but clear, and she allowed herself the opportunity to forget her mission for a while and enjoy the scenery. She passed by a number of remote estates similar to the van der Jagts', stately country homes dating back three centuries or more, but what dominated the landscape were massive tulip fields that would be ablaze with color in another two or three months' time.

As she walked along the Spaarne canal toward the small city, she spotted a young Dutchman and his son in a small fishing boat, their pale blond hair iridescent in the morning sunlight. She paused for a few seconds to enjoy the sight. She was no stranger to the Netherlands, having been based here before the EOO transferred her to London. During that time, she'd gotten to know the country quite well. She'd spent many evenings out in Amsterdam, either looking for brief encounters or taking in the city by night. She enjoyed the beauty and versatility of the small metropolis known as the Venice of Northern Europe. Even after moving to London, she often spent long weekends back in the Netherlands.

But in moments like this, when she'd pause by some picturesque canal watching boats full of families go by, or sit sipping cappuccino at a sidewalk café as passersby strolled hand in hand, a melancholic yearning for something she couldn't quite identify rose up in her. Normally she could suppress this feeling of an ever-present void in her life by keeping constantly on the move. Working, and racing cars in her other life as a professional driver, provided opportunities for fast, thrilling, exhilarating performances. Her casual trysts with women were another outlet. She liked to push her lovers to their limits, the way she did her cars, giving them the kind of rush she felt behind the wheel. But the experience was never the same for her. Her sexual encounters were fun and killed the boredom, but she was always aware of simply going through the motions, as she did with most everything else in her life. It was only when she allowed herself to slow down for a moment that her lonely existence became completely real.

The giggle of a woman drew her attention to a young couple approaching on a bicycle. The boy pedaling had a big smile on his face; his girlfriend was riding sideways on the rack behind the seat, her arms wrapped tightly around his waist. She let go with one hand to wave at Allegro as they went past, and Allegro waved back. Was this what she needed to really feel alive? Could it be that all it took was someone to hold onto, someone to make her giggle and love her unconditionally? Was that what she was missing?

She returned to the hotel room she and Nighthawk had booked, and gathered up her things to take back to the estate. Slinging her duffel bag over one shoulder, she checked out and headed back the way she came, past stately manors and quaint shops, and through the remnants of the ancient wall that had once surrounded Haarlem. She was barely to the city limits when she heard a car approaching and saw a small Renault with Kris at the wheel. When she raised a hand to wave, it slowed to a stop and the passenger window rolled down.

Allegro smiled and shifted the duffel bag on her shoulder as though it were a lot heavier than it really was. Here was the perfect opportunity to try melting the ice between them. Time to use what information she had about Kris to gain her trust. "Are you offering me a lift back to the house?"

"I suppose," Kris replied. "I'm done here."

"Thanks." Allegro threw her duffel into the backseat and got in the passenger side. "I picked up the rest of my stuff."

"You walked?"

"Jogged. It's not far."

They were silent for a while as they resumed the journey toward the estate.

"Any chance we'll get some snow out here?" Allegro asked when Kris showed no interest in talking.

Kris glanced at her. "We don't have to do this, you know."

"Do what?"

"Polite conversation."

Allegro sighed loudly. "Listen, I know you must be upset by your father's death and having to take care of the house and who knows what else." She half turned to face Kris. "But it's just you and me there most of the time until your place is fixed up, and I'm only trying to be civil. I don't know why you—"

"Who *are* you?" Kris interrupted.

"Jesus." Allegro shook her head in amusement. "Up until now I thought you were kidding when you refused to remember my name."

But Kris wasn't smiling. "I mean, who are you really? Why are you here? What do you want from me?"

The questions, and Kris's expression, instantly placed Allegro on her guard. Kris couldn't possibly know anything, could she? "Like I told Hans," she said casually, "I'm looking to extend my time here. Postpone my return to the States. And I don't want to waste my money on hotels."

"Aren't you too old to be…as you Americans say…doing Europe on a shoestring?"

"Maybe. But we all have our reasons. I needed to get away from home for a while."

Kris's eyes narrowed. "Are you in some kind of trouble?"

"No, nothing like that." Allegro waved the idea off as if the possibility was ridiculous. "I figured it was time for a fresh start, that's all." She gazed out the window, attempting to sound like she had secret regrets and a past she couldn't discuss. In a sense, she was telling the truth. "That was a year ago, but it never happened because I stayed where I was. Turned out that *willing* things to change, while I was still stuck in the same place doing the same things and seeing the same people, didn't work. So…I decided on a different approach. Find a way that made going back to old habits impossible." She could feel Kris staring at her, but she kept her attention on the countryside they were passing, a mix of farms and woodlands.

"So you're running, then," Kris surmised. "From your family? Husband? Boyfriend? What?"

"I really don't want to talk about it. Not while I'm still in rehab, anyway." At Kris's sudden intake of breath, Allegro met her eyes. "That's what I call it. This addiction of not being able to let go of what I don't need but depend on, in an unhealthy way." She smiled inwardly when she saw Kris's small nod of acknowledgment, as though she understood this all too well.

"Fair enough." Kris returned her attention to the road. "I think I can empathize with that."

I bet you can. "How about you? Are you married? Engaged? I don't see children."

"None of the above," Kris answered. "I've had some relationships in the past, but nothing significant. They were either a means to kill the boredom, or the 'wayward' sort, if you know what I mean, to frustrate my father. I guess any attention was better than none."

The house came into view and Allegro realized she didn't want the ride or the conversation to end. Not only because Kris was finally opening up a little, but also because she was really enjoying this civil and easy exchange between them. As they turned into the gravel drive, she caught a glimpse of someone, a man running from the back of the house into the woods. Jeroen wasn't due for another hour, so it couldn't be him. And this guy wasn't some prospective buyer checking out the place or he would have waited for them to return instead of taking off like a scared rabbit.

She was instantly on high alert, scanning the area of the trees where he'd disappeared for a hint of movement or color. Outwardly, she kept her body posture relaxed and her voice matter-of-fact. Kris had given no indication she'd seen the man, and Allegro didn't want to alarm her and risk getting the police involved. "Yeah, bad boys can be fun," she agreed, "but tiresome pretty quickly, especially if they're just there to make a point."

"Bad *girls*," Kris corrected.

Despite her preoccupation with the fleeing stranger, Allegro was intrigued by Kris's revelation. This interesting little tidbit was certainly not in her dossier. Sure, Kris had let her kiss her in Venice, but Carnival time was infamous for loosening inhibitions. People engaged in behavior that might not be the norm. "Excuse me? I thought you said bad *girls*."

"I did." Kris pulled up to the house and parked.

Much as Allegro wanted to pursue the turn this conversation had taken, she had to let it drop. Now was not the time. She had more pressing matters to attend to. "I'm going to get things ready for Jeroen. Need help getting this stuff inside?" In the backseat, beside her duffel, was a large sack of groceries.

Kris shook her head. "I think I can handle it."

Allegro hauled her bag up to her room, hurrying once she was out of sight. From her window, all seemed quiet. She went to one of the unoccupied bedrooms that faced the rear of the estate and studied the view from there. There was no sign of the man she'd seen running from the house. Making her way back downstairs, she made sure Kris was occupied in the kitchen before she slipped out the front door.

There were fresh boot prints in the soft dirt along the side of the house. Smooth, with a diamond imprint in the heel, not like the rubber-soled workman's boots that Jeroen wore. She followed the prints to the back of the house and frowned when she saw that they led to a large wooden crate beneath one of the high windows leading to the den. The man must have dragged it there so he could see inside.

The only good news was the fairly scant number of boot prints. The absence of trampling suggested he probably hadn't been there long before they'd arrived and surprised him, and the wide spacing between them as they led into the woods confirmed that he'd been running fast to get away. The prints became more difficult to track in the densely packed earth of the forest, but she was able to follow other clues, the occasional broken tree limb or disturbance in the undergrowth. She trailed him to the next road, where he'd probably left his car.

That someone else wanted the diamond enough to risk breaking into the mansion was not unexpected, since she'd been briefed the Afghans were going after it as well. But Allegro was stunned that they'd gotten here so fast. Their intel must be pretty damn good. They knew Kris had the diamond and where she lived. They'd also ascertained that no one was home and the house had no security, if the man was willing to approach it in broad daylight. Had he been watching them? For how long?

She'd have to be extremely vigilant from now on, especially since she was acting solo. This development put even more pressure on her to find the stone quickly. She had to get to it before he did. She returned to the mansion and found Kris still in the kitchen, digging into bacon and eggs, toast, and coffee. It smelled heavenly.

"Snooze, you lose, isn't that the expression?" Kris greeted her with a wry smile. "What happened to you? I called up and asked if you wanted some breakfast. For future reference, I don't ask twice."

"No prob. Not really hungry." Allegro tried to ignore the savory smells and the way her stomach was growling. "Say, were you expecting anybody this morning?"

"Expecting anyone? You mean, besides Jeroen? No. Why?"

"No neighbors or anything?"

"No. We've never socialized with any of our neighbors," Kris said. "My father valued privacy. Most of the time Hans was his only visitor. They were like brothers."

Allegro made herself a cup of coffee. Hans Hofman again. He was there when Jan got the diamond, and apparently was his only friend when he died. She needed to get back in his office and photograph more of that diary. Perhaps she'd find another clue. Perhaps Hans kept his own records.

"So, why are you asking about visitors?" Kris pressed.

"Oh, I thought I saw a guy outside," Allegro replied offhandedly. "Must have been someone passing by." The last thing she needed was to put Kris on alert. "Could be that word's out in town that the house is going up for sale."

She lingered over coffee only until Kris finished her breakfast and went upstairs. Jeroen was due anytime, and she had a task to do that required a few minutes of solitude and improvisation. In Jan van der Jagt's desk, she found pencils and transparent tape and a couple of his business cards, pristine and white. It took her a few minutes to split three pencils and remove the lead. A mortar and pestle from one of the kitchen cabinets quickly reduced the lead to a fine powder.

She used a makeup brush from her toiletries kit to apply the shavings to the outside of the window above the crate. The intruder was obviously not a pro. As she suspected, he'd pressed his face against the glass to peer into the darkened interior of the house and flattened his hands on the pane as well, to shield his eyes. It looked like she had a usable set of prints. She photographed them first with her pocket camera, set on macro zoom, then used the transparent tape to lift them slowly from the glass and apply them carefully to the back of the business cards. With her cell phone cam, she photographed the black-on-white version of the prints and sent the images to EOO headquarters for identification.

When she was finished, she wiped the window clean, returned the crate to where it had been, and lightly raked the area to obliterate the boot prints. She expected Jeroen to park his van back here, as he had the day prior, to more conveniently unload the supplies they'd need through the rear entrance. No need to alert him, either, that anything was amiss.

❖

Angie was a damn attractive woman, even in her work clothes and covered in plaster. Hers was the kind of toned, fit body Kris had to admit she'd always favored. And she seemed to have a mischievous playfulness about her. A twinkle in those beautiful caramel eyes, like she didn't have a care in the world. All Kris's life, she'd done and been the opposite. She glanced out her bedroom window at the grounds of the estate and surrounding woods. There'd been no swing set there for her, no tea parties with the neighboring children, or games of hide-and-seek. She'd spent much of her youth alone in her room, reading.

It hadn't been much fun in this household. She wondered what kind of childhood Angie must have had, to turn out the way she had. So different.

It was foolish, she realized, to entertain any kind of interest in the American. Once the work on the house was done, Angie would be on her footloose way again and on the other side of the world, only a distant memory. It was all these sudden changes that prompted such musings. Her father's death, selling the houses, having to support her mother.

When she'd left home at eighteen to move into the villa, her father had gifted her with a sizeable endowment to maintain the lifestyle he'd insisted was necessary and befitted their social status. In recent years, however, she'd come to loathe her dependence on her father's funds, so as the money dwindled, she'd built up a lucrative Web design business to avoid having to ask for more. A wise move, in retrospect, since her father was in bad shape financially and too vain to admit it, even to her or Hans. He'd gone deeply in debt rather than sell off his prestigious properties.

Now Kris's Web design business was all she had, and it wasn't enough to relieve her worries about the future. She was restless and looking for a distraction to keep her from thinking too hard about the fact she had no idea what she was going to do next with her life. She knew that was why she was fascinated by the American. But she also knew it was best to seek distraction in something or someone a little safer than some transient stranger. Before she'd left Venice, she'd gotten an e-mail from Ilse Linssen, an old friend and former lover, inviting her to catch up on their lives over dinner the next time she was in the capital. Perhaps that invitation couldn't have come at a better time.

Allegro waited only a half hour after Kris had retired for the evening to begin a more thorough search of the mansion, alert this time for any further unexpected forays her hostess might make to the kitchen for a late-night snack. But after an exhaustive search she concluded that the only way she was going to get to the safe was to drill through the wall. And that noisy solution was certainly not an option if she wanted to obtain the diamond discreetly and avoid implicating herself as the culprit.

When she retired to her room for a couple of hours' sleep, the ticking of her bedside clock reminded her she had rigid time constraints to complete her mission. She needed to return to Hofman's office, and soon, to see what else Jan van der Jagt might have revealed in his diary about his favorite hiding places for the diamond.

Chapter Eight

Monday, February 11

"I see you're finding your way around the kitchen." Kris stepped gingerly over debris and plaster dust and looked up at the ceiling Allegro had been working on. "Which is fortunate, because you're on your own tonight."

It was clear from her choice of attire that Kris wasn't planning to spend the evening at home. Her charcoal slacks and dove gray silk blouse were the latest designer fashions, as were her matching charcoal pumps and purse, and she'd taken exceptional care with her makeup. Champagne eye shadow and brown mascara and eyeliner brought out the blue of her eyes, and muted mauve rouge and lipstick added just the right amount of color to her fair skin. Her blond hair, sleek and shiny, had been curled in soft waves to frame her oval face. She was stunning.

Allegro got to her feet, ignoring the stiffness in every muscle and joint in her body. She tried not to stare at the provocative way the soft silk of the blouse hugged Kris's high, round breasts. "I'm sure we can manage without you. Got a hot date?"

Kris gave her a frosty look. "I have some business to attend to in Amsterdam, that's all. I probably won't be back until very late."

Allegro grinned, rather enjoying the look of agitation her remark had provoked. She couldn't resist teasing Kris a little more. "What kind of business keeps you out till late?"

"The kind that doesn't concern you."

"If you ask me—"

"Which I'm not."

"You *should* be going on a date," Allegro continued, ignoring the interruption.

Kris exhaled a loud sigh of exasperation. "Do I look that desperate?"

Allegro brazenly assessed her body with an appreciative leer, as though Kris's comeback had been an invitation to do so. "No. You look that good. It'd be a waste to spend the evening with boring conversations."

A flush of pink heightened the color in Kris's cheeks. "I have been accused of many things. Boring is not one of them."

"I don't doubt that. Your presence alone provides me with plenty of excitement."

"You mean you enjoy aggravating me," Kris said.

"I mean you're a very attractive woman." When Allegro let her gaze linger on Kris's cleavage and licked her lips, she was rewarded by a marked increase in the rise and fall of those perfect breasts as Kris's breathing accelerated.

"Isn't there some *work* you should be doing?"

Letting her reluctance show, Allegro tore her focus away from Kris's chest and met her eyes. "Screwing," she deadpanned. The shocked look on Kris's face made it nearly impossible for her to keep from cracking a smile. She pulled a screwdriver out of her back pocket and held it up. "I should screw that chandelier back in place," she said innocently.

Without waiting for a reply, Kris stalked out of the room and a few seconds later the front door slammed shut. Allegro waited for her to drive off before hurrying upstairs for a shower and change of clothes. By the time she biked to Haarlem and retrieved her rental car, dusk had fallen and she hit heavy traffic heading into Amsterdam. Hans Hofman's office was closed by the time she arrived in the city center. Still, there were too many pedestrians and bicyclists about for her to pick the lock without being noticed.

She claimed a bench where she could keep an eye on the neighborhood, biding her time by amusing herself with a game of "peg the tourist," a favorite pastime in cities like Amsterdam. Most of the time she could guess the origins of passersby before snippets of overheard conversation confirmed her assessment. Americans were always easiest, with their backpacks, white sneakers, and slogan sweatshirts. Delineating some of the Mediterranean ethnicities wasn't difficult either. Spaniards were generally shorter than their neighbors, with more rounded faces. Greeks had angular features. French men favored a very distinctive haircut, and their beards were also trimmed in a way that set them apart.

In recent years, British and Dutch housewives, especially those over fifty, had begun favoring the same cropped hairstyle that once set American dykes apart. Among the Asian visitors, the eyes were often the distinguishing feature. The Japanese had a downward slant from nose to temple, the Chinese the opposite. The native Dutch were fair, with weak chins, the men tall and stork-like, the women pear-shaped. Such generalities weren't always reliable, of course, but she was right much more often than wrong.

She played her private game until the street was momentarily devoid of traffic and pedestrians, then let herself into Hofman's building and made her way to his ground floor office. Happy to find the diary right where she'd left it in the lawyer's file cabinet, she immediately began to photograph the remaining fifty or so pages. Now and then, when she spotted the word "diamond" in the text, she would read a few paragraphs, then force herself to resume shooting, conscious that she had to get back to the estate before Kris returned. As she reached the final few pages she was startled by the sound of voices in the outer office. She clicked off her penlight, shoved the diary back into the file, and ducked behind a massive armoire. Her alarm grew when she realized she wasn't overhearing a couple of cleaners getting started on their evening chores. Kris and Hofman were approaching.

"Have you gone to see your mother?" Hofman asked as he flipped on the light and they entered the room.

Allegro heard the squeak of his office chair as he settled into it, and Kris's loud sigh. Though unnerved at nearly being discovered, she was grateful that her Dutch was fluent enough for her to eavesdrop on their conversation.

"Not yet," Kris answered. "I'm afraid seeing me might only make her worse. The doctor says she's still unable to distinguish her fantasies from reality. Since Father's death she's retreated further inside her own little world. She's refusing even to talk at her therapy sessions."

Allegro caught a glimpse of Kris moving toward the window

overlooking the canal. She pressed her back against the armoire to avoid being seen.

"Her psychiatrist doesn't think she'll be up to leaving anytime soon," Kris continued. "Every time she seems to be getting better, something sets her off again. This is the worst bout of depression she's ever had."

"I know you don't want to upset her by moving her," Hofman said. "But there are less expensive alternatives than where she is."

"I'll think about that if it becomes absolutely necessary," Kris promised. "But not now. I can't deal with another suicide attempt on top of everything else, and it sounds as though she's in that frame of mind again. I wish she'd talk about it instead of holding everything in. I don't know what's made her this way."

"There's no need to make a decision now," Hofman said. "Her care is paid for through the end of next month."

"If the villa sells quickly, that should resolve that problem. The house certainly looks like it will take a lot longer. Speaking of which, I really should be annoyed with you for hiring that American. She's... irritating beyond belief. So smug."

Allegro bit back a smile.

"She's definitely a confident woman," Hofman said. "How is she handling the work?"

There was a pause. "I guess I have no complaints there. She did work very hard yesterday, and was at it again early this morning. Though I suspect she might have been pounding on the ceiling at nine a.m. because she knew I was still asleep right above her."

Hofman laughed. "It's saving you a lot of money having her work for room and board. I find her quite charming."

"So you said." Kris sounded dubious.

"Kris, have you given any thought about what you're going to do once both places have sold?" Hofman asked. "I know the difficulties you're facing, and you're welcome to stay here, of course. I have a spare room upstairs if you need it."

"That's very generous, Uncle. I hope it doesn't come to that, but I'll keep your offer in mind. Let's hope the sale of the house can solve most of my problems. Then I can get an apartment nearby and visit you instead."

"Either would suit me. Will you live in Amsterdam, then?" The pleasure in Hofman's voice was unmistakable, revealing the affection he had for Kris.

"I'm not tied to anywhere. As long as I have my computer, I can do my job. At least if I'm here I can visit you, and keep an eye on Mother."

"I wish I could do more to help," Hofman said. "I know I told you I'd be out to the estate to look in on things, but my current case will prevent that for a few more days. Is there anything you need?"

"No, it's fine." Kris was standing close enough to the armoire that Allegro could smell the lavender of her perfume. "Although I did want you to show me how to get to the vault. I know you explained it in your phone call, but I've been so preoccupied with the debts that I'm afraid that part is just a blur."

"You know where the room itself is, correct?"

"Yes," Kris replied. "Father told me the history of the mansion, and pointed out the wall around the priest's room. But I thought the only entrance had been sealed up years ago."

Priest's room? Why hadn't she thought of it earlier? The estate had been built in the seventeenth century, during the Reformation, when Catholics throughout the Netherlands had to worship in secret. Some of the so-called "hidden churches" built within homes were still preserved in Amsterdam, drawing steady streams of tourists. Most of them had a priest's room, a small alcove with a secret door, where the priest could be hidden if authorities discovered the church.

"The room was originally accessed through a trapdoor to the cellar," Hofman said. "Jan sealed it up. I imagine he must have been afraid if anyone learned of the diamond, the vault would be too easy to find, so he reconstructed, probably while you and your mother were in Venice. Very clever of him to put the new entrance through the garden."

The garden. Allegro would have found it eventually, but she was thankful she wouldn't have to waste time ruling out all the alternatives now.

"I spent so many years playing out there, getting into everything," Kris said. "It's just amazing I never stumbled across it. Or that the gardener didn't, either."

"That was the general idea," Hofman said. "Hiding in plain sight."

Kris said something Allegro couldn't make out, then added, "I must run. Thanks for everything, Uncle."

"I'll walk you down. I need to stop by the night store for a few things."

Allegro heard Hofman's chair squeak, followed by the sound of the door closing. She went to the window and discreetly watched them leave. They stood talking for a few minutes in the dim light provided by a street lamp several yards away. There were a few pedestrians out on the street, most moving with the sense of purpose people had at night when they were on their way to meet someone or heading home after dinner.

Allegro noticed the one person standing completely still, a dark figure in the shadow of a tree not far from Hofman's building. From the way his attention was fixated on Kris and her uncle, he might as well be holding up a LOOK AT ME sign. Allegro had worked on surveillance ops often enough to know he wasn't some tourist or a local out having a smoke or enjoying the view. Trying to measure his intentions, she watched him closely as Hofman and Kris embraced and kissed good-bye. As they set off in opposite directions, both on foot, the man watching them lifted the collar of his beige trench coat and glanced around before walking quickly in Kris's direction. Allegro couldn't get a clear enough view of his face to know if he was the man she'd seen at the mansion the day before, but he sure seemed to be stalking Kris. She hurriedly checked her Walther P99 and left the building.

Could this be the same man she'd seen running from the estate? If so, he knew a lot about Kris and where to find her. She had nothing to base any assumptions on, but her gut told her this guy was either after the diamond, or after Kris as a way to get to the stone. Would he go so far as trying to kidnap her?

❖

Kris tucked her scarf into her long woolen coat in an effort to ward off the February evening chill, and headed toward the Rembrandtplein, a small green space surrounded by cafes, bars, and nightclubs, and one of the city's most popular destinations after dark. She'd chosen to walk, knowing she'd have trouble finding a parking spot close by, and she also wanted to clear her head. Hans Hofman's offer of a place to stay had driven home how drastically her life was changing. The renovations would consume the last of her savings. If she couldn't sell her houses quickly, she'd soon be without funds and totally reliant on her Web design business. She could probably support herself in a modest style, but she would not be able to pay for her mother's expensive care.

The prospect of losing her life of privilege wasn't the devastating blow it might be to another in her position. The trappings of wealth and title had only drawn the wrong sort of attention, especially from women whose motivation for getting close to her was all about what she could do for them. A simpler existence had a certain appeal. No more gala parties and keeping up appearances. No more living up to anyone's idea of how she should behave. Change was good, she told herself, but she still felt overwhelmed and restless. An evening of blowing off steam with a friend was long overdue.

She'd agreed to meet Ilse Linssen at De Kroon, a second-floor café bar in a landmark white brick building more than a century old. The front dining room, where she'd reserved a table, was a glass-enclosed terrace that allowed patrons a splendid view of the busy square below. Several stairs led up to the bar, a spacious lounge area filled with comfy leather chairs and couches. The décor was eclectic: large screen hi-def monitors covered one wall, all airing the same nature video. Around the other walls an array of taxidermy trophy heads vied with busts of famous philosophers.

Kris glanced around, surprised at how busy the place was for a Monday night. The reason became clear at once. Most of the patrons were forty- and fifty-something Italians, probably all from the same tour bus. Ilse was waiting for her at their table. She got to feet and smiled as Kris approached.

"You look wonderful," Kris said, embracing her friend and one-time lover. Ilse hadn't changed much in the nine months since they'd last seen each other. She was model thin and beautiful, chic in a tan cashmere turtleneck and chocolate leather skirt with matching boots. Only her platinum hair was different. She'd cut it several inches shorter, to her jawline, and the style suited her.

Ilse stepped back to arm's length and studied Kris's face. "Everything all right?"

"Is it that obvious?"

"Sit." Ilse let her go. "And tell me all about it."

"Wine first. And some pleasant conversation before I unload all my troubles." Kris got the waiter's attention and ordered a bottle of Chardonnay. "Tell me what you've been up to since your last e-mail. Great new look, by the way."

She listened to Ilse's latest gossip as they sipped their wine and tried to forget for a while how surreal her life had become. Halfway into her second glass, she realized she'd barely listened to a word. Deciding she needed to splash her face, she excused herself and cut through the lounge toward the ladies room, ignoring the usual glances, with one exception, a man watching her from one of the wing chairs. He was alone and not unattractive, with medium brown hair. Probably not Dutch, and not one of the Italians either. But though his gaze was fixed on her, he didn't smile. When she returned to her table, he was still there and still watching her every move.

"I hate the way some people stare." Kris dropped into her seat. "At least do it discreetly, if there's no encouragement."

"Male or female?" Ilse inquired, looking toward the rest rooms.

"Does it matter?" Kris waved a hand absently in the man's direction. "It's the trend that's irritating."

"You sound stressed," Ilse said sympathetically.

"The last few weeks have been a challenge, to say the least." Kris poured herself another glass of wine. "It was very sweet of you to send flowers when Father died. And I got your phone messages. But I wasn't up to talking to anyone."

"I understand," Ilse said.

Kris gazed out the window. A tram braked abruptly below, clanging its horn and narrowly missing a trio of tourists on bright red rental bikes. "My father and I were never close, but I'm only beginning to realize how little I really knew the man. He had a lot of secrets."

"Everyone does. That's human nature."

"No doubt. But I don't think everyone leaves a massive amount of debt for their families to deal with."

Ilse's eyes widened in surprise and she frowned. "I'm sorry. Is it very serious?"

"Well, the villa's already up for sale, and the estate soon will be. And even that may not be enough." A pained laugh escaped Kris. "On the plus side, I'll probably be getting an apartment here in the city, so we can have a cup of coffee now and then."

"Is there anything I can do?"

"You're here, listening. That helps."

Kris felt a pang of regret that she hadn't been open to a real relationship with Ilse during their brief affair four years earlier. But she was already disillusioned with women by then and had kept Ilse at a distance. Looking back, she could see that she hadn't questioned her own behavior at all. She'd rejected Ilse's attempts at greater intimacy automatically, and Ilse had been hurt, perhaps even insulted, by her mistrust. Ilse had long since moved on to someone more willing to open her heart, and Kris had continued having brief, meaningless affairs with women who would cause no ripples in her life. This predictable course had kept her sailing in quiet waters, and even though she missed excitement and passion, she'd learned to be content with anything as long as it lacked drama. Recently however, she'd started to realize she'd mistaken predictability for reliability, and tediousness for peace. She now saw that she'd deluded herself into believing she felt contentment when, in fact, she'd simply settled for a poor imitation of life.

"I'm serious," Ilse reiterated. "If I can help…"

"This is something I have to handle on my own. Not like that's anything new."

Ilse leaned closer and placed a hand on the side of Kris's face. "You don't have to pretend with me, you know. I can see how upset you are."

The gentle touch was all it took. Tears sprang to Kris's eyes and the dam of frustration that had been building inside of her threatened to burst. Unable to conceal her bitterness, she said, "I'm just so fucking tired of playing the countess and doing what's expected of me, Ilse, I want to scream."

CHAPTER NINE

From her vantage point in the adjoining lounge area, half hidden behind a pillar, Allegro watched Kris's companion reach out to touch her cheek. The intimate gesture sent an unfamiliar twinge of something twisting through her stomach. Jealousy? Envy? The turmoil in Kris's expression was clear. Allegro wished she were near enough to hear what the two women were talking about. But as intent as she was on trying to read their interaction, she was equally focused on the man who had followed Kris here. Sitting in a wing chair not far away, he hadn't taken his eyes off her in the last hour. Thankfully, he seemed to be oblivious to everything else, including the fact that he was also being watched.

Allegro studied his face in profile. He was forty or so, with medium brown hair, thin lips, and a slight crook in his nose. Though she still couldn't be absolutely certain it was the guy she'd seen at the estate, he was similar enough in height and build that it was a pretty safe bet. He was sitting with one leg crossed over the other, so Allegro was able to get a good look at the bottom of his boot. The marking on the heel resembled those left in the mud. What was he planning? And was he working alone?

She glanced back toward Kris. From her restless body language, and the abandon with which she was drinking her wine, Allegro could see something was definitely not right with her. She was upset and preoccupied, her usual poise absent. With her guard down she reminded Allegro of a trapped animal or child, helpless to deal with a situation she had little control over. She was vulnerable in her condition, somewhat intoxicated and apparently emotional. It wouldn't be possible to return to Hofman's office tonight. Allegro would have to photograph the last few pages of the diary at another time. Her priority had to be looking out for Kris, and hopefully discovering the identity and purpose of the man following her.

She realized that her decision to make Kris's safety her first concern was a departure from her normal procedure. Ordinarily, she could approach her missions with a detachment that allowed her to focus solely on her objective. But on occasion, a protective instinct she could not ignore made her stray from the cold calculations that usually governed her work. Over the years, she'd seen too many innocents suffer the repercussions of other people's choices, and she'd always felt the need to comfort them, to offer what little she could to make their situation bearable. Something about Kris spoke to that part of her. Allegro already cared more for her than she should. Operatives were taught to pay attention to the warning signs of attachment, emotion that could cloud judgment and lead to self-serving rationalizations for dubious decisions. It was her job to ensure nothing happened to Kris, at least until the diamond was secured, but the truth was, she would protect her, regardless.

When the two women began putting on their coats to leave, Allegro hurriedly donned her jacket and left ahead of them, ducking into the shadowed doorway of a closed flower shop halfway down the block. Kris and her friend walked away from the café arm in arm, still deep in conversation. The man from the lounge emerged soon after and followed them, the collar of his beige trench coat pulled up to partially obscure his face. Allegro tracked them from a distance.

After a couple of blocks, the women paused so Kris's date could unlock a bicycle from a crowded rack. They kissed good-bye and Kris strolled toward a tram stop while her companion pedaled off in the opposite direction. Allegro kept to the shadows, watching the man narrow his distance from Kris, now that she was alone. The street they were on was far enough away from the bustling nightlife around the Rembrandtplein that there were few other pedestrians. Kris reached the shelter of the tram stop and stood waiting, her arms folded against the cold. The man paused a short distance away and lit a cigarette, but tossed it away after only a couple of puffs when the tram came into view.

Allegro's alarm grew when she realized the tram was empty except for the driver. She broke into a run as Kris pulled a ticket from her pocket and pushed the button to open the door at the back, while the man in the trench coat hurried to the open door in front to pay the driver. Allegro's timing had to be perfect, and it was. She reached in and snatched Kris off the tram just as she was mounting the steps. The doors closed, trapping the man inside, and the tram started on its way.

Kris whirled around angrily. A shocked look crossed her face when she recognized Allegro. "What the hell do you think you're doing?"

"Hi to you, too," Allegro said with a broad smile.

Suspicion hardened Kris's features. "Did you follow me?"

As if the accusation made no sense to her, Allegro frowned in a show of bewilderment. "Why would I follow you?"

As she'd hoped, the challenge made Kris pause to examine her own reactions. Even in the hazy lamp light, her reddening cheeks were obvious. She responded, "You tell me," but self-doubt made the question hesitant.

Allegro gave a flippant shrug. "Because you're gorgeous?"

Her sarcasm seemed to hit home. Kris blinked as though trying hard to keep her eyes focused. "Very funny."

"Seriously, I didn't think I was supposed to work day *and* night," Allegro teased. "I thought I'd check out the city by night sort of thing. Anyway, I saw you heading for the tram and I figured I'd offer you a ride back home."

"First of all, it's not *home*, not for me and definitely not for you. And secondly, who says I have plans to go back there tonight?"

Allegro kept one eye on the street. No doubt the man in the beige coat would get off at the next stop, which wasn't far. She had to stay with Kris until she was safe. "You told me you wouldn't be back until very late. I guess I took that to mean you weren't going to be away overnight." Trying to prove she had no agenda, she added, "Look, I don't know anyone here and when I saw you I was happy, that's all. It seemed only right to offer you a ride back to the estate. My mistake. I didn't mean to piss you off."

She watched self-doubt flicker in Kris's eyes. Their shine reflected how much alcohol she'd consumed. "I wasn't aware you had a car," she said with wobbly dignity.

"I rented a car in Haarlem."

"How convenient." Her words were slurred. "Thanks for the offer, but I don't need a lift. In fact, the last thing I need right now is someone else trying to tell me what to do. I'm perfectly capable of getting home by myself." She settled onto the nearest bench with a determined expression.

Allegro was close to losing her patience. Kris was acting like a petulant child, and had it not been for the fact that she was tipsy and agitated, Allegro would have said that to her. But now was definitely not the time. "Look, I made you miss the tram. The least I can do is wait with you for the next one."

"Do what you wish."

As she settled onto the bench beside Kris, Allegro glanced down the rail line. There was no sign of the stalker yet, but he'd be on them any moment. She had to get Kris away from here. "I really wish you'd reconsider and let me give you a lift. The trams don't run very often at this time of night, do they?"

Kris glanced at her watch and frowned. "Oh, perfect. It's nearly one. That was probably the last tram."

Allegro spotted the man in the beige trench coat a few blocks away, heading toward them at a jog. "In that case, just let me drive you back to Haarlem."

"I told you I'm perfectly capable of finding my own way home," Kris snapped as she got unsteadily to her feet. "I can walk to my car."

"Kris, I know you've been drinking tonight. I don't think you should get behind the wheel."

Kris glared at her, fury glinting in her eyes. "Fine. I won't drive, then. But I'm not going with you. I'll stay at my uncle's."

"I hope you have a key. He's got to be asleep."

"Hans won't mind," Kris asserted angrily. "He's very understanding."

"Then at least let me drive you there," she offered.

"There's no need. It's not that far. I can walk."

"He lives in the area?" Allegro feigned surprise. "Even better, then. I'll just walk with you."

"I don't need a tourist to escort me." Kris sounded offended.

Allegro laughed softly. "I wouldn't be escorting you. I'd only be tagging along. You know, sucking up the nocturnal atmosphere."

"Suit yourself." Kris shrugged her off and started walking a bit unsteadily toward Hofman's office.

The stalker had caught up and was watching them surreptitiously from the shadows of a building not far away. Tucking her arm into Kris's, Allegro marched her along the Keizersgracht, the canal to their right, at a brisk pace. She had to make sure that Kris was safe indoors before she confronted the man. She needed to find out what he was up to and attack was always the best defense.

They were crossing a small bridge when Kris stopped, almost out of breath. "Slow down. I know you Americans take pride in doing Europe at breakneck speed, but this is ridiculous."

"Oh, hey, I'm sorry. I didn't realize."

Kris leaned against the railing of the bridge, and Allegro did the same beside her, suddenly mindful of the awesome view in every direction. The bridges were outlined with strings of small white lights, and the amber street lamps and lighted windows of the homes lining the canal were mirrored in the placid waters. Under different circumstances, this would have been the kind of moment to lose herself in, standing here with a beautiful, somewhat intoxicated woman, but all she could think of was the man closing in on them. She needed to get Kris somewhere safe.

Kris looked around, seemingly appreciative of their surroundings, and there was an expression on her face Allegro had never seen before. She appeared neither sad nor worried; the look of dread and uncertainty that seemed to be permanently etched on her brow was gone. For once she didn't seem haunted, or even melancholic, but content. Allegro wanted so much at that moment to tell her how breathtaking she looked.

"You don't seem the sightseeing tourist type to me," Kris finally said. "Why is that?"

Allegro turned to face her while surreptitiously watching the stalker get nearer and nearer. "I'd ask you what kind of tourist type I do seem to you, but I shiver at the thought of you replying. Anyway, you don't have to be any particular type to appreciate this." She could see that Kris was trying to suppress a smile.

They stood there in silence, listening to a handful of geese noisily cutting through the calm water beneath them. When he reached them, the man paused a few yards away, smoking a cigarette, to all appearances as captivated by the view as they were. Allegro was mulling over how she was going to make the guy aware that he'd been spotted, and maybe scare him away as a result, when Kris took matters into her own hands.

Glancing over Allegro's shoulder, she said in a low voice, "I know this sounds strange, but I think that guy's been following me. He was staring at me in the cafe, and now, here he is."

Allegro was surprised that Kris had noticed her stalker, especially since she'd been drinking and was obviously caught up in her own problems. Perhaps she hadn't given the countess enough credit. "You're a very attractive woman," she said nonchalantly. "I can't say I blame him for checking you out."

Kris seemed momentarily pleased by the compliment, but her smile was short-lived. "Well, I blame him. I don't care for creeps who follow me around, and that's what I'm going to tell him."

Allegro knew Kris's bluster was the wine talking, but she couldn't let her do something foolish. The guy had been content to merely tail them so far, but if confronted, all bets were off. What if he produced a gun? She would have to act, and she couldn't risk blowing her cover. "Let it go, Kris. He's not important."

"No. I'm sick and tired of attracting the world's users. It's time I made that clear. Besides this guy looks like he's after more than just a good time and I intend to find out what that is."

She started toward the man, but Allegro grabbed her by the arm. "Wait, just wait."

"Wait for what?" Kris jerked free and glared at her. "I'm always fucking waiting, always having to do the right thing, be the right person, say the right thing, put up with any bullshit loser that comes my way so I don't have to be alone." She was so angry she was almost shouting. "Well, you know what? I don't care anymore. I don't care if I have to be alone for always. It stops here."

The man was staring openly now, and so was another couple passing by. Allegro was desperate to stop her, so when Kris started toward the man, she grabbed her by the shoulders and pushed her up against the railing. They looked at each other. Kris's face was flushed and her eyes were glinting fire.

Allegro did the only thing she could think to do. She kissed her.

Obviously startled, Kris resisted at first and tried to pull away, but Allegro persisted, trapping Kris against the rail with her body. When she pushed her tongue into the warmth of Kris's mouth, Kris melted against her and returned the kiss in kind. For a long moment, Allegro allowed herself to enjoy the fierce and hungry joining, surrendering to the wave of arousal building within her. At the same time, she remained alert to the man, listening for every sound.

When they finally parted, Kris gaped at her in confusion. She was breathing hard. "Why did you do that?"

"You looked like you wanted me to."

"I did not," Kris stuttered. "I was barely tolerating your presence, if you must know."

"Then why are you still holding on to me?"

"You're so full of yourself."

"So they tell me." Allegro smiled.

Kris pushed her away roughly and glanced around as though to regain her bearings. She peered over Allegro's shoulder at the man still watching them. "Fuck him," she said tiredly.

"Look, Kris, let me drive you home, okay?"

"No. I can't deal with being there tonight." She ran a hand through her hair. "Too much thinking about the past. If you want to walk me, fine. Let's go. I just want to sleep."

They walked in silence to Hofman's office, fifteen minutes away. Despite having been spotted, the stalker was undeterred. No longer bothering to conceal himself, he trailed after them, keeping about ten yards behind. He was either an amateur PI or a hired goon too stupid or desperate to care that he'd been seen. If he fell into the last category, that made him unpredictable and very dangerous. It was time to find out who he was, and soon, she'd create that opportunity.

It was nearly two a.m. when they reached the attorney's building, but there was a light on in his upstairs apartment.

"Oh good, he's awake. Well, you've seen me here. You can go now," Kris said as she mounted the steps to ring the bell.

"I'll just hang around to make sure you get in okay."

"I don't know whether to be infuriated with you or pleased."

"Sleep on it. Pleased will win out, I'm sure."

Kris rolled her eyes, but she was smiling. Before she could reply, Hofman opened the door, dressed in his pajamas and robe. Surprise and concern crossed his face when he saw the two of them standing there. "Kris, are you all right?"

"I'm fine, uncle. I saw your light on, and the truth is I really don't feel like being back at the mansion tonight."

"I offered to drive her back," Allegro added, "but she insisted on spending the night here."

Kris shot her a withering look before returning her attention to Hans. "Forgive me for disturbing you so late."

"Don't mention it, child. I was awake anyway. Please come in." He stepped to one side to admit them, and the two women stepped into the foyer. Allegro glanced back before Hans shut the door, and glimpsed the stalker, waiting outside beneath a tree.

"My years are turning me into a night owl," Hans continued, "When I can't sleep, I always have a case I can work on."

"Well, I can definitely sleep." Kris yawned and headed unsteadily toward the stairs leading up to Hans's apartment. "Good night."

"You know where the guest room is," Hofman said.

"See you tomorrow," Allegro called after her, but Kris didn't respond.

"You have to excuse her. She's had a lot to deal with lately." Hofman watched his niece disappear from view, then turned toward Allegro. "Nice of you to see her here safely."

"Nothing to excuse," she said. "Mr. Hofman…"

"Please, call me Hans."

She smiled. "Hans, would you mind if I used your toilet before I head back?" It was an excuse to stay a bit longer. She didn't trust the stalker. He obviously intended to stick around, and she wondered how far the obtrusive idiot was willing to go.

"Please. Go right ahead." He gestured forward. "It's at the end of the hall to the right."

When she emerged a few minutes later, Hans was nowhere in sight, but the light was on in his office. She stood in the doorway. "It must be a serious case if you're still at it this time of the night."

"It gets harder to keep up at my age, but I so enjoy my profession." He reached for a mug on his desk, but paused when it was halfway to his lips. "I just made some coffee. Would you like some?"

"Sure, thanks."

He rose to pour her a cup from a pot he had brewing on a side table. "How are the renovations going?"

"We're making good progress, I think." Allegro was happy for the small talk because it gave her the opportunity to stick around and make sure the stalker didn't do anything stupid. She carried her cup to the window and discreetly kept an eye on him. He'd moved to a nearby bench.

Hofman seemed pleased with the company and in no hurry to turn in, so they chatted on about the mansion and about how she and Kris had run into each other and made their way here. An hour later, she saw the stalker get up off the bench and start away, down the street.

She yawned as though suddenly tired, and checked her watch. "Wow, is it really three a.m. already? I'd better get back. Lots to do tomorrow. Today, actually," she corrected herself, getting to her feet. "Thanks for the coffee and conversation."

"My pleasure." Hofman followed her to the door. "You are welcome to sleep over, Angie. I'm sure Kris wouldn't mind sharing the guest room with you."

Yeah, right. I don't think so. "No need. There's no traffic at this time of the night, so it won't take long to get back, and Jeroen will expect me first thing in the morning. Good night, Hans."

"Drive safe, Angie."

The man who'd been stalking Kris was halfway down the block, headed away, when Allegro hit the street. As she hurried after him, he pulled a cell phone from his pocket and made a call.

She approached him but his voice was so low she couldn't make out what he was saying. She waited for him to finish and put the phone away. "Excuse me, sir."

He turned around. His face registered surprised recognition. "Yes?"

"I was wondering if you could tell me how to get to the Leidseplein." She slurred her words; she didn't appear outright drunk, but definitely tipsy. "You see, my vacation love affair decided that a kiss was all I get tonight and didn't even bother to drop me off at my hotel." She could see the contempt in his eyes.

"I don't know where this place is. Now leave me alone." From his strong accent, it was clear he was German.

Allegro took a half-step toward him, stumbled, and dropped her gloves. She reached for his arm to steady herself as she bent to retrieve them. "I'm not drunk," she mumbled, as her hand closed over the first one. "Clumsy, not drunk." She sniggered and reached for the second glove, losing her balance. "Damn." The hand that had been on his arm slipped down his coat as she fought to regain her feet.

"*Mein Gott.*" The German shook her off, his irritation evident.

Allegro stuck her hands in her pockets, wavered slightly on her feet and gave him a grin. "Well, thanks anyway, mister."

"Good-*bye,*" he snapped and strode off.

He was a few feet away when she spoke again, this time with a hint of threat in her tone. "*Auf Wiedersehen.* No doubt we'll meet again."

The German cast a sharp backward glance at her before hurrying off. She waited until he disappeared around the corner then followed him at a distance. As she kept pace, she pulled out the cell phone she'd lifted from his coat pocket and checked it for clues. The man had received two calls that day. Caller ID showed both as coming from a "Manfred." She didn't risk a callback until she knew more about the man she was trailing. The owner identification details had not been added in the usual places but the cell's address book gave her another way to learn his identity.

"*Guten Abend,*" she replied when a woman answered sleepily. "My name is Helga, and I found this mobile phone here on the street in Munich. I assume that it belongs to either your son or daughter since I dialed 'Parents.'"

"Munich? What's he doing there?" came the reply. Allegro could hear a male voice in the background, probably the woman's husband asking who was on the phone. "My son would lose his head if it wasn't attached to his body."

Allegro laughed. "My mother says the same of me," she continued in fluent German. "Would you like me to drop it off at the nearest police station? The one on the Ettstrasse is the closest to where I am. He can pick it up there." As she spoke, she watched the stalker climb into a car and speed away.

"How sweet and honest of you. That would be wonderful."

"Who should I say it belongs to? They will probably ask for ID when he picks it up."

"Yes, of course," the woman said. "My son's name is Gunter Schmidt."

"And his address. If I don't get time to go there, I can post it."

Allegro disconnected as soon as she'd keyed the details into her own cell phone. With a flick of her wrist, she tossed Schmidt's cell into the nearest canal.

CHAPTER TEN

Allegro sat in her rental car, staring at the exterior of Hans Hofman's building across the canal, debating whether to return to the mansion in Haarlem. All the lights were off, now. Hans had gone to bed. Protected from the wind, she wasn't uncomfortably cold. It would be no real hardship to remain there overnight keeping vigil over Kris, but her priority was the diamond. She had a good window of opportunity at the moment. The mansion was empty, and she had a clue now about where to find the entrance to the vault. Jeroen usually didn't arrive until eight a.m. to begin work, so she had a good three hours or so to find and retrieve the diamond. She would then be free to leave, her task complete. If she wasn't successful, she'd try again tonight. Meantime, she needed to maintain her cover and make sure no one else discovered the stone before she could secure it.

But try as she might, she couldn't ignore the growing urgency she felt to protect Kris from harm. There was something very personal about this need to keep her safe. She simply couldn't bear the thought of anything happening to her. She was certain the German would probably return to continue his surveillance, but Kris knew he was watching her. She would most likely emerge in broad daylight, when lots of people were about, and if she noticed him, she would be on her guard. Her car was parked only a few yards from Hofman's door. She should reach it without incident and be safe enough on her drive back to the estate.

Allegro wished she knew why Gunter Schmidt was interested in Kris. She'd called the name into the EOO and was waiting for a response. It was late afternoon in Colorado, and they'd had enough time to process her high-priority request. She adjusted the scrambler on her phone and called again. Montgomery Pierce answered.

"Good timing. I was about to contact you," he said. "We have an ID on the prints you sent us."

"Let me guess. They belong to the same Gunter Schmidt I'm following around Amsterdam." She smiled inwardly at the snort of exasperation that preceded the EOO Chief's reply.

"They do. Schmidt's a known member of a violent neo-Nazi group Interpol is tracking, called the Aryan Brotherhood."

"What's his problem with van der Jagt?"

"Unknown. The group is led by Erhard Baader and we were able to identify several other members." He reeled off a list of names.

"Back up. You mentioned a Wolff."

"Manfred Wolff," Pierce repeated.

"Yes, I need you to check what his connection is to a deceased Geert Wolff."

"Give me more."

"Geert Wolff was a Gestapo officer during World War Two. He tried to buy van der Jagt's silence in exchange for the Blue Star in order to avoid trial and execution."

She heard a shuffling of papers in the background, and Pierce's voice as he ordered someone to work up a history on Wolff. Then he came back on the line. "You found all this in that diary Hofman's holding on to?"

"Something tells me the Afghans aren't the only ones after the diamond," Allegro said. "Schmidt's keeping a close eye on Rocky. A really close eye."

"Do you think he's a threat?"

"I'm not sure, but I'm not about to risk it."

"Good. Until we're ready to shut this down, you need her."

"Yeah, that's right. I…need her." As she said the words, a twitch of something personal behind the sentiment nagged at her, and out of nowhere, the memory of their kiss blossomed in her mind. She shoved the thought aside. "I need to know Schmidt's game."

"We'll run a check, see if he's registered at a local hotel," Pierce said.

She thanked him and signed off, bothered by the possibility that there could be a personal agenda at work. The two calls on Schmidt's cell had come from a "Manfred," probably Wolff. Was the last a coincidence or was the caller connected to Geert Wolff, the Gestapo officer? If so, and if he knew what Jan van der Jagt had done, he must bear a grudge. Yet he hadn't hunted van der Jagt down in all the interceding years. Why?

Allegro stared out into the dead quiet of four a.m. It was far too cold for anyone to be out. February temperatures in Amsterdam routinely dipped below freezing, and the bitter gusts of wind blowing in from the North Sea were powerful enough to knock bicyclists over. If Gunter Schmidt had returned to Haarlem by now, he was probably tucked up warmly in his hotel bed. She started the car and drove through the dead streets of the city, working through various scenarios. By the time she reached the highway, she was sure there had to be a family connection and that Wolff would have come looking for the diamond sooner if he'd known where it was.

Perhaps he didn't know van der Jagt's name or had assumed the diamond was sold long ago. Or perhaps personal vengeance wasn't important to him. Why get interested now? There was only one reason. He had discovered that the van der Jagt family still had the stone. How? That was the most puzzling and unsettling question. The diamond had only recently resurfaced. Who else knew?

Allegro picked up her cell and called Monty Pierce again. "If Wolff knows Rocky has the diamond and Schmidt is his errand boy, he had to find out somehow. Who are our contacts and which one talked to him?"

Pierce promptly confirmed her suspicions. "Manfred is Geert Wolff's son. As to the leak, we haven't nailed that down yet. It's a short list of possibilities. The lawyer, the jeweler who examined the stone, and the professor he consulted. I suppose the mole in Afghanistan could have made the connection indirectly, and there are a few people at MIS we're checking."

So Wolff had sent his Aryan goon after Kris in order to reclaim the diamond taken from his father more than six decades earlier. He certainly had cause to pursue Kris. Aside from his interest in the gem, he obviously shared his father's Nazi sympathies and would be seeking vengeance for Jan van der Jagt's betrayal. Allegro was tempted to confront him at once to remove the immediate threat to her mission and to Kris. But she had to do so in a way that didn't alert Wolff, who possibly had other violent confederates waiting in the wings to call upon if needed.

Americans, Afghans, and now Germans. The international race for the *Setarehe Abi Rang* was clearly escalating. And at whatever cost, she intended to be first across the finish line.

❖

Kabul, Afghanistan

"Che khabari baraje mandarid?" What news do you have for me? Afghan Culture Minister Qadir asked as soon as he admitted Yusuf into his office. The efforts to recover the *Setarehe Abi Rang* from the Dutch countess had become his singular obsession since the phone call from Professor Rafi Bayat, more than a week earlier.

"I checked with my staff again at the museum," the Deputy Arts Minister replied in Farsi. Yusuf's face reflected the complex ethnicities that had influenced Afghanistan's rich history—the angular nose and chiseled jaw of a Greek, the slight tilt of Asian eyes, and the dark hair, skin, and characteristic turban of a native Pashtun. "No one has expressed any unusual interest in the crown, and they will report any future inquiries to me immediately. Of course I took all precautions to ensure the utmost discretion about this whole affair, as you instructed."

"I knew I could depend on you. That will be all, Yusuf."

Qadir's telephone rang as the man departed. It was Azizi, the loyal soldier he'd chosen to retrieve the diamond. He had wanted to send the man at once, but it had taken several frustrating days to make the proper arrangements. Now the Americans were no doubt involved, interfering in the matters of others while ignoring bigger problems on their own shores.

"I am at the airport. My flight to Amsterdam leaves in forty minutes," Azizi informed the minister. "Everything is in place at the other end. I will report in as soon as I have something further."

Qadir stroked his beard, already envisioning the myriad of Allah's works that al-Qaeda would accomplish with the proceeds from the gem. And he would no longer have to wonder and worry about the repercussions to his country if the truth be known that the centerpiece of the crown was a fake. His thoughts slid to the need to ensure that the professor never divulge what he knew. "Very good, Azizi. I'll have another task for you, when you complete your primary objective."

"I am honored to provide whatever services I am called upon to do," Azizi replied.

"May Allah strengthen your hands." Qadir disconnected and dialed Rafi Bayat. "Have you talked to the family yet?" he asked after greeting the professor politely.

"*Salam, Agha.*" Hello, sir. The professor's tone was respectful, as was befitting when addressing a man of great importance.

Qadir leaned back in his chair, reassured that the academic knew his place. He had only a moment's regret that the loyal professor who had made all this possible would also have to be silenced. But Qadir had long ago reconciled himself to doing whatever needed to be done to advance the greater cause of the righteous, the *khilafat*. For now, however, Bayat was his one connection with the countess. It would not do to lose him prematurely.

"I spoke to the woman's attorney," Bayat continued, "and urged discretion in this matter. He was understanding and promised to speak to the countess."

"Well done. And did you learn anything about where this replica diamond is being kept?" Qadir asked.

"Not yet, unfortunately. But he gave me information that enabled me to trace its origins back through two families." Bayat paused, interrupted by another voice in the background, a man, speaking English. "One moment, sir."

Qadir sat up straight. So the professor had ignored his instructions to leave the inquiries to the Afghan government. This wouldn't do at all. A couple of minutes passed before Bayat returned to the line.

"Please forgive me, Qadir. I just arrived at the university. That was one of my students. As I was saying, the countess's father acquired the diamond from a Gestapo lieutenant during the Second World War. I spoke to the man's son. He told me this diamond originally came from a Jew named Moszek Levin. He's dead and I'm trying to trace any descendents."

"You are to keep me, and only me, apprised of every new find," Qadir instructed. "This is a very sensitive matter, one which I regard seriously. The less men involved, the better for our country, especially at times like this."

"Of course, *Agha*. My country and its reputation are my priority."

❖

Soon after Qadir dismissed him from his office, Deputy Arts Minister Yusuf hurried to one of the phone booths recently installed in the Afghan capital. Placing his periodic calls to Washington DC always made him nervous. He didn't identify himself. He'd been passing information to MIS Deputy Director Cliff Norton long enough that the U.S. intelligence officer knew his voice. He was never asked to reveal his identity, but Yusuf suspected Norton knew who he was.

"Time is running short," he said. "The terrorists have already begun to put their plan into motion, and will act very soon against the West."

"How soon? Where?" Norton asked. "Can't you be more specific?"

"You have a matter of days only," Yusuf replied. "I will give you the targets, the timetable, everything you need to stop this, as soon as I have the diamond. If you do not return the stone, tens of thousands, maybe millions, will die."

He heard the major's sharp intake of breath.

"Our emissary will arrive soon in Amsterdam," Yusaf said. "He has instructions to take all necessary steps to recover the diamond."

"We're doing our best," Norton said. "But if we can't get to the diamond within your time frame, you can't possibly let so many innocent people die by withholding this information."

"The deaths of innocents is always very sad. Your country had to endure such a nightmare not too long ago. Unfortunately, such nightmares are ongoing in my country."

"You sound very flippant. I was under the impression that you were among the noble men trying to stop al-Qaeda and those who dishonor the Qur'an by using it to justify the killing of innocent people."

"I am," Yusuf said. "And I hope to make a difference by giving you the information you need."

"But you're willing to make that difference only if the price is right."

"Do not insult me, Major. The money I have asked for in the past was not for personal gain. It was in fact used to feed our people and restore our war-torn country. But this time, money cannot buy what is at stake. Our honor. The *Setarehe Abi Rang* must be returned to the crown before the world discovers that we have been perpetuating this deception."

"It sounds like your motivations have less to do with noble religious reasons and more to do with misplaced patriotism," Norton said. "Is the honor of your country worth millions of lives?"

"You cannot give a value to honor. Do you not send countless young men to war in the name of honor and patriotism?"

There was a long silence on the line. "We do," Norton admitted, "but our goal is justice and not to save our government from humiliation."

"I would rather not get into the topic of justice with you," Yusuf said. "I have seen too many innocent people killed by American bombings."

"We do what is necessary to ensure peace."

"As I am sure you will this time. Get me the stone, Major. The clock is ticking. And in exchange, you will get your peace."

❖

Allard Pierson Archeological Museum, University of Amsterdam
Tuesday, February 12

Rafi felt energized as he gazed around his cluttered office. He opened his browser and checked his e-mail as he did every morning before his classes, bypassing the usual student requests and academic inquiries. He'd arrived at work much sooner than usual, hoping for several hours of tranquility before his colleagues and students began making their demands. Finally, he saw what he'd been anxiously awaiting, a reply from the grandson of Moszek Levin. Upon his return from Berlin, Rafi had spent hours researching the Jew and had discovered a Web page Levin's grandson had created as a tribute to his ancestor. Rafi had used a link to send an e-mail and had been on tenterhooks ever since. The Web site was in English, evidently so it could be viewed internationally, and he took it as a good sign that they could communicate without difficulty.

He closed the door and returned to his desk. Taking out a fresh yellow pad and sharpened pencil, he read the brief e-mail and dialed the number the grandson provided. He doodled on the pad while he waited for the connection to go through. By the time a woman answered, he'd absently sketched a fairly good representation of the *Setarehe Abi Rang*, exactly to scale.

"May I speak to Pawel Levin, please?" he asked in English.

After a moment, a man came on the line. "This is Pawel. Who is speaking?"

"Mr. Levin, this is Professor Rafi Bayat at the University of Amsterdam. I sent you the e-mail about your grandfather?"

"Yes, Professor. How may I help you?" The man's Czech accent was thick, and Rafi had a little trouble understanding him.

"I am researching the history of a diamond that was once in your grandfather's possession. I was told it was taken from him by a German lieutenant during World War Two, right before your grandfather was sent to the concentration camp."

"I know of this diamond," Pawel Levin replied. "My father spoke of it when he told me stories about the war. He said it was our family's most treasured heirloom, a magnificent blue stone passed down through several generations. He went to Auschwitz as well, but survived because he was very strong. They sent him to a work camp."

Rafi had no interest in Levin's story of the Holocaust, but he remained polite. "He was very fortunate to have survived. So many died during that horrible period."

"He was forever scarred by the experience. They only had a week together at Auschwitz before my grandfather was taken to the gas chambers."

"How horrible," Rafi said solemnly. "It is a fine thing that you have done, this tribute to your grandfather for all the world to see."

"Thank you. Because of the stories my father told, I'm very much interested in my family's history. My brother and I have spent many hours tracing our genealogy." Levin spoke a few words to whomever he was with, then returned to the line. "About this diamond. What is it you want to know?"

"Do you know how and where your family acquired the diamond?" Rafi asked.

"Oh, yes," Levin replied. "My ancestors came from Persia, from an area that is now part of Iran. Our people were traders. For hundreds of years they carried silk and spices across the east. In Persia they dealt in carpets, of course. And antiquities. My family left Persia in 1839 when the government imposed forced conversions. Thousands of Jews emigrated to Afghanistan then."

"That was during the First Anglo-Afghan war," Rafi supplied. He was thoroughly familiar with the history of his homeland. How odd, he thought, to have this in common with a Czech Jew. "During that time, the British colonists placed Shah Shuja-ul-Mulk back on the Afghan throne but much of his wealth was gone, except for the royal jewels."

"That is also what I have heard," Levin said. "The story told to me was that Shah Shuja met my ancestor, and agreed to exchange the blue diamond for other goods that could be easily sold. My ancestor had to swear on his life that this bargain be kept forever secret. He and his family planned to leave Afghanistan immediately, but—"

"Shah Shuja was assassinated." The story made complete sense, Rafi thought, fascinated. "So they did not need to flee."

"They left about thirty years later, when the anti-Jewish laws were enacted. That's how we ended up in Prague."

"And your family kept the secret of the diamond through those years."

"Yes, the story was passed down. Fortunately my father survived or I would not have known anything about it." Levin sighed. "My grandfather thought he could protect the family when the Nazis came. He had friends in the government so he didn't leave when most of the Jews fled the country. But his profession made him even more of a target. He was a watchmaker, you see, so when the roundups began, they broke into the homes of the wealthy first, ransacking for valuables. My grandfather tried to hide the diamond on himself, but a Gestapo officer searched him and found it. He never knew the man's name."

"A fascinating story," Rafi replied, more calmly than he felt. "Thank you so much for the information, Mr. Levin. It helps me a great deal."

"What happened to the diamond, Professor?" Levin asked. "Do you know?"

"Unfortunately, that is a mystery," Rafi lied. "It was one of several jewels from the royal collection that has been lost forever. I am doing research on them all, for an exhibit at my museum. Thank you again, sir."

"Of course, Professor."

Could it be so? Rafi asked himself as he hung up the phone. If Levin's story was true, the gem Rafi had examined was almost certainly the real *Setarehe Abi Rang*. Yet Minister Qadir had immediately dismissed that possibility. And Qadir, in his esteemed position, would certainly be privy to the truth. Wouldn't he?

Rafi considered calling the minister back immediately with the news, but he felt uneasy. He didn't want to cause offense by implying Qadir was lying about the stone, or worse, deliver the bad news that the famous gem in Kabul was a fake and the real stone was not even the legitimate property of their nation. He had been relieved, back in Berlin, when he discovered that Manfred Wolff had no idea the diamond his father stole had any historic significance. It was merely a spoil of war. Wolff was unlikely to speak of the matter, but what of Countess Kristine? She had agreed to be discreet, but once the stone was authenticated would she remain silent?

The *Setarehe Abi Rang* was worth a fortune, the kind of prize a collector would pay a large sum for. The money shouldn't go to her, and the stone shouldn't vanish into some illicit collection. It rightly belonged to the people of Afghanistan from whom it had been stolen by an unworthy ruler. Rafi was mystified by Qadir's insistence that all further inquiries be left to the government, effectively shutting him out. Who was better qualified to ascertain the truth than he, a loyal Afghan and one of the world's foremost experts in this field? *And* he was the only one who had actually seen the countess's stone. Surely there was more he could do to secure a just outcome. This was, after all, a matter of national pride.

CHAPTER ELEVEN

Haarlem, Netherlands

Allegro did a thorough check of the rear exterior of the mansion, searching with her penlight for the hidden way to the vault, but the ancient brick wall was unmarred. She wandered among the topiary, trying to make sense of the cryptic clue she'd gleaned from Hans Hofman's conversation with Kris. *Very clever of him to put the new entrance through the garden.* On her second pass by the shed, it hit her. Was it possible that this was the way to the secret room? Through a tunnel? *Jesus.* Staring her right in the face all this time. She tried the door. Locked. It took her no time to get inside the small storage building, which was crowded with gardening tools and bags of potting soil, clay pots, and hoses.

She found the hidden trapdoor beneath the wide rubber mat at the back. It was padlocked, no challenge at all for her talents. Elation mixed with dread. She was about to accomplish her mission, but she'd have to leave as soon as she secured the diamond. The thought made her limbs feel leaden as she returned to the house to fetch her tools. She hated sneaking off without saying good-bye. The memory of Kris's lips on hers flashed into her mind.

When she got to her room, she spared herself a moment to look longingly at the bed before digging through her duffel for her stethoscope and gloves. She was exhausted to the bone, but dawn was approaching and sleep was a luxury she could not afford. Forcing herself back downstairs, she made her way through the kitchen and out the back door.

She'd taken only a few steps toward the shed when she heard the crunch of tires on the gravel drive. Darting back inside, she peered through the window and was startled to see Jeroen's van pull up. *Damn.* She took off her jacket and ditched the stethoscope and gloves in one of the pockets as he exited the vehicle with a large bucket in his hand.

"You're here awfully early this morning," she said as he came through the door.

"Angie," he replied, surprised. "I told Kris you didn't need to start until our usual time."

"You talked to Kris?"

"Yes, I told her I needed to leave early today for another job, so I'd make up the time this morning. She didn't tell you?"

"No, actually I just got home. I was in Amsterdam."

Jeroen smiled. "Hope it was fun. You look like hell."

"I've been getting that a lot lately," she replied, stifling a yawn.

"Why don't you get a few hours' rest?" he suggested.

"Sure you don't mind?" She was aggravated at not being able to immediately retrieve the diamond, but it was prudent she get some sleep since she'd have to make another attempt that night.

"Go," he said, shooing her with a dismissive gesture.

Halfway up the stairs, her cell phone rang with an update from Monty Pierce. She took the call, stripping off her clothes as she listened, but when it was done she was still too edgy and frustrated to sleep. She took out her camera and skimmed through the additional diary pages she'd photographed. It was dull reading, mostly a recounting of Jan van der Jagt's wartime exploits and later business affairs with no further mention of the diamond. She got the distinct impression the man had been a self-involved narcissist, as there were few mentions of his wife and daughter.

She stashed the camera in her duffel bag and closed the curtains, her mind churning with thoughts of Kris. She pondered what had made her the way she was—always guarded and often melancholic. Kris had obviously led a privileged life, getting whatever she wanted, coming and going as she pleased, exploiting all the possibilities available to her. Such a different existence from her own. So many more options. Most of her life, Allegro had had to get permission for her every move. Everything she did and said was monitored and analyzed.

Yet all of Kris's opportunities didn't seem to have brought peace or real happiness. She didn't appear to be contented or fulfilled. A closer look into her background helped explain why. With a self-centered father and a mentally sick mother, she must have had the freedom to do as she pleased, but only because they didn't care. She didn't appear to have many friends and hardly ever received phone calls. Except for that one time on the bridge, she seemed haunted by something. Sure, she took her teasing well and never shied away from a response, but Allegro could tell such interactions made her uneasy, almost suspicious, and Kris was quick to put an end to them.

Although she'd known her only a few days and Kris hadn't gone out of her way to be particularly friendly, Allegro sensed her standoffishness was almost beyond her control. Every time Kris got close to opening up and relaxing around her, she'd immediately close up again and go back to her defensive and distrusting self. What was she trying to hide? What was she running from? She'd been through a lot lately with the death of her father and losing her fortune, but what Allegro saw in Kris's eyes was not the pain of recent mourning. It went a lot deeper. Whatever it was that had made Kris so wary and troubled had been with her long enough to form her.

She shouldn't care, and she wasn't in the habit of trying to read people for personal reasons, but Kris intrigued her in a way that was new. She didn't have the luxury of being able to put time and effort into solving the mystery that was Kris, but she was unable to stem her curiosity. Was Kris so compelling merely because of her looks? Allegro met plenty of beautiful women, but none made her want to find out what was going on beneath the attractive exterior. She didn't have those answers.

Surrendering finally to her exhaustion, she dozed until a noise from below awakened her. The bedside clock informed her it was after eleven, so she forced herself out of bed and into a shower. The thought of spending another long day of house repairs while she had so much to do, and so many questions to answer, made her long to be back at Silverstone, racing through the turns. Life made sense when she was behind the wheel of a Ferrari F2008, where she could, for the most part, control how fast she got to the finish line. The track had predictable twists and turns, and her mastery over the 900-horsepower monster beneath her allowed her to maximize her rate of acceleration. In her work as an operative, she hated being at the mercy of so many human variables and having to move at a pace dictated by others.

Dressing in her work clothes, she headed downstairs. She hadn't heard Kris's car drive up and was relatively certain she hadn't come back, but she was still disappointed to find only Jeroen's van parked outside. Was Kris too tipsy to remember their kiss on the bridge? Had Allegro been the only one affected by it? Kissing a woman as part of her job was a practiced chore. She never expected to get as caught up in the moment, but something odd had happened. She wasn't sure if it was the romantic setting or her physical attraction to Kris, but had the circumstances been different she knew she would not have ended the evening alone in bed. Although Kris had made it clear that their explorations were at an end, a part of Allegro wished she had wanted to come back to the mansion immediately and pick up where they'd left off. She found it hard to accept that her feelings were completely one-sided.

When she reached the front room, she greeted Jeroen with a pleasant, "Good morning." He was on a ladder, busily patching plaster on the ceiling.

"That your car outside?" he asked.

"Yes. A rental." She set another ladder in place beneath the high ceiling.

"I wondered where Kris was."

"She stayed in Amsterdam last night," she told him. "But I thought she'd be back by now."

"Hate to work without her since she seems to think we need her supervision." He chuckled. "I don't know why she bothers to watch. She doesn't know anything about restoration."

"It's her money, I guess."

He shrugged. "It's you she's watching. Probably thinks a woman can't handle this type of work, but you seem to know what you're doing."

Allegro wondered what Jeroen would think of some of the things she'd put her body through while on assignment. "It helps that I try to stay fit. I'm used to hard work."

For the next several minutes, they labored mostly in silence, allowing Allegro the opportunity to consider her options regarding Gunter Schmidt. Her call from the EOO had contained the useful information that Schmidt was registered at a small hotel in Haarlem. As soon as she had the diamond she would pay him a visit and ensure the clumsy stalker was no further threat to Kris.

Shortly after noon, acute now to every small nuance of noise from outside, she heard the crunch of tires on gravel and began to relax, releasing knots of tension from her shoulders. She descended her ladder and wiped her hands clean on a rag. "Kris is back," she told Jeroen. "I'm going to make a pot of coffee."

She paused in the hallway on her way to the kitchen, waiting for the front door to open. Kris walked in wearing the same charcoal slacks and dove gray silk blouse from the night before, but her ensemble was rumpled and her face wore the slight puffiness of her overindulgence.

"Need coffee?" Allegro asked, sounding more chipper than she felt.

Kris walked past without responding and took a few steps toward the room they'd been working on, then stood looking around at the repairs, hands on hips, as though determined to ignore her.

Allegro remained where she was, equally determined to get Kris to acknowledge her. Seconds passed. "Kris?"

Finally, Kris turned and met her eyes, but only briefly. "Whatever," she replied dismissively as she resumed her apparent assessment of their work.

Allegro hesitated, studying Kris's body language. Although the countess was trying to avoid eye contact and appear her usual distant self, she couldn't stop herself from the occasional surreptitious glance in Allegro's direction.

"Love the enthusiasm," Allegro said over her shoulder as she continued on toward the kitchen. She filled the coffeepot with water and dug through one of the cabinets in search of a filter. By the time she was measuring out the coffee, she could sense Kris behind her, watching her from the doorway. Without turning around, she asked, "Sleep okay?"

"Could have been better," Kris replied wearily.

"Too much to drink?" Allegro hit the brew button.

"Everything about last night was too much."

Allegro leaned back against the counter with her arms folded over her chest. "Including us?"

"There is no *us*." Her tone was aloof, but Allegro could see the response was feigned. Still avoiding eye contact, Kris shifted her weight restlessly from foot to foot.

"I'm pretty sure that was you I kissed."

"Oh, that." Kris reached out to pluck a piece of loose paint from the wall at her elbow.

"Denial, much?" Allegro replied cheekily.

Kris glared at her. "Not denial. Get over yourself. Why would a kiss be too much?"

Allegro gave Kris her most charming smile. "Are you saying it wasn't enough?"

"What I'm saying is that it was just a kiss." Kris's slight stutter suggested she was anything but blasé about their heated exchange the evening before. "Nothing new."

"I get that. I realize we didn't invent the wheel last night, but I'm trying to say I'm sorry if I offended you." Allegro could see Kris visibly soften, though she tried to mask it immediately.

Gesturing dismissively, she said, "Like I said, it was just a kiss."

The aroma of coffee wafted through the kitchen, and Allegro checked the progress of the brew. The pot was nearly filled. "So, what was too much about last night?"

"Let's see." Kris took a deep breath and let it out. "A heavy discussion with an ex-lover. A strange man staring at me all night, then following us." Her eyes narrowed. "I still don't know how to place him. He wasn't the usual looking-to-get-laid type."

Allegro poured two coffees. "Guys are guys. They come in all forms."

"I guess."

"And what else?"

Kris studied her face. "Why did you kiss me?"

"I couldn't resist," Allegro said. "What's your excuse?"

"I didn't start it."

"But you didn't stop it either."

"I can't really remember much of what happened," Kris replied, rubbing her temples.

"Maybe you should take the day off and get some rest."

"And maybe you should get back to work and let me be the judge of that."

"Whatever you say." Allegro handed Kris one of the mugs. She smiled as she looked Kris over, her gaze trailing over the low-cut blouse, the form-fitting slacks, to the charcoal pumps. "Should you choose to come watch, I suggest you change your clothes. And shoes." She met Kris's eyes again. "But that's up to you. If not, we could always use some comic relief."

Kris smiled.

"Looks good on you."

"Comic relief?"

"Smiling." Allegro headed back toward the living room, but paused a couple of yards away to turn to look back at Kris. "And the heels."

She heard a soft laugh behind her as she left to find Jeroen.

An hour later, Kris joined them, dressed in jeans, Prada boots, and a sweatshirt. "I could help," she offered. "What would you like me to do?"

Allegro climbed down the ladder and brushed herself off. "We were just discussing what to tackle next."

To her horror, Jeroen walked over to the wall that adjoined the hidden room and ran his hand over a particularly large crack in the plaster at one corner. "You know, this looks like it'll need more than a quick patch. I bet the framing needs reinforcement. Some water may have gotten to it, maybe from the other side." He examined the walls enclosing the hidden room. "You hear about this kind if thing but never see it. Like revolving library shelves." He turned to Kris. "Did you know that this was a fake wall?"

"Huh? Oh, that. Yeah, it's an old closet or something." Kris bit her lip, plainly uncomfortable with the question. "There was a way to get in there from the cellar, but Father sealed that up years ago. We'll deal with it later. I'm sure there are other things to keep us busy in the interim."

"Oh, certainly. I wasn't suggesting we do it today," Jeroen said. "But soon. Why don't you two get started scraping up there," he suggested, gesturing toward another area of the ceiling that was pitted with peeling paint. "And I'll mix up another batch of patching compound."

Kris helped move the large ladders over and caught the wry look her companions exchanged. Why the hell weren't they taking her seriously? She went to the toolbox and snatched up one of the tools. How hard could it be?

She hadn't taken two steps up the ladder before she began to see what they were sniggering over. The slippery soles of her boots made it almost impossible for her to climb the rungs with any grace at all. She clutched at both sides of the ladder, nearly losing the tool in the process, and inched up one rung at a time. It was as though each step was covered in grease. If she didn't know any better she might have thought they had deliberately sabotaged her.

It took a silly amount of time and effort to reach the top, where she came face-to-face with the American, who seemed to have thoroughly enjoyed watching her ungainly ascent. Kris looked down, and then immediately wished she hadn't. She'd never liked heights. A momentary dizziness overcame her, and her feet started to slip. She clutched at the ladder for dear life but felt herself beginning to fall. It was only Angie's arm around her waist that steadied her.

"Thanks," Kris said once her breathing had reached normal. She met Angie's eyes, determined to show confidence. The American winked at her. *Winked*. She nearly lost her footing again. Ignoring the woman's warm appraisal, she held up the tool in her hand. "What do I do now?"

Angie grinned as if she'd said something funny. "Well…"

The tone seemed laced with innuendo, but Kris could hardly complain about her teasing since the woman had just saved her from a nasty fall. "You said remove the plaster, right?" she asked indignantly.

"Yup. So why don't you start by going back down and replacing that screwdriver in your hand with a scraper that's big enough to actually accomplish something?" Angie broke out laughing and Jeroen joined in.

Kris looked at the wide scrapers they were holding, comparing them with the tool she'd carelessly picked up. She then stared down again at the incredibly long distance back to the floor. "You could have said something before I climbed up here," she mumbled.

Her descent took as long as the climb, as the sound of more raucous laughter rang out. *Comedians.* She'd never enjoyed being the brunt of a joke, but it didn't seem to bother her quite so much when Angie teased her. Despite herself, she found something about the American very intriguing. There was a lot more to her than Kris had first thought. Beneath that cocky exterior, she seemed vulnerable and genuinely kind. The night before had certainly been evidence of that, with Angie's thoughtful offer of a ride home when they ran into each other. Instead of being grateful, Kris had rudely brushed her off. The alcohol had been a factor, and her conversation with Ilse had stirred up old wounds. Kris felt guilty that she'd taken her feelings out on Angie, and even guiltier that Angie had responded to her churlishness by insisting on seeing her safely to her uncle's.

The memory of their heated kiss on the bridge flashed into her mind. Though her initial reaction had been to resist Angie's unexpected and presumptuous advances, the feel of her lips had made that impossible. Just thinking about those few moments of surrender stirred up butterflies in Kris's stomach.

❖

Schiphol Airport, Amsterdam

Azizi stretched out his arms as the Dutch security official ran the handheld metal detector down his body and up again, taking his time. The passport control officer had taken an extraordinarily long time with his Afghan passport as well, as he expected, but he managed to avoid speaking of the contempt he felt at being pulled aside for the additional scrutiny merely because of his heritage. He picked up his bag at the luggage carousel and proceeded to the rental car counter, selecting a dark Peugeot that would not draw undue attention.

It was midafternoon as he drove to Haarlem. After checking into his hotel, he washed and changed his travel clothes for dark pants and a black button-down shirt. An hour later, the receptionist telephoned him in his room to say a deliveryman was waiting in the lobby. He went down and accepted a large bouquet of flowers with a card that said *Welcome to Haarlem*. The deliveryman also handed him a gift-wrapped box, its ribbon bearing the name of a well-known local chocolatier. Azizi carried both gifts back to his room and tossed the flowers into the wastebasket.

He unwrapped the candy box and extracted the gun and silencer from beneath their packing tissue. After screwing them together, he pulled a sheet of paper from his jacket pocket. Written in Farsi, it contained directions to the van der Jagt mansion. He calculated that he had at least another four hours before it would be dark enough to approach the estate. He'd use that time to reconnoiter the area, have a meal, and get some rest.

CHAPTER TWELVE

Haarlem

"God, I'm tired." Kris collapsed onto a couch in the salon, apparently unmindful of the white dust from her clothes that wafted onto the embroidered cushions. Dusk had fallen, and Jeroen had long ago departed for his other job.

"Working with a hangover will do that to you." Allegro threw her scraper into the toolbox and brushed herself off before settling into a comfy wing chair nearby.

"It's the physical exertion, all this bending and reaching. Are you saying you're not tired?"

Allegro shrugged. "I'm more hungry than tired. I need to eat something, and soon."

"Well, guess what? I'm not cooking." Kris leaned her head back and briefly closed her eyes. "Matter of fact, I think I'm going straight to bed."

"You've hardly eaten, aside from that one sandwich hours ago. That can't be healthy. Why don't we order a pizza? They deliver out here, don't they?"

Kris didn't move, but a smile twitched at the corner of her mouth. "We're not in Timbuktu, Angie. We do actually have delivery service."

"If I didn't feel so blessed at the moment, your sarcasm might bother me."

Kris looked at her curiously. "Blessed?"

"That you remembered my name." She grinned.

"Would it kill you not to have the last word?"

"Too hypothetical to answer."

Kris sighed dramatically, rolling her eyes. But she was clearly enjoying the exchange. "Let me get the takeout menu."

They argued over the toppings, compromising on a large pizza with pepperoni, black olives, and extra mozzarella, and were told it would take thirty to forty minutes for delivery.

"I'm going to run upstairs for a quick shower," Kris said, forcing herself off the couch. Plaster dust had insinuated itself into every orifice of her body.

"You don't need to doll yourself up for me, you know," Angie said.

Even as tired as she was, Kris couldn't help wondering if Angie's playful banter was all in jest or a sign of sincere interest. To her surprise, she hoped it was the latter. She'd never met anyone quite like this infernal American before. "You can't possibly be that self-involved."

"A girl can hope. They say it springs eternal."

Kris felt her cheeks warm. "As eternal as your arrogance," she replied, with what she hoped was just the right amount of comeuppance.

"Do you mind if I heat things up in here?" Angie asked.

The words immediately brought back the kiss of the night before and sense memories overtook Kris with such force she almost forgot to breathe. Several seconds passed as she searched her mind for a suitable reply. Angie watched her from the wing chair with annoying self-satisfaction on her face, as if she knew exactly what effect she was having. As though she was remembering their kiss as well.

"Get your mind out of the gutter," Angie said in a soft, slow drawl. "I was talking about the fireplace."

The playful look in her eyes brought that eerie sense of déjà vu back, but try as she might, Kris couldn't account for the feeling. More and more, Angie was getting to her, in a good, but very unsettling way. Why was she always attracted to exactly the wrong type of woman? "Don't flatter yourself," she retorted as she left the room. Pausing at the door, she turned. She couldn't help herself. "And yes, a fire would be nice."

Kris hated the fact that she actually spent time selecting what to wear to eat a damn pizza in her own home. She rejected her first choice, oversized sweatpants and sweatshirt, as she caught a glimpse of herself in the mirror. Hoping for the careless chic she envied in women who looked good in anything they threw on, she settled on a pair of low-cut jeans and a pale blue long-sleeved T-shirt that hugged her breasts and showed some cleavage, and made her way back to the salon.

Angie was in the armchair in front of the fireplace, seemingly lost in thought, her legs outstretched, her attention on the flames. She greeted Kris with a vague smile. Annoyed that the tepid reaction disappointed her, Kris bent to warm her hands by the fire. When a few moments elapsed without a smart-ass remark, she stole a sideways glance at Angie and caught her staring at her ass. The appreciative look on her face told Kris two things. The change of clothes had been well worth the effort, and the American's playful flirting was most definitely a sign of real interest.

"Sleepy?" Kris asked.

Angie looked at her for what seemed like hours before she responded. "Hungry."

The expression in her eyes said she was hungry for more than just food. But before Kris could decide whether to openly acknowledge the inference, the doorbell rang. "Lucky for you."

"Or not," Angie replied. "I'll get it."

They picnicked in front of the fire, making small talk and enjoying a bottle of Merlot with the pizza. Kris was surprised how relaxed she felt, and how easily Angie could make her laugh. And it didn't escape her attention that Angie couldn't seem to take her eyes off her breasts, though she admired them discreetly. She'd had so many dinners with women who sought to curry her favor that Kris had long ago lost count of the number of white linen tablecloths and candlelight settings she'd endured, unimpressed. Why the heck did a simple dinner of pizza on the floor, with a near-total stranger, feel like one of the most memorably romantic encounters of her life?

She retrieved a couple of pillows from the couch and stretched out on her side. Facing Angie, propped up on one elbow, she said, "You know, when we first met you told me you were here to make a fresh start and break away from some old habits. You talked about letting go of some things that weren't healthy for you."

Angie finished the last slice of pizza before replying. "Sounds about right."

"Were you referring to a relationship?"

"Not any one in particular. Just relationships in general."

"So you don't have someone special waiting for you back home?"

"Nope." Angie busied herself refilling their wineglasses, not meeting her eyes. Getting any personal information out of this woman was like pulling teeth.

"What do you do for a living?" Kris asked. "When you're not backpacking across some continent looking for the odd job."

Angie got up to put another log on the dying embers, then stoked the fire until it was roaring again. "This and that. I don't have one of those reliable professions. Doctor. Lawyer. Teacher."

"Is it me, or are you always this evasive?"

"I don't really like to talk about my life." Angie returned to sit beside her, cross-legged. "It's boring and I want to forget about it for a while. Besides, it's not like you've offered a plethora of personal trivia either."

Kris stared into the fire, surprised to realize that she was genuinely curious about this woman and, for once, she didn't feel the need to maintain her distance. "You're right. I haven't."

"Okay, I'm now officially in shock." Angie's look of stunned disbelief was spoiled by that ever-present cocky grin. "I mean, you admit that I'm right about something? You feeling okay?"

"And there you go." Kris sighed. "Opening your mouth and killing the moment."

"Come on, I'm kidding." Angie got her own pillows from the couch and matched Kris's posture, reclining beside her with their wineglasses between them. "Go on, I'll shut up."

"I was about to say that I have been rather standoffish, but you shouldn't take it personally." Kris let her gaze drift around the room. Memories of her early years came flooding back. "Growing up in this mausoleum, with a self-centered father and a manic-depressive mother, wasn't easy. Neither of them cared how I felt, and eventually I started to feel like my emotions weren't valid. Like I wasn't valid. I so wanted them to notice me that I started excelling in everything. School, sports."

She paused for a sip of wine. "When that didn't work, I took the bad-girl approach. I did everything I could to get into trouble, but they never looked twice. I might as well have been invisible."

"How could anyone not notice you, Kris?" Angie's voice had a gentle tone she hadn't heard before. "You're beautiful, smart, funny—"

"And redundant. That's all I've ever felt. They were both so involved with themselves I often wondered why they had a child in the first place. You know, part of me lived in fear that one day they'd give me up for adoption and get it over with. I suppose the only saving grace was that they could afford to have someone cook and clean for me, so they didn't have to bother."

"I'm so sorry, Kris."

She stiffened. "Please don't. This is why I hate talking about my past. People start to feel sorry for me and I can't stand that."

They both went quiet, gazing at the fire.

"How about friends and lovers?" Angie asked after some time had passed. "Are you close to anyone?"

"The woman I had dinner with last night, Ilse, is a good friend. She genuinely cares about me."

"Ah, she's the ex you had the heavy discussion with? Does that mean you opened up to her?"

"About some things, yes. We're a lot closer now than when we were dating." Kris was feeling the effects of the wine, but in a nice way. Angie was easy to talk to, and it felt good to get some of this off her chest. "I've never gotten close to my lovers. I kept them happy with… things."

"Things?"

"Cash, trips, cars." Kris thought of the fortune she'd spent on women whose names she'd long forgotten. "I shamelessly used my parents' money to entertain and keep my lovers. I figured it was the least my dysfunctional family could give me. I'm not proud of taking advantage of their wealth, but I was angry and I suppose desperate for attention. I thought the world owed me some kind, *any* kind of happiness, even if that meant using someone else's money to buy it. I overcompensated with my lovers because I thought if I didn't give them whatever they wanted, they'd ignore me."

"Like your parents."

"Predictable, isn't it?" Kris looked at Angie expecting to see disgust written all over her face, but was surprised when she found nothing but sympathy in her caramel eyes.

"Are you still letting yourself be used that way?" Angie asked.

"Not anymore. I finally realized by doing that I was creating my own insecurity. Women were with me only because of what I could buy for them. That was three years ago. I guess I stopped throwing money around just in time, since my father left us with next to nothing. There's no way I could afford to buy love now."

"I don't see how anyone could be interested in your money after having spent a minute with you. Although I know the world is full of opportunists. I find it nauseating that you were used that way. You deserve so much better."

"Yes, I do. But I got exactly what I deserved. A fuck for a buck." Shocked by her own bitterness, and the fact that she hadn't even tried to hide it, Kris fell silent.

Angie didn't look embarrassed. Her expression was surprisingly soft, almost one of understanding. "I'm happy you don't feel that way anymore."

"I don't feel much of anything anymore." The statement had been true for such a long time Kris said it almost without thinking. But as soon as the words were out, she realized she'd certainly felt something when Angie kissed her.

As if reading her mind, Angie gave her a knowing look and said, "I don't believe that." She stretched out a little more, lying on her back with her arms up and hands linked beneath her head, eyes closed. Her dark hair, jeans, and baggy sweatshirt were so covered in plaster dust it looked like she'd fallen into a vat of flour. She was a far cry at the moment from the meticulous fashion plates Kris normally dated, but she thought Angie looked absolutely adorable. "You need to loosen up and try to enjoy life a bit without worrying about things too much."

Such advice, from anyone else, would have most certainly irritated her immensely. She hated it when people tried to analyze and offer unsolicited opinions to others on how to live their lives. A few of the women she'd dated had done it with her. But with Angie, she felt the need to defend herself. She didn't know why, but she didn't want Angie to think she was some uptight rich bitch who couldn't have a good time and who felt sorry for herself because her childhood sucked. What a cliché.

"Who said I don't have fun?" she replied defensively. "I have plenty of fun."

"Yeah, right." Angie chuckled.

Kris couldn't resist the sudden urge to punch her on the shoulder. "I *do*."

Angie's response was another snort of laughter. "Give me a for instance."

"I went out with Ilse only last night." *So there.*

Angie was unconvinced. "Yes, it's all coming back now. You mentioned her along with the stalker, as examples of your stressful evening. Sounds like a hoot and a half."

"Don't belittle her. We had a great time. Emotional, but great."

Angie's expression softened. "I didn't mean to belittle. All I'm saying is you could use a bit of fun. No heavy conversations or bad trips down memory lane."

"There's more to life than fun," Kris grumbled. "We can't all afford to indulge in a laissez-faire lifestyle."

"Okay, fine."

Silence fell between them again, the only sounds the grandfather clock ticking away the minutes and the occasional crackle of the fire.

"Why don't you like me?" Angie finally asked.

Kris had, in fact, just been thinking about how much she was enjoying the company of her unorthodox houseguest. And how surprised she was that she even enjoyed the woman's cocky teasing. So much so, that she was actually beginning to look forward to their next round of verbal sparring, though of course she was not about to initiate it. "Why won't you tell me what you're running from?"

"I never said I was running." Angie stared at the fire, her face conveniently averted.

Kris took the opportunity to study her in profile. Though her posture was relaxed, the intermittent flexing of the muscles in her jaw was a sign of that ever-present restlessness that seemed to be an inherent part of the woman. "You didn't have to. It's obvious."

When Angie turned her head, there was a flicker of pain in her eyes. "I'm preoccupied, that's all."

"It's like you don't dare sit still," Kris said carefully. "You even rock back and forth when you eat. Sometimes it looks as though it's almost painful for you to relax, and when you do, it's not for long. Most of the time you look like you want to run."

"And that's why you don't like me?" As if she'd just pulled down a curtain, Angie's expression was suddenly blank.

Kris knew the technique, she used it herself to mask her feelings. But the pain was still there. She could sense it. "I never said I didn't like you," she said softly. "It's just that your arrogance can make you a pain in the ass."

Angie blew out a breath, as though in surrender. "Oh, great. You think I'm a self-absorbed, arrogant pain in the ass." The vulnerability returned to her expression. "What *do* you like about me? Anything at all?"

The question was an invitation to open scrutiny. Kris couldn't resist. Angie was a beautiful woman, even in her work clothes, her glossy dark hair salted with plaster dust and her face devoid of makeup. She was so different from Kris, in so many ways. Exotic, almost. Her angular features, olive complexion, full lips, and caramel eyes, framed by long lashes, suggested a Mediterranean heritage. And she had the soft musculature in her shoulders, arms, and legs that Kris envied and had been unable to duplicate despite her efforts in the gym.

If she were to answer with complete honesty at that moment, she would have said *I like your eyes, your mouth, your body. The way you kiss, and the fact that your kiss made me feel so alive.* But she was in no way ready to go there. "You're…handy around the house."

"I'll try to take comfort in that." Angie got up abruptly and started to pick up the empty plates and glasses. "I'm going to get my arrogant, self-absorbed ass to bed. It's late."

She didn't look Kris's way or speak further before departing for the kitchen. Kris wondered whether she was as hurt as she appeared or if her show of sulking was yet another prelude to a joke. She got up as well and returned their pillows to the couch, then closed the screen to the fireplace and turned off the desk lamp. As she headed out of the room, she bumped into Angie. Her expression was unreadable and her voice held none of its usual frivolity when she spoke.

"Good night, Kris. I'll see you tomorrow."

Kris grabbed her by the arm as she turned for the stairs. "Angie, wait. I didn't mean to hurt your feelings."

"Don't worry about it. You were being honest."

Kris was shocked by the disappointment that clouded her face. She realized, as they stood face-to-face, that Angie's arrogance was a thin veneer, a shield masking some kind of hidden anguish. She ached to do something—anything—to make that pain go away. Under the glare of the hallway light, she noticed a white chunk of plaster stuck to Angie's hair. Without thinking, she reached over to remove it.

"You have this big piece of..." She stopped mid sentence when she saw the way Angie was staring at her. She'd seen that smoldering look of arousal and desire many times in her life, but rarely did it ever have this kind of effect on her. It was a visual caress that she felt clear to her toes.

She was about to pull her hand away when Angie covered it with her own. "Why is this so hard for you?"

They continued to stare at each other for a long while, both breathing heavily.

Kris didn't bother to pretend the question confused her. She knew exactly what Angie was asking. "I'm not sure," she replied, finally, her voice so low she hardly recognized herself.

"Let me know when you are...sure." Angie's hand dropped and she bolted up the stairs to her room without waiting for a reply.

CHAPTER THIRTEEN

Kris returned to her room and stripped for bed, but although her overworked body begged for slumber, her mind would not allow it. The memories of Angie's kiss and the hunger in her eyes stirred her up and left her wanting. And somehow that glimpse of vulnerability within the American's tough, carefree exterior had driven home her attraction. Kris really wanted to get to know her better, and she was sure the interest was mutual.

Like a persistent jackhammer in her head, the events of the past twenty-four hours kept pounding away. Angie. Jerking her off the tram and kissing her like that. No warning, no reason. Like she had every right to, like she knew Kris wouldn't object. *Pompous American.* But Kris hadn't objected at all, had she? Despite herself, she'd enjoyed it very much. Too much, as a matter of fact.

The memory of those warm lips against hers kept intruding relentlessly on her consciousness. She told herself it was only a kiss, but something about it, something other than the fact that Angie was a mystery, troubled her. She might have been tipsy, but their close proximity had brought on a sense of déjà vu that excited and puzzled her. Tonight's strained conversation was even more confusing.

They were dancing around each other, on the very cusp of something that felt innately powerful and right, and Angie was apparently leaving it entirely up to her to decide whether they would act upon the spark of attraction that was building by the day. Yet again she thought about those moments on the bridge, and her body reacted with a hollow flutter. Trying to shift her focus away from the woman who'd invaded her consciousness, she thought about the weird guy who'd been watching her in the restaurant. Why hadn't he approached her? Spoken to her? He seemed content to watch, and follow. The behavior was far from typical for the usual predatory male.

Kris tried to place his face. Perhaps she'd encountered him before and he was simply hanging around her, waiting to be recognized. Feeling restless and wanting to soothe her aching muscles, she padded into the bathroom. A double dose of ibuprofen took the edge off the tension headache closing in on her, but she still couldn't relax enough to fall asleep. She gave up after a half hour of tossing and turning and went to the window to look out on the grounds of the estate. Too long neglected, the once-elegant topiary appeared as shapeless silhouettes in the moonless, overcast night, and she could barely make out the tall evergreens that ringed the perimeter.

The earlier conversation with Jeroen about the hidden room had been nagging at her all afternoon, and she decided it might be prudent to move the diamond from the vault. There seemed no better time than the present to take care of it, so she dressed, adding a heavy sweater and jacket to the clothes she'd worn earlier. Retrieving the combination to the vault that Hans had given her, she headed downstairs.

❖

Allegro paced in her room, allowing enough time for Kris to fall asleep. She couldn't put off recovering the diamond any longer and tonight was the right time to make her move. She wished like hell she had a sports car, an open road, and some alone time with an uncomplicated woman. Anything to help her escape this confusion. She'd never questioned her choices before and stood behind her lifestyle with complete conviction. But Kris, with a few careless words, had managed to make her feel inadequate and superficial. What others thought of her was something she never even considered, never mind cared about. The fact that a woman she barely knew could make her doubt herself threw her completely off balance. And what she hated more than the unusual ebbing of her confidence was the fact that Kris thought about her in such unflattering terms. An arrogant pain in the ass?

Allegro conceded that she'd intentionally played the role of an insouciant American to make her cover work. But she hadn't expected to be quite so convincing. At the same time Kris had obviously looked close enough to notice her constant need to run. The only other person who had ever commented on her restlessness was Luka Madison. They'd grown up together in the academy and each was the closest the other had to family. Luka had noticed because she cared, but why had Kris? Why had she looked at her with such tenderness tonight, yet dismissed her so casually with that comment about her being "handy"?

Allegro was so absorbed in her thoughts that she didn't realize something in her environment had changed until a few seconds after she heard a noise outside her window. Footsteps. Just as they registered, they were gone. She turned off the light and hurried to her window. It was too dark to make out anything but vague black shapes. Trees, hedges, the fence. She waited a few seconds and heard the noise again. Unlatching the window, she eased it open, careful not to make any sound. Nothing seemed to be moving on her side of the house.

She thought of the German and knew she should have acted sooner to confront him. Maybe he knew more about the diamond than they thought. Was it possible that he knew about the vault? And how to get to it? It seemed far-fetched, but she had no reason to discard the possibility. Never eliminate an option without proof. She couldn't risk him recognizing her from the night before, so she went to her duffel, withdrew her ski mask, and put it on. Next came her gloves and Walther P99 and silencer. She also took a moment to substitute a heavy black sweater for the plaster-covered T-shirt she'd worked in.

There was a large oak tree outside her window, its nearest branch a few feet away. She perched on the windowsill and jumped, landing with her arms wrapped around the branch. Swinging her legs up around the limb, she shimmied silently to the trunk and worked her way to the ground.

Keeping to the tree line that ringed the estate, she moved low and fast, alert to any further sound or movement. If the German was out here, he wasn't keeping to the gravel pathway that led from the house to the garden shed against the opposite wall. He could be hiding behind any of the shrubs and topiaries, or keeping to the trees, as she was. It occurred to her that if Schmidt knew how to get to the diamond, her mission would be over. She would have to take the stone before he could, and then she'd never see Kris again. The prospect saddened her in a way she hadn't imagined possible.

When she reached the rear wall where the trees were few and

farther apart, she darted from one topiary to another, maintaining a clearer view of the walkway. That's when she spotted Kris. She began to relax, but then everything happened so fast her instincts and training took over.

Kris stopped walking. "Is anybody there?" she called out.

Allegro froze. There was no way Kris could have heard her. She heard a faint sound near the shed. Kris heard it, too, and started running toward the house. She fell, and Allegro heard her cry out as a flash of gunfire flared from beside the shed. There was only a wisp of sound, a dull, fizzing pop she would recognize in her sleep. The intruder had a silencer, too.

She ripped off her mask and let it drop to the ground. Gun in hand, she raced toward Kris in a crouch, her heart hammering in her chest. Relief and fear battled for dominance when she saw her start to rise, a sitting duck for a second shot. Allegro tackled her from behind, letting her momentum carry them both forward. They landed at the base of a broad shrub that would provide decent cover.

As Kris started to scream, Allegro gave her shoulder a sharp shake. "Kris, it's me." She aimed the Walther in the direction of the shooter and made her voice loud enough to be heard by whoever was out there. "I saw you and thought you were an intruder. I called the police. Are you okay?"

"Aside from being face down in the mud, you mean?" Kris sounded pissed but not hurt.

"We really need to stop meeting like this," she said jokingly. "What are you doing out here in the middle of the night, anyway?" Allegro kept Kris in her grip, wanting to make sure the shooter had gone before they both stood.

"I forgot to check on the firewood supply and it looks like we'll have some bad weather tomorrow."

Bad weather? Prevarication didn't get any more feeble. February was Amsterdam's coldest month, but they weren't facing an imminent freeze. Replenishing the firewood could have waited till the next morning. "In the middle of the night? It's so dark out here you could have fallen."

"It would appear that I already have, and not by my own fault. Besides, what could you have done about it, had there really had been an intruder out here?"

"I'd have pointed him in your direction so you could insult him to death," Allegro said, still bothered by Kris's earlier assessment of her.

"Are we really having this discussion out here, while I'm choking on sludge?" Kris shifted to get up, but Allegro kept her pinned while she shoved the gun into the back of her jeans. Kris craned her head around. "Can I get up now, or is this your idea of foreplay?"

"You'd know if this were foreplay," Allegro replied. With her attention fixed in the direction of the intruder, she held out her hand to help Kris up. Once they were on their feet, presenting a clear target, they needed to move fast. "Come on, let's go. The police should be here any moment."

Allegro put an arm around Kris's waist and hurried them toward the house, the whole while keeping watch on the shed. They reached the mansion without further incident, but she knew the danger was far from over. As Kris turned on the lights to the kitchen, Allegro instinctively swung her gaze to the window that overlooked the back of the estate. "You're going to track mud all over," she said, keeping her voice nonchalant as she reached into her pocket for her cell phone. "Why don't you strip down right here and head upstairs for a shower while I call off the police."

Kris paused where she was and looked at herself. Her clothes were covered in muck, and they'd already left a trail of muddy footprints from the door. By the time she'd removed her shoes and socks, Allegro was done with her faux phone call to the police.

"Did you stop them on time? I wouldn't think it would take this long to get here from Haarlem."

"Busy night, I guess."

Kris kept her eyes on her bare feet. "I'm sorry I worried you and got you out of bed." She turned and headed for the living room.

Allegro kicked her shoes off and followed her. She didn't want to leave her alone until she knew for sure that no one was in the house. "I'd be happy to help you get some more firewood tomorrow if you're running out."

"That won't be necessary. I think we're all right for now."

Once she heard Kris's shower running, Allegro took the opportunity to thoroughly search the house, making sure every window and door was tightly bolted. As she carried out her security measures, her heart refused to slow down. She was shaken by the gravity of what had just occurred. Kris could have been killed. Nearly was. And what weighed on Allegro was the profound sense of loss she would feel if that had happened. She knew it was foolish to think they had any real future together, yet she couldn't stop herself from panicking at the thought of leaving Kris here to fend for herself, not even aware of the danger she was in. *Future together?* Since when did she ever think in terms of a future with anyone? What was happening to her?

For the first time, one of the dictums of the EOO truly drove home. There was peril in becoming personally involved in any way in an assignment. But she couldn't help it. Somehow, someway, Kristine van der Jagt had become a very important priority in her life, and she felt powerless to change that, at least until she'd fulfilled her mission. Then she could run again, speed away as she always did. Time and distance always worked, taking her far from her inner landscape to the only world she really understood. Her work.

Allegro finished her rounds of the house at the window of a vacant guest room that overlooked the back of the estate. She stared down at the dark shapes of the trees and shrubs below, looking for signs of the intruder and hoping it was mere coincidence that he'd been standing by the shed. She braced herself for what was ahead. If all went well, she would be gone before Kris woke up. She would leave a note, of course, but things were so awkward between them that Kris would probably be relieved. Trying not to feel despondent over that likelihood, she slipped along the hallway to her bedroom and retrieved her lock-picking tools and stethoscope from her duffel bag. Tucking them into her jeans, she donned a pair of latex gloves and slipped downstairs and out the back door, locking it behind her. She withdrew her gun and took cover behind the nearest hedge, listening intently. The windows of the mansion remained dark and several minutes passed without sound or signs of movement. Reasonably certain that she was alone, she advanced to the tree line and skirted the perimeter of the estate until she was satisfied that no one was about.

The locked shed door was no obstacle. She was inside within seconds and had the padlock off the trapdoor almost as quickly. As she'd suspected, the tunnel led toward the house. Her penlight skimmed over a couple of crates and an old trunk, all so covered with dust and dirt it was obvious they hadn't been opened in many years. She descended and, keeping her back to the cool, damp wall, moved cautiously to the end. Another steel ladder led upward to the hidden room. The small rectangular space contained only the vault, which sat nestled against one wall. A dark brown standing safe five feet tall, two feet wide, and two feet deep, it was an Austrian-made Wertheim model at least fifty years old. As she started in on the combination, she tried not to think of Kris, sleeping one floor above, and the fact that if the Blue Star was indeed on the other side of this thin steel barrier, she would never see her again.

Five of the six numbers came easily. The last took more time, because she was struggling as she never had with the possible repercussions of a mission successfully accomplished. She'd be on the first plane out of Amsterdam and Kris would be left alone to deal with whoever had shot at her tonight. When she felt the final tumbler engage, she held her breath and reached for the lever.

She was almost relieved to find the safe empty.

Allegro left everything as she had found it, the vault locked up again, the padlock and mat back where they were. As she relocked the door to the shed, she heard a noise across the yard, near the house. Slipping back into the dark shadows of the tree line, she moved slowly and carefully toward the sound, gun at the ready. Two minutes passed, then three. She spotted a shadow pass between two shrubs, not far from the rear corner of the mansion. A silhouette too large to belong to Kris.

She stalked him, slowly closing in, careful not to alert him to her presence until she was within striking distance. Then she sprang from behind, wrapping her left arm around his throat as her right thrust the end of her gun hard against his cheek. He froze. It was only this close that she was finally able to confirm his identity. He reeked of fear and stale sweat.

In German, she said, "Good evening, Gunter. What are you doing here?"

He barked out a demand to be let go. She cocked her gun and poked it harder against his cheek, repeating the question. No response.

"Are you searching for the diamond?" she asked.

As soon as the words were out, Schmidt struggled to get loose, and she hit him in the back of his head with the butt of her gun. He crumpled to the ground, dazed, and she trained her Walther on him.

Recognition crossed his face. *"Die Amerikanerin."*

She'd hit him hard, but he wasn't dizzy for long. Moving faster than she thought possible, he wrenched his gun from his coat and brought the weapon up to fire.

Allegro pulled her trigger first and got him between the eyes. He fell back, inert, and although he was clearly dead, she adhered to protocol and fired a second shot into his head. As she bent over his body and searched his clothes, her mind raced through the options for body disposal. The ring on his car keys told her he'd rented a Fiat. She suspected he'd parked his car where he had before, on the road behind the woods adjacent to the rear of the estate, so she headed there first, hurrying the quarter-mile as best as she could in the dark shelter of the trees. Once she got to the road, she pulled out the keys and hit the remote, hoping to spot a flash of the Fiat's headlights through the shrubbery on either side of the pavement. Nothing. She ran a short distance in the direction of town and tried again before running back the way she came, and jogging along the main road in front of the estate, depressing the button on the remote.

She finally located the car behind a large hedge not far from the mansion, and drove back without headlights. Cutting the engine as she hit the driveway, she let the car roll to a stop behind the barn as close as she dared get to the German's body. After making sure the vehicle couldn't be seen from the house, she let herself in the back door, removing her shoes just in case there was blood on them. She quickly found what she needed—large plastic trash bags, a spare tarp, and a full can of spray paint from the artists' supplies in the cellar. She had to get moving. It was only two a.m., but Haarlem came to life long before sunrise.

There wasn't much blood. The first shot had killed the German instantly. She pulled a bag over his head to contain what remained and glanced around for his gun. The weapon wasn't next to the body; it had evidently landed somewhere in the blackness around them, and there was no time to look for it now. The dead man was too heavy to carry to the car, so she laid the tarp over the garden cart they'd been using to haul renovation supplies and hefted the body onto it. She was out of breath by the time she got the German positioned in the passenger seat, his body slouched forward and his head to the side where it couldn't be seen.

Panting, her clothes wet with sweat, she started the car and reversed quickly onto the main road to Haarlem. Once she reached the city she searched systematically for an isolated side street, away from traffic and devoid of lights and possible witnesses. When she found the perfect spot she parked the Fiat, dragged the German's body into the driver's seat, and removed the bag from his head. Using the spray paint, she drew a large swastika on the side of the car, jammed the can into her coat pocket, and left the scene at a walk, keeping her head down whenever a rare vehicle passed by.

On the outskirts of town, Allegro paused to scratch the serial number off the can with her house key and wipe it clean of any van der Jagt fingerprints before dumping it into the nearest sewer along with the plastic trash bag she'd turned inside out so any DNA would be destroyed. She covered the final distance to the mansion at a brisk jog, every muscle in her body screaming in protest. Near the shed she drew a bucket of water to wash the tarp she'd used, which she then folded and dropped into the garden cart where no one would be surprised to see it. Later, she would burn it along with her clothing. She sluiced the area where she'd killed Schmidt, eliminating visible blood. Her last task was to retrieve her ski mask and locate the German's gun. Her breath caught in her throat as she pulled the weapon from a nearby shrub. There was no silencer, and she'd already searched his pockets for anything that might connect him to the van der Jagts without finding one.

Incredulous, she sniffed the barrel. The German hadn't fired a shot. He was not the man who'd tried to shoot Kris earlier. Someone else had been here tonight. Someone who'd now had at least a couple of hours to finish what he'd started while she was disposing of Schmidt's body. She bolted to the house, frantically shed her shoes, gloves, and the outer layers of her clothing before entering, and rolled them into a bundle around her ski mask and the German's gun as she raced upstairs to Kris's bedroom. Her heart boomed like thunder in her chest as she gripped the doorknob.

CHAPTER FOURTEEN

Haarlem

Azizi reported in not long after he left the van der Jagt estate and returned to his hotel room. Kabul was three and a half hours ahead of Haarlem time, so he knew he'd catch the Culture Minister as he was rising for Fajr, the dawn prayer. He regretted that his first attempt to recover the diamond had gone so badly that the police might now be watching the van der Jagt mansion. But he had escaped to try again, and there was some positive news that would help redeem him in his superior's eyes.

Qadir got right to the point. "Have you found it?"

"I am afraid not, *Agha*. I was close but got interrupted. It would appear that a female companion is staying with the countess. This guest got in the way."

"Did they see you?" Qadir asked.

"I am certain that they did not, but they called the authorities when they thought someone was on the property. I left before the police arrived."

"I find this conversation less than satisfactory." The minister's irritation was clear. "You allowed two *women* to stand in your way?"

Azizi flinched at the insult and automatically bowed his head. "Please, *Agha*, I have good news as well."

Qadir ignored the entreaty. "I sent you there to honor your country. If you cannot handle this mission then I will have to replace you."

Azizi tried to hide the fear in his voice and replace it with confidence. He knew what the repercussions would be if he failed in this assignment. "That will not be necessary. I am a tested soldier and will do what I have to, to live up to this honor."

"If you value your family's future, that would be wise. What was the good news?"

"I know where the *Setarehe Abi Rang* is," he replied. "The countess retrieved it from its hiding place while I was there."

Again the minister became enraged. "You should have taken the stone then. What could two women do to stop you? Were you not armed?"

"I was, but so were they. The woman who joined her looked like trouble and I did not want to take any chances. I am aware of the dire situation but do not want to involve our country or your name in any kind of scandal should something have gone wrong." Trying to avoid further questions, Azizi added, "She has it on her, I am sure. And she will try to move it soon. I will be there when she does."

"I hope for your sake that your next attempt will be a successful one," Qadir warned.

"I assure you it will. Have a good day, *Agha. As-Salāmu `Alayka'*."

Qadir made the requisite reply, wishing him peace, and the phone went dead.

❖

Allegro was so intent on making sure Kris was all right she gave no thought to how she might explain exactly what she was doing bursting into her bedroom, partly clothed and out of breath, more than two hours before dawn. The curtains were drawn and the room was black as pitch. It took a few seconds for her eyes to adjust before she could make out the shape beneath the covers. Relief poured through her as Kris bolted upright in alarm, crying out, "Who's there?"

"Thank God." Allegro hadn't intended to say it aloud, but fortunately the words were barely audible. She hurriedly stuffed her gun behind the bundle she was carrying.

"Angie?" There was panic in the voice. "Is that you?" The bedside lamp came on. The heavy comforter had been thrown back, and Kris was wearing only a body-hugging tank top. The rest of her was covered by a pale yellow satin sheet. She was breathing hard from her abrupt and rude awakening, staring at Allegro as if she'd gone mad. "What's wrong? What happened?"

"Nothing, why?" she said casually. *That was slick.*

"*Why?* Because you burst in here at…" Kris peered at the alarm clock on the bedside table. "Five thirty in the morning, looking like you're ready to pounce."

The word "pounce" drew Allegro's gaze involuntarily to Kris's breasts, but she enjoyed the sight only briefly. Her preoccupation with the night's events precluded any serious consideration of sex at the moment. "They say the third time's the charm." The remark was met with a scowl, so she quickly added, "I was wondering if you'd like eggs for breakfast. I'm doing some laundry and thought I'd cook afterward."

Kris's eyes narrowed suspiciously as she took in Allegro's appearance and the clothing bundle under her arm. "You expect me to believe you scared me half to death to ask if I'd like breakfast?"

"I thought you were awake. I heard noise coming from your room."

Kris frowned. "You look like hell for someone with so much zest for the early hours. Are you on drugs?"

"No, though I did have a rough time getting to sleep last night, this is just the natural high of a morning person."

"That's a high I'm not familiar with and I'd like to keep it that way."

Allegro grinned. "I thought we'd get an early start this morning, since Jeroen will be occupied with his other job. So…eggs?"

Kris dropped back onto her pillows. "I'm not going to be here today. I'll be visiting my mother. But since I'm up now, I'll jump in the shower and meet you downstairs for those eggs you're so anxious to make."

"Eggs à la Angie, coming right up." She backed out of the room, keeping her gun out of sight.

"Christ. All this enthusiasm about breakfast," Kris mumbled.

"I heard that," Allegro hollered back. "And my enthusiasm applies to everything."

She detoured to her room, hid the incriminating bundle in a drawer until she could deal with disposal, and put on fresh clothing. Then she called the car rental agency in Haarlem and left a message saying she'd be in when they opened to exchange her black economy vehicle for a light-colored, fast sports car.

❖

Kris pondered Angie's bizarre behavior as she showered and dressed. It couldn't be a cultural thing; she'd known a lot of Americans. The woman was just...odd. She knew she should be looking forward to a return to her predictable if solitary life, but she had to admit having Angie around made her days a lot more interesting. She never knew what to expect next, and despite being tackled, bruised, and scared to death last night, she felt strangely happy. It was a refreshing change to have someone in her life who wasn't interested in what she could provide for them. Angie knew she had no money and didn't seem to care about her title. She didn't hesitate to speak her mind and tease Kris about her shortcomings. As much as the banter sometimes irritated her, it also was a comfort, somehow. Like she was being viewed exactly for *who* she was, and not *what* she was.

The enticing aroma of freshly brewed coffee hit her as she headed downstairs. Angie was dishing up a plate of scrambled eggs dotted with bits of ham and cheese. As a child, Kris had always considered the kitchen the coziest, most welcoming room in the mansion. Although outfitted with the latest appliances, it retained the feel of a relaxed country home thanks to its plank wood flooring, pale yellow walls, and antique oak cabinetry. She'd taken refuge here when she felt most alone and isolated. Their Indonesian cook was always baking bread or cookies and was never too busy to ask how Kris had done in school that day.

"Take a seat." Angie indicated the small square breakfast table by the window, where two places had been carefully set. She laid slices of toast on either side of the eggs and carried Kris's plate and coffee over first.

Kris had to admit the eggs smelled heavenly. Another of Angie's hidden talents, apparently. "Oh, good, I'm actually quite hungry."

"I was thinking that since both you and Jeroen are taking off today, I should use the day to take care of some things I've been putting off."

"Like what?" Kris's mouth was watering, but she waited, an

ingrained habit of her formal upbringing, until Angie returned with her own meal and sat down.

"Like going to the immigration office in Amsterdam to apply for a temporary residency permit. I'm about to exceed my three-month limit, so I should check my options. I don't want to get in trouble."

"You could use this address as a place of residency if they ask. I would be happy to confirm that for you." Kris picked up her fork and dug in. The eggs tasted even better than they smelled.

"Great. I'm sure that would help." Angie grinned at her. "So, you're not ready to see me leave yet, huh?"

"Well, of course not. Look around, there's still so much that needs to be done."

The smile faded and Angie poked at her breakfast dejectedly. "Of course. How could I forget? Being 'handy' is my one redeeming quality."

"That's not true, and it's not what I meant."

Angie set her fork down and the smile returned, but it wasn't as convincing as before. "Are you going to tell me that you spent last night soul-searching and are finally ready to accept how profound and multi-layered I am?"

"You know," Kris replied, "someday soon, I am going to figure out why you so desperately try to hide behind humor and evasiveness."

Angie looked quickly away. "I'm not hiding behind anything." She busied herself spreading butter and marmalade onto a slice of toast, trying to appear her usual casual self, but Kris could see she was unsettled.

"We all have something to hide," Kris said softly. "We all have closets."

Angie's reply was in that same subdued, sincere tone. "I'm flattered you want to go looking into mine."

They continued their meal with another strained silence, the American avoiding eye contact. Kris had definitely struck a nerve. "Who knows," she said, trying to lighten the moment and return that spark of mischief to Angie's eyes, "I might even find your modesty somewhere in there."

The words had the desired effect. Angie chuckled as she scooped up their empty plates and took them to the sink. When she looked back at Kris, the smile was genuine. "What's this modesty you speak of?"

❖

Allegro left Kris drinking coffee in the kitchen and headed to her room, mentally mapping out her day. As soon as she'd taken care of the bundle in the drawer, her first priority was to find the diamond. She couldn't search Kris's room and the rest of the mansion now, in case she was caught. But she couldn't wait until Kris left, either. She was certain Kris had taken the stone from the vault, no doubt intending to move it to a more secure location, probably a bank lockbox where such valuables ought to be housed. It would be foolish to leave it unguarded with two strangers around every day. Kris had come downstairs wearing a sheer silk blouse and form-fitting skirt, so she probably didn't have the diamond hidden on her. And Allegro had searched the purse and coat waiting on the chair at the base of the stairs. Kris usually put her stuff there when she was planning to go out.

Still, it seemed likely Kris would take it with her. And with a second stalker on her tail, someone who had already taken a shot at her, Allegro's only choice was to keep close to her today. The lines between her mission and her own desires were blurring, but either way she had no choice but to stick with Kris until she could arrange for some backup or until she took possession of the diamond.

Her pride did not allow her to ask Pierce for help directly, at least not yet. She was afraid he would see her request as more personal than professional. There was only one person Allegro trusted enough to help protect Kris at any cost, and fortunately, the chances were good that she could be in the Netherlands in a matter of hours. She'd spoken to Luka Madison a couple of weeks earlier, and Luka had been in Malta, between assignments, working at a cathedral in her civilian job as an art restorer. She and Allegro were among the Organization's most versatile ETF operatives, and Luka—aka Domino—was an especially skilled sharpshooter and master of disguise. When they were younger Allegro used to call her Shape-shifter, because of her ability to pass as anyone she had to.

Their friendship had begun during their early teens, when they were assigned to share a dorm room, and it had blossomed during their intense, grueling training. They kept each other motivated during the dark times of doubt and debilitating exhaustion. And each provided the other with the kind of absolute, unquestioned familial support only orphans can truly appreciate, having been unable to take it for granted.

Their bond had been cemented forever during a fateful assignment three years earlier. The Elite Operatives Organization had been hired by the FBI and its Russian counterpart, the FSB, to eliminate a spy who'd been feeding American and Russian intel to the Middle East. The mission involved a helicopter drop into northern Mongolia, in December, where a contact would meet them and take them across the border to Siberia. Domino had asked to go and only Allegro knew the real reason why. Domino's previous assignment, in Sumatra, had been particularly horrific and she'd made up her mind to quit the Organization. Pierce wouldn't let her leave voluntarily; it was never an option for an ETF. So Domino had decided to disappear. Allegro knew she planned to use the Siberian mission as her means. She also knew that Monty Pierce would search until he found her. The EOO had a long reach, and once a rogue agent was located the outcome was preordained.

The last operative who'd wanted to leave came back from a Middle East assignment in a body bag, supposedly killed by a land mine. But a pro like Agent Harrison, the dead woman, was trained to spot mines a mile away. The truth would forever remain clouded, but the message was clear. If operatives thought they could leave whenever they wished, if they thought they could sever the ties of commitment that bound them to their controllers, they were naïve. Allegro knew better than to delude herself that the EOO was capable of mercy when it came to mutiny. Whether Domino disappeared of her own volition or the EOO's, Allegro couldn't bear the thought of never seeing her again, so she'd quickly volunteered to go along on the Siberian mission.

They'd boarded the C-17 Globemaster III cargo plane at the Kimhae Air Base near Pusan, South Korea, not long after dusk, attended by the minimal number of U.S. Air Force personnel necessary to get them airborne. Their pilot and copilot were also U.S. military, but the man who sat with them in the rear of the plane was another EOO operative, assigned to relay information back to headquarters and make sure everything went as planned.

The temperature at the drop zone was bone-chilling, and the sky at thirteen thousand feet was at least thirty below zero. They wore white accuracy jumping suits with thermal suits beneath, white arctic boots, heavy gloves, neoprene facemasks, helmets, and goggles. When they entered the skies above Mongolia, both strapped on their parachute vests. They'd done this so many times it was second nature to double-check every strap and connection on their rigs. The gear they would need for their mission would be in the Jeep that picked them up.

When the pilot gave them a five-minute warning, they rose from their steel benches to stand before the large cargo door aft. Almost immediately, Domino seemed fidgety and unfocused. She paced and pulled up her goggles to rub at her eyes.

Allegro came up beside her and put a hand on Domino's shoulder. "Are you okay?"

When her friend didn't answer, she turned her until they were face-to-face. "Luka, what's wrong?"

"I can't do this." Domino looked down at her feet and shook her head.

"What are you talking about?" Allegro glanced at the other operative, who was watching them intently.

"We have an assignment to take care of," he said. "Get yourself together, Domino."

She went to the nearest bench and sat, putting her head between her legs. "I can't. I'm dizzy." She was breathing so fast her harness visibly rose and fell with each exhalation.

Allegro squatted in front of her. "You can't be serious. Are you telling me you've suddenly developed a fear of heights?"

The male op regarded Domino suspiciously. "Your last tests were all clean. There's no reason for you to be feeling like this."

"Listen, I can't do this," Domino repeated, rubbing at her eyes again. "I think it's the altitude. It's making me sick."

"Are you refusing this assignment?" The male op asked angrily.

"I've been complaining about these spells for weeks, and getting the same response about my routine tests being fine. It's time the EOO paid attention and got me an MRI or something."

The pilot called to them from the cockpit, "The drop is in two minutes."

A loud rasping sound echoed through the plane as the massive aft cargo door began to open and arctic air rushed in on them. The noise of the wind and machinery was enormous. Even standing close together, they had to shout to be heard.

"I said I *can't*," Domino declared.

"Shit." The male op glared at her. "Allegro, get ready," he hollered. "You're going solo. I need to advise that we have an agent down." He proceeded on to the cockpit to radio headquarters.

Allegro's insides began to twist as she realized the extent to which Domino had been preparing for this opportunity. "I'm not letting you do this," she said, just loud enough for her to hear.

"I don't know what you're talking about." Domino stared at a spot over her shoulder.

"You're about to sabotage yourself. Aborting a mission with no proof of medical reason."

"This is none of your business," Domino replied. "And I have plenty of other reasons."

Allegro could feel the clock ticking. "They'll know, Luka."

Domino's determined expression didn't change. "I don't give a fuck. I can't do this anymore."

"They'll find you. However long it takes."

Domino leaned back until her head rested against the curved steel interior wall and closed her eyes, as though that would preclude any further discussion of the matter. "I know what I have to do."

"Thirty seconds to drop," the pilot screamed back at them, his voice barely audible.

"Suit yourself," Allegro yelled. "But you're not taking me down with you. I'm not going back to headquarters having to prove I didn't plan an abort mission with you, or trying to explain what I knew or didn't know about your plans. Either way, I'll end up with a red flag on my file, and never mind the damn PER they'll put me through." She shuddered at the prospect of undergoing yet another psychological evaluation review. "And you…" She unbuckled her vest and tossed the parachute toward the open cargo door. The wind took it out and away in an instant. "You'll get black-flagged and you know what that means." A black flag was no mere disciplinary measure. It meant interrogation and then elimination. "You'll never get away with this."

"What are you doing?" Domino shouted in alarm.

Allegro took a step toward the door, where the wind was so strong she was barely able to keep her footing. She stared at her friend. "I know what I have to do as well."

She took another step and let the wind suck her out of the plane, feeling the full force of the enormous pressure as she started to drop. She was plummeting to earth at ninety miles an hour, but because of her body's resistance to the air she felt like she was flying. Belly to the earth, she spread her arms and legs in an effort to slow down, but the ground came toward her with surprising speed. She should have been terrified, but she felt no fear at all.

The impact when Domino slammed into her from behind knocked most of the wind out of her. The arm locked around her waist squeezed out the rest. Domino hooked their harnesses together and immediately pulled the cord to release her chute. They jerked upward as the chute deployed.

"Miss me already?" Allegro screamed at the top of her lungs.

Domino didn't reply.

The combined weight of their bodies increased the acceleration of their descent until they were plummeting way too fast, especially for a parachute designed for one. The ground rushed up to meet them so fast Allegro knew they were going to have a very hard landing. Her hips and ass took most of the impact as they landed in a heap. Under her, Domino was cushioned somewhat by the waist-deep snow. The parachute had wrapped around them, and as soon as they caught their breath, Domino unhooked their harnesses and they struggled to untangle themselves.

"Happy you could join me," Allegro said.

"Fuck you!" Domino lunged at her, wrestling her to the ground and pummeling her with her fists.

Allegro fought back with a trio of hard punches. "No, fuck you." She pushed her friend roughly away. "Did you think I was going to let you go on a suicide mission?"

The words were barely out of her mouth when Domino threw her down again. "What in the hell do you call what you just did? You could have killed us."

"But I didn't," Allegro replied calmly, holding her off. "I saw the size of the chutes. I knew we would manage."

"Do you understand the risk you took?" Domino shouted.

"All of a sudden you care about whether you live or die?"

"I always have, you reckless idiot." Domino punched her again, hard.

"I'm the idiot? You're the one sabotaging yourself and sealing your destiny."

"Listen, it's my damn life," Domino insisted.

"That's your problem, Luka. You think your life belongs to you. News flash. It doesn't. It never has and never will." Allegro looked up at her friend. She didn't feel the cold, but this close to Domino, she could see her rapid breathing as short, angry bursts of white vapor. "None of us gets to walk away. We're bought and paid for. They own us, and our destiny."

As the words sank in, Domino's firm pressure against her wrists eased, and she finally released Allegro and sat back on her ass, arms wrapped around her knees. "How do you do it, Misha?" she asked eventually. "How can you live with what we see?"

Allegro remained sprawled where she was, propping herself up on her elbows. "By not feeling it."

"Bullshit. You feel and live like no one I've ever known."

"Look closer, Luka. I simulate every emotion that comes out of me. The good and the bad. I've become a pro, not just in faking my identity, but my feelings as well."

Domino shook her head. "How can you live like that? Not let anything touch you?"

"Who said anything about living? This is survival. The only thing that makes my heart beat faster is speed. I push myself, just to see if I feel the fear of mortality." She shrugged. "Sometimes, it works."

"You've had to fight for your own life on more than one occasion." Domino leaned closer, studying her face. "Are you telling me you've never felt afraid?"

"I've felt a need to survive. Something purely instinctual."

"Come on, Misha. We've been on missions together. I've seen the fear in your eyes."

Allegro looked away. She took a long breath and let it out, watching the vapors disappear into the darkness. "Yes, and that's why I can't let you do this to yourself. Or to me." The admission was more difficult than any assignment and her words came out in a rush. "At least when you're with me, when we're together, I feel the fear. Not for myself, but for you. Having you, the one person in my life I give a damn about, makes me feel like I have reason to be afraid. I'm afraid of losing you. While I have you I feel like there's someone out there who cares."

"And you're right. I do."

Allegro sat up and met Domino's eyes. "Don't fool yourself, Luka. They wouldn't hesitate to eliminate us if it meant protecting their precious Organization. They've invested in making us trained killers, not in family values. If we had to be eliminated, the only thing they'd mourn is the money and time they've spent on us."

"Why don't you run?" Domino asked. "If you're not afraid of anything?"

"I do run. Every chance I get, preferably as fast as possible. Always looking for that finish line in case it's the final one. They never are."

"I mean *really* run," her friend pressed. "From this life."

Allegro didn't answer. The faraway sound of a motor pierced the silence. She got to her feet and started to gather up the parachute, but Domino's hand on her shoulder stopped her.

"Mishael?"

"I'm not crazy, Luka," she replied in a tired voice, staring off in the direction of the approaching Jeep. "I'd never find rest. I'd have to spend the rest of my life looking over my shoulder. Besides," she faced Domino again, "what's the point in running when there's no finish line? When there's nothing to run to?"

Allegro exhaled slowly and called herself present. Three years had passed since that day, but the memory was still so fresh her lips almost felt numb. She flipped open her cell and dialed Domino's number.

"Hello?" her friend answered cautiously, and that didn't surprise her. Few people had her number, but Allegro had engaged her scrambler, so the caller ID would not have displayed who was on the line.

"Isn't payback a bitch, especially when the bitch calls to collect?" she said.

Domino laughed. "Do I need to bail you out? Have they finally arrested your ass for exceeding the speed of light?"

"No, that's on next week's agenda. Are you still in Malta?"

"Yes, and I'm about to leave for Tibet." Domino sounded more relaxed than Allegro could ever remember. "Are you in trouble?"

"In more ways than one." With a pang of guilt, Allegro recalled

Domino's planned vacation with the new love in her life, journalist Hayley Ward. "Can Tibet wait? I need your help ASAP."

Domino's voice was instantly serious. "Work?"

"Sure as hell not pleasure." Allegro gave her the address of the Haarlem estate. "How soon can you get here?"

"One moment." There was a short pause and some muffled sounds. "I'll be there in a few hours. Call you at this number when I get there."

"Thank you. Oh, and by the way," Allegro asked, "do you think I'm a self-absorbed, arrogant pain in the ass?"

"No, no, and yes." Domino's tone was amused. "Why?"

"Just something someone recently accused me of. Obviously they don't know what they're talking about."

"Obviously."

Allegro ended the call with renewed confidence. She'd had little doubt that Luka would drop everything to help her, but it was still a great comfort to know her friend would soon be there to watch her back. They were an unbeatable team, and she felt certain that together, they could handle anything and everything that might arise to jeopardize her mission and Kris's safety.

CHAPTER FIFTEEN

Haarlem
Wednesday, February 13

The Saint Francis Institution didn't open to visitors until nine a.m., so Kris lingered over coffee in the kitchen after Angie headed upstairs saying she needed to shower. The sun was coming up and the sky beyond her window was a faint pink color. The same subtle tone reflected off the metal trim of the garden shed, drawing her gaze. She was puzzled to notice the garden cart sitting only a few feet from the door. She didn't recall it being there the previous evening, but she had her mind on other things. Jeroen occasionally used ladders and carts that were stored in the shed, and the fact that he often left the door unlocked as he worked made her even more confident that she'd done the right thing by removing the diamond. The trapdoor wasn't obvious, but if anyone were snooping about they would probably find it.

As soon as Jeroen had started talking about knocking down a wall of the secret room, she'd decided it would be prudent to house the stone elsewhere, at least for the time being. She'd felt secure about leaving the gem in the priest's room when there was no access from within the house, but the vault would be exposed for who knew how long during the renovations, and although she trusted the people she invited into her home, she was also careful. She'd placed the stone in the pocket of a blazer in her closet, certainly not the safest overnight hiding place, but other options had seemed even more obvious—under the mattress or inside an ornamental vase. She would be relieved when she could transfer it to a bank deposit box after visiting her mother.

Kris went upstairs and retrieved the diamond. She briefly considered hiding it on her person but there was nowhere in her clothing that a lump the size of a cherry wouldn't be noticeable. Checking her watch, she placed the stone in the inner pocket of her purse before returning to her coffee. It was nearly eight. She always had to mentally prepare herself for her infrequent visits to the Saint Francis Institution, for she never knew what to expect of her mother. One day, Wilhelmina would be quiet and distant, barely acknowledging her presence; and the next she would be ranting endlessly about her treatment by the staff, all indignant and superior, begging Kris to take her home where she belonged.

The latest doctor's report had not been good and the staff had been alerted to watch her closely for another suicide attempt. She'd tried twice during her two years at the institution. Kris had no doubt that her mother's determination to end her life was genuine. Wilhelmina had slit her wrists in the bathtub on an otherwise uneventful day at home. Kris's father had broken the door and saved her life. Not long after she was admitted to the institution, guards had intercepted her attempting to jump off the roof. She'd also been found stockpiling drugs. But meds dispensation was so strictly monitored she couldn't hoard more than a few pills before she was caught. Kris had no doubt that if she were at home she would find a way to take her own life. She only wished she knew the reason why.

"You're a million miles away." Angie's voice brought her out of the past and back to the present. "And from your expression, I'd say it's not in a very good place. Anything I can do?"

The gentle inquiry touched Kris in a place that felt raw and for a second she was close to tears. Blinking away the signs of emotion, she looked up. Angie was watching her from the doorway. Kris was so used to seeing the American in work clothes, usually with plaster in her hair, that she was quite unprepared for the sight before her. Angie was dressed in low-cut brown corduroy trousers that hugged her slim hips, and a tan turtleneck that fit like a second skin, accentuating her high round breasts, flat stomach, and the soft muscles of her biceps. Her straight dark hair, which fell to the top of her breasts, shone in the sunlight, and a hint of gloss on her lips invited kissing.

She was so lovely that Kris succumbed to speechless appreciation for several seconds. Knowing her appraisal must be comically obvious, she said hastily, "I was just thinking about my mother. There's nothing anyone can do. But thanks."

"I have an idea," Angie said, dropping a duffel bag onto the floor at her feet. "Is your mother far away?"

"She's in the Saint Francis Institution. Right outside Amsterdam."

"Then why don't you let me take you out? I thought since we both have the day off we could maybe grab a bite and a dance in the city? Nothing fancy, and we won't be too exhausted later."

The picture that formed in Kris's mind had them dancing so close she'd get the chance to taste that lip gloss after all. The prospect made her almost giddy with anticipation. "That's the best offer I've had in months."

Angie looked surprised. "Is that a yes?"

"I believe it is." Kris couldn't believe how easily Angie had managed to dispel her melancholy. "I assume this is part of a Machiavellian plan to loosen me up and show me how to have real fun?"

"No, it's just a sincere invitation." Angie gave her a smile that she could only describe as wicked. "But should you feel the overwhelming urge to relax and enjoy, feel free. I'll be there to intercept you if you go completely wild."

Wild was not a word she'd ever have used to describe herself, at least until now. But the idea of losing some of her inhibitions suddenly had a definite appeal. "I could surprise you."

Angie's wicked smile got bigger. "You could surprise us both."

"How about we meet up at the Rembrandtplein at five for cocktails? You know where it is, don't you?"

"How about we meet at the bridge instead?" Angie suggested. "I certainly remember where *that* is."

Kris found herself distracted again by the way Angie's apparel defined her exquisitely sculpted body. She'd never fully appreciated how fit and toned Angie was, like an athlete, but when Angie was dressed in such form-fitting clothes she couldn't help but notice. Even that evening on the bridge, Angie had been mostly hidden in her heavy coat and Kris had been too tipsy to note those firm thighs and toned abs. Averting her head to hide the blush she felt coming on, she said, "The bridge is fine."

"Sounds like that crazy enthusiasm has started to creep up on you," Angie teased softly.

"I'm going to leave now before you make me rethink my decision to go out with you." Flustered by her nagging fascination with Angie's body, Kris rose and headed for the doorway, but just as she reached it, Angie blocked the way with her arm.

"How about you stay clear of thinking tonight and let me take the lead?" she said when Kris's eyes met hers. Then she leaned in close, her breath a soft caress against her ear. "I promise to be good. *Very* good," she whispered.

Kris's body reacted instantly to the provocative tone and words. A warm rush of desire and anticipation poured through her, settling low in her abdomen. Unnerved, she ducked under Angie's arm to escape before Angie could see the effect she was having. Heat rose to her cheeks as she scooped up her purse and coat and fled through the door, not looking back.

She fumbled for her keys, cursing the delay, and cursed again when she had trouble finding first gear in her father's Renault Clio. Thoroughly exasperated, she squealed the tires as she shot out of the driveway and headed away from the estate. She immediately turned on the car radio, desperate for a distraction to her jangled nerves. The top news story concerned a local murder the night before. A street-cleaning crew had discovered a man shot to death in his car. A swastika was painted on the side of the vehicle. He'd been identified as a German citizen, but authorities were withholding his name pending notification of next of kin.

The reporter mentioned an Anne Frank Foundation study that chronicled a seventy-five percent increase in the amount of extreme right-wing violence in the Netherlands the previous year. Apparently the police thought the man's murder could be in retaliation for recent neo-Nazi hate crimes. So far the rise in neo-Nazism in her country had been confined to centers like Amsterdam and Oss, so Kris was dismayed to hear that the cycle of violence was extending to quiet towns like Haarlem. She hoped it was an isolated incident, and not a foreboding of more trouble so close to home. Her life already had more than enough turmoil in it. Any more, and she feared she might come completely unglued.

❖

The Audi TTS coupe waiting at the car rental depot was silver and capable of more speed than anyone would ever need on the open road. Over 250 kilometers, or 150 miles per hour. Allegro threw the duffel bag into the passenger seat, slipped into the two-seater, and started up the engine. She put on a ball cap and sunglasses and checked the signal from the tracking device she'd planted in Kris's coat when she returned downstairs after calling Domino. She needed to get rid of the bloody clothing and the German's gun, but she could leave the evidence in her duffel for now. Kris was fifteen minutes ahead and she could easily make up the time if she followed immediately. The Renault Clio was a lackluster ride with a 1.2 liter engine, and not the latest model. Kris would be plodding along the highway in the slow lane with countless European hatchbacks of the same ilk. With any luck the Clio would stall suddenly, for no apparent reason, something they were renowned for, and Kris wouldn't get it started again for a few minutes. Or maybe she would get stuck behind a van and not have the power to zip into the next lane easily.

As Allegro sped out of Haarlem, overtaking cars like they were going backward, she reflected, as she often did, that vehicles with low horsepower were more dangerous than the high-powered cars she usually drove. The Audi handled like a dream and had so much acceleration she could take a few risks. *Now we're talking.*

She spotted Kris's Clio a few miles from Amsterdam. Sure enough, she was driving under the speed limit, sandwiched in a line of fuel-efficient cars. Following at a discreet distance, Allegro realized immediately that she wasn't the only driver pacing the Clio. Ahead of her a dark Peugeot wove in and out of traffic, keeping three or four cars behind Kris. Allegro got close enough to get the license plate number, then dropped well back again and adjusted the scrambler on her cell.

It was nearly one in the morning in Colorado, so she wasn't too surprised when the EOO operator told her that Montgomery Pierce was not in his office and had left instructions not to be disturbed except in an emergency. That usually meant he was away, occupied with a high-priority case, so Allegro asked to be patched through to Joanne Grant's home instead. When the EOO Director of Academics came on the line, her voice was groggy from sleep.

"It's Allegro. I need an ID, ASAP. Do you have a pen and paper?"

She paused when she heard a male voice in the background say, "What's up, honey?"

It took a scant few seconds for realization to sink in. "What's Monty doing there and why is he calling you 'honey'?" she asked.

Joanne Grant sounded wide awake now. "That was the TV."

"Unless he got his own reality show, that was definitely Monty."

There was a long silence, then, "What can I do for you, Allegro?"

"Oh, my God. Are the two of you doing it? I *knew* it."

"That wasn't Monty."

"Yeah, and those weren't my speeding tickets on your desk. Anyway, why don't you put me on speaker. It'll save us all time."

Allegro heard muted whispering.

"She knows." Grant's anxious hiss was followed by a few terse words that could only have come from Pierce.

"Mom, Dad, stop arguing," Allegro yelled. "You're going to traumatize me. And there's something very wrong about you getting more action than me."

The phone went to speaker. "What can I do for you?" Monty Pierce was definitely not amused.

Allegro laughed, loud and long. "I hope you're decent. I'd hate to think you're naked on the other end of the line."

"Allegro, you'd better have a good reason for this call." Her boss's tone had escalated from peeved to furious.

"I need a name. Driver of a two-year-old rental Peugeot I'm following." She gave him the make and license plate number and briefed him on the incidents the night before involving the German and the shooter who got away. "I'm pretty sure the ID will tell us the Afghans have arrived."

The next thing she heard was Pierce on his cell phone calling into the Organization with her information, then Joanne Grant came back on the line. "I'm going to ask you to keep this situation between Monty and me to yourself. It's a very new and delicate matter."

"Sure, Joanne," Allegro replied. "But I gotta tell you, no one would be surprised. I, for one, am happy for you guys. Monty could sure use some—"

"Stop right there, young lady," Grant cut her off.

"I was going to say some good company. Any luck with the ID?" Pierce joined in again. "Azizi. Just the one name. He's a fanatic. Madras educated. Ties to one of the more radical mosques. Afghan National Army. This guy is dangerous."

"Got it," she said. "I'll let you two get back to having wild sex."

"Is there anything else?" Pierce didn't sound amused. He also didn't bother with a denial.

"No, that's it." Allegro could hear Grant's laughter.

"Then when can you expect to conclude this?"

"Rocky moved the diamond from the vault last night. It has to be somewhere on her or in the house, so I'm going to tail her everywhere today and search the mansion when we get back. With the Afghans in the picture now, I need to stick with her."

"Don't let her deposit it in a bank," Pierce said. "We don't have time to stage a major extraction op. We've just had additional intel and the timetable has tightened up."

Allegro's mind raced. It had been no surprise to learn that the shooter was an Afghan. She wondered how much this Azizi knew and where the tip-off had come from. How was it possible that both the Afghans and Manfred Wolff knew where the stone was? Was the same source selling information to everyone? And now it sounded like Pierce had new actionable intelligence. "Are you saying we have a date for the terrorist attack?"

Pierce was cagey. "I'm saying you need to get the diamond as soon as possible, by any means necessary. Countless lives are at stake."

"I'll keep you advised."

Allegro was thankful that she'd called Domino in for backup. The situation was already too complicated for a lone operative. The Military Intelligence Service was no doubt positioning resources at this time, and EOO personnel were in place in the Middle East, ready to move on the intel they would get in exchange for the diamond. She had to neutralize the Afghan fanatic, Azizi, and get Kris and the diamond out of harm's way before the Germans tried again. Once Wolff found out his friend was dead, he would be even more determined to avenge himself and get the diamond. And he would probably have a hard time convincing another Aryan Brotherhood thug to risk his life, so maybe he would come after the stone himself.

Allegro smiled. She couldn't wait to get acquainted with this guy, to give him something no amount of precious stones and money could. Something people like him experienced only after death. She wanted to give him a taste of what hell felt like.

CHAPTER SIXTEEN

Berlin, Germany

Manfred Wolff slammed down the phone, cursing loudly enough that his mother tore her attention from the fireplace to gaze blankly in his direction. He raised his bulk out of his chair and went to the window. It was a miserable morning. A brisk wind blew sleet against the pane in an annoying, uneven cadence that was giving him a headache. But the weather matched his mood.

Gunter Schmidt had been found murdered in Haarlem. Apparently the fool had drawn attention to himself and had been targeted for his racial pride. Now that Europe was infested with vermin and race traitors, a good German could no longer hold his head up for the Fatherland. The authorities sided with the worthless scum that had invaded the Continent, and were turning the heat up on Aryan groups. It would be risky sending another man to Haarlem so soon, so Manfred had offered to make the journey himself, claiming he would try to make arrangements for his frail mother.

As he'd anticipated, Erhard Baader, the leader of the Aryan Brotherhood, didn't think it was a good idea for him to leave his mother, the wife of a Third Reich hero. Baader also had more pragmatic reasons for remaining involved. There was money at stake, and he would get his cut when they recovered the stone. Baader already had a man lined up to buy it, a loyal German living in Argentina. This wealthy collector and his elderly father, a former SS colonel, assisted friends by purchasing art and jewelry hidden since the war. With the passage of time, Nazis and their descendents had found it easier to liquidate these valuables without having to explain their history and prove ownership—after all, the original owners were usually dead, along with their close relatives. Who could account for possessions acquired in the chaos of war? Besides, the German government had paid ample compensation to supposed "victims."

Of course, no one compensated families like Manfred's for all they'd lost. No one paid for the bombing of their homes or the crimes perpetrated by the Red Army barbarians when they marched through Germany. Military commanders had anticipated what the Russians would do and had tried to protect the German people by surrendering only to the Western Allies, but it made no difference. Manfred had never asked his mother how she survived the occupation of Berlin. He didn't have to. Friends of the family said she was never the same afterward.

When Erhard Baader suggested the name of another loyal solider willing to finish what Schmidt had been sent to do, Manfred made no objection. Baader said the man was young, but well trained and eager to prove himself worthy. He would be briefed this morning and instructed to keep a low profile among the Dutch. Manfred wished he could be there to see the countess's face when she realized who she was dealing with. He wished he could watch as she was executed in her cheating father's place.

❖

Outside Amsterdam

The Saint Francis Institution was a modern two-story, red brick building with ornate wrought-iron balconies. The same wrought-iron also barricaded most of the windows, appearing at first glance to be an innocuous design feature. The landscaped grounds were dotted with wood and iron benches, and the day had warmed enough that several of the residents were out enjoying the sunshine, monitored by a pair of burly security guards.

Allegro steered the Audi into an empty spot on the street in front of the institution where she could get a clear view of the parking lot. Through her binoculars, she watched Kris park the Clio and get out. The Afghan in the Peugeot pulled into the lot as well, but he was being careful and drove to the opposite end. He idled there until Kris was inside the building, then he parked right next to the Clio. After ten minutes or so, he got out and stood between the cars, allowing Allegro a good look at him for the first time.

He was tall, average weight, with a long face, much of it covered by a black beard. He had a long nose too, and large lips, but his eyes were small and set close together, mere slits that made his face seem disproportionately wide. He had on Western clothes under a long dark coat, and his black hair was cut very short. Instead of a turban, he wore a Karakul, a traditional Afghan peaked wool cap.

He tried both doors of the Clio, and the hatch at the back. Was he foolhardy enough to attempt something drastic in broad daylight, in plain view of the institution? There were enough people around that there would be witnesses if he attempted to abduct Kris or take another shot at her. Allegro's alarm grew when he disappeared from view, crouching down between the two cars. A couple of minutes passed, long enough to plant a bomb or tracking device, or perhaps disable the brakes.

She started the Audi and turned into the lot. She backed into a space a reasonable distance away and ticked off a mental checklist. Only one of her instructions gave her any pause. The order "by any means necessary" meant she could, and should, use force or threats to obtain the diamond. Her present options were very simple. She needed to kill the Afghan before he could get the diamond or harm Kris. Then she had to seize the Blue Star, no matter what. If Kris didn't give it up willingly, she might have to hurt her. It consoled her a little that the sooner the stone was out of Kris's hands, the sooner she would be safe. But in the process of taking the diamond, Allegro would lose Kris's trust forever. Even if Kris was willing to listen to an explanation sometime in the future, Allegro would never be able to tell her the whole truth. It didn't matter how she handled this phase of her assignment, she was going to lose Kris's respect. If she imagined any other outcome, she was heading full speed toward a hopeless finish line.

She checked her Walther and focused again on the Afghan, Azizi, planning the shot she might have to take. There could be no untidy mistakes. She would prefer to take care of the Afghan more discreetly, but she'd carried out quick, clean executions in worse surroundings. If he attempted to harm Kris, she would do whatever was necessary to end the threat. Azizi lit a cigarette and leaned against the Peugeot as he watched the building. When his posture stiffened, Allegro followed his gaze to the front entrance. Kris and her mother emerged and slowly descended the stairs. They walked along a concrete path, passing by the parking area, not five yards from the cars, before settling onto a bench slightly farther away.

Wilhelmina van der Jagt seemed to be paying little attention to Kris, her gaze always elsewhere, her face expressionless. Kris took a scarf out of her coat and put it in her mother's hand. Allegro recognized the scarf, having seen it earlier that morning when she'd searched Kris's coat pockets. Wilhelmina seemed to recognize the accessory and started to give it back, but Kris pressed it on her, tucking it into her pocket as they stood up. Azizi hadn't moved.

There was no way Allegro could let Kris get into the Clio until she'd had a chance to see what he'd been up to between the cars. She pulled out her cell phone, slid down in her seat, and dialed Kris's number.

❖

Kabul, Afghanistan

The door to his office was locked and his blinds were drawn, because Culture Minister Qadir was studying the plans for al-Qaeda's most ambitious and devastating attack yet against the Western infidels. His covert patronage of the group had earned him the honor of being able to anticipate and enjoy their works in Allah's name, and his esteem with the devoted brethren would be greatly heightened once he turned over the *Setarehe Abi Rang*. The diamond would pay for many attacks against the U.S. and its allies. He stroked his beard and imagined how the world would react when the plans before him came to fruition. The time was very near.

Qadir's telephone rang, breaking his quiet contemplation. He'd told his assistant not to disturb him unless it was matter of the utmost urgency. The caller was Professor Rafi Bayat. Frowning, he snatched up the phone. "Yes?"

"I have located relatives of the Jew who had the countess's diamond before World War Two, sir," Professor Bayat informed him. "And the story they tell is very disturbing."

Qadir stiffened, anticipating more difficult facts to respond to. He hoped Azizi would soon complete his primary task, so that he could deal with the overly inquisitive academic. Bayat's information confirmed what Qadir already knew, that the diamond in the Netherlands was the real *Setarehe Abi Rang*. But the story learned from the Jew added new urgency. The diamond had been traded for goods by the puppet king, Shah Shuja ul-Mulk, before his assassination. If this history could be verified, the stone's provenance would be established. It could not be surreptitiously sold once the whole world knew the story. It would have to be returned to the crown. The plan would be ruined. Al-Qaeda would let it be known that he was unreliable.

"How can this be so?" the professor asked. "Perhaps there has been a great cover-up for reasons of pride. How could it be admitted that an Afghan sold the *Setarehe Abi Rang* to a Jew?"

"No, it's impossible, as I told you," Qadir said without hesitation. "The story is a lie invented to make this similar stone appear more valuable."

"As you say, Minister," Bayat answered respectfully, but Qadir could hear the doubt in his tone.

"You have done well, Professor Bayat. Now return to your world of academia, and let us take care of this delicate matter."

"If I might be of further service—" Bayat began, but Qadir cut him off.

"That will be all. I have urgent matters of state awaiting me, professor." With that, he disconnected, then immediately dialed Azizi's number.

Recovery of the *Setarehe Abi Rang* would have to be delayed. The troublesome professor had to be silenced at once.

❖

"Hi. I got my stay permit and am done for the day." Allegro rested her gun on her lap as she spoke on her cell phone. "Can I come pick you up?"

"There's no reason for you to drive all the way here," Kris replied. "Besides, I'll have to leave my car behind if you pick me up."

"It's really no trouble at all. I can take you back to your car later." Allegro perched the phone on her shoulder and screwed the silencer onto the Walther. Her target had stubbed out his cigarette. He was talking on his phone. "I got myself a new rental, the fun kind, and wouldn't mind driving it some. It's really not that far."

"Well if you don't mind the drive." Kris gave directions to the building Allegro was looking at. "How long do you think it will take you to get here?"

"Ten minutes at the most. I'm headed your way and traffic is light."

"Good. I'll see you soon, then. Do you mind running by my uncle's? I promised to stop in."

"Sure, no problem. See you in a few."

Allegro slid the gun into her coat pocket and checked her surroundings. She couldn't waste any more time, but this was far from an ideal place to take care of Azizi. The shooting could be witnessed. Her car could be identified. The EOO didn't appreciate loose ends. But they also expected their operatives to take initiative. She'd spent too long on this assignment already and it sounded like the terrorist threat was real and imminent. She could not allow a loose-cannon fanatic to derail the operation at this critical stage. And if she thought about it, something she preferred to avoid, she was afraid that he might act unpredictably and simply shoot Kris. She didn't know what his instructions were. She was only assuming they were the same as her own. What if he was part of a cell and knew nothing about the diamond? He could have been ordered to kill Kris while some other cell member went after the stone. How could she be sure of anything?

One thing she could depend on was her observation skills. Azizi had straightened up and his face became more intent when he took the call on his cell phone. She recognized his body language. He'd just received new orders. She got out of the car, put her duffel in the trunk, and started walking uneasily toward the Peugeot. To her surprise, Azizi got into the car in a hurry and started the engine. She deliberated, the gun in her hand. As he backed out, she started to lift the weapon free of her coat and was about to raise it for a clean shot through the driver's window, when she heard her name being called.

Kris waved from the sidewalk. "Perfect timing," she said as she approached.

"I told you I wasn't far away. Like the new wheels?" Allegro pointed toward the Audi. "I have a thing for fast cars."

From the corner of her eye, she watched Azizi speed away from the institution. His departure could mean one of several things. Either his assignment had been cancelled or his instructions altered. Or he had the diamond, although she was certain he didn't. Or he'd just been tipped off that she was coming after him, in which case where was the EOO leak?

"Why am I not surprised?" Kris said. "So did my father. Do you get as many speeding tickets as he did?"

Allegro smiled. "You mean you've never seen me on *America's Most Wanted*?"

Kris looked at her with a serious expression. "Maybe we should take my car, or let me drive."

"I was kidding. All I mean is that *many* is such a relative term." She opened the passenger door. "Trust me, you're in very capable hands."

As they buckled up, the enclosed space seemed to fill with the subtle lavender of Kris's perfume, the same scent she'd worn in Venice. Allegro stole an appreciative glance at Kris's sexy ensemble. Her low cut silk blouse was beige and she'd paired it with an aubergine-colored skirt and matching pumps. At one point, she shifted, and the hem of her skirt rose to expose a bit of her smooth ivory thigh. It was all Allegro could do not to reach over and caress it.

By the time they reached the outskirts of the city center, the sun had come out, and locals and tourists alike were taking to the streets to enjoy the wintry warmth. Bicycles filled every lane, far outnumbering the cars. In front of the Rembrandt museum, a horde of Japanese tourists milled around two buses, all of them with cameras around their necks or in their hands. Allegro drove evasively just in case anyone was tailing them. A tram was nearing from her right as the traffic light turned yellow. She darted across the intersection just ahead of the tram, and zigzagged through the narrow streets until she was sure they were not being followed.

"What are you doing?" Kris asked.

"Scenic route."

"You seem to know your way around the city pretty well."

"I have a good sense of direction and I was here for a few weeks before I headed into the countryside. Got around quite a lot." Allegro parked on a side street, around the corner from Hans Hofman's place on the Prinsengracht. Just in case they were being watched, she didn't want their stalker to know which building they'd gone into if he cruised the area looking for the Audi.

Hofman seemed pleased to see her, and after exchanging a warm embrace and requisite Dutch three-kiss hello with Kris, he did the same with her. "I am happy you could join us, Angie. Come in. I picked up some wonderful scones from the baker down the block this morning."

"Sounds perfect," Kris said. "And the coffee smells wonderful."

He led them upstairs to his apartment, a two-bedroom flat with a living room that overlooked the canal. Sunlight streamed in through the tall windows, transforming what would have been a dark, almost cavelike bachelor's residence into a cheery, welcoming nest. The paneled walls were a medium brown, and the antique furniture was dark, almost black, oak. The leather sofa and matching wing chairs he steered them toward were dark brown as well, and so were the blinds. And the light pine floor had been almost entirely concealed beneath a deep burgundy and navy Persian carpet. Hofman was obviously not a man who believed bright colors belonged in the home.

Nor did he care for disarray or clutter. As she passed the matching glass-fronted bookcases lining one wall, Allegro noticed that all the books were carefully sorted by language, topic, and author. Three small oil paintings—ducks—were perfectly equidistant and squared. There were no frilly knickknacks, just a handful of sentimental touches, a few framed photographs, and a highly polished soccer trophy. But whoever did the dusting had missed a spot here and there, and the morning sunlight accentuated that oversight.

Allegro realized the extent of Hofman's devotion to comfort when she and Kris sank into the deep cushions of the couch, and leaned back against fluffy charcoal pillows that looked like gray marshmallows. The couch was positioned near enough to the large picture windows that they had a marvelous view of the Prinsengracht neighborhood and the brave boaters passing by, clad in several layers and huddled low to minimize the wind.

Hofman laid out the coffee and scones on a low, narrow table in front of them and took a seat in one of the plush wing chairs, next to Kris. "Before I forget." He reached into his pocket. "I had another key made for you. Please feel free to use it, anytime you need to stay over in town again."

Kris took the key from him and put it in her purse. "That's very kind of you, Uncle. I'll try not to lose this one."

She and Hofman exchanged pleasantries for a while, speaking mostly in English, no doubt for her benefit. Kris described her visit with her mother, who'd spoken little and seemed almost unaware that she was there. Discussion then moved onto the renovations at Haarlem and the big news item of the day, the murdered German.

"There was a swastika painted on his car, wasn't there, Angie?" Kris sounded dismayed.

Allegro mumbled something vague.

"This tourist was definitely a German?" Hofman asked.

Allegro wasn't surprised by the strain that tightened his face. He had the diary and knew the story of the diamond's past. In his shoes, Allegro would be uneasy to hear about a German neo-Nazi in Haarlem doing something that had led to his murder. She didn't want him to spook Kris by panicking suddenly and handing over the diary. She was about to change the subject when she felt her cell phone vibrate. Taking a glance at the caller ID, she excused herself and went into the next room. At the sound of Domino's voice, she felt her shoulders relax.

"I'm in Rome," Domino said. "I took a private plane to get here so I could bypass airport security and bring what I need. Best if I drive the rest of the way, which means I'll arrive very late tonight or early tomorrow. Have the others been informed?" she asked in a cryptic reference to Monty Pierce.

"Negative. Text me when you get here, and I'll brief you."

Allegro disconnected and started back to rejoin Kris and Hofman. They were speaking Dutch, and she caught the word *diamant,* so she paused in the hallway. Even though they were unaware that she understood the language, she thought they might be more open to discussing the gem without her present. But they were apparently through with whatever they'd been saying about the Blue Star, because now they were on to talking about *her,* still in Dutch, and loudly enough for her to make out every word.

"I never said I didn't like Angie," Kris said.

"I believe the first words you used to describe her after you yelled at me for hiring her were *arrogant* and *smug.*"

"Because she is, and I've told her as much."

Hofman laughed. "I'm sure that went down well."

"Not really." Kris paused. There was a note of remorse in her voice. "I told her I was sorry, but…I don't know what to make of her. Every time I ask her anything personal she gets evasive and shuts me out. It seems like she's running from something."

"We all have our reasons, Kris," Hofman said gently. "And we all react differently to them. Look at yourself."

"What's that supposed to mean?"

"You stopped living a long time ago. While you were fighting for the acceptance of your parents or lovers, you were at least fighting for something. These past years, it's as though you've given up."

"At least I'm not running from my responsibilities."

"Even worse," Hofman said in that same fatherly tone, "you're running from life."

Allegro wanted to stand there and listen to more but figured a longer absence would seem suspicious. "Please don't mind me," she told them as she entered the room. "I can imagine you have some catching up to do. I'll check out your collection of books, if you don't mind."

"Of course, Angie. Go right ahead." Hofman pointed toward the nearest bookcase. "All the English ones are over there."

Allegro inspected the bookcase with her back to them. She plucked a rare first edition of *Crime and Punishment* off the shelf and carefully turned the pages.

"She may have her issues," Hofman continued to Kris in Dutch, "but I think she's adorable and very beautiful. I dare say she's exactly what you need."

"Uncle!"

Allegro had to bite her lip to stop herself from laughing at the chagrined response.

"Don't tell me you haven't noticed. She's certainly a much better catch than all the others you've associated with," Hofman continued. "Damn deadbeats."

"I'll give you that," Kris agreed. "But it was my fault for letting them use me."

Hofman loudly sipped his coffee, then set down the cup. "Too bad you don't find our friend here attractive."

"I didn't say that." There was a shyness to her quiet admission that Allegro found endearing.

Hofman's response was the animated Dutch equivalent of *Eureka!* "I knew it."

"Knew what?"

"I've seen the way you look at her. Even now, you can't take your eyes off her behind." Allegro kept her head averted so they wouldn't see the grin spreading over her face. She was really beginning to like Hofman. Kris was lucky to have him in her life, considering the relative absence of her parents.

"Do you have any idea how embarrassing it is to talk about this with you?" Kris's exasperation was evident.

"It would be more embarrassing and…frustrating, if the appreciation wasn't mutual," Hofman offered, chuckling, "But you don't have to worry about that. Trust this old man, he knows what he's talking about. She looks at you the same way."

"Uncle, please stop. Besides, she's leaving in a few weeks."

"Which gives you two options. Either enjoy this short time with her or you make her stay."

Allegro waited for Kris's response.

"The first I can definitely do. In fact, we're going out for dinner and dancing later."

"And the second?"

"I can't *make* her do anything," Kris said. "All I can do is give her reasons to *want* to stay."

CHAPTER SEVENTEEN

Azizi sat patiently in his rental car outside the Allard Pierson Museum at the University of Amsterdam. Allah had granted him a new opportunity to prove himself, and he had no doubt that his new mission would go exactly as planned. Since leaving the mental institution, he'd spent hours in preparation. He'd acquired all the tools he needed, then drove around the northern outskirts of the city, in the sparsely populated shipyard district, until he found a perfect spot to execute his plan. Two hours before nightfall, he circled the museum building until a parking spot opened up near the door leading to the administrative offices. He then went briefly inside the complex to get a good look at his target. Allah was with him, for he didn't need to come face-to-face with the professor. The man's picture was on the museum brochure at the entrance.

Azizi checked his office hours. If the professor kept to his schedule, it would be dark by the time he left. But it also meant he had to be vigilant, because he needed to catch Bayat before he caught a tram or got into a car. Azizi acquired his objective, and for that he was grateful.

When the professor exited the complex twenty minutes later than expected, Azizi recognized him easily as he passed beneath the bright lights illuminating the exterior of the building. He started the Peugeot and pulled up beside Bayat as the professor fumbled with the locks on his bicycle at a rack beside the street.

He rolled down the passenger window. "Professor Bayat?"

"Yes?" Bayat abandoned his bicycle and came over to lean into the window.

"I've been sent by Minister Qadir," Azizi said in Farsi, smiling genially when he saw a flicker of concern cross Bayat's face. "I'm here to help you authenticate this duplicate diamond. Will you get in, please?"

"The minister did not inform me he was sending anyone, and I'm not at liberty to discuss this subject," Bayat answered, making no move to get in the car.

"You can talk to him yourself, if you like." Azizi took out his cell phone, dialed the number, and passed the phone to the professor.

"I'm sorry to disturb you, sir," Bayat said into the phone. "There is a man here who…" He listened for a few seconds. "Yes, sir, of course. I understand." He seemed more relaxed as he got into the passenger seat and returned the phone. "I apologize for my hesitation. These are highly sensitive matters, as I am sure you know, so it's prudent to be cautious."

"I take no offense, Professor." Azizi pulled away from the curb and headed toward the remote spot he'd selected.

"Where are we going?" Bayat asked.

"To a place where we will not be overheard. As you said, these are highly sensitive matters."

In an effort to keep the professor at ease, Azizi asked about his family as they drove through the congested streets toward the shipyards. The ploy worked quite well, until they pulled into the parking lot of an abandoned brick building, and he parked the Peugeot not far from the water's edge. There were no other vehicles about, and they'd long passed the last pedestrian or cyclist. Bayat's body language changed abruptly. He sat rigid in his seat, glancing about.

"Get out of the car, Professor," Azizi ordered.

"Get out? Why?" Bayat shrank away, pressing up against the passenger door.

Azizi took the keys from the ignition, and as he rounded the back of the car, he pulled the knife from his coat. He opened the passenger door, dragged the professor out of the car, and before Bayat could say another word, slit his throat, careful to keep himself clear of the sudden spurt of blood.

Bayat made a gurgled, strangled sound as he dropped to the ground, and then lay lifeless. Azizi retrieved a coil of rope and two large cement blocks from the trunk of the Peugeot and set them at the water's edge. He dragged the professor's body to the spot, bound and weighted it, and let it sink into the dark water. On the way back to town, he dialed the minister's number to confirm the deed was done, then he resumed his search for the diamond.

By now, the countess was probably back in Haarlem, he reasoned, but it was risky to chance breaking into the house tonight, not knowing who might be with her. So he decided to eliminate the only other place the diamond could possibly be if the countess did not have it in her possession. With the woman she called "Mom."

He arrived at the Saint Francis Institution at nine thirty p.m. and parked on the street. He approached on foot, keeping to the periphery of the grounds to avoid the bright lights that illuminated the front façade of the building. A van was parked outside the delivery entrance while a man came back and forth with a hand truck full of laundry bins. Azizi hurried to the door and glanced inside the building. The deliveryman was nowhere in sight, so he slipped in and hid behind a column until the worker had completed his task and the van had pulled away.

Moving cautiously down the hallway, Azizi passed several unoccupied offices. He could hear two women talking in a nearby hallway, then footsteps receding, then silence, so he risked stepping into one of the offices and hunting on the computer and the desk until he found a list of names and room numbers. Wilhelmina van der Jagt was in 209. The emergency fire stairwell was clearly marked, a bit farther along the hallway he was in. He made it inside just as he heard the footsteps coming back.

❖

"It's still a little early for dinner," Kris said as they left Hofman's building. "Most places don't open until six."

"Would you like to walk a while?" Allegro suggested. "I've been in the country long enough to know you have to enjoy the sunshine while it lasts, because things could be very different in five minutes."

Kris laughed. "All right."

As if by tacit agreement, they avoided the busy shopping thoroughfares and requisite tourist stops, keeping to the quiet, picturesque streets along the canals. "The architecture is amazing," Allegro said, pointing to the ornately carved gable atop the nearest building, which had been converted to private apartments. A black and white plate embedded in the brickwork told them the place dated back to 1483.

"I never tire of walking the streets," Kris agreed. "It's a feast for the eyes, if you care to look for the details."

"Speaking of feast." Allegro glanced at her watch. "Do you have a place in mind for dinner?"

"We're very close to Pasta e Basta," Kris said. "Do you like Italian food and opera?"

"Sounds great."

Pasta e Basta was in a red brick building on the Nieuwe Spiegelstraat, a busy street lined with antique shops. A few steps down, past a cluster of potted greenery and a pair of stone columns, and it was as though they'd been transported into a sophisticated and cozily romantic restaurant in the heart of Venice. Allegro flashed back to Carnival, and her first glimpse of Kris in her purple ball gown. She recalled the porcelain perfection of her skin and the way people reacted to her smile. Kissing Kris's neck had been more than just a distraction ploy. Allegro had been seduced by her beauty, propelling her inexorably forward. She'd almost resisted the temptation, but the sorrow she glimpsed in Kris's eyes made her ache to erase that pain. When her lips found the delicate hollow at the base of Kris's throat and Kris leaned into her in sweet surrender, Allegro nearly came undone. It had taken all her willpower to pull away, to keep her hands from exploring that soft skin and those enticing curves.

The urge to touch Kris was no less strong now, and the ambience of the restaurant wasn't helping. The lighting was subdued: a few chandeliers, muted sconces along the sides, and long tapered candles on each of the white linen tablecloths. Mural portraits in oil had been painted directly onto the crème-toned walls at the back, while other fine art in gilt frames, and tasteful Italian antiques completed the décor. The dramatic velvet draperies at the windows were the same deep scarlet as the comfortably padded seating. High-backed chairs and upholstered couches dated from the turn of the century.

Rectangular tables in the center of the restaurant accommodated larger groups, while small round tables at the edges provided more private intimacy for couples seeking an evening of flirtation. They passed by the grand piano, and Allegro was surprised to see the man at the keyboard playing merrily away while diners served themselves from a buffet of appetizers nestled inside the instrument. A dozen large platters were filled with such delicacies as salmon, carpaccio, antipasto, caprese salad, and insalata di riso. The food was both enticing to the eyes and irresistible in its aromatic allure.

The pianist had been playing Mozart as they arrived, but as they took their seats at a table for two near the bar, one of the waiters launched into an aria from *La Traviata*, his rich baritone filling the space and casting a hush over the patrons.

"He's really good. When you said opera, I didn't think we'd hear it live," Allegro said.

"That's one of the major draws of this place, besides the excellent food," Kris replied softly. "Most of the servers are trained singers, and they also have professional vocalists on staff. They do everything—opera, jazz, pop, rock, you name it."

Over the next ninety minutes, they feasted on pasta and shared a bottle of Amarone, a dry red wine produced not far from Kris's Venetian villa. Allegro was surprised to find they were so relaxed in each other's company that when Kris asked how she liked her tagliatelle with grilled red snapper, she scooped some onto her fork and held it out. Kris smiled as her mouth closed around the offering. Soon they were sampling off each other's plates without hesitation, laughing as they did so, like lovers long together. It was a small thing, but still a kind of familiar ease that had been lacking in Allegro's brief affairs, and she delighted in every moment.

The entertainment continued throughout their meal, each of the wait staff taking a turn. Operatic arias were followed by Broadway musical numbers and pop tunes. When their darkly handsome waiter brought their tiramisu and cappuccinos, he launched into a romantic ballad in Italian, serenading both of them in a clear tenor.

Allegro was so absorbed in Kris—in the way the candlelight enhanced the golden tones in her hair and made her eyes sparkle—that she paid no attention to what the man was singing. His voice seemed to put Kris into a dreamy state, and Allegro couldn't help but stare at her. She looked so exquisitely lovely right then, Allegro very much wanted to kiss her.

"Do you speak any Italian?" Kris asked.

"I'm afraid not," Allegro lied, trying not to stare at Kris's lips. "How about you?"

"Yes. We have...*had* a house in Venice for years. I visited as a child, and moved there when I was eighteen." A hint of smile tugged at the corner of her mouth as Kris reminisced, making her even more beautiful. But her eyes were sad, just like they'd been that Carnival night. "I love Italy, especially Venice."

Something vulnerable in her expression made Allegro ache inside. "Do you still go back a lot?"

"I recently had to put it up for sale. We need the money since father left us with so much debt." Kris's voice sounded more melodic than any serenade they'd heard that night.

"Why don't you translate some of the song for me?" Allegro asked.

"What's the point?" The smile faded and Kris sighed. "It's Italian, and like most Italian songs, it's about love and drama." She leaned toward Allegro, never breaking eye contact. "When we met the first time, your face was hidden in the shadows of the night. All I could see, all I can still remember, is the smile on your lips before you kissed me. It left me breathless. I regret not that a stranger made me feel that way, I regret that you left."

As the words registered in her mind, transporting her back to Venice, Allegro tried to hide her shock. "What?" It came out as a croak.

"The song." Kris gave her an odd look. "You asked me to translate it."

Relief poured through Allegro, making her almost dizzy. Of course her Italian was fluent, but she'd been so lost in Kris that she hadn't registered a word of the song. "Of course. Yes, love and drama."

She tore her gaze away, pretending a sudden interest in the nearest painting. It was an eighteenth-century portrait of a nude woman reclining on a divan, which didn't help her current state one bit. Silence fell between them as Allegro struggled to free herself from the memory of her lips against Kris's neck. She wondered if Kris remembered that kiss with the same unfulfilled longing she felt, and couldn't resist asking, "Has a stranger ever kissed you breathless in the dark, someone you never knew, and never saw again?"

"Yes," Kris said wistfully. "An Italian woman. And as a matter of fact, not that long ago."

"You don't say." Allegro hoped she sounded more nonchalant than she felt.

"In Venice, the night before I left the house for good," Kris said. "She never kissed me on the mouth, but it was still…unforgettable."

Allegro warmed from within until she realized that leaving such an indelible impression was possibly a disadvantage. How could she compete with a mysterious stranger who had bestowed an "unforgettable" kiss? Her next words were out of her mouth before she could arrive at a strategy. "Would you like to meet her again?"

"Why, what for?" Kris asked. "She apparently wasn't interested in more, and I'm done feeling needy. How about you? Have you ever shared an exciting kiss with someone you never saw again?"

Allegro smiled. "I've recently shared a very exciting kiss with a beautiful woman, but I get to see her every day." Kris blushed and looked away, giving Allegro the confirmation she needed. Perhaps she could compete with herself, after all. She faked a sigh. "Looks like I'm alone in that sentiment."

"I can be just as evasive as you."

"Why would you want to be evasive?"

"Because you frustrate me." Kris sounded more confused than annoyed. "Why can't you answer simple questions?"

A brief silence fell between them as they finished their cappuccinos. Finally Allegro folded her arms across her chest and said, "Okay. Go ahead, ask me something. Anything."

Kris took her time coming up with the right query. "What was your most memorable Christmas present as a child?"

Allegro was used to thinking on her feet. On the job and in her private life, she served up the answers that got her what she needed. But she never expected such a sensitive, innocent question, and it took her completely by surprise. She could say it was some ball or doll, but that didn't feel right. Not now, with Kris. "I never got any Christmas presents as a child." She looked away.

"I'm sorry. I shouldn't have taken for granted that—"

"Hey, it's no big deal. What do you say we go for a walk and get some fresh air?" Allegro motioned for the waiter.

"I didn't mean to upset you."

Kris leaned forward and took her hand, looking deep into her eyes. What Allegro saw in that intent gaze was something she'd rarely seen before. True compassion. A human connection that affected her more than she thought possible. She had to look away to compose herself. "Don't worry about it, I'm fine." She stood quickly. "Let's go find a place where I can collect on that dance."

The response felt inadequate and she hated feeling so ill-equipped to cope with the situation. But the EOO had never taught her how to deal with sincere emotion.

❖

Night had fallen, but the skies remained clear. They kept to the side streets along the canals, admiring the curved strings of lights on the bridges and the reflections of the houselights in the placid water. It had gotten colder with the setting of the sun, and normally she despised the cold, but Allegro was so completely distracted by her beautiful companion she barely noticed the chill. She did think to keep an eye on her surroundings for any sign of someone following them, but the only people around were couples, gay and straight, many arm in arm. The romantic atmosphere was contagious, and when they paused to watch a boat go by, Kris slid her hand through the crook of Allegro's elbow, and it seemed the most natural thing in the world. They stood there for a long time, not moving, as though neither wanted to break the closeness.

"I promised you a dance," Allegro said at last. "Do you know a good place?"

"Café Sappho is popular and it's close by, on the Rokin," Kris suggested. "It's very crowded on weekends, but tonight shouldn't be too bad. The deejay plays good music and they change the artwork every month to spotlight some young new artist, which is always quite fun to see."

"Lead the way."

They set off again, arms still linked. Kris led them on a route that passed by the bridge where they'd kissed. At the same spot where they'd lingered before, she tugged at Allegro's sleeve. "Do you mind if we stop here for a moment?"

"Not at all." The lavender of Kris's perfume filled Allegro's nostrils. "I have very fond recollections of this bridge. Do you think about that night at all?"

"Why don't you refresh my memory?" Kris released her arm and turned to face her.

The amber light from the street lamp played across her delicate features, masking the expression in her eyes and drawing Allegro's gaze to the deep shadow beneath her slightly parted lips. Their first kiss, two nights ago, had been fierce, born of necessity, or that was how Allegro justified it. She'd needed to silence Kris, not seduce her. But Kris's heated response had stoked an inferno and the flames still hadn't died down. This time, Allegro's lips danced over Kris's so lightly, it was the barest of touches at first. She withdrew a few inches, and they breathed the same air. Allegro lifted one hand to Kris's cheek and leaned in to kiss her again, caressing her lips with her tongue, so sweetly and gently that Kris moaned.

"More?" Allegro whispered.

"Yes." Kris whispered back, and her soft breath sent a shudder of arousal through Allegro. "Much more," she added, as she slowly kissed her way to the base of Allegro's throat, then began to trace an agonizingly slow trail of kisses upward, back toward her mouth.

Allegro couldn't wait for the slow torture to reach its conclusion. She cupped Kris's jaw in her hand and brought her face up until their lips met. It was an unhurried and exquisitely delicate kiss. Almost chaste, were it not for the growing throb that stirred low in her abdomen.

"You're driving me crazy," Kris whispered, breathing hard.

Allegro smiled her cockiest grin. "Really? I hadn't noticed."

"Just shut up for once and kiss me." The mischief and longing in Kris's eyes were irresistible.

Allegro took another quick glance around before moving in to give her a proper kiss. This time there was nothing slow or gentle about it. Locked in each other's arms, they pushed together urgently. The ferocity of that first kiss couldn't match the intensity of this one. Kris's mouth yielded in sweet surrender. Their tongues stroked wetly, and Allegro's heartbeat doubled. Kris sucked hard, taking Allegro's tongue deeper into her mouth. The throbbing in her belly became a painful need. She cursed the layers of clothes between them and pulled back long enough to finish unbuttoning Kris's coat, so she could thrust a muscled thigh between her legs. Kris groaned into her mouth as they kissed again.

Suddenly, the sound of applause broke the silence, and they parted to find a long, glass-topped tour boat full of passengers below them, about to cross under the bridge. Most of the tourists were on their feet, staring up and smiling at them. There was more applause, and a beefy man wearing a New York Yankees jacket yelled, "Get a room!"

As the boat disappeared, Kris straightened her coat. "You still owe me a dance."

"Is that what you want?" Allegro tried to keep the disappointment from her voice, unsuccessfully.

Kris smiled and gave her another kiss, but all too briefly. "For now. I want this night to last as long as possible."

The disappointment was gone, as quickly as it had arrived. Allegro grinned and took Kris's arm. "Then dance we shall."

CHAPTER EIGHTEEN

Because it was a weeknight, Café Sappho was only about half full and the proprietors had opted for quieter music and candlelight instead of the usual disco ball and bright spots. In other words, it was perfect for the mood Kris was in. If they were going to dance, she wanted it to be body to body, picking up where they'd left off at the bridge. Angie's kisses had inflamed her, almost dangerously so. She felt delightfully out of control and she wanted to stay that way as long as possible. It had been tempting to go right from the bridge to bed, but there was a lot to be said for the sense of anticipation that had been building between them all night.

"Can I get you something to drink?" Angie said as she surveyed the room. There were tables to the left and right, and built-in padded seating along the walls. The bar was farther back.

"I've had enough alcohol," Kris replied, taking her by the hand and leading her toward the dance floor in the rear. "What I haven't had enough of is your body against mine."

They dropped their coats at the nearest table and joined a dozen other couples. The ballad that came on as they reached for each other, "You Give Me Something," seemed almost too perfect for their first slow dance together. James Morrison's soulful lyrics made her realize how hard she was falling for Angie, and how empty her life had been before they met. She wanted to believe that Angie felt the same way, and it seemed so, from her tight embrace. They danced, not speaking. The next song was another slow one, Dana Owens singing "If I Had You."

Kris wrapped her arms around Angie's neck, and Angie's hands, which had been caressing her back, slid down and began to massage her ass. As they swayed to the music, they found a natural rhythm together, their bodies perfectly in sync. One slow song followed another, and they made no move to leave the dance floor, their caresses and gyrations getting bolder with each number. Kris entwined her fingers in Angie's hair, and when she looked up into those half-lidded, caramel eyes, she saw the arousal burning there. This time, she was the one who initiated the kiss. Slow and sensual, like the music. Angie's hands gripped her ass even harder as she slipped her thigh between Kris's legs again and sent her heartbeat fluttering. Dizzy with desire, she rocked even closer until the pressure building between her legs was unbearable. Much more, and she might come right there on the dance floor.

"I think you should take me home," she whispered in Angie's ear.

There was no hesitation whatsoever in Angie's reply. "Let's go."

They grabbed their coats and headed back toward the Audi, parked several blocks from the bar. The streets were nearly empty of pedestrians and bikes, and Kris glanced at her watch, surprised at how much time had passed while they'd been lost together dancing. It was well after midnight and the trams had stopped, so they had to walk the distance. Angie placed an arm around Kris's shoulder, and they strolled slowly along, leaning in to each other, not speaking at first, just enjoying the beautiful evening.

Sliding her arm around Angie's waist, Kris envisioned them naked together within the hour, and her pulse raced at the very thought of it. But she realized with a start that she didn't want this to be some brief and meaningless affair. She was beginning to develop strong and undeniable feelings for Angie, despite the fact that she still knew almost nothing about her. Beneath her cocky self-assuredness, there was a vulnerability she identified strongly with. She sensed that Angie hadn't had an easy time of it, growing up. Her answer about Christmas presents hinted at the same kind of early isolation Kris had experienced.

"What are your plans when the repairs are finished?" she asked, recalling her uncle's advice that she consider asking Angie to stay in the Netherlands.

"I don't know if I can stay until the house is done," Angie replied softly. "There's still so much to do."

How soon must you leave? she wanted to ask. It felt as though an invisible clock somewhere was counting down this rare gift of happiness. "What will you do back home?"

"I'm not really sure. I've been trying to push any long-term plans away."

"Are you looking forward to going back? I can imagine you must be homesick by now."

"I guess." There was a long pause before Angie continued. "I mean, I miss a few people but it's not like I get to see them that often anyway."

That ticking clock got louder in Kris's head. The prospect of perhaps never seeing Angie again seemed unthinkable. She tugged on Angie's coat to force her to a stop. They were on another bridge. "Do you think you'll be coming back again?"

"It's crossed my mind, but I really don't know." Angie wouldn't meet her eyes. "It's not that simple."

"Why not?"

"Because I have to get my life back on track." Silence fell between them as they gazed out over the water. Angie's sigh was audible. "Beautiful night, isn't it?"

"Yes." Kris had walked these same streets countless times before, and had long thought Amsterdam one of the most beautiful cities in the world. But she was seeing it and feeling it much more profoundly tonight, with Angie. She absorbed every nuance of the city's romantic allure with a new appreciation. "Quite frankly, I can't remember the last time I enjoyed myself this much."

"Does that mean you actually like my smart-ass company?"

The question was pure Angie, but it lacked the usual cockiness, and Kris sensed—she hoped—that there was a serious inquiry hidden in the feeble attempt at humor. "Too much, I think," she admitted, hoping for some similar sentiment in response.

But Angie grew quiet again, staring down at a couple of swans passing by below them.

"Tonight, all of it…" Kris took a deep breath. She had to know. "Does it mean anything to you?"

"Kris, I think you're an incredible woman, and I'm enjoying every minute with you."

"That's great, but it doesn't answer my question. What does tonight mean to you?"

Angie faced her, and her voice grew serious. "It means I'm right where I want to be, with exactly whom I want to be with."

Kris could see the sincerity in her eyes, and something else. Something she wanted to believe was an acknowledgment of the growing depth of their connection. "Would you come back to see me if I asked you to?"

A flicker of surprise crossed Angie's face, and she turned away again. "Why, is there another house you need to renovate?"

Once again, the question was devoid of Angie's usual arrogance, a halfhearted attempt to lighten the moment. Kris began to understand how much Angie had come to rely on humor as a way to deflect questions she didn't want to answer. Her growing irritation at the woman's elusiveness had begun to stem the feelings of arousal and excitement that had driven them from the bar. She pulled roughly at Angie's coat, until they were face-to-face again.

"Angie, you've evaded every question I've asked you about yourself and your life, and that's your right. I suppose you have your reasons. We all do. But *please*, don't evade me, not right now. It's taking a lot of courage for me to ask these things. I'm actually surprised with myself for being this forward, but...but you make me feel..." She fumbled for the right words to describe what was inside her, then realized she'd just said it all. She'd been numb before they met. "You make me *feel*," she repeated. "I don't usually—"

"Kris, I don't know if I can give you what you—"

"Please, let me finish. I don't usually jump into bed with women, and I've never been a fan of one-night stands. I understand you have to leave, and I know that this night could be the only one we ever share, but...what I'm trying to say and failing miserably at is, I don't want it to end with tonight. I know you can't make promises, and I gave up on the concept of always a long time ago, but you make me feel too much to let it end."

Angie's hands curled into fists. "I can't promise anything. I can't give you a guarantee that I'll come back...or even for a tomorrow." Frustration was evident in her tone. "Like I said, things are complicated."

"Will you at least tell me what's so complicated?" Kris asked gently. "Are you in trouble? Are you married? What?"

"Nothing like that." The restlessness was back. Angie shifted her weight from one foot to the other, and gripped the rail, as though anxious to leave.

Without a word, Kris resumed walking toward the Audi, and Angie fell quickly into place beside her. She said nothing further for three of four blocks, and Kris's exasperation grew with every step. She stopped abruptly when she could take it no longer. "I think I just made a complete fool of myself."

"What? Why?" Angie asked.

"I'm standing here asking you to come back because I want more," Kris said angrily. "I got so wrapped up in the hope that the feelings were mutual that I didn't for a moment consider the fact that you were just out for a fun night."

"Kris, it's not like that," Angie protested. "I do like you. A lot. But—"

"But what? Help me understand. Stop being so damn vague for once and try the straightforward approach." Kris didn't care that her voice was loud enough to carry to the apartments surrounding them. "You don't need to play mystery woman to avoid telling me the truth. All you have to say is that you were hoping to get laid."

"It's not like that," Angie repeated. "I can get laid anytime I want."

"So tonight was simply about proving yourself right? Showing me how to loosen up and enjoy life. This whole seduction plan was about showing Kris how to live a little. How altruistic of you."

"Come on, Kris. I said I like you."

Her fury boiled over at Angie's attempt to pacify her. "Well, that's great. I feel so much better now that I know you don't fuck women you dislike."

"You're overreacting."

"I'm overreacting?" She was nearly shouting now, stunned by Angie's total disregard for the risk she'd just taken. It was difficult to open up the way she had. "Christ, Angie, I'm fall—" She stopped herself from any further admissions, since it would clearly get her nowhere. "Oh, forget it. What does it matter?" Abruptly, she turned and started back the way they had come.

"Where are you going?" Angie called after her. "The car is this way."

Kris stopped and pivoted to face her. "I know it sounds crazy, but all of a sudden I'm not in the mood for a mercy fuck."

"Okay, I get that." Angie took a couple of steps toward her, and held out her hand. "But let me take you home."

"I really don't want to be around you right now, nor do I want to go back to that house."

"I'll drive you to your car," Angie offered, taking another step nearer.

"No, thanks." Kris waved her off dismissively. She was suddenly exhausted. "Go…please. I want to be alone."

"Will you let me walk you to your uncle's?"

"He'll want to know why I'm there again in the middle of the night, and I'm not in the mood for conversation."

"You can't wander around the city alone this late," Angie protested. "It's not safe."

Kris's anger flared anew, an almost involuntary response when someone tried to tell her how to live her life. "I can do what I damn well please. I'm very capable of taking care of myself. I've had thirty-eight years of practice."

"Kris, will you come to your senses?"

"I did. About ten minutes ago, when I realized what a stupid mistake I was about to make."

"I'm sorry it came out that way," Angie said gently, moving still closer until they were face-to-face. She started to reach out for Kris's shoulder. "I didn't mean to hurt your feelings. And tonight was not about getting you into bed."

"Stop. Just stop." Kris raised a hand to keep Angie from touching her. "Angie, go home…where ever the hell that may be, since I'm not privy to that information."

Angie's hands dropped to her sides, and she replied in a resigned voice. "Fine. Suit yourself."

Kris stormed off at a fast pace, with no particular destination in mind. What a fool she was. Tears began to flow, streaming down her face, and she wiped them angrily away. The city around her faded from her consciousness, its romanticism now only increasing her pain.

❖

Haarlem

Azizi arrived at the van der Jagt mansion a little after midnight. Relieved to find the place dark, with no cars about, he hid the Peugeot in the shelter of some trees by the roadside and approached from the side of the building. Minister Qadir had told him to do whatever was necessary to obtain the diamond, so he did not hesitate to break one of the small windows in the rear door to gain entry. He tried to muffle the sound by placing his coat over the pane as he struck it. Then he moved quietly through the house in the dark, up the stairs to the bedrooms, to ensure he was alone.

Satisfied, he clicked on his flashlight and began searching for the gem. He started in the countess's bedroom, taking care to search every possible hiding place—her bureaus, the pockets of the clothes in her closets, even the boxes of personal items stacked against the wall, still taped shut from her move from Venice. Then he tried her bath, searching among folded towels, opening prescription bottles, even peering into shampoo and perfume bottles with large enough openings to slip the diamond into.

Having no luck, he searched the other bedrooms thoroughly. The vacant bedrooms were quick to work through, the mattresses stripped and the drawers in the dressers empty. Returning to the ground floor, he walked among the rooms, scanning for any obvious place to try next. The den, he decided. He went through the desk, and ran his hand behind the books on the bookshelves to see if the gem was concealed behind them.

Still no diamond.

He was beginning to get frustrated. It would be impossible to search every conceivable hiding place in this enormous mansion, even if he had several undisturbed days to do it. He had to confront the countess, and force her to tell him where the stone was. Azizi decided the front coat closet was the best place to wait. He could hear the approach of a car best from there and grab her as she entered the house.

He hunched down into the corner of the closet, with a heavy coat cushioning his back. He was bone tired, but he knew what would happen to him if he failed, so he had no trouble staying awake, listening for her return.

❖

Amsterdam

Allegro watched Kris storm off into the night until she was nearly out of sight, then set off after her. She knew she couldn't leave Kris alone, with all that was going on. She hadn't spotted the Afghan all night, but was she looking hard enough? Was her mind where it should have been? Was she concentrating on getting that diamond like she was supposed to? She'd searched Kris's purse and hadn't found anything, but after that it all became a bit of a blur. She found herself completely enraptured in the evening and their time together.

Her assignments had always been her priority, and she had never disappointed. Emotional involvement had been carefully removed from her world. In part because of her training, and also because it had become her only means of coping with what she'd been trained to do. She knew that often there was no alternative to the inevitable death or pain that some missions required, and she'd found her own devices to deal with her actions. The ghosts that came to her on occasion, especially in the beginning, were impediments that needed to be dealt with. She knew there was no escape from her life, so she'd trained herself not to feel.

In the beginning it took effort. She had to compartmentalize what she'd seen or done, but later this coping mechanism became a fact of life. Her life. Lying, stealing, and killing were all part of the game, and as long as she thought about it as a game it was all doable. The times that this theory didn't make sense, when she couldn't convince her conscience that she was doing the right thing, she turned to speed. Speed was the only comfort she knew that could take her away from the things she didn't understand. But she knew that no amount of horsepower could make a difference this time. It wasn't an option, and most of all—it wasn't what she wanted.

Tonight, she'd managed in the space of a few hours to lie, steal, and kill. She'd lied about her intentions, stolen Kris's hope, and killed Kris's feelings. She didn't have a choice. She couldn't deceive Kris into thinking that she was a woman who could come back and see her, be with her, dream with her, and give her hope for a future together. Though she'd had to play this game before to get what she wanted, tonight, with Kris, it didn't feel right. Kris deserved better because she...she was like *her*. She'd lived her whole life feeling convenient but unloved, needed but not wanted. A trophy, and one not earned because of the effort put into it, rather one that was bought to shine when necessary.

Kris was as much a random victim of her life as *she* was. A victim turned prisoner in a prison she'd created to protect herself, to prevent herself from having to feel. Kris had already been damaged in so many ways, Allegro hated herself for adding to that list. Very often when she looked at Kris, she saw herself. A woman wanting so desperately to live, but not knowing how to. The memory of pain on Kris's face when she told her not to overreact, and of her own response to Kris's admissions, burned her eyes. Kris finally dared to feel and open up, and she'd shot her down. Made her feel ridiculous for having hope. God, it hurt so much to see her like that. To not be able to tell her...what? What, damn it?

She wanted to tell Kris that she wasn't alone, that she understood how much courage it took to say what she did. To admit to wanting the impossible. To admit to dreams of a life with someone who needed her not because of what she could do for them, but because of what they made her feel. Wanted all of her, because it made sense. Because it hurt too much to be without her. Tonight and every other night with Kris had made her feel like she had a right to dreams. Sharing a house with her, waking up with her, laughing and arguing with her made her...*feel.*

Was that why her assignment had taken a backseat? Why she'd been relieved to find the diamond was not in the safe last night? Why the possibility of Kris not liking her hurt, and why she had run to her in fear when she realized that someone might still be in the house? Why she'd even been willing to shoot a man untidily, in a parking lot, for fear of what he might do if she allowed him the opportunity? That he might take Kris from her. Allegro hadn't felt fear in years. Lack of fear was what made her so good at her work. What was there to fear when she had nothing to lose? Her heart started to pound. Was she afraid of losing Kris?

She found herself walking faster, closing the distance and keeping to the shadows in case Kris turned around. Several blocks from where they'd parted, on the Nieuwezijdsvooburgwal, she watched Kris enter a small hotel. Allegro stood under the street lamp for what seemed like forever, looking up at the windows, wondering which one Kris might be in. Her heart broke over and over again at the thought of how alone and disillusioned she must feel. *I'm so sorry, Kris. Sorry for everything.* But most of all she felt sorry for herself. For having lied to herself about her intentions. For her stolen hopes and for killing her own dreams of a future with Kris. How much longer could she live like this? How many more sacrifices would she have to make, and how much longer would she deny herself what she knew nothing about, but longed for so damn much?

She hadn't cried since she was a child. But tonight, as she stood under the lantern looking up at the hotel windows, she let the tears fall until there was only one thing she could do. Be with the one person that made *something* make sense.

She entered the building and asked the man at the reception desk for Kris's room number. He told her because of the late hour, he'd have to call Ms. van der Jagt to tell her that someone was looking for her. When he reached for the phone, Allegro put her hand on his, and looked at him for the first time through swollen eyes. It was a family matter, she told him, and it would be best if he didn't alarm her unnecessarily. That what she was about to tell her was a delicate matter that was better discussed in private.

He looked at her for several seconds, and his face softened.

❖

Kris slowly opened the door and stood there, blocking the entrance. The room behind her was dark, the only illumination provided by the ambient light of the city streaming in through the windows. Kris was still dressed. Her eyes were red from crying. "What do you want?"

Allegro could feel her own eyes burning but she didn't care. "Let me in?"

"I did, and you humiliated me." Kris's voice was edged with pain.

Allegro ached with every word. "I'm so sorry, for everything."

She didn't know what made Kris break down and let her in, but finally she did, retreating back into the room a few steps. Allegro shut the door behind her. Neither moved or spoke for what seemed like forever.

"I never meant to hurt you." Allegro struggled to keep her tears from falling again. "I never meant for any of this. It's just that—"

"It's just that you don't feel the same way," Kris said.

"It's just that I don't have a choice." Allegro stared at the dark floor at her feet.

"Why not?"

"Because I just don't."

"Christ, Angie." She heard Kris's loud sigh of frustration. "Did you come here only to be vague again?"

"I don't really know why I'm here or what I can say that will make a difference." Her voice was loud in her ears, her own exasperation evident. "There's a lot about my life I can't talk about, but I need you to know that I'm terrified. There, I said it. For the first time in my life. I'm afraid."

"Afraid of what?"

"What I feel for you." Her voice broke with emotion. Still she couldn't meet Kris's eyes. She held her breath, waiting, hoping, but the silence that followed her admission was deafening. "I know it's late," she said, when she could bear it no more. "I'll let you get back to sleep."

She turned for the door. Her fingers were on the knob when she felt a hand on her shoulder. She turned to meet Kris's eyes for the first time. She didn't care that Kris could see her tears.

Kris stepped close and cupped her face, wiping the tears away with gentle caresses of her thumbs. "I'm afraid, too," she whispered.

Chapter Nineteen

Allegro wrapped her arms loosely around Kris's waist as their lips came together, tentatively at first, in a tender kiss of healing. The tip of Kris's tongue danced over Allegro's mouth, and the ache of loneliness and guilt that had consumed her began to melt away.

She let Kris take the lead in their exquisitely slow seduction, humbled and grateful for her forgiveness and tacit acceptance of her need to remain secretive. Her hands were gentle, stroking Allegro's hair, then slipping behind her head to caress her neck. She coaxed Allegro's coat from her shoulders, never ceasing her almost timid kisses of exploration as it fell to the floor. Their bodies barely touched. Kris's fingertips traced long, light paths across Allegro's back, descending with torturous delicacy to her hips. Her slow deliberation was intoxicating. She seemed just as determined as Allegro, to prolong and savor this night.

Her lips teased Allegro's. Gentle bites and nips were punctuated with brief tongue-tip caresses, until the need to deepen the kiss began to drive Allegro mad. As though Kris could sense her growing hunger for more, she withdrew, and Allegro felt the loss of contact as a sudden, dull throb in her chest. She ached for the warmth and taste of her mouth again, for their tongues probing firmly against each other. The powerful compulsion to kiss Kris went far beyond mere lust. The feeling of intimacy in the joining of their mouths was unprecedented for her.

"Stay with me tonight," Kris whispered.

Allegro consented without words. Taking her by the hand, she led her to the bed and unbuttoned her skirt at the back. Kris stepped out of it and kicked off her pumps. Very slowly, Allegro slipped the silk blouse over her head, relishing the first sweet touch of soft skin beneath her fingertips and the shiver of delight her touch produced. Kris wore a lacy beige bra and panties. Her curves and valleys were highlighted by the faint light streaming in through the window.

Allegro's breath caught in her throat at the loveliness before her and it was a moment before she could speak. "You're so beautiful."

She caught the slight downward turn of Kris's head at the compliment, and though she couldn't make her features out clearly, she knew Kris was probably blushing. The response delighted her. Kris undoubtedly heard compliments often, and Allegro had murmured the same words to her, in Italian, the first time they'd met. But Kris didn't seem to make the connection. She went to one of the small bedside lamps.

"I want to see you." Kris's voice was low and breathy as she pulled the chain. The lamp bathed her with a warm amber light, making her even more enticing.

Allegro drank in the sculpted calves, firm thighs, round hips, and narrow waist. The swell of her high, perfect breasts. The hint of rosy nipples beneath the beige lace. And the smooth ivory skin of her chest as it rose and fell with the quick cadence of arousal. She noted a subtle trembling in Kris's hands—she was nervous, as well as excited. And Allegro was surprised to realize she was equally jittery.

Their eyes met. Kris's pupils were dilated so much the blue was barely visible, and the open vulnerability and desire Allegro could read there increased the rapid thumping of her heart. She slipped off her boots, letting her gun slide down into her right boot, where Kris wouldn't see it.

Before she could remove anything else, Kris said in that same breathy tone, "Let me do the rest. Come here."

Allegro closed the distance, gazing deep into Kris's eyes. Kris's fingertips felt cool against the heated flesh of her belly and sides as her turtleneck was slipped over her head. And when she unfastened Allegro's trousers and crouched to pull them down, she etched her fingernails lightly down her thighs. The sensation triggered a tight coil of arousal low in her abdomen.

As Kris slowly rose, her hands smoothed upward, caressing Allegro's calves, thighs, and hips, and gradually increasing the pressure until finally settling on her ass. Allegro was wearing a thong, so when

Kris's nails skimmed her bare flesh, another spasm of arousal tore through her.

"I want to caress you for hours, touch every part of this magnificent body," Kris whispered as she twisted the thong aside before slipping it off.

Allegro's bra was the next to go. She removed Kris's panties and bra in the same languorous way, though it took every ounce of her self-control not to pull Kris hard against her. She was so anxious to feel their bodies move together, breast against breast, pelvis to pelvis. With Kris, she wanted every moment of their joining to remain forever engraved in her memory. The torrent of lust she felt was not unusual, but there was so much more, a torrent of emotion. Joy, awe, longing, and more.

They moved onto the bed, facing each other, their prolonged eye contact speaking volumes about their mutual desire.

"Lie on your back," Allegro said, and when Kris complied, she began an extended exploration of her body with her fingertips and mouth, kissing and caressing her legs, hips, stomach, chest, neck. Down the length of her and back again, avoiding her most sensitive areas, delighting in her soft moans and the way her body writhed beneath her tongue.

"God." Kris exhaled loudly and reached down to entwine her fingers into Allegro's hair, gently pushing her head lower. "I don't know how much more of this I can stand."

Still Allegro avoided the place that Kris needed her most, though the scent of her arousal was unbearably compelling. She did, however, finally move to one breast, caressing it wetly with her tongue. Then the other breast, circling the rigid nipple before taking it into her mouth. Kris gasped with pleasure. It was only then that Allegro lay fully atop her, allowing the long-delayed ecstasy of their naked bodies in full contact, and they began to move together, Kris's hips rising to meet hers. Nails raked down her back and dug into her ass. Their thrusts against each other increased in tempo and pressure until the driving need to taste the wetness she could feel against her thigh was intolerable. She left Kris's breast and descended, soliciting more moans and gasps, and finally, she claimed Kris's sex with her mouth.

Their extended foreplay had made Kris so ready that she came all too quickly, crying out as her body went rigid, spasming in waves, then collapsing bonelessly beneath her. For the next few minutes, Allegro continued to lavish gentle kisses along the inside of her thighs, and at the base of her abdomen, as Kris's rapid breathing returned to normal.

"Jesus." Kris let out a long purr of contentment. "That was incredible."

Allegro smiled as she kissed her way gently back up Kris's body. "There's plenty of time for more."

"Oh, yes," Kris agreed, looking up at her, her face still flushed with excitement. "But first, it's my turn to torture you a while. Lie on your stomach."

And so she did, and Kris spent the next several minutes fulfilling that promise, lavishing her legs, ass, and back with wet swipes of her tongue, nips of her teeth, and tormentingly wonderful caresses with her hands. By the time Kris allowed her to turn over, she was ready to burst, but Kris spent several more long minutes building her higher still with more wet caresses on her stomach and breasts before finally delivering her from her agony.

The hours passed quickly as they pleasured each other to exhaustion, so that by the time they finally lay nestled together, Kris's head in the crook of her shoulder, dawn was breaking.

"I don't want to leave," Kris mumbled sleepily.

Neither do I. Being with Kris made Allegro feel a thrill far more fulfilling than the adrenaline rush she got from speed. But she had to get back to the mansion this morning to search for the diamond. Time was running out, and she thought the gem must be hidden somewhere in Kris's bedroom, after all.

Their quiet solitude was broken by a chime from Allegro's cell phone. Kris groaned as she extricated herself from their embrace to check the text message. It was Domino. She'd arrived in Amsterdam. She replied with the address of the hotel, telling Domino to meet her outside ASAP.

"A friend, asking how the Dutch are treating me," she said aloud as she closed her cell.

"And what did you reply?" Kris asked, stroking her breast.

"That the hospitality has been…unforgettable." Allegro reached for her clothes and started to dress. "Since I'm up anyway, I desperately need some coffee. Why don't you get some sleep, and I'll be back before you know it."

"What time is it?"

"Still early." She leaned over and gave Kris a quick kiss. "Now close your eyes and dream of me. I'll see you shortly."

❖

Thursday, February 14

Allegro got in the passenger side as soon as Domino pulled up outside the hotel. Domino was dressed for work, in black jeans, a black turtleneck, and black leather jacket. She hadn't changed much in the six months since they'd last seen each other. Still in top form, her shoulder-length brown hair recently trimmed. Her gray-blue eyes took in Allegro's appearance with the same assessing gaze as they sized each other up.

"Welcome to Amsterdam," she greeted her friend. "On the right side you can see a magnificent view of—"

"Spill," Domino interrupted, looking up at the hotel. "Is this where they have you staying?"

"No. I really appreciate you coming on such short notice."

"Not like I had a choice after you pointed out that I owe you."

"That's not the only reason you're here," Allegro said softly. They'd rarely ever spoken of their close bond. There was no need to, and emotions and relationships were not topics that ETFs were generally comfortable discussing.

But Domino acknowledged the rare admission with a smile. "No, it's not, and you damn well know it."

"I'm in a jam, Luka."

"I figured that much."

Allegro briefed Domino about Operation Vanish and what she'd been assigned to do. She told her about the vault, Manfred Wolff and his goon, Gunter Schmidt, and about the Afghan who was the immediate concern. She wrote down the make, model, and license plate of Azizi's car, and touched on Kris's visit to her mother at the institution. "So basically," she summarized, "I have days—who the hell knows, maybe hours—to get the damn stone to Colorado."

"What's your plan?"

"I need time to look for it without having to look out for Kris as well," she replied. "I want you to keep an eye on her while I search for the diamond. Azizi is a serious threat, and I need her alive because if I don't find the diamond back at the mansion, I'm going to have to confront her. I don't have a choice."

Domino nodded. "What do you want me to do?"

"The Afghan followed her yesterday. He got close to her car, and I couldn't check it while she was with me. We took mine when we left."

"You think he planted something," Domino acknowledged. "I'll check it out."

"After I drop her off at her car, you can't let her out of your sight. She has a tracker in her coat, but she's likely to change at some point. I want you to plant one on her car. Everything you need is in the trunk of my rental. It's an Audi." She handed Domino the keys and told her where to find the vehicle. "The gun I took off the German is in my duffel. Get rid of it for me, and return my keys to the hotel reception desk. I also need you to delay Kris, so I have enough time to search her bedroom."

"Where is she now?"

She indicated the hotel. "In room 302."

Domino raised an eyebrow in surprise. "Business or pleasure?"

Allegro's mind filled with images of the night before. She didn't answer.

"You weren't kidding when you said you were in trouble," Domino said gently. "What's going on? This is very unlike you. Since when do you give a damn about someone you've slept with?"

It took her several seconds to answer. "Since she came along."

"I'm going to go out on a limb and say that she's the one who called you a self-absorbed, arrogant pain in the ass."

"Huh? Oh, that. Like I said, she was confused." Allegro couldn't help but smile.

"Do they know?" Domino asked.

"Monty and company have no idea."

"What are you going to do?"

That was the million-dollar question, wasn't it? "I don't know. There's not much I can do."

"Does she know who you are?"

"No."

"Do you trust her?"

Allegro studied her friend's face. Her expression lacked the usual detached intensity that she'd always associated with Domino. Instead, there was compassion and empathy, as though she well understood the inner turmoil she was going through. "Trust…do we have that luxury?"

"No," Domino replied, "but we have our instincts."

"I barely know her."

"That wasn't my question," Domino pressed.

Did she trust Kris? Allegro had learned not to trust anyone, but in her heart, she knew the answer. "Okay, fine. I trust her. But I don't know how she'll react to the truth."

"Does she have reason to trust you?" Domino asked. "Despite the lies?"

"What do you mean?"

Domino put her hand on Allegro's shoulder. "Would you kill her if you had to. If they wanted you to?"

This she could answer without hesitation. "*No.* Not an option."

Domino turned in her seat to face her. "I have a lot of things I regret about my life, Misha. Things I could have done differently, choices I could have made. My biggest regret, though, is not having followed my instincts. I almost lost Hayley because I didn't think she could handle the truth. I didn't give her the chance to judge for herself, to face the truth and accept it. But then this amazing woman surprised us both by showing me that she could accept and deal with what I do."

Domino gripped Allegro's shoulder tighter. "She even helped me find a way to deal with it all. To remind me that what I do is for the greater cause. And she's always there to prove to me, time and time again, that I have a safe place to go to when I can't even stand to be around myself."

"You're a lucky woman," Allegro said. It was then she noticed a calmness to Domino, a serenity she'd never seen before. "Both of you took a hell of a chance."

"She's worth it. Is Kris?"

Allegro lifted her gaze to the third floor. "She's a wonderful woman, Luka."

"Is she worth taking that chance?"

That answer came more easily than she expected. "My gut tells me she is."

"Then I'll do whatever it takes to keep her safe."

Domino drove off while Allegro jogged to a café down the block for two coffees. When she returned to the room, she found Kris awake and getting dressed. She seemed flustered. Something had happened.

"What's up?" she asked.

"My mother's doctor called," Kris said. "Mom's upset. She claims someone broke into her room last night and searched her things. I need to get there and find out what's going on."

Allegro kept her voice calm. Had Kris left the diamond with her mother? The possibility seemed incredibly unlikely. The woman lived in a mental institution. The staff probably searched her room every day in case she stockpiled meds. "Was it a thief?" she asked. "Did he take anything?"

"I'll know more when I get there. Oh, I must call Jeroen to tell him not to expect us right away. I assume it's all right that you'll drive me, is that a problem?"

"Let's see, work with Jeroen or your company? Hmm, I think I'll go with the latter. Besides, I want to make sure everything is okay with your mother."

Kris finished dressing and disappeared into the bathroom.

Allegro pulled out her cell and sent a text message to Domino, hoping she'd had enough time to get what she needed out of the Audi and return the keys. The message read: Change of plans. Leaving now for institute. Make sure her car is clean ASAP.

"I'll head downstairs and check us out," she told Kris through the door. "Meet you in the lobby."

She was grateful the keys were at reception, and that the Audi was parked some distance away. Their walk to it would give Domino a chance to do what she needed to do. Allegro also planned to hit every red light she could.

CHAPTER TWENTY

Haarlem

His knees and back ached from his long confinement in the closet, and he'd nearly fallen asleep half a dozen times, but Azizi kept his vigil until finally, a little before eight a.m., the sound of tires on gravel and the slam of a car door alerted him that he was about to have company. He got on his feet and readied himself, grasping his gun tightly in his hand. The door to the closet was open slightly, so he could see the countess as she came in.

It was so quiet he could hear the click of the key in the lock before the front door opened. His heartbeat increased, and he peered through the crack in the door, unblinking, poised to attack. The figure that passed by his limited field of view wasn't Kristine van der Jagt. It was a man, blond-haired and in his thirties, obviously a workman, from his coveralls and the toolbox in his hand. The man vanished into the next room, and shortly after, steady scraping sounds signaled his labors had commenced.

Azizi quietly slipped the gun back into his coat pocket as he considered what to do. He could eliminate this man now, one less witness and potential impediment to his confrontation with the countess, but he knew he'd have to do it in a way that didn't immediately alarm the woman as soon as she walked in. No blood. Then he'd hide the body. She would be looking for the workman, though, since his car was parked outside, so he'd have only a limited amount of time to ambush her.

He reached for a long silk scarf hanging on a peg at the back of the closet, and quietly opened the door a bit more. The workman was not in sight. Azizi pushed the door open further, but before he could take a step, the ringing of a cell phone made him freeze. He heard the workman's voice. "Jeroen."

A long silence followed, then the man spoke again, in Dutch. Azizi caught the word "Kris" and stiffened. The phone call ended, and the sounds of scraping resumed. He slipped quietly from the closet and wrapped the scarf ends around his hands as he crept toward the next room, keeping close to the wall.

At the threshold of the room, he risked a quick glance inside. Allah was with him. The workman was turned away, occupied with peeling stubborn chunks of plaster from the wall, and the noise he was making would obscure his approach.

Azizi covered the distance separating them in a few seconds, and had the scarf around the workman's neck before he could react. He pulled the yellow silk tight, nearly lifting the man off his feet as he struggled, fumbling uselessly at the scarf with both hands. "Stop or I'll kill you," he barked in English, and it took only a moment for the man to comply.

He relaxed the scarf slightly, enough to let the workman breathe again. "Where is the countess?"

The Dutchman noisily sucked in several lungfuls of air. "I don't know," he rasped.

Azizi pulled the scarf tight again. "Do not lie to me. I know you just spoke to her. I will not ask you again. Where is she?"

The workman's face reddened and he made choking sounds as he once more struggled to get free. When he realized the futility of his efforts, he dropped his hands in surrender, and nodded his head.

Azizi relaxed his hold once more and the man gasped for air. "She's in Amsterdam," he choked. "The Saint Francis Institution."

He had what he needed. As he jerked the scarf as tight as he could, biceps straining, the workman's eyes bulged with surprise. He didn't struggle long. It was over in seconds. Azizi dragged the body into another room, out of sight behind a desk, and threw one of the work tarps over it. He might have to return here, he reasoned, if he missed the countess at the institution. He'd also hide the workman's car down the road before he left. No need for the van der Jagt woman to be alerted to danger as soon as she walked in.

Outside Amsterdam

To stall for time Allegro took every busy street she could, leaving the city. The day was notably colder that the previous day, windy, too, and the gray skies threatened rain or sleet any second. They were still several miles from the Saint Francis Institution when her cell phone chimed. The text message from Domino read: Car clean. Peugeot now in the lot. Advise.

Allegro typed back: Put tracker on him.

Three blocks from the building, her cell sounded again. Done.

Allegro pulled into the lot. Azizi was in his car, parked near the entrance. Domino's car was two rows away. She found an empty spot right in front of the steps and turned to Kris as she shut off the ignition. "Do you want me to come in with you?"

"Thanks," Kris replied, "but I think Mother will be more apt to tell me what's going on if it's only us. Why don't you wait in the lobby?"

"Fine by me."

They hurried into the building, Allegro keeping her body between Kris and the Afghan's car. The benches outside were empty.

"I'll be here if you need anything," she said as they parted.

Kris disappeared down a hallway and she went to take a seat on a couch near the reception desk. She hoped Kris's demeanor when she returned would indicate whether she'd left the diamond with her mother, and whether whoever had broken into Wilhelmina's room had taken it.

Allegro sent Domino another SMS: Could have lead on Operation Vanish. Sit tight.

❖

Wilhelmina van der Jagt was sitting at her window, staring out, as she had been the day before. But her demeanor couldn't be more different. In place of the mute lassitude she'd exhibited the day before, was a level of animation Kris hadn't seen in months.

"They won't believe me, but I swear it's true," her mother began as soon as she stepped into the room. "I saw him going through my things. I'm not hallucinating, and it wasn't a dream."

"Slow down, Mom. Start from the beginning."

Wilhelmina glared at her with irritation. "A man came into my room last night, very late." She spoke with the deliberate over-enunciation one uses with a child. "I'm a light sleeper, as you know. When I woke up, I saw him searching through my bureau." She pointed toward one of two large dressers by the bed. "It was dark, but he had a little flashlight, and there was enough light coming in through the window too that I could see his silhouette clearly. I didn't see his face, but he was tall and he wore a long coat. No hat."

"What did you do?" Kris pulled a chair up beside her and studied her face. That glazed look was gone, and Wilhelmina certainly sounded coherent.

"I was terrified, of course." Her mother's hands shook. "I should have pushed my button for the attendant, but I wasn't thinking very clearly. When he moved toward my closet, I blurted out something. I think it was, 'What are you doing?' or words to that effect. He bolted from the room."

"And then?"

"Then I turned on the light and rang for help. It took the attendant at least three or four minutes...*minutes*," she repeated with disdain, "to get here. And *then* he refused to *believe* me, I suppose because the man didn't throw everything on the floor and make a mess. He told me I must've had a nightmare and to go back to sleep." She clutched nervously at a small string of pearls around her neck. "What if he'd attacked me?" Her voice rose. "I'd have been dead long before anyone came to check."

"But you're all right, Mom," Kris replied in her most soothing tone.

"I tell you, he was here," Wilhelmina insisted angrily. "Why won't anyone believe me?"

"I believe you," Kris said, though she wasn't quite sure what to think. The story sounded fantastic and her mother had a history of conjuring up tales that were much more fiction than fact.

"You need to tell them," Wilhelmina said. "You need to take me out of here, so it won't happen again."

"I don't think you're in danger, Mom. The staff will be alert to any strangers walking about after visiting hours, and I'll ask them as I leave to check on you more often."

Wilhelmina scowled. "You don't believe me, either." She turned away from Kris and gestured with her hand impatiently. "Just go, then, if you're not going to help. I don't know why you came."

"I came because I care about you," Kris said softly. She stayed for another hour, but her mother ignored her. Finally she rose from the chair. "Have them call me, if you need me."

❖

Allegro glanced out the lobby window at the Peugeot. Azizi hadn't moved. Obviously he hadn't found the diamond when he'd broken into her mother's room. Or someone else had been here the night before. If Kris had given the Blue Star to her mother, and someone else had gotten to it, the damn stone could be anywhere by now. Finding it would be next to impossible.

Allegro cursed herself for letting her guard down and neglecting what she'd been sent to do. Time was pressing, with too much at stake, and for the first time ever she found herself in the unprofessional position of having to remind herself what her mission was. Her objective was to retrieve a damn historical rock to save the reputation of the Islamic world in exchange for information about an imminent terrorist attack, and she was acting as if she was assigned to protect and serve. Protect Kris and serve her own emotional and physical needs.

She was frustrated and irritated with herself for not giving this particular assignment the singular attention it required. How many thousands of lives did it take for her to put her objective first and foremost? When she'd realized Kris had taken the stone from the vault she should have just ended it right then, and forced Kris to hand it over. Instead she'd allowed her to leave the house, possibly with the stone. Then came her irrational response to dealing with Azizi. She'd been so ready to take him out that she'd almost blown it like an amateur. Why was she acting so unprofessionally?

"Everything all right?" a voice asked from immediately behind her and Allegro realized she'd been so preoccupied she hadn't noticed Kris approach.

"Yes, fine," she said hastily. "How is your mom? What happened?"

Kris shrugged. "Mother's fine. She wasn't hurt. But to tell you the truth, I don't know if I believe her. She claims she caught a man going through her things and scared him off."

"Did she get a good look at him? Did he take anything?" Allegro asked as they made their way outside.

"No, it was dark." Kris sighed loudly. "My mother has invented things before to get attention. But she certainly seemed agitated today, and quite lucid. I stopped to talk to her doctor. He doesn't give much credence to her story, either, but they'll keep a close watch on her and make sure security is alerted."

Kris's calm reaction told her the stone was still safe. Allegro walked her to the Clio, keeping her body between Kris and the Afghan's car. It had started to rain, a light mist. "See you back at the estate," she said as Kris started the engine.

Kris pulled out first, and Domino slipped in behind her, ahead of the Peugeot. Allegro was the last to leave, but detoured at her first opportunity, speeding down a parallel street to get ahead of them all, then racing toward the mansion.

She didn't know how long Domino could delay Kris, so she used every moment she had, screeching to a stop in front of the mansion, spitting gravel in every direction, then bolting up the stairs to Kris's bedroom. Though she tried not to disturb things as she went about her search, she couldn't take quite the meticulous care she usually did. She started with the obvious. Mattress, dresser drawers, and the pockets of the clothes in Kris's closet. Inside shoes. Then the less likely places. The diamond wasn't there. Her cell phone rang as she headed toward Kris's bathroom. She glanced at the display, expecting an update from Domino, but it was Montgomery Pierce.

"Why haven't I heard from you?" he asked. "Do you have the diamond?"

"You would've heard from me if I did."

"Maybe I haven't made myself clear. I need that stone *yesterday*." Pierce was nearly shouting into the phone. "An attack is planned for any minute. I don't care *what* you have to do at this point but get the diamond *now*. We have our people in Afghanistan ready to move. Because time is so short, you're going to have to deliver it directly to the mole. I'll give you his coordinates as soon as you're ready for the drop off."

"Any idea where that will be?"

"Probably Kabul. The MIS is on standby at the Dutch army base to fly you over. You should be there in half the time."

"Why do you need me to deliver it if the MIS is flying over there?" she asked.

"This is no time to be handing it over to other people," Pierce said. "The last thing we need is for it to fall into the wrong hands. And since she's with you, instruct Agent Domino to join you. We're going to need as many ops as possible out there."

"How did you know—"

"Because it's my job to know."

He disconnected and Allegro returned to her task. She'd nearly finished searching Kris's bathroom when Domino called.

"Rocky's detoured. She headed straight for Amsterdam after you left her, with the Afghan on her heels. I ran a red light to lose him and stay with her. She's on foot at the moment on the Kalverstraat. I'm following her as we speak."

"Are you picking up his signal?"

"Yes. He's in the area, on the move. No doubt looking for her car."

It wasn't welcome news. The district that contained all the major shopping venues and attractions was relatively small. "Damn. The city is like a big village. You have to go out of your way to not be seen."

"The weather isn't helping either," Domino said. "The rain is keeping a lot of people off the streets. She's an open target."

"Stay as close as possible."

"I intend to, but short of putting my arm around her and blowing my cover, there's only so much I can do to protect her. Have you found the rock?"

"Negative, and I've done as much searching in this place as the mission allows. It could be anywhere and I'm afraid time's up. I have to confront her."

"When?"

"ASAP. I'll call you back in a few. Don't lose her." Allegro hung up and dialed Kris's number. "Hey, there. Where are you? I thought you'd be right behind me."

"I was about to call you," Kris replied. "Since I was in town anyway, I thought I'd stop to get some software and a few other things I need. It's time I got back to some of my projects."

"Okay, cool. Are you going to be long?"

"Miss me already?"

She could hear the smile in Kris's voice. "That too, but I was wondering if you could pick up some lunch. There's nothing here."

"Sure. I should be back in thirty minutes."

"See you soon." Allegro went downstairs, considering what she would say to get Kris to surrender the diamond. Barely five minutes had passed before Domino called her again.

"Azizi's signal just stopped where our cars are parked. I think he's spotted the Clio, and Rocky is headed that way now. It's not safe for her to go back there."

Allegro immediately disconnected and dialed Kris's cell. She had to get her away from the car and keep her from walking around, direct her somewhere safe until she could get back to Amsterdam. Somewhere indoors. Crowded. And close. *The Rijksmuseum.* It had all of the above, and a bonus—security guards with guns.

"You must be really hungry," Kris said when she picked up.

"Why don't you stay where you are," Allegro suggested. "I have no idea where Jeroen is and what he wants to work on next, so maybe we could meet up and do something fun. What do you say, are you up for it?"

"I think that's a great idea."

"You're still in town, right?"

"I'm headed toward the car," Kris replied. "What do you have in mind?"

"A museum and then lunch?"

"Sounds good."

"Great. Why don't you leave the car where it is, if you have a good parking spot. Catch a tram to the Rijksmuseum, and I'll meet you there."

"Good plan. It's impossible to find a parking spot around here. See you in a little." Kris added warmly, "And I miss you, too."

Allegro hurried to the Audi, her cell phone to her ear. "I'm meeting her at the Rijksmuseum," she told Domino. "I told her to take a tram."

"Chances are he's going to be on the same tram. He's back on her heels."

"Good. If he's as obsessed as I think he is, he's going to follow us into the museum, and I intend to lose him in there."

"Then what?" Domino asked.

"Then I want you to take Kris somewhere safe. This asshole won't let up as long as he thinks she has the stone, so I need to get rid of him for good. I'll meet up with you after and get her to give me the diamond. Once she does, both you and I have to leave for the Middle East. I can't go until I know she's safe." She pressed harder on the accelerator, passing cars on the highway like they were standing still. "Get yourself a ticket for the museum, and stay close to us."

"Rewind a bit," Domino said. "*Both* of us are going to the Middle East?"

"Yeah, Monty's orders. They need as many of us as possible should this get out of hand."

"How the hell did he know—"

Allegro cut her off. "Quote. It's my job to know. Unquote."

"Why do I ask?"

"I'm fifteen minutes away," Allegro said.

"See you at the museum."

CHAPTER TWENTY-ONE

There were a half dozen people already waiting at the tram stop, and a handful more hurried toward it when they saw the long tram come into view. Kris got on at the front, ahead of a cute woman dressed in black, two Japanese tourists, and an elderly man. The rest piled into the rear, where an attendant was also dispensing tickets. The tram was fairly crowded, with few empty seats. As she paid the driver, she spotted one in the middle. A tall, dark-skinned man coming in from the back saw it as well. Their eyes met briefly. She was closer, so she started toward it to head him off, but was stopped short by a tug on her coat. She turned to see the cute woman who'd boarded the tram behind her.

"Does this tram go by the Rijksmuseum?" the woman asked in English. An American.

Kris glanced back toward the rear before she answered. The dark-skinned man had taken the empty seat and was watching her, but without the smugness she might have expected. Sighing, she gripped the nearest pole and turned to answer the American as the tram began to move. "Yes, it stops right outside. I'm headed there myself. Just get off when I do."

"Great, thanks," the American said.

Kris turned her attention to the streets they were passing. They had several blocks to travel, enough time for her to replay in her mind her night with Angie. She'd been an amazing lover, and though they'd only been apart an hour or so, Kris's heart began to beat faster at the thought of seeing her again. When they'd been dancing together, she'd envisioned their lovemaking as heated and fierce, a quick and hungry joining. But though it had certainly progressed to that in the wee hours before dawn, it had begun as the most exquisitely tender and sensual experience she'd ever known, an unhurried and undeniably sexy mutual appreciation of each other before they finally came together.

With every passing hour, the prospect of Angie's imminent departure weighed more heavily on her heart. How unjust it felt to finally feel love, to have at long last met someone who seemed to care about her in earnest, only to lose it all so quickly. She wondered whether Angie would be any more forthcoming today about her life and her plans, in light of what had happened between them. Perhaps that was why she suddenly wanted them to spend the day together.

Kris thought about how she could broach the topic of their connection in the future. She hadn't asked Angie if she could visit her in America, but she could do her Web design business from anywhere, so why not? Much would depend on how the whole financial situation turned out, once the estate sold. She'd have to ask her uncle if he'd heard back anything yet from Professor Bayat about the diamond. She didn't really count on the diamond to take care of all her financial problems, but it certainly could help.

The Rijksmuseum came into view in the distance, and she turned to the cute American, still standing beside her, gripping the pole. "Our stop is coming up. That's it, there." She pointed to the massive building, a gabled, red-brick structure in the Dutch neo-Renaissance style. "Unfortunately, the main building of the museum is closed for renovations until next year, but the major pieces, like Rembrandt's *The Night Watch* are on display in the Philips Wing. There's still plenty to see. The entrance is around the back. I can show you where, if you like. I'm meeting someone there."

"I'll take you up on that," the woman said.

They got off the tram together and headed toward the Philips Wing. Kris paid no attention to the crowds of tourists around them speaking every language imaginable, nor the chill wind from the west. Her mind was firmly on the night before and all the ways she and Angie had touched each other. Even her mother's cold dismissal couldn't dispel the sense of euphoria that had enveloped her.

The two of them got in line behind a dozen others, and she began to scan the crowd for Angie. She was a little surprised to recognize the man who had taken her seat on the tram. He was waiting in line a few people behind them, and looked less than enthralled. Kris wondered why people who were bored by art visited a museum. It was something to talk about, she supposed, and it implied a deeper, more sensitive personality than one might imagine. The dark-skinned man looked like the type who needed all the help he could get in that department.

❖

The nearest parking Allegro could find was in the underground lot of the Marriott a few blocks away, so she left the Audi there and jogged to the museum. When she neared the rear entrance, she spotted Kris and Domino, standing together, talking. Azizi was a few people behind them in line. They were almost at the entrance. Domino's choice to make contact with Kris instead of simply observing her was a red flag. Clearly she had judged Azizi's threat as immediate.

Kris saw Allegro and waved. "Over here."

When she reached her, Allegro gave her a quick kiss. "Hi, beautiful."

They grinned at each other.

Kris linked her arms around Allegro's waist. "I could get used to you calling me that."

"Good, 'cause I like calling you beautiful."

Kris glanced toward the entrance. "We should be indoors soon. It's not too busy."

"Sweet. That means we should be able to find a place where I can thoroughly kiss you."

Kris's smile got wider. "Is that a promise?"

Allegro avoided Domino's eyes. The line moved forward. "Do you trust me enough to take you to a secluded place?" she asked playfully.

"I'll take my chances," Kris said.

They reached the desk and Allegro asked for two tickets. Before they headed off, Kris turned and smiled at Domino. "I hope you enjoy your day."

"Thank you," Domino replied. "I hope you guys find that place to…get away," she added, looking at Allegro.

For the first hour or so, they ambled through the exhibit of Dutch Masters, with Allegro always aware of the Afghan, who kept with them as they moved from room to room, but stayed at a distance and pretended to be absorbed in the art. There hadn't been much of a line at the entrance, but the earlier rain had driven a lot of tourists inside, so most of the time they had ample company, including the occasional security guard. Allegro was aware, all the time, of Domino keeping an eye on them all from the periphery. As Azizi edged nearer, maintaining a distance of only a few yards, Domino compensated by sticking very close to him.

On the second floor of the exhibition, they came to a fairly quiet room with only a half dozen other tourists and no guards. The wall on their right was sealed off with a floor to ceiling curtain, and a sign in several languages read: DO NOT ENTER. RENOVATION AREA. ACCESS TO AUTHORIZED PERSONNEL ONLY.

Allegro glanced discreetly at Domino and then back to the curtain. Moments later, a loud crash echoed through the room, and as heads swiveled to find the source, Allegro put her arm around Kris's shoulders. Everyone's attention was on Azizi and the metal trashcan rolling away from him, spilling its contents on the floor. Domino did a fairly credible job of looking as shocked as the rest of the tourists, stepping far enough back that no one doubted the Afghan was responsible for the disturbance. Red-faced, he bent over to pick up the can, mumbling apologies.

Allegro quickly pulled Kris behind the curtain, into the prohibited area. They were in another large exhibition room, stripped of its art and full of work materials, but dark and dusty—obviously not a priority for workmen at the moment. Allegro could hear no sounds in the dark rooms beyond.

"What are you doing?" Kris asked.

"I told you I'd find a quiet place." Allegro grinned.

"But we're not allowed to be back here. It could be dangerous." Kris moved toward the curtain, but before she could get out of arm's reach, Allegro grabbed her elbow and pulled her into a tight embrace.

"Come on, live a little. This is exciting," she said in her naughtiest voice. "You said you trusted me." She gave Kris a quick wet kiss on the neck. "Follow me."

Taking Kris's hand, she led her across the long, dark room. They were just inside the adjoining room when Kris pulled at her to stop, glancing nervously about as though she expected them to be discovered at any moment, but she made no further move to leave. "Are we here to make out or explore?"

"Shhh. You don't want them to hear us, do you?" Allegro whispered, stroking her finger along Kris's mouth.

"We could go back to the house," Kris whispered. "We'll have plenty of privacy there, and to tell you the truth, I have been thinking about undressing you all day."

Allegro pulled Kris to her and kissed her soundly, mostly to keep her from going anywhere, but also, she had to admit, merely because she couldn't stop herself. Kris kissed her back with equal enthusiasm, and the small shopping bag she'd been holding slipped from her fingers and hit the floor. Their lips parted at the noise.

Kris stooped to pick up the bag. "Can we go home now?"

Allegro's keen hearing picked up the sound of slow, deliberate footsteps in the next room. She stiffened. It was too dark to see anyone.

Kris, still pressed against her, felt the change and froze too. "What is it? Is someone coming?"

Allegro put her hand over Kris's mouth to quiet her. They stood very still for a few seconds until she was sure the footsteps were gone.

"We should really get back to the museum," Kris whispered.

"This way," Allegro said, steering her further into the dark recesses of the renovation area.

"Where are we going?" Kris asked, clearly exasperated.

The sound of someone stepping on broken glass in the room they'd just left startled them both.

"We're trying to find our way back out, sir," Kris blurted out in Dutch before Allegro could stop her. "We got curious." When there was no immediate reply, Kris continued, "Hello, sir. Can you show us out?"

Allegro heard the faint but unmistakable sound of a gun being cocked and footsteps coming their way. She bent over and swiftly removed the Walther from her boot. "Let's go," she whispered, pulling Kris across the room.

"Where did you get that, and what the hell's going on?" Rising fear was evident in Kris's tone.

"There's no time to explain now, but you've got to trust me, Kris. There's a guy out there with a gun and he's not security." Allegro maintained a firm grip on Kris's arm and continued to pull her along.

"I'm not going anywhere." Kris jerked free. "If this is a joke, it's not funny anymore, Angie."

"Please keep your voice down." Allegro took Kris's arm again. "Do you see me laughing? This is no joke. He's dangerous and he's after you."

"Who is he? What does he want with me?"

"I'll explain later. First, I have to get you out of here. Now please stay with me."

"This is crazy." Kris fought their forward momentum and managed to jerk free again.

Allegro roughly grabbed her by the wrist. "Damn it, I don't have time for this." Her tone changed completely, from soothing to stern. "You're coming with me *now*. End of discussion. Now move."

"I'm not going anywhere. Who the hell *are* you?"

"Not now, Kris. Please let me get us out of here." Allegro's cell phone vibrated in her pants pocket. She tucked her gun into her waistband so she could retrieve it without letting go of Kris's wrist. She flicked the phone open, careful to keep it between their bodies so the glow of the display didn't give away their position.

Domino's text message read: He=armd. 3scrty grds+u. cnt #.)! which she translated as: *He's armed. Three security guards are with you. Can't take him out. Leave now.*

"Fuck," Allegro muttered under her breath, and quickly messaged back, one-handed: TX @ EMG, which Domino would translate as: *Leave and get a cab waiting at emergency exit.*

She pocketed the cell and reached for her gun again as she tugged Kris along in search of an exit. They hadn't gotten very far when they heard security guards shouting, asking whoever was there to come out.

"It's not me he's after. I knew you were in trouble," Kris said, keeping her voice low. "Are the police after you? What have you done?"

Allegro heard footsteps very close to their left and turned to aim her gun. When the sounds ceased abruptly, she pulled Kris into an alcove where she could get a better view of who was coming.

"I can't believe I've been harboring a criminal," Kris said.

"I'm not a criminal," Allegro responded, her mouth close to Kris's ear.

"Then who are you? And why is someone chasing us?"

"I'll tell you later. First, I need to get you out of here alive."

"Alive?" Kris's voice trembled.

"Just trust me, Kris."

The footsteps started coming their way again. Much closer this time.

"Don't move," she ordered, and released her hold on Kris.

She could barely make out a silhouette edging slowly toward them, but she could tell by the way he was stopping to check around the corners that he didn't know where they were. It was only a matter of time before he reached them. Allegro braced herself and prepared to move. She couldn't tell if the man approaching was Azizi or a guard, but either way she couldn't let him find them. She estimated he was no more than six feet away when she heard Kris's plastic bag knock against the wall.

The silhouette froze. *"Wie is daar?"* Who's there? A guard.

Allegro jumped him as he came to the front of the alcove. In one quick move, she put her arm around his neck and hit him with the butt of her gun on the back of his head. He slumped to the floor. She dragged him behind the alcove, out of sight, and rejoined Kris. "Which part of *don't move* was open to interpretation? You must suck at surprise parties."

Kris was clearly in no mood for humor. "Did you kill him?" Her voice was strained.

"I gave him a hell of a migraine, but he'll be fine. Let's go."

She led Kris though several more rooms. They'd taken a winding horseshoe turn, and were headed back in the direction of the Philips Wing when she saw a green neon sign ahead indicating an emergency exit. She heard the distant voice of another guard holler in Dutch that he'd spotted a man with a gun heading to the emergency exit.

"The man with the gun is coming this way," Kris volunteered.

"I know. I heard it, too."

"But he said it in Dutch," Kris said. "I thought you didn't speak Dutch."

"Later," Allegro said as they reached the exit.

Posted on the large steel door was a sign that said NOT IN USE. She tried it anyway, but it was locked. She cursed under her breath as the sound of the footsteps pursuing them neared. He would be on them any second. Allegro grabbed Kris's arm and started running. She could hear the footsteps break into a run as well. Another floor-to-ceiling curtain loomed ahead, light spilling through around its edges. A low hum of subdued voices filtered through from the other side. They'd come full circle, to another open exhibition room in the Philips Wing.

"We're going back in, so look normal," she told Kris. "Don't panic, and don't run." She glanced through the edge of the curtain to make sure no guards were about, then led Kris out, through the crowd of tourists to the middle of the room.

"Cameras to your right," she said in a low voice. "Keep looking down and away."

Kris followed her instructions while they stood still for a few moments. Allegro scanned the room and spotted what she was looking for next to the restrooms, a door to the fire exit. She took Kris by the elbow and steered her across to the door. Fortunately there was no alarm. She pushed Kris through and they started to run down the stairs. They'd taken the first turn and were halfway to the ground floor when they heard footsteps on the concrete stairway. Allegro looked up and saw the Afghan peering over the rail as he closed the distance.

"Go!" she hollered at Kris as she drew her gun from the back of her waistband and raced after her. She'd only gone two steps when she heard the ping of a bullet hit the railing beside her hand. She hadn't heard the shot, which meant Azizi was using his silencer.

"Oh, my God, he's shooting," Kris yelled.

"Keep going," Allegro barked.

She returned fire when Azizi rounded the turn in the stairs. She got him on the shoulder, but could tell from his minimal response that it was probably only a flesh wound. He had his gun up, ready to fire again, but this time he was aiming at Kris, a couple of yards ahead of Allegro. Without thinking, she leapt down the stairs, putting her body in the line of fire, and nearly knocked Kris over. They landed near the door to the street.

"Son of a bitch," Allegro said through gritted teeth as a bullet pierced her leg.

She fired back toward Azizi as they scrambled up. Kris pushed the door open and they made it outside into a narrow alley behind the museum. It was raining again, a downpour this time. Allegro kept her gun at the ready, glancing back for their pursuer, as they bolted down the alley. The cab was waiting half a block away. Domino stood on the opposite curb. They reached the car just as Azizi came running out into the street. His eyes locked on Allegro's.

"The Marriott hotel, please," she told the driver, and they pulled away.

She heard Kris gasp. "Angie, your leg," she whispered urgently. "It's bleeding."

Allegro glanced down at the widening stain of scarlet on her right thigh. At the center of the circle was a small tear in the brown corduroy of her trousers. "It's nothing. Only a flesh wound."

They rode in silence, watching the police cars race by in the direction of the museum. The cab let them out at the front of the Marriott and Allegro led them to the underground parking garage, making sure they weren't followed. She took her duffel bag from the trunk and settled Kris in the passenger seat. As she got in the driver's side, she put the duffel on Kris's lap, then raised the lever to push her own seat back as far from the wheel as it could go. She unfastened her trousers and wriggled them down past her knees.

"I need to take care of this," she said, inspecting the wound. It didn't look too bad; the bullet had taken a small chunk of flesh from her outer thigh, halfway between her knee and hip.

"Shouldn't you go to the hospital?" Kris asked, pale-faced.

"There's no time for that."

"We need to go to the police."

"That's out of the question. We can't involve them," Allegro said firmly. "I'll explain later." Reaching into her bag, she dug through it for gauze and antiseptic fluid. She poured some of the fluid straight out of the bottle into the wound. The sting was unbearable and she shut her eyes for a few seconds, waiting for the pain to subside.

"Here, let me," Kris offered.

"No, it's okay. I've done this before."

Kris took the duffel and placed it on the narrow bench behind their seats. Then her hand closed over Allegro's, where it loosely gripped the gauze. "Please. Let me help. All right?"

Allegro didn't answer, but neither did she object when Kris took the antiseptic and gauze from her. She watched Kris's profile as she carefully and gently cleaned away the blood. Her face was unreadable and her whole demeanor was subdued. "Are you okay, Kris? I mean, are you hurt?"

"I'm fine," Kris answered, but her hands started shaking almost as soon as the words were out of her mouth. She stopped what she was doing. "No, I'm not," she finally said, her voice rising as her eyes met Allegro's. "I'm confused and I'm scared and I want to know what the *hell* is going on."

Allegro studied her injury as she considered how much she was going to tell her. "That looks better." She took the antiseptic from Kris and poured more of it into the wound. "Son of bitch, that burns."

Kris leaned over until her face was just above Allegro's thigh and blew on the wound for several seconds. The pain subsided. "Is that better?" she asked, looking up at her.

"Everything with you is better. Even this."

Kris sat up and she frowned. "Angie, what's going on?"

"Let's finish this first, okay? Are you any good at sewing?"

Kris's eyes widened. "You're kidding me."

"No, I'm not. If you can't do it, I will. Hand me the duffel." Allegro pulled out a bottle of local anesthetic spray, a wide roll bandage, and a sealed sterile packet containing silk thread and a needle.

"Are you serious?"

"It's not the first time." Allegro sprayed the anesthetic on her leg and broke open the sterile pack. She'd just finished getting the thread through the needle's eye when Kris stopped her hand.

"I can do it."

When the anesthetic took effect, Allegro did the first stitch herself, gritting her teeth, to show Kris how deeply to insert the needle in the flesh. Then Kris took over, stopping now and then to check with her and wipe away the blood. Each stitch was placed with meticulous care. Five was all it took.

"You're very good at this," Allegro said. "You've been holding out on your talents."

Kris almost smiled. "I've never even sewn a button in my life."

Allegro lifted her leg so Kris could wrap the gauze around her thigh and secure it. Her hands were as gentle as they'd been on her body the night before, and Allegro had to fight to keep those images out of her mind. Kris looked at her a long time before she spoke. "Will you tell me what's going on, Angie?"

"Mishael." Her voice was so soft, she barely recognized it.

"What?"

"My name is Mishael Taylor."

Chapter Twenty-two

Kris stared in bewilderment. "Are you with the police or something?"

Allegro shook her head. How was she going to answer this? "It's complicated. I work for a private organization."

"Doing what?"

"Whatever is necessary. I can't talk about that."

Kris studied her face for a long while. "Are you a spy?"

"Not exactly. I don't work under any one government."

"You're some kind of mercenary?"

"I try to make this place a safer world to be in."

Kris shied away from her, her body pressed against the passenger door. "Christ. You kill for money?"

"I sometimes have to get rid of scum," Allegro said. "And sometimes I have to defend myself. Or others."

Kris eyed her warily. "Who was that man?"

"He's here for the same reason I am, except that he plans to kill you once he has what he wants." Allegro hesitated, trying not to scare Kris any more than was necessary. She almost laughed at herself. How much worse could it get. They'd already been chased and shot at. "I was sent here to retrieve a diamond that went missing a long time ago and belongs to the Afghan government. It's the one your father left you."

"Are you saying I have the real Blue Star?"

"Yes."

"How do you know?" Kris looked stunned. "My uncle has a specialist looking into it."

"Your stone's authenticity has already been confirmed by Professor Bayat," Allegro said. "He may not have admitted it to you, but he told the Afghans it was the real deal. The guy in the museum was sent by them. He's been stalking you for days. I'm almost certain your mother was not hallucinating. He probably went into her room looking for it. She's lucky to be alive."

Kris inhaled sharply. "And I discredited her because of her illness." Her shock and incredulity finally seemed to be giving way to dismay. "I don't understand why they would go to such lengths. Why didn't they just ask for it if they want it bad enough to kill for it?"

"Because only a handful of higher-ups there know it's missing," Allegro said. "They've been displaying a fake gem for decades, and they would be disgraced if the Arab world found out. They couldn't run the risk of you or Mr. Hofman going to the press."

"We wouldn't do that," Kris said with painful naïveté.

"I know, but we're talking about a mistrustful government," Allegro said gently. "The way they see it, if they steal the stone, no one will ever believe you had the real one in the first place. But that's not the worst. There's a corrupt Afghan politician trying to get his hands on the diamond before it ever makes it back into the Persian crown, so he can use it to fund al-Qaeda operations. He figures no one will ever know about the fake jewel as long as the real one never shows up."

Kris looked horrified. "So you came here to steal the diamond from me and give it to the Afghans?"

"I need to get the stone to someone who will return it silently to the crown. In return, he's going to give us information on an imminent terrorist attack against Western targets."

"How do I know that you're telling the truth?" Kris asked. "Why should I believe you? How do I know that you're not like this maniac who is after me? A common thief, an imposter?"

"Because you've seen what a common thief is capable of," Allegro said. "The maniac, as you called him, has no problem putting a gun against your head to get what he wants. Have I forced you? Have I threatened you?"

"No."

"If I were like him, I'd just put my gun to your face and demand the diamond and you'd give it up, wouldn't you?"

"Why haven't you?"

That Kris could believe she'd even consider that option stung, but Allegro kept her hurt well masked. "For various reasons," she said. "To begin with, I don't believe in harming innocent people. Even if you'd turned the diamond over to the man who shot at us, this politician he's working for couldn't take the chance that you'd make all this public. Too many people would be eager to check the crown and they'd find out the stone on display is a fake. My mission was to steal the diamond without you knowing, and give it to someone who will discreetly put it back in the crown."

Kris went quiet and looked away, out the window, obviously considering all she'd just learned. Two men passed close behind their car, headed toward their own, and Allegro kept her eye on them in her mirrors, as she had everyone who'd come into the garage since they'd arrived. The men were speaking Russian, replaying an evening with two blondes the night before.

Kris turned toward her once more. "So that story about coming to Europe to get away from your family in the States and get some emotional rehab was all bullshit."

"I live in England and I don't have a family," Allegro said. "I was born in Iran and placed in an orphanage there. Five months later, I was adopted by the organization I work for."

"You sat there and listened to me talk about my screwed-up life and pretended to identify with me, and sympathize, when in reality, you don't give a fuck."

"That's not true, Kris. I do care. And my life is plenty screwed up."

"Why didn't you just ask me for the damn thing? It would've saved you the trouble of having to fuck me." Kris's tone was scarily calm. She didn't rant. She didn't curse. On the contrary, she looked sad and defeated. Like a boxer who'd received the final blow and had resigned himself to the fact that the game was lost.

"Please don't say that, Kris."

"You know what's crazy?" Kris blinked hard against the tears that were beginning to stream down her face. "If you'd asked me for it, I would have given it to you. Even without knowing why you wanted it. God knows I need the money for my mother and all the other debts, but…I thought I'd found something a lot more precious than a damn stone. When am I going to learn?"

Allegro's heart ached at the pain on Kris's face. "I'm so sorry. I was only doing my job. I never expected…this."

But Kris continued as though she hadn't heard, talking more to herself than Allegro. "I thought I'd learned my lesson after all these years of users. You made me believe you were different. Christ, what a fool." She put her head down and started to sob, jerking away when Allegro gently touched her shoulder. "Don't you dare," she warned, glaring at her with red, swollen eyes, furious. "Don't…you…*dare* touch me."

Allegro ran her hand through her hair in exasperation. She thought she knew what pain was, but nothing could compare to the sting of Kris's disgust and hurt.

Kris turned to stare out the front window, her gaze unfocused. When she spoke again, the defeated tone was back, the anger gone as quickly as it had flared. "My uncle recently said to me that I'd let myself die. That I'd stopped living, and you were just what I needed, the right person to bring me back. I believed him. I believed him because I wanted to. I needed to believe that you could help me feel again. And you did."

"You made *me* feel, too," Allegro said, leaning toward Kris but careful not to touch her. "For the fir—"

Kris turned to face her, and the anguish in her eyes stopped Allegro cold. "You've made me feel more dead than I ever have. God, this *hurts*." The tears streamed down her face. "And I *hate* you for it," she shrieked, beating her fists repeatedly against Allegro's chest. "I hate you."

Allegro made no move to stop her. She sat there taking it, because she deserved it. She couldn't feel any physical pain beyond the pain in her heart, and in the midst of the tirade, she whispered, "I love you, Kris," not sure if Kris even heard her and not caring if she did.

It was the first time she'd said those words to anyone, and now she'd said them to a woman who hated her. A woman who'd placed her trust in her, and whom she'd betrayed. The pummeling against her chest slowed, then stopped. The sound of Kris's loud, rapid breathing, punctuated by sobs, also eased as she collapsed back against her seat and closed her eyes. She looked thoroughly spent. The front of her blouse was wet from her tears. After couple of minutes, she dried her eyes and sat up straight again, but she didn't look at Allegro.

"Let's go get your diamond, Ang…Mishael. God, I can't even say your name. Just get me out of here."

Allegro started the Audi and headed out of the garage. Her thigh ached, but she'd been conditioned to ignore such pain, and had dealt with far greater injuries than this. "Where am I driving us?"

"Back to the house," Kris replied, staring straight ahead.

Allegro called Domino. "We're headed to the mansion. Where are you?"

"I'm still in the city," Domino replied. "Are you okay?"

Allegro glanced at Kris. "She'll give us the diamond. But no, I'm not okay."

"Sorry to hear that," Domino said.

"Are you still picking up his signal? Where is he?"

"I lost him half an hour ago," Domino informed her. "He's out of range."

"Damn. Meet us back at the house." She signed off.

"Who was that?" Kris asked, her attention still focused out the passenger window. They were in stopped rush-hour traffic, still a couple of miles from the A20 on ramp.

"A colleague," Allegro replied. "She's meeting us back at the estate."

"Am I the *only* one who's been living in the dark?" Kris asked, her voice dripping with sarcasm.

"Actually, very few people know about this," Allegro replied seriously. "And you have to keep it that way, Kris. For your own sake."

Traffic began to move again. When she got onto the highway, Kris finally turned to look at her once more. "How long have you been following me?"

"Since Venice."

"Venice?" There was a long silence. Allegro could almost hear the wheels turning in Kris's head as she began to make the connection. "That night. In the den. The mask. You kissed me. You'd been in the cellar."

"Yes. That was me."

"You were looking for the diamond?"

"Yes."

She heard Kris's snort of disgust. "You were playing with my emotions even then."

Allegro glanced her way again. "I didn't have to kiss you, but I couldn't help myself. You were the most beautiful thing I'd ever seen."

Kris didn't respond. Her eyes grew moist and she turned away, looking forward almost wistfully, like she wanted to believe it was true. Allegro darted in and out of traffic, keeping an eye on her rearview mirror for any sign of someone following them.

"What will happen after I give you the diamond?" Kris asked.

"My colleague and I have to return it, in exchange for the intel about the attack."

They drove in silence through the vast stretches of farmland between Amsterdam and Haarlem. The bucolic scenery was right off a postcard. Lazy cows and cozy stone farmhouses with tidy gardens outside, the occasional glimpse of a windmill in the distance, the pastoral serenity in sharp contrast to the tense atmosphere inside the car.

"There's something you need to do after we leave with the diamond," Allegro said.

"I don't know that I'm in the mood to do anything for you."

"It's not for me. It's for the safety of your family. As long as interested parties think you still have the diamond, they'll keep sending people after you."

That got Kris's full attention. "What do you mean? Once you return the diamond, the Afghans will know they have it and they'll leave us alone."

"The Afghans will, but not the Germans."

Kris's forehead wrinkled in confusion. "Germans? I don't understand."

"Your father got the diamond from a Nazi lieutenant during World War Two," Allegro explained. "His son, a guy named Manfred Wolff, knows you have it. He also wants it back. I know for a fact he sent one of his cronies from a neo-Nazi group after you."

Kris seemed lost in thought for a while. "The German killed in town…"

"I found him snooping around at the estate. I took care of him, but I wouldn't be surprised if Wolff sends others." In her peripheral vision, Allegro could see Kris watching her during the long silence that followed. "I didn't have a choice. He was going to kill you, and when I interrupted him, he tried to shoot me."

"When did all this happen?"

"Two nights ago." It seemed a lifetime had passed since then. "The Afghan was there, as well."

"The night you tackled me in the garden," Kris recalled.

"I heard him shoot, and jumped on you to protect you."

"You weren't protecting me, you were protecting the diamond," Kris said, with that same disquieting tone of sad defeat she'd had earlier. "The only reason you kept me alive is because I know where the damn thing is, and you don't."

"That's not the only reason," Allegro said. "Before I go, I'll make sure the Afghan isn't a threat, but I need to know you'll be safe after I leave as well. You and your uncle need to make a statement to the police and the press tomorrow morning, saying you recently inherited a diamond from your father. You were going to have it appraised, but it was stolen before that could happen, so you have no idea of its history, value, size, anything like that."

"Do you think that will keep this Wolff guy from sending anyone else after me?"

"It should. And you can't stay at the mansion until that statement gets out. Why don't you stay with Ilse tonight?"

"How sweet of you to care," Kris said bitterly.

"I do care, damn it," Allegro gripped the steering wheel so hard her knuckles went white.

"Is there *anything* you've said to me that wasn't a lie?"

It was a fair question. And it deserved an honest answer. Allegro glanced over at Kris, who was staring out the window again. "Yes," she said softly, unconsciously relaxing her grip. "Fifteen minutes ago. When I said I loved you. I've never said that to anyone before."

"And you expect me to believe that?"

"I don't have the right to expect anything from you. And I have nothing to gain by saying that I do. All I can do is hope that you believe me. Last night was not about the diamond. Was not about work. Last night was not about taking anything from you, it was about giving myself to you."

Kris didn't answer or look at her, or in any way acknowledge what she'd said. The Audi ate up the miles as dusk began to fall, and just as they reached their exit, Allegro's cell phone broke the unbearable silence.

"I've picked up Azizi's signal," Domino reported. "He's stationary, in Haarlem."

"The bastard is waiting for Kris."

"Why don't we let him follow us to the house and take care of him there?" Domino suggested.

Allegro glanced at Kris. "I don't want to do it there, for obvious reasons." She didn't want Kris to witness what she was capable of.

"Want me to take care of it?"

"No. You're here eyes only, without a cover." Since she'd pulled Domino away from her civilian job, she had only her real passport with her. If the situation went wrong, and the police got involved, Domino's well-guarded, true identity would be compromised. "This operation is mine, and that includes taking care of whoever stands in the way of its completion."

"What do you want to do?" Domino asked.

"Give me his exact coordinates." They were off the highway, and Haarlem was only a couple of miles farther, so Allegro slowed her speed dramatically, grateful there was no one right behind her. Since Domino was following the Audi's position as well, from the tracker in Kris's coat, she could relay their proximity to Azizi.

"He's on Gedempte Oostersingelgraacht, a mile ahead, on your right."

"Where are you?" Allegro asked.

"I'm at equal distance behind you," Domino replied.

"Keep a bigger distance," Allegro told her before disconnecting. She reached the intersection and turned onto the two-lane, one-way street. There was parking on either side, and the Peugeot was five hundred yards ahead. She increased her speed slightly and headed straight for him.

CHAPTER TWENTY-THREE

Haarlem, Netherlands

"Oh, my God, is that the Afghan?" Kris gasped.

Allegro nodded. She did a U-turn, Azizi following. But just before she got back to the highway, she turned onto a side road that led away from Haarlem to the pastureland beyond. It was a flat two-lane, with deep, water-filled ditches on either side to keep animals from crossing over. Now and then there was a break in the ditch to accommodate the driveway to a farmhouse or barn.

The sun had just set. She could barely make out the vague white shapes of cows sleeping in the fields to her left, and the occasional silhouette of a tractor or stacked bales of hay. There was no local traffic on the country road; the only headlights were hers, Azizi's, and Domino's, far behind them both. The speed limit was thirty miles an hour, but they were going seventy or more. When the Afghan got too close, she'd gun it to keep him out of shooting range but always within sight.

"Where are we going?" Kris kept glancing back at their pursuer.

"You'll see." Fifteen minutes into the chase, Allegro pulled out her phone and called Domino. "There's a gas station with a car wash a couple of miles north on the highway. Meet me in there."

Without waiting for a response, she disconnected, then glanced into her rearview and saw the distant headlights of Domino's rental make an abrupt U-turn. A couple of minutes later, when she neared a circle intersection with another country road, she slowed to let Azizi close the distance. When he got a couple hundred yards behind them, she accelerated, screeching around the circle just as he came to it and heading back the way they'd come at ninety miles an hour.

Kris shrieked in terror during the wild turnaround, but calmed when she realized Allegro's maneuver had left the Peugeot's headlights far behind. "We're losing him," she said, glancing back.

"Can't have that." Allegro eased her foot off the gas until the Afghan got within five hundred yards again, a distance she maintained until they could see the highway in the distance. As she'd hoped, the traffic had cleared substantially.

She stomped the gas pedal and the Audi shot forward with alarming speed. Kris shrieked again when she realized Allegro wasn't going to brake for the on-ramp, a sharp curve to the right. The Audi's tires protested with a deafening squeal, and the smell of burning rubber filled Allegro's nostrils. When she reached the highway, she pushed the gas pedal to the floor.

Kris clutched the overhead handle with both hands. "We're going to die!" she screamed, when Allegro swerved around another car, going well over a hundred miles an hour.

"Don't worry," she said calmly. "I do this for a living."

"Do what for a living?" Kris's breathing was so rapid and loud Allegro was worried she might hyperventilate.

"I have a regular job as well," she said, checking her rearview to make sure she'd lost the Peugeot. She was fast outdistancing the few cars behind her. "I test-drive and fix race cars. Formula One. This is nothing."

The gas station was coming up fast, so she braked hard and drove directly into the car wash. Domino was sitting in her car, parked directly in front of them.

"Do you really think this is the right time to be worrying about the shine on your car?" Kris asked, flexing her hands.

"I'm glad you got your sense of humor back." Allegro unbuckled her seat belt. "Kris, you need to get out."

"What are we doing here?"

"Come on, you'll see."

They walked around to the front of the car as Domino got out of hers.

"Kris, this is Luka. Luka, Kris. But I know you've met," Allegro said.

Domino smiled.

Kris stared. "You're the woman from the tram."

"She's been following you when I couldn't, to protect you from the Afghan," Allegro explained.

"That's why you stopped me from going to that seat," she said to Domino. "And he was behind us in line at the museum."

"Hi, Kris," Domino said.

"If we're done with the introductions, I need you to get her out of here," Allegro said. "Go to the mansion."

Kris tugged her sleeve. "Where are you going?"

"To take care of him."

Kris frowned. "You're going to kill him?"

"We need to go, Kris," Domino said.

But Kris kept her full attention on Allegro. "What about the diamond?"

"Give it to Luka. I'll meet you at the house."

Kris looked as though she was going to say something else, but after a few seconds, she started toward the passenger door of Domino's car. She paused there and turned back toward Allegro. "I…I'll see you later."

Domino handed Allegro the tracking device. Azizi had passed the car wash and was heading away from them on the highway. Allegro took off after him, caught up to the Peugeot within a few minutes, and shot past him so he couldn't see into the Audi. She was certain he'd recognized the car, though, when he took off after her.

She made sure to keep ahead of him, grateful that the high seats of the sports car made it impossible from the rear to see whether there was anyone in the passenger side. They were passing more farmland, the next big city still miles away. She took the next exit, with Azizi on her tail, and quickly found another back road much like the one they'd just left. Steep, water-filled ditches on either side, as before, the pavement more pitted, but flat. And this road had two advantages: it was narrow and had even fewer farmhouses than the one outside Haarlem.

Allegro gunned the engine to leave him well behind, and once she passed a long stretch without barns or farmhouses, hit the brakes at the next driveway and quickly turned around. His headlights in the distance were coming toward her at a high rate of speed. *Okay, son of a bitch. Time to see who's got the bigger balls.* She accelerated and headed straight for the Afghan, driving down the middle of the road. She clicked on her brights to blind him.

She could almost feel his panic. The Peugeot slowed dramatically. But Allegro kept her speed steady, calmly closing the distance between them. He had only two options: stop, or get out of the way. He was on a mission, and she knew what that meant in his world. A soldier never disappoints, it could mean his head. There was nowhere for him to go. He had ditches on both sides, and the road was too narrow to avoid her. She kept her speed constant.

Mere seconds before impact, he swerved. She shot past him as he careened into the ditch to her right. Allegro braked hard and skidded to a stop, then hit reverse and shot backward until she was beside the vehicle. The car was half submerged, and Azizi, gun in hand, was trying to pull himself out of the passenger window.

Still in the Audi, she hit the button to lower the passenger window with one hand and reached for her Walther, equipped with its silencer, with the other. Aiming through the open window, she fired at the gun in his hand. Azizi screamed and fell back into the Peugeot as the gun broke in two and took part of his hand with it. Allegro got out of her car and walked to the edge of the ditch, looking down at him through the open window.

Good-bye, son of a bitch. She raised her gun and fired, hitting him cleanly between the eyes. A shot to the head was the traditional way. Always make sure you aim to kill. A second shot, and she was done. She removed the tracker from the Peugeot and sped back to the mansion.

❖

"Are you part of this…organization, too?" Kris asked Luka as they left the car wash and headed toward the mansion, thankfully at a normal rate of speed.

"Yes. That's how we know each other. What has Misha told you about us?"

Kris noted the nickname. *Misha.* A sign these two women were close. "Nothing. Just that you're getting rid of scum and making this a better world."

"Sounds about right."

"I still don't know what that makes you."

"It makes us necessary," Luka said. "What we do…what Misha does, is not who she is. It's part of her, but she's so much more."

"That's right. She's a Formula One mechanic," Kris said drolly. "How about you? What's your cover story?"

Luka laughed. "It's not a cover story. We have actual jobs, and we're called to duty when things get out of control. When we have to go where others can't. I'm an art restorer."

Kris studied Luka in profile as they drove through the lighted streets of Haarlem. She looked like the artsy type, but her toned physique, like Misha's, made it also entirely believable that she was capable of taking care of herself in a fight. "Why didn't she pick something safe, normal, like you did? If she's not out playing Rambo, she's on the track racing killing machines."

Luka's smile faded as she glanced toward Kris. "Because she needs the adrenaline to feel alive. We lead rather complicated lives that deprive us of the usual emotional highs. Highs that matter."

"How do you get your emotional highs?"

"I used to try the most ludicrous things, not caring what might happen to me." They stopped at a traffic light and Luka turned to look at her. "When that didn't work, I turned into a shut-in. But recently, I found what I'd been missing all those years. What I'd been depriving myself of, thinking I didn't deserve it."

"What's that?" Kris asked.

"Love." Luka smiled and, for a moment, looked past Kris, as though her thoughts had taken her elsewhere. "I found someone who accepts who I am and what I do. Accepts my moods and takes away the pain by giving me warmth and understanding. Loves me unconditionally although she knows I can't give her answers or explanations. All she asks is that I love her unconditionally in return."

"Do you?"

"I would risk my life for her. Misha is like that as well." The light changed, and Luka returned her attention to the road.

If anyone knew about the women in Misha's life, Kris thought Luka the most likely candidate. "Is there someone she would risk her life for?"

Surprise registered on Luka's face. "What do you think she's doing now? The only reason she asked me to come here was to protect you.

She wasn't ordered to protect you, Kris, and nobody asked her to get rid of the Afghan. Her mission was to get the diamond. That's all."

Kris's mind was whirling. "What are you saying?"

"He's a danger to you, so she won't leave until she's dealt with him," Luka said. "I've known her all my life, and I've never seen her more afraid of losing someone. She's always been fearless because she's had no one she cared enough about to fear *for*. Except me, but we're like family."

They turned onto the road to the mansion. Kris remembered the morning she'd picked Angie…Misha…up here, carrying her duffel bag. The cocky American tourist she'd already decided not to like. So much had happened since, in such a short time, it hardly seemed possible. She'd only known Misha for a few days, and hadn't known her at all as it turned out. Yet she couldn't ignore the feelings that threatened to engulf her. Even in the confusion and shock of the events swirling around her, she could find a strange calm deep within, a sense of certainty she could not explain. She was in love. Impossible, illogical, and undeniable.

"Is she going to be all right?" she asked.

"She'll be fine. Don't worry." Luka said it with such confidence it did help calm Kris's nerves.

"How do you know?"

"Because she's one of the best." Luka pulled into the driveway. "But also because she has reason to come back."

"The diamond?"

Luka shook her head and smiled. "You. She loves you, Kris."

Kris dug in her purse for her key, as they mounted the steps to the mansion.

Luka closed her phone and said, "She'll be here in twenty minutes."

"Thank God."

"She wants you to get the diamond. We'll have to leave immediately, as soon as she grabs her things."

Kris slid her key in the lock. *Immediately*. If she'd known their conversation in the car might be their last, would she have done anything differently? Misha *had* known, she realized, and that was why she'd poured her heart out. Somehow that made the words she'd said easier to believe.

Luka's hand on her arm stopped her as she reached for the knob. "Allow me." With her gun in her hand, she pulled Kris behind her, then opened the door with one hand and pointed her gun inside with the other.

"The light switch is on the right," Kris said.

Luka reached around to switch on the light, then stood still, scanning the interior and listening. There was no sound from within. They moved as a pair, until they could see into the next room, where the renovation work was being done.

"Aside from the mess, does everything look like it should?" Luka asked.

Kris glanced past her. "Yes. As far as I can tell, anyway. It feels like I haven't been here for months."

"A lot has happened. Where's the diamond?"

"In the vault," Kris said. "The entrance is through the garden shed. It's faster if we go out through the kitchen. But I have to get the keys first. One to the shed, and one to the trapdoor." As she started toward the den, Luka stopped her.

"Please stay with me. I'll walk us there."

They moved as one again, Luka with her gun pointed, and Kris behind, her hand on Luka's back. When they reached the den, Luka turned on the lights. The room was empty, and it didn't appear that anything inside had been disturbed. Kris started around the desk, Luka close beside her. One of the work tarps blocked the bottom drawers because there was something large beneath it. Kris's heart began to beat faster.

Luka touched the edge of the shape with her foot. "Stand back, Kris." She crouched, her gun pointed, and swiftly pulled back the tarp.

Kris screamed when she saw it was Jeroen, his eyes open and unnaturally wide, blue lips frozen in a permanent grimace of pain. "Oh, my God." She put her hands over her eyes, but she could still see his face, burned forever in her memory.

"Do you know him?" Luka asked gently.

"Jeroen. The…the handyman." A wave of dizziness washed over Kris. "He was a friend of my uncle's."

"I'm sorry. From the looks of him, I think he was killed late last night or early this morning."

As Kris backed away from the body, her knees started to buckle. She stumbled to the nearest chair and collapsed into it, then put her head down. "When will all this stop?"

"Tonight," Luka said. "It stops tonight. By tomorrow, everything will be back to normal."

Kris rocked back and forth in her chair while they waited for Misha. The only sound she could hear was the faint ticking of the grandfather clock in the next room until finally a car pulled into the drive.

"I'll be right back." Luka departed, leaving her alone with Jeroen.

❖

Allegro had raced back to the mansion, her heart growing heavier with each passing mile, knowing she'd have only mere minutes with Kris before they had to leave for the Middle East. She'd said everything she'd needed to say to her, how she felt and what Kris meant to her. Everything except the fact that knowing her had changed everything. For she knew in her heart that her escapes with fast cars and anonymous women would never be enough any more.

Domino met her at the door and briefed her on what they'd found. Tucking her gun into the back of her waistband, Allegro hurried into the den and found Kris rocking back and forth in her chair, her head in her hands. She knelt in front of her, but didn't dare touch her.

"He's dead." Kris started to sob.

"I know," Allegro said. "He was a sweetheart. He never deserved this."

Kris wiped at her eyes and looked up at her. "I'm so scared."

"You have nothing to fear anymore. He won't be bothering you again."

"You killed him?"

"He was a ruthless, sick bastard."

"And you killed him," Kris repeated.

"Yes."

Kris's eyes swept over the tarp. "Good."

"Kris, I know this is difficult," Allegro said gently, "but we're running out of time. Luka and I have to leave. The sooner we go, the faster you can call the police to notify Jeroen's family. We can't be here when the police arrive."

Kris acted as though she hadn't heard. She was still staring at the body.

Allegro placed a hand lightly on her cheek and turned her face until their eyes met. "You can stay here with Luka while I go get the diamond. Just tell me where it is."

"It's in the vault. Through the garden house."

She's in shock. She's not thinking clearly. "No, it's not, Kris. I've already checked there."

Kris looked puzzled. "When?"

"The night before last," she said. "The night you went out to get it."

Kris bit her lip, and went quiet for a moment, as though trying to focus her thoughts. She was staring at her feet. "I gave it to my uncle when we went over there yesterday. I was going to put it in a lockbox because Jeroen..." Her voice broke at the mention of his name. "Because Jeroen wanted to start working on the fake wall. But because I'd made plans with you and couldn't get to the bank, Uncle offered to return it to the safe last night. He didn't think it wise to keep it in his office, and he had to be in Haarlem to visit a friend anyway. He was going to ask Jeroen to wait to work on that wall."

"The keys to the shed and trapdoor are in the desk drawer," Domino interrupted. "It's best that you get them."

Allegro opened the top drawers and quickly scanned for the keys without luck. She had to move the body slightly to get access to the bottom drawer. The keys were hanging on a hook. She passed by Domino on the way out. "Stay with her. I'll be right back."

"Of course."

She went out through the kitchen door, her boots crunching over the broken glass where the window had been shattered. Fumbling for the penlight in the pocket of her coat, she ran to the shed with her gun in her hand. It took only a minute to unlock the door, throw aside the mat, and get through the trapdoor and into the tunnel. She raced the length of it, blocking out the pain in her thigh, and scrambled up the ladder to the vault.

In her line of work, success was all in the details. She remembered the combination; it was one of those things operatives memorized automatically. She spun the dial with the penlight in her mouth, and reached for the lever.

"What the hell?" she said, staring at the empty safe in disbelief.

CHAPTER TWENTY-FOUR

"He must have changed his mind about driving out here," Kris said. There was only one place her uncle would keep the Blue Star, she was certain. In his safe. And she knew how to get into it. When he'd told her where the key was, he said it was because he was getting on in years and she was his only family left. Using that information now felt like such a betrayal of his trust. A violation of his privacy. "It's only a matter of time before he realizes it's missing."

"He'll call the police and they'll eventually come to the conclusion that someone stole it. Remember when I told you to go to the press? You don't have to, now. The German will find out you don't have the diamond this way."

Kris ran her hand through her hair. "All these lies."

"I don't like lying any better than you do," Mishael said. "Not to people I love. Lying to you is one of the hardest things I've ever had to do. But you don't have a choice. Try to take comfort in the fact that thousands, maybe millions of lives will be saved because of these lies."

Kris sighed. "I'll try."

There was little traffic and they reached her uncle's quickly and found a parking spot halfway down the block.

"We'll wait here," Mishael said. "Please be fast."

Kris hurried to the door and let herself in with the spare key he'd given her. Using it now felt like another betrayal. "Uncle?" she called out. "It's me. I thought I'd drop by since I was in the area."

There was no answer.

"Uncle?" she repeated, louder.

Still no answer. But she could make out the faint sound of the television in his apartment upstairs. He hadn't heard her and perhaps that was for the best. She could do what she needed to do and be out again without him ever knowing she was here. She went through the reception area to his office. It was dark, but there was enough light coming in through the window for her to do what she needed to do. The key was right where he'd told her it would be, stuck in a book on Dutch art that she'd given him. Kris went to the safe behind his desk. It wasn't that large, and she had to crouch to open it. She couldn't see inside the dark interior, she had to reach in and search. Her fingers skimmed over papers then felt velvet. She pulled out the bundle and opened it. The Blue Star, hard and cold, lay in her hand. She closed her fist over it and started to rise, but before she could, she was yanked hard, by her hair, backward. She tried to regain her footing, clutching at her scalp with her free hand, but the grip on her hair was too strong. She was too startled to scream.

"*Geben Sie mir das*," a man's voice said from behind, and then he pushed her head forward, hard, toward the safe.

Kris couldn't stop herself. Her world went black.

❖

"She's been in there twenty minutes," Domino said, checking her watch. "And it's five minutes since we sent the last text message. We have to go in."

The lights were on in the upstairs apartment. The office remained dark. Allegro's sense of alarm grew, until her heart was thundering against her chest. "This can't be good. She would have sent a text back by now, even if she didn't have it yet."

They hurried to the door and rang the bell. No answer. It was locked, so Allegro pulled out her Walther and shot the lock.

"I'll take the first floor," she told Domino. "You look upstairs."

Allegro ran down the hallway, through the outer office into the dark room beyond and flipped on the light. She saw Kris's feet sticking out from behind the desk. Not moving.

"Kris!" A scream of anguish and disbelief. She held her breath as she hurried behind the desk. There was a gash on Kris's forehead, spilling blood into the carpet. Allegro felt for a pulse. When she found one, she released the breath she'd been holding. She put her hand against Kris's cheek, and gently swept the hair away from her face. There was no response. Carefully, gingerly, she slipped her hands beneath Kris and shifted so she could cradle Kris in her arms. "Come on, baby. It's me."

Finally, Kris began to stir. "Angie?"

"Misha. But right now, I'll settle for anything." The heavy weight on her chest lifted, and her thumping heart began to calm.

"What happened?" Kris mumbled.

"I was kinda hoping you could tell me."

The sound of Domino's footsteps drew her attention to the doorway. "Her uncle needs to go to a hospital. Whoever did this banged him up badly. They got in and left through the garden. The door is still open."

"Use the phone on the desk to call 112," Allegro said. "Speak in Dutch and say you're Kris van der Jagt. Tell them there's been a break-in." While Domino made the call, she asked, "Who did this to you, Kris? Who was here?"

Kris took a couple of deep breaths. "I tried to get the diamond. I had it in my hand when this guy came from behind and grabbed my hair."

"Did you see who it was? What did he look like?"

"I don't know. He was behind me. It was so dark. I didn't see him."

"Did he say anything?"

Kris reached up with an unsteady hand to touch where her forehead was gashed, "God, my head really hurts."

"I know. But you'll be fine." Allegro gently stroked her hair. "Thank God."

"*Geben Sie mir das,*" Kris mumbled.

"What, honey?"

"That's what he said."

"In German?"

"Yes." Kris started to rise, and Allegro helped her into a sitting position, but stayed on her knees beside her.

"The ambulance is coming," Domino said. She stood at the window, looking out onto the street. "I can hear them."

"Kris, we have to go, but the ambulance will be here soon. Tell them you called and that your uncle is upstairs, okay?"

"Yes." Kris put her hand over the wound and winced.

"I have to go now." But Allegro didn't get up. They looked at each other for several more seconds, their faces close together.

"Will you come back?" Kris asked. "Will I see you again?"

"I'll contact you, okay? I don't know when, but I will."

"Misha?"

"Yes?"

"For a difficult woman," Kris said, "You're very easy to love."

"I am?"

"Yes, damn you." Kris smiled, but her eyes were filled with tears. "So please be careful. Even if I don't see you again, I never want to lose you."

"They're almost here, Misha," Domino warned. "We have to move *now*."

Allegro leaned forward and kissed Kris, all too briefly. "In a single week," she told her, "You've given me more reason to live than anyone has in a lifetime."

They left through the garden door as the ambulance attendants were coming in the front.

❖

By the time they hit the highway, it was after ten p.m., and they were able to make good time in the Audi in the sparse traffic. Allegro's wounded thigh was protesting, so she took a pain pill and let Domino drive the first stretch. Once they crossed the border and got on the German autobahn, with no speed limit, Allegro took over and pushed the pedal to the floor. She engaged her scrambler and called in to headquarters at one a.m, five p.m. Colorado time. They were ninety minutes from Berlin, she figured.

Montgomery Pierce answered immediately. "Where are you?"

"In Germany."

"What the hell for?" Pierce shouted into the phone.

"The stone." Allegro briefed him on what had happened and asked him to get Manfred Wolff's home address. They were driving, she explained, because they'd decided it would be faster than going by air.

They couldn't take a commercial flight with their guns, and she knew it would be time-consuming to get the right clearances to detour the military plane waiting for them at the Dutch airbase. If Wolff's latest thug was driving, they'd pass him and be waiting at Wolff's, since he had a half-hour lead at most. If he'd gone to the airport, he would probably arrive ahead of them, but not by more than ninety minutes or so.

When she'd finished, Pierce gave her Wolff's address in the city center. "I'll have a helicopter ready to take you from Tegel airport in Berlin to the American base in Frankfurt."

"I'll contact you as soon as we're ready for takeoff," Allegro said.

"You had better be sure the diamond is there," Pierce warned. "We're out of time. Do you understand that? So far, Operation Vanish is a disaster."

"It's not over yet, Monty. I'll make sure the mole gets the stone."

"Yes, you will," he said. "This is not the time to have your first failed assignment."

❖

"I was so busy getting involved in things I know nothing about, I let myself become distracted," Allegro said bitterly. "This work doesn't allow distractions or emotional attachments. Now I know why."

"Oh no. You are not going to look for excuses to run," Domino objected. "Don't blame yourself for allowing yourself to be human. I made the same mistake, and I know for a fact running doesn't work. You think you're getting further away, when in reality you're running in circles."

"What do you mean?"

"That you're not dealing with any of your issues by leaving them in the dust," Domino replied. "You're merely running into the same problems over and over."

"What problems? I didn't have any until I let myself get attached."

"Bullshit. First of all, you have plenty of problems. No one can do what we do and not. When you asked me on the phone in Malta if I thought you were arrogant, I answered honestly when I said no.

Because I know for a fact that you're not. So I know you're not being conceited when you say that your lifestyle leaves you cold. Which leads me to believe you're in denial." Domino let the words sink in before she continued. "Second of all, you didn't *let* yourself get attached. It happened because the right person came along and you had no choice other than to lie to yourself. That's not your style, so don't start now."

"I learned long ago that the only way to survive and maintain some semblance of sanity is to shut it all out," Allegro said. "Let it all go."

"That doesn't mean it doesn't leave scars," Domino said gently. "That it doesn't break something in you every time you have to look evil in the eyes."

"Maybe something does break, Luka. But it heals after a while because it has to."

"Time alone doesn't heal. Time makes it bearable. When you break your arm and do nothing about it, eventually with time it will mend, but it will mend crooked and leave you with a lifetime of pain. That's why you need a cast to help it heal and mend properly."

"I don't think they make casts for these kind of breaks."

"They do. I found mine, and now you have, too. Don't run from her, Misha."

They arrived at Wolff's apartment a little after two, and parked on the next block, facing the building, where they had a clear view of the entrance. It wasn't a large complex, and they knew he was on the second floor, so it was a fairly safe assumption that the single lighted window they were looking at was his. There was no one on the street.

"I bet the bastard's up ogling his loot, or waiting for it to arrive," Allegro said.

Domino looked out the front window, scanning the exterior. "Doesn't look like there's much security here."

"Good. It's not like we have time for an all-nighter. I'll get my gear on." Allegro stuck her Walther in the back of her waistband and dug through her duffel bag for her ski mask, lock-picking tool, and Bluetooth earpiece. She adjusted the Bluetooth and dialed Domino's number. "See you in a few."

"Yes, you will, slick."

Domino remained in the car while she got out and went to the main entrance. Allegro used her long pin to open the door, and checked the immediate area for security cameras. There were none. "It's clear," she relayed to Domino.

There was an elevator down the hallway to her left, but she bypassed it to take the stairs. Before she got to the second floor, she paused to pull her ski mask over her head and draw her gun. The hallway to apartment 223 was empty. She crept along it, listening for noise. A hint of light spilled out from under Wolff's door. She peered through the peephole. Though the view from this side was distorted, she could see there was no one directly opposite, no movement at all.

She slowly turned the knob to see if it would make noise. It didn't. Allegro used the pick again to open it and slipped inside. She was in a hallway, with doors leading off either side. The last one on the right was open; it was where the light was on. She took a few steps forward and the floor beneath her squeaked. She froze. A man's voice demanded to know who was there. She saw a shadow disturb the light in the last room, so she quickly opened the nearest door and disappeared inside.

"Mutter?" the man called, addressing his mother.

Allegro looked around the room she was in. It was very dark, but she could make out a figure in the bed and a wheelchair, nearby. She stood behind the door, her back pressed up against the wall, as the heavy footsteps came down the hall. The door opened, shielding her. A stockily built man stepped into the room and paused for several seconds while Allegro held her breath. Apparently satisfied that nothing was amiss, he closed the door again and retreated back down the hallway.

She remained where she was for a few minutes. Then she opened the door and crept out. She peeked into a living room. Wolff was in front of the fireplace, closing the screen, his back to her. The diamond was nowhere in plain view. He turned off one lamp and moved toward another, to the right of the fireplace.

Allegro crept up on him as he moved to extinguish the second light. She clamped one hand over his mouth, while the other pressed the end of her gun beneath his chin. "Where's the stone?"

Wolff tried to scream, but she only tightened her grip, and shoved the gun harder against his throat. "Try that again, and I'll shoot. Do you understand?"

He nodded, his nostrils flaring as he breathed loud and fast through his nose in his panic. She wrestled him to the chair in front of the fireplace and pushed him down into it. Releasing her grip on his mouth, she kept her Walther on him and stood in front of the chair.

"Who are you?" he asked.

"Let's not bother with introductions. I'm going to ask again. Where is it?"

Wolff had his hands on the armrests, and he started to push his bulk out of the chair, trying to rise, but she put her hand on his shoulder and shoved him down roughly, then cocked her gun. "What stone? What do you want?" His voice was getting higher by the second as his fear rose.

"Has he delivered it to you yet, or not?"

"I think you're talking to the wrong person."

"And I think you're fucking with the wrong person. Is it here yet, or not?" She placed the Walther, with its silencer, against his knee. "You know what's great about this gun?"

Wolff didn't answer, but she could see he was starting to sweat. His face glistened with it.

"I can give you an extra asshole and nobody needs to hear a thing."

"It's not here yet," he said hastily, as the sweat really began to pour.

"Are you sure?" she asked. "I find it hard to believe that you were about to go to bed if you're expecting company. I'd be all nervous anticipation if it were me."

"He's going to bring it to me tomorrow." Wolff's slight hesitation was all she needed to hear. "He did not get back until very late," he added, looking away. "So we agreed that he would bring it to me tomorrow."

"We have two problems," Allegro said. "One problem being that you're lying. Second being that my ass is too close to the fire and it's really starting to get on my nerves. I tend to get irrational when things get on my nerves. Now I want you to choose your next words very carefully, because I feel that irrational streak coming up. Where is the diamond?"

"I told you I won't have it until tomorr—"

She pulled the trigger and shot him in the knee before he could finish. He sprang out of the chair from the pain, clutching at his knee, and starting to scream, but she'd anticipated that and had her hand over his mouth quickly. She shoved him back in the chair.

"I don't have anywhere I need to be," she said calmly. "I can go on putting holes in you all night. And when I'm done with you, there's always your mother."

Tears ran down his face. He was clearly in agony. He cursed at her in German between gritted teeth.

"Okay, here we go. One more try. Wrong answer, and you'll have two knees to worry about. Where's the diamond?"

He glared at her, groaning in pain and fury. "In the bookcase."

"Point."

Wolff pointed to one of the three bookcases in the room.

"Give me a title," Allegro said.

"The drawer at the bottom."

Keeping the gun aimed, she went to the bookcase and searched through the tablecloths and napkins in the drawer until she felt something hard. There, wrapped in one of the napkins, was the Blue Star. She stared at it for a few seconds, then rewrapped it in the napkin and stuck it in her pocket. "See, it wasn't that difficult."

Before she left, she ripped out the phone cable, and took his cell phone and smashed it with her boot. She contemplated finishing Wolff off, but she hadn't been ordered to make the kill, and the thought of the wheelchair lingered. Someone had to look after the old lady asleep in that room. As she made her way back down the hallway, she spoke into her Bluetooth. "I'm on the way out."

"I know," Domino replied. "I'll be out front."

Allegro took off her ski mask and tucked her gun away as she ran down the stairs. The car was waiting for her outside the entrance.

❖

"We're on our way to the airport," Allegro told Montgomery Pierce as soon as the EOO Chief came on the line.

"Good," Pierce replied, in a much calmer tone than the last time they'd spoken. "You should be in Kabul by fifteen-hundred, local time. You are to wait on the northeast corner of Salang Wat and Shir Ali Khan with a plain white envelope. A Fouad will approach you. Your name is

Sayeh. He'll hand over a mobile phone. The mole will contact you on that phone to give you his location. When you hand him the diamond, he'll give you the location and targets in exchange. You're to pass the intel on to me ASAP. The MIS is ready to move. We're *all* ready to move."

"What do you want us to do then?"

"We don't know what the terrorists will be using, or where the targets are," Pierce said. "In the worst case, we'll have to notify the Western targets for immediate evacuation. In the best case, we get there in time to stop them. You're on standby after the drop-off, and awaiting further instructions. I can't be more specific than that at the present time. The mole hasn't given us anything yet. He contacted the MIS an hour ago to say the terrorists are in position and ready to start countdown in twelve hours. Make sure you get the diamond to him on time."

"I will." When Pierce disconnected, she turned to Domino. "Time to rock and roll."

She briefed her as they turned onto the road leading to the airport. They were on the helicopter twenty minutes later, headed to their military transport in Frankfurt.

CHAPTER TWENTY-FIVE

Kabul, Afghanistan
Friday, February 15

In his home in the outskirts of Kabul, Afghan Culture Minister Qadir slammed the phone down angrily, frustrated at his failed fifth attempt to contact Azizi to find out the status of his recovery of the *Setarehe Abi Rang*. The clock was ticking, and his al-Qaeda brothers would not be pleased if he failed to turn over the diamond as promised. His sponsorship of the group had given him the rare opportunity to be involved in, potentially, the greatest attack to date against the West, and he wanted nothing to jeopardize that. Especially since the attack was now just eleven hours away.

Qadir intended to commemorate the occasion by remaining at home with his wife and daughters this day, though he would spend much of it here, in his home office, awaiting updates. Azizi should have reported in long before this. He would have the man's head when he returned. Qadir stroked his beard as he considered his alternatives. He didn't have many. The best option was to tell his fundamentalist brothers that delivery of the gem was merely delayed, that he would have it for them very soon, and immediately dispatch another man, perhaps two, to recover the diamond. A loyal member of al-Qaeda, a noted Kabul jeweler, had already been contacted and was prepared to cut the stone and liquidate it for quick cash.

He stared down at the plans before him, admiring the thoughtful and meticulous preparations. Soon, two cities would lie in ruins. No, he hadn't done all that he had, only to miss this golden opportunity to see the West brought to his knees. Whatever it took, he would have the *Setarehe Abi Rang* within a matter of days, at most.

❖

The U.S. Army jet that flew Allegro and Domino from the Frankfurt airbase to Afghanistan was a Gulfstream IV C-20F, a fourteen-seater with a two-man crew. Capable of Mach .80, it traveled the thirty-two-hundred-mile distance to Bagram without refueling. They made it in six and a half hours.

Below them, the view was a moonscape of endless steep, rugged mountains, brownish red, with a dusting of snow here and there. There were few signs of civilization. Finally they glimpsed Kabul, nestled in a narrow valley between high, jagged peaks. As they approached the air field, Allegro donned a long black burka over her clothes. The traditional full-length garment covered her from head to foot. A small oval cut around her eyes was covered by a thin mesh netting, reducing her clarity of vision. But it was necessary to blend in. She had her Walther and was wired up. Her tiny earpiece transmitter would allow everything she heard and said to be heard by both the MIS and EOO command centers. Domino wore a burka too, only in blue. She was also wired so that she and Allegro could communicate with each other if necessary. She was instructed to follow from a far distance and move in only if instructed to. They couldn't give the mole a reason to bolt before they got the intel they needed.

EOO Operative Lynx, a fresh-faced younger operative Allegro had seen on occasion in group ETF briefings, was waiting for them at the air field in a nondescript older sedan. Lynx's burka concealed her golden blond hair. Only her dark brown eyes could be seen; she'd torn away the mesh netting on her veil since she was driving. Beside her was a large duffel bag filled with gear, including night vision binoculars, an MSG-90 sniper rifle, and two mini Uzi submachine guns.

There were few words exchanged on the half-hour ride into Kabul. The journey provided the women with a kaleidoscope of images of the city's struggle to recover from years of war. They passed through endless neighborhoods of ruined stone and mud-brick buildings, riddled with bullet holes and littered with abandoned wrecks of cars, where children searched through trash, and beggars swarmed the car.

As they neared the city center, they began to see signs of recovery in new hotels and shops, and construction crews at work laying pipe and smoothing pavement. Merchants lined the sides of the road in carts and canvas tents, selling overripe bananas and giant flatbreads, brass and silver bracelets, beaded lapis lazuli necklaces, and embroidered robes and hats. The wind covered everything with a fine dust of sand from the surrounding desert, muting any vivid colors with a patina of ochre.

Domino exited a block from the address Pierce had given them to cover the remaining distance on foot. Allegro got out at the contact point and waited with the white envelope in her hand. Two minutes went by before a man approached her. Fifty or so, dressed in a black wool chapan and beret-like Pakol hat, he had a white beard and green eyes, which stood out as bright beacons against his dark skin. He spoke in Farsi. "Are you waiting for someone?"

"My brother," Allegro replied. "He is coming to take me to my uncle's." Her fluency was so perfect she could have passed for a local.

"My name is Fouad," he said.

"I am Sayeh," she replied.

Very discreetly, he slipped a cell phone into the pocket of her burka. "He will call you in five minutes," he said, and took off in the direction he'd come from, blending quickly into the crowd on the street.

Exactly five minutes later, the cell phone rang. "Is this Sayeh?" the caller, a man, asked.

"Yes."

"This is your uncle. You are to meet me inside the entrance of a deserted building on Jadayi Suhl." He read off the address. "It will take you fifteen minutes to walk," he added before disconnecting.

Allegro walked to the meeting place, a two-story former office complex, and waited inside. The building had lost part of its front wall to a bomb, and the interior and exterior both were pitted with bullet holes. She turned when she heard someone approach her from behind. The mole had been waiting in a room further inside the building. He wore a turban and high quality chapan with intricate embroidery. He'd covered his face with a scarf, so only his dark brown eyes—a hint of an Asian tilt to them—and the curve of an angular nose could be seen. "Sayeh?"

"Hello, uncle," she said. "Please confirm the name of your alliance."

"Major Norton." He provided the name of the MIS man he'd been feeding information to. "Show it to me, please. And keep in mind that I am not alone here."

"Of course," she replied. "I am only here to deliver and pass on what you give me. Please remember that I also am here with company and Major Norton will not take kindly to any type of misinformation."

"I assure you, I am no terrorist," the mole said. "These extremists have plagued and disgraced our country for too many years. I will be happy to see them stopped."

Allegro removed the diamond from her pocket, unwrapped it from the napkin, and held it up. The afternoon sunlight streaming in through the broken window nearby glinted off the gem, radiating sparks of white fire onto the pitted walls of the room. "Beautiful, isn't it?"

"Indeed," he replied, staring at the Blue Star as though in a trance. "And soon it will be where it belongs."

"But before that, I need the information," she said. "Please hurry."

He returned his attention to her. "They intend to launch missiles at nineteen-hundred hours. European targets. One to the center of London, the other to Rome."

"Where are they operating from?"

"There is an underground base in Naghrak, on the outskirts of Jalalabad," he said, before giving her specifics on how to find it.

"What kind of missiles?"

"Russian. RT-2UTTKh Topol-M," he said matter-of-factly.

Allegro's training included a familiarity with nearly every type of nuclear device. She knew the Russian missiles had a range of nearly seven thousand miles and could be modified to carry up to six warheads.

She could hear a commotion in her earpiece as the information she was getting was passed along and acted on. Almost immediately, a voice in her ear said, "Codes, we need codes."

"The deactivation codes?" she asked the mole.

"I'm sorry," he said. "I cannot help you with that. I am not privileged to that information."

"Who is?"

"Very few, and only those directly involved in this mission." He was the picture of calm, as if he was reciting the weather forecast.

"Names, please." She could hear in her own voice that her patience was wearing thin. His seeming indifference to the whole matter was getting on her nerves.

"I do not know them all. But I know for a fact that Culture Minister Qadir is one of those behind the plan."

"Where is he now?"

"At his home. He will wait there and go on with his day as planned. He will be informed about the mission after the missiles have been launched, and then feign surprise while an extremist group takes responsibility for it."

"Let him go," a voice in her ear ordered. "We have what we need."

Allegro handed the mole the cell phone she'd been given, and then the Blue Star, once again wrapped in the napkin she'd taken from Wolff's house. "You can return this to your country now."

"Thank you. And thank Major Norton for me."

"I will. I'm sure he went to great lengths to get this for you." It was what a simple messenger would have responded, but Allegro almost had to force herself to say the words. It was thanks to her and the EOO that this had been made possible.

She left the building and walked out into the street. Pierce's voice in her ear instructed, "Allegro, Domino. You are to visit Qadir for the codes. The MIS is on its way to Jalalabad as we speak. We need the codes ASAP."

Domino spoke first. "To gain access to the computer in the bunker and deactivate the missiles, we'll need him alive."

"I don't care if we need retinal or print recognition to access it. Rip his fucking eyes or hand off if you have to," Pierce commanded. "Understood?"

"Yes," Domino answered.

"Check," Allegro said.

The EOO Chief relayed Qadir's address on the outskirts of the city, and said Lynx would pick them up when they were ready to leave for Naghrak. "Rome and London are on red alert and are being evacuated," he told them. "And we're ready to deploy intercept missiles if necessary. The Brits will try to down theirs over the North Sea, and U.S. carriers and bases in Europe will track the Rome missile and try to get it somewhere over the Mediterranean."

Allegro and Domino met up a bit further down the street and stopped a taxi to take them to the minister's residence. They got out a block before to briefly recon the area, its security, and entrance and exit points. Passersby paid them little notice as they approached Qadir's house and stood across the street. From all appearances, they were just two local women making small talk.

Qadir lived in a residence befitting his status, a large and handsome two-story yellow-brick domed structure, with ornate iron trim and marble columns.

"I'm going in through the balcony," Allegro said, as they watched a woman—either Qadir's wife or cleaning woman—hang a small Persian carpet out to air, then walk away toward the main thoroughfare. "Wait here on the bench until I'm in."

She crossed the street, ran a few steps, and jumped to grab the bottom railing of the balcony. As soon as she'd pulled herself up and over, she heard Domino in her ear, "All is clear."

Allegro hid behind the wall until she was sure the room was empty. She entered and quietly walked across to open the door. She heard children's voices coming from upstairs. "Meet me at the front door," she told Domino.

She hurried down a short flight of stairs and let Domino in. "Kids are upstairs," she said. "I haven't seen anyone else yet. Follow me."

They hurried to the bedroom where the children's voices were coming from. Two little girls, probably five and six or so, were playing on a fine old carpet as large as the room. Embroidered pillows and several dolls lay scattered around them.

Allegro pulled her veil away and smiled. "Hello," she said in Farsi. The girls stared up at them, too surprised to respond. They both had long black hair and dark eyes. "What a beautiful doll," she told the older of the two, as she knelt beside her, still smiling. "Can we join you?"

"Who are you?" the girl asked.

"Friends of your father. He sent us to say hello."

"You can have this one," the younger girl said, placing her doll in Allegro's hand. "Her name is Samara."

"We'd love to play, but let's go tell your daddy first that we'll be up here." Allegro held her hand out as both girls stood. She took the older girl's, and Domino the other's.

"Daddy's downstairs in his office," the younger one said.

"Yes, that's where we left him," Allegro agreed.

The girls pulled the two of them down the stairs, giggling and talking about what games they could all play together. Allegro drew her gun but kept it hidden between the folds of her burka. She knew Domino had done the same.

The door to Qadir's office was shut. When they got to it, the eldest girl knocked on it with a tiny fist. "Daddy, it's us."

"I'm busy now," said a man's voice patiently from inside, as Allegro stooped to scoop up one child into her free arm, and Domino did the same with the other.

"But your friends are here."

Allegro didn't wait for the girl to finish. She opened the door and both she and Domino walked in, each with a child and guns drawn.

Qadir, seated behind his desk, glared at them. "What is this?" he asked in Farsi.

"What, you don't like our fashion sense?" Allegro replied in English. "I think these sacks are pretty fetching."

"This is the deal," Domino said. "You give us what we need to access the computer and deactivate the missiles and we give you your daughters back...alive."

Qadir got to his feet. "I don't know anything about missiles."

"Now is not the time to go into denial, prick." The child in her arms started fidgeting, and Allegro tightened her hold.

Qadir smiled. "Such a decline. A country that has its women fighting a man's war when they should be at home with their children. They must be desperate."

"Not as desperate as you're about to get. Now, unless you want me to put one right here," she pointed her gun at the girl's head, "like I did with your guy in Amsterdam, I suggest you stop stalling and give me what I want."

The smile froze on Qadir's face as the girl started to cry. "Daddy, help."

"Get that away from her!" he shouted.

"Qadir, what's going on?" a female voice behind them called out, and a few seconds later, a young woman walked in. She wore no veil, so Allegro knew it was the minister's wife.

Domino was closest to the door. She had her gun pointed at the woman's head the moment she walked in. The woman screamed. "Go and sit in the chair," Domino ordered, gesturing with her gun to the chair nearest Qadir.

The woman complied, her eyes wide with fright as she took in the scene before her. Both children were crying. "Qadir, what's going on?"

"Stay out of this," he said.

"Your husband is responsible for funding and helping al-Qaeda plan a terrorist attack against Europe. We are here to stop him," Domino told her.

"What is she talking about?" the woman asked.

"Nothing. She doesn't know what she's saying."

"Thousands, maybe millions of innocent people are going to die in a few hours, and he's responsible for it," Allegro told her. "Do you understand me? Innocent children are going to die because of him."

"My children are innocent, too," the woman pleaded. "Why are you pointing guns at them?"

"If we have to sacrifice two children to save millions, we will," Domino bluffed.

The woman looked up at her husband. "Stop them, Qadir. Is it true, what she says?"

"Yes, it's true. We've been monitoring and listening in on his conversations for weeks," Allegro bluffed. The mole was too important to the U.S. government to be implicated, and she knew that by saying they had evidence against Qadir, it should scare him into thinking that not only was his career over, but his life was on the line as well.

The woman stared at her husband like she was seeing him for the first time. "What have you done? Why would you do this to us, Qadir? And to your country? Haven't we suffered enough?"

"We're running out of time. Either you tell us how to stop the missiles or you get to sit there and watch us kill your family in the name of whatever you think justifies your cause. What's it going to be?" Allegro pulled hard on the girl's hair, making her squeal.

"Stop. Please, stop," Qadir's wife pleaded. "In the name of Allah, give them what they want."

"I am a dead man if I do," Qadir said. "They will kill me if they find out I betrayed the cause."

"You're a dead man either way," Allegro told him. "If they don't kill you, your government will."

"So why should I tell you anything?"

"For our children!" his wife screamed, furious. "They are going to kill our girls unless you talk."

"Your destiny was out of your hands the moment you decided to work with these animals, and there is nothing that can change that." Allegro pointedly looked from one child to the other. "But their destiny is still in your hands. Let them remember you as a father who made a big mistake but the right decision. The decision that saved countless lives."

"Do it, Qadir. Do it for them," his wife begged, tears streaming down her face.

The eldest girl, the spitting image of her father, was following the scene with rapt attention. Allegro could tell that though she understood little of what was going on, she could sense the danger, her mother's distress, and that her father was doing nothing to stop it. "Daddy, why won't you help us?"

Qadir looked at the girl, and then at his other daughter, still crying, and then at his wife. He dropped into his chair and buried his face in his hands. "726272 237426," he said wearily.

Allegro repeated the numbers out loud to make sure that Monty picked everything up from her earpiece.

"Lynx and Nighthawk are in position," Pierce told her.

"How do we access the computer?" Allegro asked Qadir.

"My fingerprints."

"You know what that means," she said.

Qadir wordlessly pulled up his sleeve and stretched out his hand on the desk.

"You're not getting off that easy," she told him. "Get up, you're coming with us." As he stood, Allegro spoke into her earpiece. "Nighthawk, join us."

A minute later, Nighthawk was standing next to them.

"My friend here will stay with your family and wait for my call," Allegro said. "What he does with them depends on how accurate the numbers and your prints are."

❖

Lynx was waiting for them outside in the sedan. Allegro pushed Qadir into the backseat, between her and Domino.

"The MIS is halfway to Naghrak," Pierce told the ops in their earpieces. "Go back to the airport. We're going to helicopter you in. We have less than four hours to countdown."

"Blade and Cameo are being flown to Naghrak as well," Lynx informed them as she headed toward the airport. "They may get there ahead of us."

"I was betrayed, wasn't I?" Qadir asked.

Allegro turned to look at him. "What are you talking about?"

"Naghrak was the location we used in case someone leaked information about the mission to an outsider," he said. "We have many people on our side, but very few can be trusted. For this reason, only the leaders know the actual location. The rest are just soldiers, most of them dedicated, but sometimes one gets an offer or threat and talks. The actual location of the missiles is revealed to the soldiers last minute."

There was a long silence in the sedan as the ops stared at Qadir in disbelief. The only sound Allegro heard was Pierce's curse in her earpiece, then his shout to someone to get Major Norton on the phone.

"The SS-27 Topol can also be deployed with a mobile launcher," Allegro said, almost to herself. Then to the other ops, "The missiles are somewhere on trucks. They can launch them from anywhere. There is no base." Allegro pressed the gun hard against Qadir's temple.

"Where are they?"

"I don't know," he said.

"Nighthawk, come in," she said loudly into her earpiece while she stared at Qadir. "Start with the youngest."

"I swear I don't know. They are scheduled to arrive in Mir Bacheh Kowt within the hour for preparation," he said.

"Where are they operating it from?" she asked next.

"A big truck. It will be following behind the missile," Qadir told her. "The equipment is on there."

"Who's operating it?"

"One of the leaders."

"The other missile?"

"Charikar," he said.

"God damn it," Pierce said into her earpiece. "The MIS is hours away from there now. They'll never make it there in time."

"How far are these places from here?" Domino asked.

"Mir Bacheh Kowt is forty-five minutes or so north of Kabul," Pierce answered before Qadir had a chance to. "Chariker is another twenty miles farther, on the same road. The MIS is going to turn around, but it'll take a while before they get to you."

Night fell as the sedan sped along the desert road to the first village as fast as Lynx could manage without losing control. They all braced themselves against the holes and gaps in the road, devastated from decades of war. At the speed they were traveling, stirring up the desert dust, they couldn't see the bone-jarring potholes in their headlights until they were almost on top of them.

They neared the outskirts of Mir Bacheh Kowt with less than two hours to go before the launch. From a distance, the village appeared to be a virtual ghost town. The Taliban had burned down ninety-eight percent of the homes and poisoned the wells, and al-Qaeda had moved in later, to use the ruins as a terrorist training ground.

Lynx cut the headlights and slowed as they entered the village. There was no sign of the trucks.

"Where are they supposed to be?" Allegro asked Qadir.

"Just off this road, a little farther. There's desert on one side, and huts on the other," he said.

"Take this street," Allegro told Lynx, pointing to a road ahead that led upward to a hilltop that overlooked the area. Lynx parked as close to the crest as she could without their vehicle being seen from below. The three women shed their burkas, and Allegro and Domino got out. Allegro had her pistol and one of the Uzis, Domino the sniper rifle and a pair of night vision binoculars. Lynx remained in the car, her gun trained on Qadir.

They'd chosen a good vantage point, and gotten there without much time to spare. A few minutes later, they spotted the two trucks coming toward them on the road below. The mobile launch vehicle, in front, was massive, some seventy-five feet long. Its missile was concealed beneath a tarp. The operations truck, a military troop carrier with a canvas canopy over the bed, followed close behind.

The vehicles pulled off and stopped at the bottom of the hill. They had a clear view of both trucks. Domino scanned them through the binoculars as the men inside got out and stretched their legs. "Two men from the launcher, and nine from the truck."

"Domino, Lynx, stay here," Allegro told them. "On my mark, take as many out from here as possible. Lynx, I'll contact you when I'm ready for him. Bring him to me."

"You got it," Lynx replied.

"Be careful," Domino added.

"I will. I promised someone I'd call them soon." Allegro ran quietly down the hill, using the ruins of the village as cover, careful of her footing in the dark.

Once at the bottom, she got as close to the trucks as possible, taking up a position behind a half-burned hut. One of the men walked straight in her direction. She stayed very still and he finally stopped to empty his bladder a short distance from where she was hiding. She aimed straight for his head with her silencer. When he went down, she hurried over to drag him into the hut. She stripped him of his robe and scarf and put them on, covering her face. "I'm moving in."

"The driver of the launcher is sitting alone in the truck," Domino informed her.

She approached the truck casually, opened the door of the passenger seat, and got in. The driver was about to say something to her when Allegro shot him in the head. "Two down."

"Nine to go," Domino said in her ear. "There's one alone on the right of the truck."

Allegro got out and quietly walked up to him. He was bent over, checking something on the vehicle. She shot him in the heart from the back, and he collapsed. She couldn't leave the body there, the others would see it. She heard someone approaching in the dark, and hurriedly shoved the dead man under the truck.

"Where is Mustafa?" the newcomer asked.

"I don't know," she answered in his language, keeping her voice low.

"Here, take this." He held something out to her, but she couldn't make out what it was in the dim light from the truck. She reached out for it, but the man stopped abruptly as he was about to give it to her, and seized her hand in his. "Blood. You have blood on your hands." He looked closer at her, and when he saw she was a stranger, he pulled out his gun.

Allegro moved faster, and shot him first, but he'd gotten off a shot as well, and the sound of it echoed through the desert. All was still again for a few seconds, then she heard people running toward her. "Domino, *now!*"

Bullets started to fly in the dark. She saw another man go down, but most had taken cover from the hill where Domino was positioned.

"I'm coming in," Domino relayed. "I can't see them from here."

Six were left and it sounded as though all of them were shooting. Men had started to move around the back of the truck from both sides, coming toward her. Allegro ran forward to the nearest hut to take cover, threw down her gun, and ripped off the robe to grab the Uzi that hung around her shoulder. She opened fire the moment one came around the corner of the truck and took him down. The others with him scattered, most bolting up the hill where the shots were coming from. Bullets flew from all sides now.

"Another one down," she heard Domino say. That left four. Just then, an explosion shook the earth and lit up the sky on the hilltop where they'd parked their car.

She stared up at the ball of fire and felt her heart constrict in her chest. "Lynx! Are you okay?"

"I'm in one of the huts," Lynx replied. "I have Qadir with me, but they blew up the car. Grenade launcher."

"Stay where you are," Allegro told her. More shots rang out in the dark.

"One more down," Domino reported.

"Three left." The words were barely out of Allegro's mouth before she heard a twig snap behind her. Automatically, she turned and fired a rapid burst with the Uzi. One of the terrorists stumbled forward out of the darkness, clutching his chest, and collapsed a yard from her.

"Two left, and that was a close one," she said.

"Make that one." Domino had gotten another. They waited where they were five more minutes, all of them silent.

"We don't have time to fuck around trying to find the last one," Allegro said. "I don't hear anything. He probably took off."

"I don't hear anything either," Domino reported.

"All clear here," Lynx confirmed.

Allegro stepped out from behind the hut. "Lynx, bring him out."

Lynx came into view, one hand dragging a tied and gagged Qadir, the other holding an Uzi. Domino emerged from the darkness to the right of her, covering her back with the rifle. Allegro moved to the front, covering them from there.

Domino glanced at her watch. "We have a little over an hour left."

"Let's go." Allegro led them to the operations truck and cautiously opened the back to make sure it was empty.

Lynx cut Qadir's bindings and Allegro grabbed him by the arm and hauled him roughly up into the truck. The other two ops stayed outside to make sure there were no surprises. Keeping her gun on him, she shoved the minister into a chair and fired up the computer. When the screen asked ENTER ID, she pushed the chair forward until Qadir was in front of it. "Do it."

He placed his palm on a plate next to the computer and accessed the missile control program. The screen read: TARGET: ROME. 59 MINUTES TO LAUNCH, and asked for a password to access the deactivation control. She didn't wait for him to start typing. She pulled the chair away and looked at him.

"Remember, their destiny is in your hands." Allegro said, a final reference to his family in case he had lied to her. He didn't blink.

She punched in the numbers he'd given her, and bright red letters flickered on the screen. DEACTIVATE MISSILE? She confirmed by hitting the Enter key, and the program asked for the password again. She typed in the numbers a second time. MISSILE DEACTIVATED. TERMINATE OPERATION? the screen read.

"I'm gonna go with yes," she said, and pressed the Enter key.

"Mission accomplished here," she told Pierce in her earpiece. "Missile one deactivated, crew dead."

"Roger that," Pierce replied. "I'll divert all MIS to second location except for a crew to pick you up."

Minutes later, the sound of an approaching plane broke the silence.

"Stay where you are," she heard Domino say. "I can't see if it's MIS." Thirty seconds passed before Domino reported, "A small MIS cargo plane."

Allegro hauled Qadir to his feet and took him outside, and the four of them took cover behind the truck.

"We still have time. We can make it." Lynx had to nearly shout to be heard over the roar of the small plane as it touched down on a flat bit of packed sand at the edge of the village.

Eight MIS soldiers emerged from the plane, all but one quickly taking up positions around the two trucks. The other remained by the plane, and they ran toward him. "Well done," he said. He had lieutenant's bars on the collar of his fatigues. "All of you get in. We need to get him," he gestured toward Qadir, "to Charikar for the other missile."

Lynx pushed Qadir forward. They were a few steps from entering the cargo plane when a shot rang out and Qadir dropped to the ground. They all took cover as a voice nearby screamed "Traitor!" in Farsi, and then all was silent again.

"Come on," the lieutenant said, "We have to go."

"Probably the one that got away," Domino said.

"We need him," Allegro said, looking down at Qadir's body. "But not all of him. Lynx?"

Without hesitation, Lynx pulled out her heavy combat knife and with one swift movement chopped off Qadir's hand at the wrist. Then she sliced a piece of material from Qadir's robe to wrap around it. She gave the gruesome package to Allegro and turned to the MIS officer. "Now we can go."

CHAPTER TWENTY-SIX

Amsterdam

In a private room at the Academisch Medisch Centrum hospital, Kris gently stroked her uncle's hand, comforted by the steady beeping of the machines tracking his heartbeat and breathing. He'd come to, briefly, when they'd brought him back from the operating room, but was so heavily sedated he'd immediately drifted off again. Hans Hofman's face was so swollen and covered with bandages he was nearly unrecognizable, and his left arm and right wrist wore casts from broken bones. He'd also been bleeding internally, but the surgery had been a success and the doctors said he would fully recover.

"I'm so sorry, Uncle," she whispered. "I never meant for this to happen to you."

The guilt she felt, however, took a backseat to worry, both for him and for Misha. Where was she now? It was torture not knowing. She prayed for God to protect the woman she'd come to love with all her heart. *Just be all right. Even if I never see you again. Just be all right.*

The television was on, playing an old film, the volume turned low. A blare of noise from it drew her eyes to the screen. A news bulletin, interrupting the regular broadcast.

"Millions are fleeing London and Rome in a panic at this hour," the commentator announced soberly. "Mass evacuations have been ordered because of a confirmed imminent terrorist attack, involving nuclear missiles." Live video popped up on the screen, showing massive road jams from both locations. "U.S. officials in Washington alerted British and Italian authorities to the threat, and said efforts are underway to disarm the missiles, or intercept them if they are successfully launched."

Kris stared at the screen in shock as the report continued. *My God. It's all true. Oh, Misha.*

❖

Near Charikar, Afghanistan

The MIS lieutenant informed them that their men were already in position in Charikar, and they would land as close as possible to the missile launcher to get Qadir's hand delivered. Blood was seeping through the robe material, so Allegro had placed the hand beside her on the bench seat. The plane was above the location in twenty minutes, flying low. She looked down. This village had also been hit hard by the war and was mostly black from above, but here and there were cooking fires and other lights where residents had returned to rebuild. The mobile launch vehicle and operations truck had parked in the desert, outside the northern edge of the city. All around them were flashes of light, and several small vehicles were on fire.

"It looks like a damn war zone down there," Allegro said. The MIS troops and terrorists were shooting at each other. "A lot more Afghans. Somehow they must have realized we got to the other missile and called in reinforcements here."

"Jesus," the MIS officer said. "When did all this happen? Our guys just got here."

A metallic *ping* rang out as a bullet pierced the exterior of the plane not far from where Domino was sitting, and she flinched. "Shit, they're shooting at us."

"We're taking shots," the lieutenant radioed in. "We can't land like this."

Allegro stood and walked over to him. "Do you have parachutes on board?"

"Well, yeah. It's a cargo plane, but…" He went a little white as he hesitated.

"You don't have to," she said. "I will. Get me the gear."

"I have to clear this first," he said, reaching for the radio.

"We don't have time for that. We have thirty-five minutes to deactivate that huge mother of a missile before millions die. Now get me the gear."

He hurried out of his seat and walked to the back of the plane.

"I'm coming with you," Domino said, getting to her feet.

"No, you're not. I can do this alone."

"Looks like you can't go with her even if she let you," the MIS officer interrupted, holding up a parachute vest. "I only have one chute here."

Domino looked at Allegro. "We've done it before, we can do it again."

"No. I said I'm going alone."

"Take this, too," the lieutenant offered, stripping off his bomber jacket and handing it to Allegro. It was a little big, but much better protection against the cold than the one she was wearing. She took it from him with a nod of thanks and put it on, zipping the hand inside, against her chest, then strapped on the parachute.

When the man had retreated back toward the front, Domino took a couple of steps nearer until they were standing face-to-face. She spoke in a low voice, so the others couldn't overhear. "You don't have to prove anything to anyone."

"I don't have time for this conversation, Luka." Allegro finished adjusting the chute. "Besides, should anything happen to me, I need you to tell her I'm sorry and that I really do love her."

"You're good to go," the lieutenant shouted from the front, as he pressed the latch to open the rear cargo door and cold air rushed in.

"Please let me go with you," Domino pleaded.

"Promise me you'll tell her."

"I promise, you idiot."

"Later." And with that, Allegro let herself drop.

She landed smoothly at the edge of the village, a safe distance from the trucks and the shooting, and was out of the chute in seconds. Moving toward the chaos, she tried to stay out of sight, keeping low and taking cover wherever possible behind abandoned houses.

The launch truck had already lifted the missile in place to fire. Terrorist soldiers were guarding the doors to the truck and the back hatch very literally with their lives, while the rest of them were fighting the MIS. Allegro checked her watch. Fifteen minutes left. She spotted an MIS soldier nearby. He'd been hit in the leg and was lying low, shooting from that position.

She yelled in his direction. "American here. Don't shoot!"

"Who are you?" he yelled back.

"I'm with the MIS as well. Don't shoot." She couldn't say she was EOO. Very few in the government knew about them. "I'm new, they just flew me in. I have the fingerprints."

"What the hell took you so long?" he shouted.

Allegro moved to him in a crouch. The MIS had been avoiding direct fire at the operations truck for fear of hitting the computer before they could deactivate the missile, which was why there were several terrorists still around it. "Listen, I need your help to get to the truck. Do what you have to, to get everyone on this side of it away from there. Shoot all around it, use a grenade as close as you dare if you have to."

"I've got you covered," he said.

"Thanks."

"Good luck, soldier."

Allegro took off toward the truck, staying low and dodging dead bodies on both sides. She had her Uzi, with a silencer attached, but she didn't use it so the flash from it wouldn't give her position away.

The soldier did a good job at scaring away or killing any terrorist who'd been positioned on her side of the truck. When she reached it, she opened the door of the driver's side and pulled herself up until she was lying on the roof of the truck. Glancing at her watch, she saw she had just seven minutes left. She heard someone at the driver's door, but before he could get her, a shot took him out, probably fired by the soldier covering her. Allegro removed the knife that was strapped to her calf under her trousers and quickly slashed a long slit in the tarp on the roof of the truck bed. The shooting around her was deafening.

Uzi at the ready in her hands, she stood and jumped onto the slit. The momentum and her body weight tore her through it, and she started shooting even before she landed, aiming high so she wouldn't hit the computer. Two men were inside, a terrorist soldier and the leader who'd been positioned at the computer. She hit both with her burst of fire on her way down, killing them instantly. The terrorist leader, she saw, would likely have escaped injury even if the MIS had fired on the truck.

He'd been shielded from the back by his suicidal soldiers, and on two sides by thick metal panels that reached the canvas roof. She'd come in from just the right angle. He'd evidently thought the thick metal behind the driver would be ample protection.

Allegro ran to the laptop and removed Qadir's hand from her jacket, unwrapped it, and placed it on the optical plate next to the computer. It registered the handprint, and brought up a screen that read TARGET: LONDON. 4 MINUTES TO LAUNCH and asked for the password, as expected. She entered the numbers, got the DEACTIVATE MISSILE? screen, and hit the Enter key to affirm. Then she typed in the code a second time when prompted to, and waited for the last screen, the confirmation to abort the operation. It was no go without confirmation.

Someone shouted something in Farsi, and the flaps at the back of the truck flew open. She wheeled around and fired a burst from her Uzi, hitting three surprised terrorists. They went down, but so did she.

Allegro saw the blood a millisecond before the pain in her chest and leg registered. It overwhelmed her, leaving her gasping for breath, dizzy and disoriented. She struggled to her knees, clenching her teeth to try to block out the unbearable agony.

As if in slow motion, she turned to face the monitor. MISSILE DEACTIVATED. TERMINATE OPERATION? was blinking. She stared at it hazily, trying to focus, but her consciousness was fading fast. She grabbed at the table to stay upright. The screen changed. 5 SECONDS TO CONFIRM TERMINATION. 3 SECONDS TO CONFIRM TERMINATION. "I'm gonna go with yes," she said to herself as she gathered the last of her strength and punched the Enter key.

She smiled before she let herself collapse.

❖

"She did it?" The tone in the copilot's voice was that of disbelief as he waited for the answer. "Well, I'll be damned." There was a short pause as he listened, "Roger that." Without turning to look at Domino and Lynx, he said, "She deactivated the missile on time. The Afghans have started to disperse and are running for the mountains. She really did it."

"Is she okay?" Domino bent close to his ear as she gripped the side of his seat. When the copilot didn't answer, she placed her hand firmly on his shoulder. Because his back was turned to her she couldn't read his expression. "Is she okay?" she repeated, louder.

"That's a negative," he replied. "She's been shot. I'm sorry."

"Is she alive?" Her voice shook.

"I don't know. But it didn't sound like it."

She turned toward the pilot. "Get us down there right now," she ordered.

"I have orders to return to the air base," he argued.

"Listen," Lynx said from behind Domino, "I don't give a damn what your orders are. If there's any chance at all that she's alive, we're going to get her."

"Dead *or* alive, I'm not leaving her behind. Just get us the fuck down there." Domino wiped away a sudden rush of tears.

"I need to clear permission for landing," the pilot said.

Domino put her face near his. "Then what the hell are you waiting for? Tell them we're going down *now*."

The pilot turned to his copilot. "They're right. She's a goddamn hero." With that, he radioed in that they were returning to the site for a recover landing.

CHAPTER TWENTY-SEVEN

Amsterdam
Two months later

"Still nothing?" Hans Hofman inquired gently.

"No," Kris answered. They were seated beside each other on the couch in Hans's living room, looking out over the canal. "I still run to the door when I hear the postman. And hold my breath every time I see there's a message on the answering machine. But there's been nothing at all. Only that one brief call from Luka that Misha was safe and would contact me when it was possible. She couldn't tell me any more."

"There was no mention at all of this group you say she was with, in the newscasts after all this happened," Hans said. "They said it was the U.S. Military Intelligence Service that stopped the attack. Perhaps she wasn't there at all."

"They wouldn't have said anything about her organization," Kris replied. "It was an undercover type of thing, very secretive. I doubt they'd allow any publicity about it."

Hans put his arm around her. They'd finally taken his casts off two days earlier. "You mustn't give up hope, Kris."

She put her head on his shoulder, and they stared out at the passing boats for several minutes.

"How's your mother?" he asked.

"Better. She's opening up to her therapist, and to me. We've talked about the things in Father's diary. Thank you for giving it to me. It helped me to understand why she is the way she is. She had a lot to deal with."

"Your father was a complicated man," Hans agreed. "And the estate?"

"The renovations are done and it will go on the market next week," Kris said. "The agent says it should get the asking price, which will settle the rest of the debts Father owed and allow for Mother's care for several more months." She turned to look at her uncle. "I'm all packed up. I appreciate your letting me stay here until I can look for a place of my own."

"I should thank you. For being here with me during those first days out of the hospital. I couldn't have managed so well by myself."

"Of course, Uncle."

"I've been thinking," he mused aloud. "A change of scenery would do us both good. What do you say about taking this old man to Venice?"

Venice. Tears came from nowhere. Immediately she thought of the last night of Carnival. She could almost feel Misha's kisses. *Oh, Misha.* It would be a bittersweet return to the city she loved, without Misha there, and without the home she'd loved so dearly, but it might help give her some sense of closure.

"Perhaps you're right," she agreed. "It may be just what I need."

❖

Venice, Italy

Her uncle seemed in a glorious mood as they approached the city by boat, but Kris fought a rising tide of melancholy. The day was warm, the sky a bright blue, and it didn't help that it would soon be dusk, her favorite time of day in Venice.

"Why don't we pass by the villa first?" Hans suggested as they stared out over the rail.

"What for?"

"Call it curiosity," he said. "I would like to see what they've changed."

Kris cringed. "I don't know if I'm ready for that."

"I understand, but please humor me."

"Whatever you like."

Kris sighed. Though her heart longed for a look at her beloved former home, she also dreaded seeing the villa again, with new owners. The fact that they might have made changes, that it might look different, felt like an intrusion on her past and memories. But her uncle insisted, and coming here had been his idea, after all. Something he needed. Maybe it *was* better to go there first and get it over with. Then she could take him to her favorite restaurant around the corner and console herself with one of its excellent pasta dishes and a good bottle of wine.

They strolled arm in arm from the dock, walking slowly, enjoying the view along the way. A gondolier waved at them, and she waved back, but kept her focus on the canal until they got directly in front of the villa. Even then she had to force herself to look. It hadn't changed. Not one bit.

Hans went to the front door and knocked.

"What are you doing?" Kris asked.

"I'd like to see inside, wouldn't you?"

Not really, no. But she could see his enthusiasm, so she nodded. To her relief, there was no answer, but Hans wasn't ready to depart. He tried the door, and it opened. He peeked inside.

"We can't just go in there," she protested.

"But it's empty." He opened the door fully so she could see, and indeed, there was not a stick of furniture or anything else within.

She followed him into the villa, puzzled. "I thought the new owners would have moved in long before now."

They heard a noise from upstairs.

"Is anyone here?" Kris called out.

"Sì," came the reply. A woman's voice. Familiar? "Up here."

Hans smiled at her. "Why don't you go take a look?"

Kris raced up the stairs, her heart pounding. *It can't be.*

But it was.

Misha was standing on the balcony, smiling that wonderfully cocky smile of hers. Behind her, the sun was just setting, casting an orange hue on the water below. She had a cane, and there were dark circles under her soft caramel eyes, but she was the most beautiful sight Kris had ever seen.

"Misha! What are you doing here?"

"Waiting for you."

Kris ran into her lover's outstretched arms and they embraced, holding tight to each other for a very long moment. Misha's heart was pounding; Kris could feel it against her chest, as fast and strong as her own. She pulled back just enough to look at her. "I don't understand. I thought I'd never see you again. When two months went by, and you never called, I assumed the worst but didn't know who to call."

Misha gently put a finger against her mouth to stop her. "I'm here now. And I'm alive and kicking. That's all that matters. I needed to let myself heal before you saw me."

"Was it bad?"

"It's over now."

Kris glanced at the cane. "Are you all healed?"

"For the most part." Misha took her hand and placed against her chest, over her heart. She covered Kris's hand with her own. "But I'm going to need you to help me heal here."

Kris brought Misha's hand to her mouth and kissed it. "I want that, too."

"So…you're okay with everything?" Misha asked softly. "With who I am? What I do?"

"What you do is not who you are." She caressed Misha's cheek with her hand. "Luka helped me see that."

"It would appear that Luka helped us both see a lot. Maybe we should invite her over to dinner."

Kris frowned. "The mansion has been sold, Misha."

"That's why we're going to invite her and Hayley here." With a mischievous grin, Misha took a small ring of keys from her pocket and placed them in Kris's hand. "You love this place so much, I thought you could stay here."

Stay here? She couldn't believe what she was hearing. "What are you saying?"

"I bought it back from the new owners. It's yours again."

Kris's heart, already overflowing with the joy of their reunion, seemed to burst wide open. Tears of happiness streamed down her face as she leapt into Misha's arms and kissed her. "It's *ours*?"

"*Ours*," Misha repeated softly. "Really?"

"Really."

They kissed again, long and fiercely. And then Misha's mouth left hers, and descended to her neck. *"Sei così bella,"* she whispered, between kisses. *"Sei così bella."*

EPILOGUE

Colorado
Six months later, October

"Yeah, I got here just fine," Misha told Kris in her Bluetooth as she steered her rental Jaguar up the steep, isolated mountain road that led to the EOO headquarters.

"Oh, good. I miss you already. I don't know how I'm going to get to sleep without you."

Misha had wondered the same on the long flight over. She pictured Kris stretched out naked on their antique Italian Renaissance bed, draped in the burgundy silk sheets and plush down comforter she'd climbed out of that morning with great reluctance. The doors to the balcony would be slightly ajar. Kris liked the fresh air, even when it was cold, and Misha couldn't help but indulge her. At eleven p.m. there would be frequent snatches of conversations drifting in on the breeze from the tourists passing by below. And music, from the boats cruising along on this starlit autumn night.

"I think you'll have a lot more success sleeping without me there. We don't seem to get a lot of sleep when we're in the same bed."

"Are you complaining? We can try separate bedrooms," Kris said playfully.

"I don't care if I have to staple my eyelids to my forehead to stay awake. We are not going to screw around with the sleeping arrangements."

Kris laughed, then made an appreciative purring sound. "Staples? You turn me on when you get all tough. I like that bad and dangerous girl image of yours, by the way."

"Then why don't you lie back in that big bed, close your eyes and touch yourself, and imagine this bad, dangerous woman's mouth on you."

"Hmm," Kris murmured. "I like the sound of that."

Misha knew exactly what was happening when Kris's voice got all velvety like that. "Are you already touching yourself?"

"Yup."

"Aw, *man*." The images that flooded her mind stirred up a lovely hum of arousal between her legs. "Okay, I'm going to hang up before I make a U-turn for the airport and the boss man puts a price on my head."

Kris moaned provocatively. "Spoilsport."

"Tease."

"Love you."

Misha had heard the words often in the past six blissful months with Kris, but each time still felt wonderfully new. Like they'd both been storing up the declaration for years and wanted to relish each occasion when it was finally spoken. "I love you, too."

Their first two months together had been spent in London, while the villa was brought back to its former furnished glory and as she continued to recuperate. Then in July, they returned to Venice, to host Luka and Hayley for a month. They'd had a wonderfully memorable time simply relaxing, taking walks and boat rides, and spending the evenings in front of the fireplace in each other's arms. Mishael and Luka had stolen moments to talk about assignments of the past and probable future ones. And Kris and Hayley had exchanged their thoughts and feelings about how it was to share their lives with far from ordinary women.

Allegro gripped the steering wheel harder as the high, razor-topped fence surrounding the sixty-three acre EOO campus came into view. The compound had been home to her for nearly half her life, but she'd never known the real meaning of *home* until she'd met Kris. She parked the Jaguar outside the administration building, a massive neo-Gothic structure with bell towers like those of medieval cathedrals, and got out. She hadn't taken two steps before another car pulled up a row away and Luka emerged.

They walked toward each other. It had been three months since Luka and Hayley bade farewell to what they called their "Venice honeymoon." During that time, Luka hadn't changed at all, but Misha had finally gotten rid of her cane.

"I'm happy to see you all healed," Luka said, smiling. "So how is life in the not-so-fast lane?"

"Now I know you're not referring to cars." Misha smiled back.

"Very perceptive."

They started toward the main entrance. "I never thought I'd hear myself say this, but she's taken away any need to be in a fast lane, period. I'm so happy it's ridiculous."

"She's an amazing woman, Misha. Hayley thinks so as well. She keeps talking about what a pity it is that you guys are so far away, in Europe."

"Things could change," Misha said. "I mean, who knows where you or I will end up? Puppets on a string, remember?"

"How is it living between London and Venice?" Luka asked. "Is Kris adjusting?"

"She feels the same way I do. It doesn't matter where we live, as long as we can be together."

"You old softie," Luka said, punching her on the shoulder.

"Look who's talking." Misha laughed.

They put their coded ID badges into the security panel and the front door opened to admit them.

"So what do you think today is about?" Luka asked.

"Couldn't tell you, but Monty sounded pretty severe."

Luka glanced in the direction of three other ETFs who were just getting on the elevator across the wide entryway. "It must be if he wants so many of us here."

"You'd think he'd mellow out what with all the action Joanne's giving him."

Luka laughed. "Did wonders for you."

"You have no idea. It's like we can't stop." Misha knew she was grinning like a madwoman, but she couldn't help it. She punched the elevator button.

"I know what you mean," Luka replied as the doors opened. They used their IDs again to access the floor containing the EOO executive offices. "Great. I'm about to stand in front of him and now I can't get the image of him and Joanne out of my head."

Misha chuckled. "Burns the retinas, doesn't it?"

"Plain scary."

"I know. It's like a car accident. You know you shouldn't look, but you do anyway."

"Dinner later?" Luka asked as they got off and stepped onto plush carpeting. "If we don't have to leave right away, that is."

"Sure."

In the large conference room next to EOO Chief Montgomery Pierce's office, the Organization's top ETFs took seats around a round mahogany table. In addition to Allegro and Domino, eight other Elite Operatives were also present, as were Joanne Grant and David Arthur, the other two members of the Governing Trio. It was a rare occasion for so many ETFs to gather and share info on one assignment. But the operation they were discussing was a complicated one, and backup operatives would likely be necessary.

Pierce started off by explaining the severity and danger of the mission, and the need to make sure the right operative got the assignment. The rest of them would be on call, to be summoned as necessary.

"Send me," Allegro volunteered when he had finished. "Let me send the sick fuck to the netherworld."

Domino rolled her eyes. "Christ, she saves the world and now she thinks she owns it." The others laughed. Then she added, more seriously, "I'm offering as well, Monty."

"Thank you ladies," Pierce said. "But I have someone else in mind. I'm sending in the one with the most fitting profile."

"What profile is that?" Allegro asked.

"Someone with less experience, but not as openly controversial as you," he answered, looking at Allegro. "And someone who is not likely to be recognized by the Asian skin traders," he added to Domino.

Placing his hand on the dossier in front of him, he slid it across the table. Everyone's gaze followed the file until it stopped in front of the agent it was intended for.

"Lynx," Pierce said. "Operation Mask is yours."

About the Authors

Kim Baldwin has been a writer for three decades, following up twenty years in network news with a second vocation penning lesbian fiction. In addition to *Thief of Always* and *Lethal Affairs*, her collaborative efforts with Xenia Alexiou, she has published five solo novels with Bold Strokes Books: the intrigue/romances *Flight Risk* and *Hunter's Pursuit*, and the romances *Force of Nature*, *Whitewater Rendezvous*, and *Focus of Desire*. Four of her books have been finalists for Golden Crown Literary Society Awards. She has also contributed short stories to five BSB anthologies: The Lambda Literary Award–winning *Erotic Interludes 2: Stolen Moments*; *Erotic Interludes 3: Lessons in Love*; IPPY and GCLS Award–winning *Erotic Interludes 4: Extreme Passions*; *Erotic Interludes 5: Road Games*, a 2008 Independent Publishers Award Gold Medalist; and *Romantic Interludes 1: Discovery*. Her eighth novel, the Alaskan adventure romance *Breaking the Ice*, will be released in August 2009. She lives in the north woods of Michigan. Her Web site is www.kimbaldwin.com and she can be reached at baldwinkim@gmail.com.

Xenia Alexiou is Greek and lives in Europe. An avid reader and knowledge junkie, she likes to travel all over the globe and take pictures of the wonderful and interesting people that represent different cultures. Trying to see the world through their eyes has been her most challenging yet rewarding pursuit so far. These travels have inspired countless stories, and it's these stories that she has recently decided to write about. *Thief of Always* is her second novel, following *Lethal Affairs*. She is currently at work on *Missing Lynx*, the third book in the Elite Operatives Series. For more information, go to her Web site at www.xeniaalexiou.com, or contact her at xeniaalexiou007@gmail.com.

Books Available From Bold Strokes Books

Sistine Heresy by Justine Saracen. Adrianna Borgia, survivor of the Borgia court, presents Michelangelo with the greatest temptations of his life while struggling with soul-threatening desires for the painter Raphaela. (978-1-60282-051-7)

Radical Encounters by Radclyffe. An out-of-bounds, outside-the-lines collection of provocative, superheated erotica by award-winning romance and erotica author Radclyffe. (978-1-60282-050-0)

Thief of Always by Kim Baldwin & Xenia Alexiou. Stealing a diamond to save the world should be easy for Elite Operative Mishael Taylor, but she didn't figure on love getting in the way. (978-1-60282-049-4)

X by JD Glass. When X-hacker Charlie Riven is framed for a crime she didn't commit, she accepts help from an unlikely source—sexy Treasury Agent Elaine Harper. (978-1-60282-048-7)

The Middle of Somewhere by Clifford Henderson. Eadie T. Pratt sets out on a road trip in search of a new life and ends up in the middle of somewhere she never expected. (978-1-60282-047-0)

Paybacks by Gabrielle Goldsby. Cameron Howard wants to avoid her old nemesis Mackenzie Brandt but their high school reunion brings up more than just memories. (978-1-60282-046-3)

Uncross My Heart by Andrews & Austin. When a radio talk show diva sets out to interview a female priest, the two women end up at odds and neither heaven nor earth is safe from their feelings. (978-1-60282-045-6)

Fireside by Cate Culpepper. Mac, a therapist, and Abby, a nurse, fall in love against the backdrop of friendship, healing, and defending one's own within the Fireside shelter. (978-1-60282-044-9)

Green Eyed Monster by Gill McKnight. Mickey Rapowski believes her former boss has cheated her out of a small fortune, so she kidnaps the girlfriend and demands compensation—just a straightforward abduction that goes so wrong when Mickey falls for her captive. (978-1-60282-042-5)

Blind Faith by Diane and Jacob Anderson-Minshall. When private investigator Yoshi Yakamota and the Blind Eye Detective Agency are hired to find a woman's missing sister, the assignment seems fairly mundane—but in the detective business, the ordinary can quickly become deadly. (978-1-60282-041-8)

A Pirate's Heart by Catherine Friend. When rare book librarian Emma Boyd searches for a long-lost treasure map, she learns the hard way that pirates still exist in today's world—some modern pirates steal maps, others steal hearts. (978-1-60282-040-1)

Trails Merge by Rachel Spangler. Parker Riley escapes the high-powered world of politics to Campbell Carson's ski resort—and their mutual attraction produces anything but smooth running. (978-1-60282-039-5)

Dreams of Bali by C.J. Harte. Madison Barnes worships work, power, and success, and she's never allowed anyone to interfere— that is, until she runs into Karlie Henderson Stockard. Aeros EBook (978-1-60282-070-8)

The Limits of Justice by John Morgan Wilson. Benjamin Justice and reporter Alexandra Templeton search for a killer in a mysterious compound in the remote California desert. (978-1-60282-060-9)

Designed for Love by Erin Dutton. Jillian Sealy and Wil Johnson don't much like each other, but they do have to work together— and what they desire most is not what either of them had planned. (978-1-60282-038-8)

Calling the Dead by Ali Vali. Six months after Hurricane Katrina, NOLA Detective Sept Savoie is a cop who thinks making a relationship work is harder than catching a serial killer—but her current case may prove her wrong. (978-1-60282-037-1)

Dark Garden by Jennifer Fulton. Vienna Blake and Mason Cavender are sworn enemies—who can't resist each other. Something has to give. (978-1-60282-036-4)

Shots Fired by MJ Williamz. Kyla and Echo seem to have the perfect relationship and the perfect life until someone shoots at Kyla—and Echo is the most likely suspect. (978-1-60282-035-7)

truelesbianlove.com by Carsen Taite. Mackenzie Lewis and Dr. Jordan Wagner have very different ideas about love, but they discover that truelesbianlove is closer than a click away. Aeros EBook (978-1-60282-069-2)

Justice at Risk by John Morgan Wilson. Benjamin Justice's blind date leads to a rare opportunity for legitimate work, but a reckless risk changes his life forever. (978-1-60282-059-3)

Run to Me by Lisa Girolami. Burned by the four-letter word called love, the only thing Beth Standish wants to do is run for—or maybe from—her life. (978-1-60282-034-0)

Split the Aces by Jove Belle. In the neon glare of Sin City, two women ride a wave of passion that threatens to consume them in a world of fast money and fast times. (978-1-60282-033-3)

Uncharted Passage by Julie Cannon. Two women on a vacation that turns deadly face down one of nature's most ruthless killers—and find themselves falling in love. (978-1-60282-032-6)

Night Call by Radclyffe. All medevac helicopter pilot Jett McNally wants to do is fly and forget about the horror and heartbreak she left behind in the Middle East, but anesthesiologist Tristan Holmes has other plans. (978-1-60282-031-9)

Lake Effect Snow by C.P. Rowlands. News correspondent Annie T. Booker and FBI Agent Sarah Moore struggle to stay one step ahead of disaster as Annie's life becomes the war zone she once reported on. Aeros EBook (978-1-60282-068-5)

Revision of Justice by John Morgan Wilson. Murder shifts into high gear, propelling Benjamin Justice into a raging fire that consumes the Hollywood Hills, burning steadily toward the famous Hollywood Sign—and the identity of a cold-blooded killer. (978-1-60282-058-6)

I Dare You by Larkin Rose. Stripper by night, corporate raider by day, Kelsey's only looking for sex and power, until she meets a woman who stirs her heart and her body. (978-1-60282-030-2)

Truth Behind the Mask by Lesley Davis. Erith Baylor is drawn to Sentinel Pagan Osborne's quiet strength, but the secrets between them strain duty and family ties. (978-1-60282-029-6)

Cooper's Deale by KI Thompson. Two would-be lovers and a decidedly inopportune murder spell trouble for Addy Cooper, no matter which way the cards fall. (978-1-60282-028-9)

Romantic Interludes 1: Discovery ed. by Radclyffe and Stacia Seaman. An anthology of sensual, erotic contemporary love stories from the best-selling Bold Strokes authors. (978-1-60282-027-2)

A Guarded Heart by Jennifer Fulton. The last place FBI Special Agent Pat Roussel expects to find herself is assigned to an illicit private security gig baby-sitting a celebrity. Aeros Ebook (978-1-60282-067-8)

Saving Grace by Jennifer Fulton. Champion swimmer Dawn Beaumont, injured in a car crash she caused, flees to Moon Island, where scientist Grace Ramsay welcomes her. Aeros Ebook (978-1-60282-066-1)

The Sacred Shore by Jennifer Fulton. Successful tech industry survivor Merris Randall does not believe in love at first sight until she meets Olivia Pearce. Aeros Ebook (978-1-60282-065-4)

Passion Bay by Jennifer Fulton. Two women from different ends of the earth meet in paradise. Author's expanded edition. Aeros Ebook (978-1-60282-064-7)

Never Wake by Gabrielle Goldsby. After a brutal attack, Emma Webster becomes a self-sentenced prisoner inside her condo—until the world outside her window goes silent. Aeros Ebook (978-1-60282-063-0)

The Caretaker's Daughter by Gabrielle Goldsby. Against the backdrop of a nineteenth-century English country estate, two women struggle to find love. Aeros Ebook (978-1-60282-062-3)

Simple Justice by John Morgan Wilson. When a pretty-boy cokehead is murdered, former LA reporter Benjamin Justice and his reluctant new partner, Alexandra Templeton, must unveil the real killer. (978-1-60282-057-9)

Remember Tomorrow by Gabrielle Goldsby. Cees Bannigan and Arieanna Simon find that a successful relationship rests in remembering the mistakes of the past. (978-1-60282-026-5)

Put Away Wet by Susan Smith. Jocelyn "Joey" Fellows has just been savagely dumped—when she posts an online personal ad, she discovers more than just the great sex she expected. (978-1-60282-025-8)

Homecoming by Nell Stark. Sarah Storm loses everything that matters—family, future dreams, and love—will her new "straight" roommate cause Sarah to take a chance at happiness? (978-1-60282-024-1)

The Three by Meghan O'Brien. A daring, provocative exploration of love and sexuality. Two lovers, Elin and Kael, struggle to survive in a postapocalyptic world. Aeros Ebook (978-1-60282-056-2)

Falling Star by Gill McKnight. Solley Rayner hopes a few weeks with her family will help heal her shattered dreams, but she hasn't counted on meeting a woman who stirs her heart. (978-1-60282-023-4)

Lethal Affairs by Kim Baldwin and Xenia Alexiou. Elite operative Domino is no stranger to peril, but her investigation of journalist Hayley Ward will test more than her skills. (978-1-60282-022-7)

Word of Honor by Radclyffe. All Secret Service Agent Cameron Roberts and First Daughter Blair Powell want is a small intimate wedding, but the paparazzi and a domestic terrorist have other plans. (978-1-60282-018-0)

In Deep Waters 2 by Radclyffe and Karin Kallmaker. All bets are off when two award winning-authors deal the cards of love and passion… and every hand is a winner. (978-1-60282-013-5)

The Lonely Hearts Club by Radclyffe. Take three friends, add two ex-lovers and several new ones, and the result is a recipe for explosive rivalries and incendiary romance. (978-1-60282-005-0)

Winds of Fortune by Radclyffe. Provincetown local Deo Camara agrees to rehab Dr. Bonita Burgoyne's historic home, but she never said anything about mending her heart. (978-1-933110-93-6)

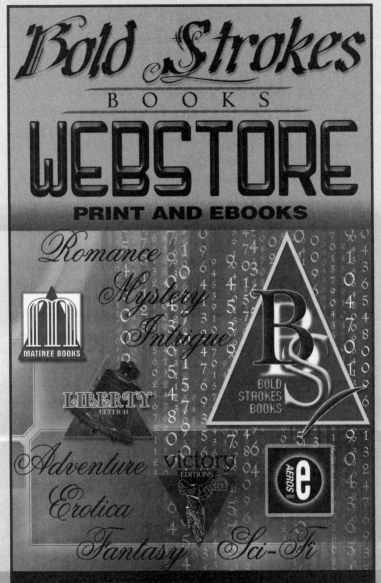

Praise

NEAPOLITAN CHRONICLES

"Anna Maria Ortese is a writer of exceptional prowess and force. The stories collected in this volume, which reverberate with Chekhovian energy and melancholy, are revered in Italy by writers and readers alike. Ann Goldstein and Jenny McPhee reward us with a fresh and scrupulous translation."

—JHUMPA LAHIRI,
author of *The Lowland* and *In Other Words*

"As for Naples, today I feel drawn above all by Anna Maria Ortese ... If I managed again to write about this city, I would try to craft a text that explores the direction indicated there."

—ELENA FERRANTE
in *Frantumaglia: A Writer's Journey*

"This remarkable city portrait, both phantasmagorical and harshly realistic, conveys Naples in all its shabbiness and splendor. Naples appears as both a monster and an immense waiting room, whose inhabitants are caught between resignation and unquenchable resilience. Beautifully translated, this lyrical gem has been rescued from the vast storehouse of superior foreign literature previously ignored." —PHILLIP LOPATE,
author of *Bachelorhood* and
Waterfront: A Walk Around Manhattan

"This beautiful book is a landmark in Italian literature and a major influence on Elena Ferrante—both as a way of writing about Naples and because Anna Maria Ortese may have been the model for the narrator of Ferrante's quartet of novels set there. Ann

Goldstein and Jenny McPhee have rendered Ortese's lively, Neapolitan-inflected Italian in vivid, highly engaging English prose."

—ALEXANDER STILLE,
author of *The Sack of Rome* and
Benevolence and Betrayal

"Naples is a vast succession of cities—Greek, Samnite, Roman, Byzantine, Aragonese, Spanish, Bourbon, Savoyard—and every phase has had its chronicler. In the aftermath of World War Two, battered, humiliated Naples found no abler witness than Anna Maria Ortese. Sixty-five years later, with international interest in Naples unexpectedly high, Ann Goldstein and Jenny McPhee have given us an essential, eloquent translation as faithful to Ortese's time as it is vividly alive for our own."

—BENJAMIN TAYLOR,
author of *Naples Declared* and *Tales Out of School*

"Anna Maria Ortese was the last great writer of the generation that produced Italo Calvino and Primo Levi. Today, few critics would disagree with the poet Andrea Zanzotto, who rates her as 'one of the most important Italian women writers of this century.'"

—THE INDEPENDENT

"Gives an essential glimpse into the origins of Ferrante's work ... A mesmerizing companion to Ferrante's Neapolitan project as well as a daring work of both social criticism and narrative inventiveness that stands, toweringly, on its own."

—SERAILLON

"An astonishing descent into the underworld ... A modern artist has rarely rendered so intensely the spectrality of all things."

—LA REPUBBLICA